DATE DUE		

Light Music

Also by Kathleen Ann Goonan

Light Music

"With the discovery of superstring theory,
musical metaphors take on startling reality,
for the theory suggests that the microscopic
landscape is suffused with tiny strings
whose vibrational patterns orchestrate the
evolution of the cosmos. The winds of change,
according to superstring theory,
gust through an aeolian universe."

BRIAN GREENE, *THE ELEGANT UNIVERSE*

KATHLEEN ANN GOONAN

This is a work of fiction. Names, characters, places, and incidents are products of the author's imagination or are used fictitiously and are not to be construed as real. Any resemblance to actual events, locales, organizations, or persons, living or dead, is entirely coincidental.

EOS
An Imprint of HarperCollins*Publishers*
10 East 53rd Street
New York, New York 10022-5299

Author photo by Joseph M. Mansy

ISBN: 0-380-97712-5

Library of Congress Cataloging-in-Publication Data

Goonan, Kathleen Ann.
Light music / Kathleen Ann Goonan.
p. cm.
ISBN 0-380-97712-5 (hardcover)
1. Colorado—Fiction. I. Title.

PS3557.O628 L54 2002
813'.54—dc21 2001055602

First Eos hardcover printing: June 2002

Printed in the U.S.A.

FIRST EDITION

10 9 8 7 6 5 4 3 2 1

www.eosbooks.com

LIGHT MUSIC is dedicated to my parents,
Tom and Irma Goonan,
on their Fifty-First Wedding Anniversary,
and to my wonderful sisters,
Mary and Susie.

THANKS AND ACKNOWLEDGMENTS

This novel is the work of several years, during which the love, support, and encouragement of my husband, Joseph Mansy, was of utmost importance. He also maintains my web page at www.goonan.com

My cousin Amy Roberts, a poet and writer, took the time to read and critique the manuscript, and her input was invaluable. Through her, Dorothy Strickland helped me adjust my portrait of Su-Chen.

Sage Walker, Steve Brown, and Michaela Roessner also read this book in manuscript, and their responses helped immensely in making it into a real novel.

Jennifer Brehl and Diana Gill helped me remove from the book that which was not necessary, and made it shine.

Devi Pillai, efficient and lively, helped things go smoothly.

Hilda Stotts, an Argentinian, provided much of the material for the Argentina section, and I thank her for the time she spent doing so.

I finished the final rewrite while spending two weeks, every day and many nights, in the George Washington University Hospital intensive care waiting room. Thanks to all of the nurses, fellows, and physicians who cared for Irma, especially Dr. Seneff and Dr. Junker.

The concept of the orerry that appears in this novel was the idea of Liz Hand and John Clute in an online story in which we participated.

The Consilience herein owes much to E.O. Wilson's book, *Consilience.* I also referred to Brian Greene's *The Elegant Universe,* Evan Walker's *The Physics of Consciousness,* Julian Barbour's *The End of Time* (the source of the Nows and the reference to Romeo and Juliet, which is from Figure 31 Space-time as a tapestry of interwoven lovers), and *The Non-local Universe* by Robert Nadeau and Menas Kafotos—all of which stand out among the seemingly hundreds of books which fertilized *Light Music.*

Light Music

2175

ELIDED NOWS

Matthew

Reverend Dania came to our town five years before I was born.

My name is Matthew. We live in the southeast corner of the Free State of Colorado, not far from the Republic of Texas, where no one ever goes. Dania came from there.

She doesn't like people to call her Reverend, and I don't. I just call her Dania. Some of the old folks call her Reverend, though, and my gramma gets mad at me if she hears me call her plain untitled "Dania."

When she first came to town, she preached what she called "seeing." It had to do with light. You might think that sounds obvious—*I* know what "obvious" means—but instead it is the least obvious thing imaginable. But it wasn't just preaching. It was a communion service and you had to drink a special wine that Reverend Dania made. She told you flat-out that it was some kind of genetic engineering stuff that would change your homeobox genes—whatever they are—and give you a new gene for the type of seeing that you would be doing. You could also find out about it with the learning slates she kept in the old warehouse she used as a church, with stuff about DNA that I couldn't figure out. She said I wasn't quite old enough.

But one day I got some of the communion stuff, I just ran up there and got some and Mom and Dad kind of shook their heads when I walked back up the aisle. It was sweet and tasted good. I was little then, but now I'm ten. I think they went to Dania's church because of Gramma, or just to be nice to Dania, or something. I don't think that they believe what she says like I do.

But it's really just like the old Jesus church because you have to take it all on faith. Nothing happened when I took it, and nothing would happen soon, and nothing might *ever* happen.

Maybe that's why so many folks did it.

I remember one Fourth of July when I was seven, which happened to be on a Sunday, everybody in town squeezed into her church-room and drank her communion stuff, maybe kind of as a joke. Except that Gramma gets tears in her eyes when she talks about it; it isn't a joke to her. She says that someday the whole world and everything we know and are able to know will change because of Reverend Dania and her band from Crescent City who went on ahead while Dania stayed behind.

But she finally ran out of the stuff and said that she was too worn out to go and make more. Maybe she stopped believing in it herself.

Now she just lives right next door to us in her little white house on Third Street, which is why I spend a lot of time with her. Mom says to be nice to her, that she is a good person and maybe just a little depressed because the world is taking so long to change. Never mind that according to Gramma it has changed, and changed, and changed again since she was a girl.

We have a bird zoo, an aviary, I guess you call it. In the aviary there are all kinds of rare birds. Small brown sparrows and robins, who have red chests. Some meanish black birds called grackles and huger black birds called crows.

We're only a block away from the aviary, and in the summer, in the mornings, I like to lie in bed and listen to the singing of the birds. Grandma says we're lucky to live so close. She says that when she's in bed with her eyes closed, it reminds her of when there were birds everywhere, in all the trees. But something that happened before I was born, the Silence, made them forget where to go when they migrated, and millions and millions of them died. They almost became extinct. A lot of other things are extinct too.

For a long time there was something called nan that changed everything, but people like my grandparents stayed away from it, back in this little mountain town, to stay safe. But someday I think that I want to go out looking for nan and find out what it is. Gramma told me a lot about how things used to be a long time ago, when there was television and radio and a lot more people. She's real, real old, a hundred and fifty years old, I think. Dad says that Gramma's stories are true, even though it all sounds very strange.

Dania says that someday everything will be like it used to be, only a whole lot better. She says the birds will be able to migrate again.

Anyway, we go to school in a big brick building a few blocks away. Mom is a teacher in another classroom, and I'm in the second set, but at the top, and next year I'll be the youngest in the third set. Well, that's hows come I know so much about birds. Mom taught me.

Dania comes to our set once a week and teaches us songs. She even goes around to the houses where there are babies and teaches them songs too. She says that the songs organize their brains in a special way. Dania is crazy about music. Dad said that she's purely crazy, but Mom always frowns at him when he says that and it's that frown that makes him be quiet right away.

One day when she was supposed to be teaching us music, way back when I was in the first set, she drew some kind of complicated picture with a lot of corners to it and talked about superstrings and things she called "dimensions." The picture was supposed to be about how just one point contains . . . well, I can't explain it because I didn't really understand it. But she sees things that other people don't see, everybody knows that. Then she told us kids about how there were more colors and sounds than we could see and hear, but one day we would have a new sense like her so that we could know all of that and the moms and dads got mad and had a meeting and told her she couldn't talk to the kids about things like that. Not my mom and dad, but some of them. The next day she started packing her stuff to leave and there was a big uproar and finally they told her she could stay. She didn't want to at first, but they told her it was all right, she could say whatever she wants, and she does. She talks about a new time that is coming when we will know more and be connected with everything and be able to communicate with each other and everything and even with people who live in the sky extremely far away, like farther than the sun, like in the stars. People laugh at her behind her back, but I don't. I love her.

Dania is pretty. Her eyes are gray-gold and sad a lot, especially when she talks about Crescent City. Her hair is long and light brown and she wears it in a ponytail. Mom says that she's one of those people who will never get old, and that the time she was in Crescent City was a long, long time ago, before even Mom was born. Gramma is old, but she looks old, and has white hair. She's not very good at walking. Dania is different.

Crescent City was way out in the ocean. Dad's brother went there, or at least left to go there. I think that if Dania could remember Dad's brother, he would like her more.

She said that a lot of people lived there. Almost a million. She had to leave because of a war. She says that she is going back, sometime, and that they are all going to outer space.

That's when Dad laughs loudest, and Mom frowns strongest. That's when I think that the Nows are confusing her, because at other times she seems to think that everyone went to space a long time ago, and she decided to stay behind to be a reverend and a teacher. Gramma says she knows the true story and that Dania stayed because of love, but Dad says that Gramma's just an old romantic and that nobody ever left.

Dania says that the reason that everything is happening is because it's an average. When she drew her drawing, she said that because of quantum indeterminancy, we actually have something to do with what is happening. We average everything with consciousness. But there are other kinds of consciousness. Other levels. I'm not sure what consciousness is, but she says that we'll all learn that eventually. Especially because we got some of the communion stuff before it ran out.

She is very strong and goes walking around in the mountains a lot by herself. I think that when she goes for those walks, for weeks at a time, carrying a pack and heading out toward James Mountain, she is looking for the Nows, and for the things made of light that are stuffed full of Nows. I think that they are so stuffed full of Nows that they leaked Nows into her when she touched them. And fried her brain, too, maybe, like Dad says. Because once I asked her what she does in the mountains and she said, "I look for a good place to jump."

She calls them light-beings, and they lived in the Republic of Texas. All kinds of strange things go on there. Everybody knows that if you head into the Republic of Texas, anything can happen. That's why we all stay here in Colorado. Anyway, they were very bright, and told her all about many things when she touched them. Even though they didn't talk in words but in pictures and in sounds. That's when she learned that time is made of Nows.

Nows are like the points on the diagram she drew. They have something to do with superstrings that are vibrating really, really fast, and that are really, really small. Like beads that fill up a room when there are a million of them are made up of trillions of things themselves. It's hard to picture this, but Mom says it's true, and that a lot of things that Dania says are true, but just hard for most people to understand. Everything we see and feel and hear is because of this, though. And they are all like music, elided music, which is when you slide your voice up and down. It's what makes everything so beautiful, like the shapes of the mountains, the colors of flowers, the sounds of the birds singing.

One summer day I went to Dania's house and she was drinking gin out of a big clear bottle, and that day she told me about cities with flowers on tops of the buildings where things that looked like giant bees flew around, and that helped everybody communicate. She had a photograph of one, and it was old and faded and the things she was calling bees were just black dots in the sky like gnats. I told her and she laughed and said it was true. But that there were other kinds of cities in the world, cities of light and cities that were giant antennae, and then she said that she was supposed to be doing some work here but she was so tired and sometimes it didn't even seem true any more. She said that it was entirely possible that she was just a holy fool and that she was sorry for everything, that I had to remember that she was sorry for everything that she had done because it would affect my children too and finally it was hard to understand her and she told me I'd better go home.

I did, but I went back later that evening and was going to visit, but through the open window I saw that she was sitting in a chair in her living room crying and I decided not to. Next to her was a tiny old radio that she keeps and it was just hissing away. In the summer nights I hear her turn it on, because my bedroom window is above hers, and the only sound it gives off is that hissing sound. We have an old radio too, and there is a radio tower on top of Golden Peak, and it keeps on broadcasting, and maybe once every two months the signal gets through. But the same old thing is playing over and over again: singing, an old old news show, what Dad says are commercials that we're all better off without, and more singing.

I like the singing, myself. She said that the notes come from the girl in the moon. She says weird things like that.

I want to see what she is seeing, when I grow up. I hope that she is right, and that we will all know this thing that she knows, and that this will make her happy. I told her I was going to marry her when I grow up and she just laughed and ruffled my hair and said that she would be way too old for me.

I want to marry her because she looks so lonely sometimes. She tells me about the different things that happened back then, what she knew about them. She says that stories are the curled-up dimensions in superstrings, and that humans are the only creatures that can tell stories and have this special kind of sentience—I think that sentience is kind of like consciousness—and that is why they can see this light, and that is why some of them went away. She talks about the ones who went away a lot. She talks about the girl who played light music, and a South American woman she calls The Storyteller, and the people who are waiting in the sky. She always ends up talking about somebody called Radio Cowboy.

That's when she looks the most sad.

I tell her I wanted to write the stories all down for a school project and she looks far off and says they are all in her head and maybe she'll tell them someday. Maybe.

One day I followed her out to James Mountain. It was summertime and windy and the leaves made a lot of noise and so she never heard me. Or maybe she did and decided to let me follow and let me see.

Because she took a turn off the main trail that I hadn't noticed before whenever Mom and Dad and my sisters and I went hiking and it was awful steep and hard to follow. Finally, when I was really, really tired, she came to a little meadow of golden grass with pine trees all round and in the meadow was a white cylinder about as tall as she was standing in a patch of wildflowers. I know what a cylinder is, and a cube and an ovoid too. She pressed some things on it and then she leaned her head against it and pounded on it with one fist and looked like she was crying. I ran away then.

But I went back last month and the cylinder is still there, and has a band of glowing lights around it higher than I can reach. I haven't told anyone about it.

I still want to marry her when I grow up.

THIS SIDE

"The evolution of the brain . . . allowed us to construct a symbolic universe that seems more real and more vast than the universe itself."

—Nadeau & Kafatos, *The Non-Local Universe*

February 2115

A wave of information-packed light swept through space and washed across the moon and Earth.

More waves followed, moving behind one another at precise intervals which would translate, on Earth, into months.

July 8, 2115

Radio Cowboy and the New Frontier

The pirate attack on Crescent City was swift and brutal, and came while Peabody was visiting the elephant.

Peabody lived for night, and slept through most of each hot, blue-struck tropical day. The small tower in which he lived alone, high above the floating city, bristled with antennae and was crammed with the accouterments of radio reception and transmission: tuners, amplifiers, devices that he had designed and built or grown, and much older electronics garnered from the mainland, all patrolled by rust-eating bacteria else they would have had a life of months instead of years in the corrosive sea air.

Peabody had been in Crescent City so long that most people referred to him as, simply, the Engineer—a reclusive though not unfriendly man who knew everything about the operation of the city.

This suited Peabody.

After he woke, at sunset, he picked with chopsticks at his usual bowl of brown rice and sipped jasmine tea, gradually becoming alert. Several thunderstorms shaded the jade sea in patches. One veered close and darkened the sky.

Cold wind washed the tower. Lightning shot to the sea; thunder cracked. Rain dropped in silver columns, brushing the edge of the city. The spidersteel windows, which he usually kept in mesh form, thickened automatically at the first drops of rain to keep his electronics dry.

A line of whitecaps five hundred feet below looked, from this height, like a standing wave, breaking on grass-stabilized beaches. Coconut palms bent beneath gusts of wind. Aquamarine farming lagoons, filled with fish and mollusks and surrounded by nodes of fabricated land, roughened. Peabody watched a white sail furl.

Crescent City, afloat in the Caribbean Sea, grew on acres of artificial land, its sweeping, tentlike lines reaching an apex just above his windows.

On the other side of his tower, the vast bulk of the city stretched out so far that he could not see the end of it, and was home to about one million people and perhaps half as many modified animals. It was quickly obscured by the deluge.

There was within the city, Peabody knew, an impulse to metamorph into a space city, for that had been the original design. Crescent City had been created to be an environment where humanity could learn complete self-sufficiency, and invent technologies which would propel and support them in space. The spacefaring vision of its founder had been long in maturing, for it lacked several vital features—one of them being a destination, and, at least now, sufficient reason to leave. It had been growing for about seventy-five years, and Peabody had lived here for the past forty years as the anonymous Engineer.

He had been born at the very end of the age of broadcasting. Scientific advances in physics, genetics, biology, and chemistry resulted in technological wonders that promised to turn humans into a new species and send them to the stars. Radios and telephones and the Internet accompanied people everywhere, like a new human sense, forming a new mind that spanned the planet.

When Peabody was born, this mind began to shatter. By the time he was an adolescent, it was gone. Radio communication became sporadic and undependable.

Crescent City had been established, in part, to preserve information and further science and learning. Those not born here were refugees from a world blasted back to varying levels of civilization by a mysterious Signal from space which had been washing Earth for just over a hundred years now, creating the radio vacuum called, in Crescent City, *El Silencio.*

Life was salubrious in the vast tropical gardens, on the sheltered beaches and bays, where the best of all that nanotech had to offer enhanced the intelligence and health of the city dwellers. Since there were no private possessions there was nothing to steal. If desired, a citizen could form any style of clothing, any type of furniture, any kind of material possession. When she was tired of it, she could leave it for others, or return it to the matter bank. One's personal territory was small, but most of life was lived in public plazas.

As the population grew, the city itself grew, establishing more pavilions, and building more land via electrostatic webs that catalyzed minerals from seawater.

Growth of new land was a slow process. In the past few decades it had been necessary to establish a waiting list for admittance into the city. Several factions had attempted to grow floating cities in other locations, but Crescent City had been established during the first phase of *El Silencio,* when all the wealth, know-how, and support of a still-extant civilization spurred its growth. Now such an endeavor would be more difficult. Peabody did not know if any other cities had suceeded, though he fervently hoped that they had.

Children occasionally dropped by his tower to learn of the wonders of radio, which still sputtered to life after the glow of sunset left the horizon, its brief transmissions captured by Peabody and added to decades of similar information. Towers throughout the world still transmitted, but *El Silencio* disrupted the waves. Occasionally, pulses of energy swept through space in what had so far proven to be a nonrepeating pattern.

Peabody himself went on the air almost every night from four to five in the morning, or longer if he felt like it, but lately he had found himself with little to say and played some of the multicultural synthesis music that had a way of changing overnight in the style-conscious hothouse of the city.

He could not say that the city had failed.

But humanity, perhaps, had failed the city—the *idea* of the city. It sometimes seemed that he was the only person here who still wondered why radio no longer functioned predictably.

His own mind held a map of the stars, formulated through painful developmental stages during which his corpus colossi had grown larger than that of most people. This curious map was also present in the minds of many children conceived the same day as Peabody. For much of his life, he had tried to forget that it was there. The process of its acquisition, as unsought and as unwanted as a cancer, had been unpleasant.

He and others like himself had been sought for study by the government, who linked their existence to the Silence; his early life had been marred by the constant need to hide from those trying to find him.

Indeed, there was a link. Developmental spurts, generally accompanied by intense, unbearable headaches, bore the same temporal pattern as the pulses. It amazed him that many children here, when they reached the age of majority, actually chose this modification, as if it were a rite of passage.

All of that information, including the star maps, were a part of the Consilience, as was other navigational information, developed by NASA, which he had stolen from Johnson Space Center in Houston when he was young.

Any individual in Crescent City could enter the Consilience, an informational stratum of the city where all of the scientific and mathematical information which made its way here—indeed, all information, no matter how seemingly mundane—was united by the city itself. The Consilience was accessible through a huge variety of interfaces.

The sun blazed briefly after the rain, an orange tongue which the blue sea swallowed. The windows thinned and a welcome cool breeze swept across the small living area, which contained a couch, a chair, a futon alcove, and an abbreviated kitchen which included a beer tap.

Peabody poured more tea and watched some kayakers put out to sea for an evening run.

He was, he had to admit, depressed. It seemed to him that none of this wonderful convergence of information would ever be used beyond making everyone physically comfortable. Nanotechnology had a way of satisfying people so that they no longer dreamed. That was his opinion. Its dourness frightened him.

In earlier days, people had flooded into the city, drawn by the Norleans Plague. The scientific community thrived.

But few new scientists took the place of older ones. Perhaps there was some tiny balance-shifting factor about the city that led children to be interested in the biosciences—sea-farming, the challenges of growing fruits and vegetables in this isolated space—much more than physics and mathematics. Their world was turned inward, toward the small, as they deciphered the riddle of matter and bid it do their will.

Perhaps the pool was not large enough, here, to produce philosophers of science, those to whom light and its great riddles were of supreme importance. There had been no new scientific revolutions here for years, though every once in a while there were mutterings of breakthroughs on some distant mainland or other, and lately a bit of excitement when the supercollider project, which ringed the city like a vast doughnut about a hundred feet above sea level, was completed and experiments begun. Though the city had survived several Category Five hurricanes, storms had wrecked previous supercollider attempts. This design, completed and implemented by the Consilience, was supposed to be an improvement. Peabody was eager to see results, which might show them a new avenue in the quest to decipher the mysteries of light.

Peabody saw everything in terms of light. His hand as he held his tea gripped light solidified, and he stood in no special place in space. This island Earth was just as empty and vibrating within its atoms and the bonds they formed with one another as any other place in any universe, though perhaps a shade more dense. The only thing that made this place special was his own consciousness, his own glance.

This was the major puzzle to him.

This, and trying to figure out what had happened to radio.

He knew there were others out there who, like him, were trying to put together a new network of broadcasting protocol. But any connections fell apart too rapidly to be depended upon.

Many, including Peabody, believed that *El Silencio,* and its disasterous effects, were the result of deliberate intelligent manipulation of Earth's atmosphere by some distant force—mostly because the sequence of pulses, the Signal, which had since washed Earth seemed to have some kind of order.

This source presumably had an understanding of the nature of light which far surpassed that of humans. Peabody had devoted his life to deriving an equation distilling the revelations into human mathematics. His good friend Zeb Aberly, a radio astronomer, was another like himself, focused on this mystery. But he had left Crescent City years ago.

Peabody's own life might have meant something if such answers had ever been found. Perhaps the answer, the closure, for him and for others in his situation, had been prepared but not sent, or had been sent and missed its target.

As he looked out over Crescent City, he succumbed to darkening intimations which all the fairylike lights of the world beneath him, now appearing as the tropical night closed down suddenly, could not brighten.

It was possible that his life with all its pain and loss was only the result of a question posed in light, and that somewhere out there those who had caused this havoc awaited their answer, the answer he had tried to formulate through a lifetime of observation, study, and puzzle-solving.

Or perhaps it was one huge improvisation and an important musician had left the stage and the tune had changed, far out there in interstellar space, leaving Earth crippled forever.

The human brain, having evolved to deal with certain environmental factors, might simply be unable to fathom the universe in the way that it so desperately wanted to. It was impossible for one mind to hold within it the entire knowledge of what humanity had discovered over the course of its scientific history. Peabody hoped therefore that the Consilience, which was nonhuman and therefore perhaps not as limited, was using that information to study possible new trajectories regarding solving the most pressing question of the age: What was causing the Silence, and how could it be stopped?

Or used.

Whether or not the city was conscious was often debated, but it did indeed act like a living organism, keeping itself and its denizens functioning as if the humans and animals were beneficial bacterium along for the ride.

Something held him in the city, but he could no longer say what, except that the city itself seemed to want him here. This was an unusual thought for a man long given to practicalities, but the idea that a system as large as this city might have a will of its own was not at all extreme. Perhaps it was wise enough to be frightened of its supposed fate of maturing into a spacefaring entity. Perhaps it was thinking things over, trying to figure out a way to leave the humans, demanding as a raft of kittens suckling an exhausted mother, behind.

If it was conscious, perhaps it was also wise, for it kept any such realization to itself.

The black cat on his couch stretched and yawned. Peabody picked up a stray image from him, a burst of metapheromones which manifested as a few lines and colors on the back of his hand.

This was another of his failures. Many islanders made it their life's work to try to communicate with animals using all kinds of methods, but Peabody, though interested, had never been able to make sense of their thoughts. Images did not dance across the Engineer's skin because his personal symbolic language remained locked within his brain. He was not able to allow it to be translated for the world to see.

His only company, for years, had been a a series of cats. They wandered into the tower one at a time and took up residence, lying striped with bands of light on the cool tiled floor, as if they had some sort of pact to keep him distant company.

Peabody did, however, feel a kinship with the elephant that lived on the new pavilion about two miles to the west. He traveled to see it every once in a while, traversing a city almost alien to him via a system of sidewalks which moved through lush orchid-laden jungle where children played without fear of other humans or of venomous creatures. In fact, it was a bit scary how free of fear they were.

It was now full night. Able to see a cosmos no longer occluded by the sun, he was finally awake. Lights and dials winked around him in a waist-high stratum banding the small room. The floor carried, like most of the surfaces of the city, a powerfully sophisticated and complex hypertextual information system. Peabody generally had it manifest a map of the world, with tiny glowing lights depicting the sources and types of radio signals he had picked up.

His roof's daylight opacity deserted it, no longer necessary, allowing starstreaked space to fill his mind. He kept the Radio Room dark except for the glow of frequency readouts, which danced through his nights in cadences that suggested something frustratingly out of his ability to understand or to know.

He settled into sampling the signals, hearing the brief thrilling blips from clear-channel stations that had broadcast automatically for almost a century while rarely riding the atmosphere for long. He felt the slight, dreamy sway of the tower in the wind and watched the dim luminosity of Crescent City grow. His hand, as he reached out to quickly twist a dial, was resolutely middle-aged in appearance—the hand of, perhaps, a fifty-year-old, though an exceedingly fit and healthy fifty-year-old. He did not wish to chance the change of younger renewal, for he had seen too many people become younger in mind as well as appearance during the various processes which brought the body the freshness of youth. As it was, he had still cheated age by fifty years or more. He supposed that effect was part of a present given him long ago by a lover.

He noticed lights on the horizon—most likely, their fishing fleet returning. He drank several cups of tea.

Sometimes, lately, Paris had skipped into range for as long as a minute at a time, with throaty singing or, more interestingly, some kind of code. He knew that Paris was a huge antenna, and that it had for many years devoted much energy to enlarging this antenna.

Suddenly, static hissed from one of his speakers.

He moved toward it eagerly as it focused into brilliant, organized sound. The scope of the sound expanded instantly and fused with the map of the radio sky which he had carried in his mind since young, its unseen dimensions picked up by senses few other humans possessed.

A light coalesced in the southern part of the room, inevitable as dawn.

It was that for which he had always waited. He knew it. This light would, at last, tell him *why*.

He took a step toward it, deeply and clearly aware, noting its characteristics.

An ovoid ten feet high. A touch of the visible spectrum wavering through it like a broad rainbow.

The music of it made his chest ache and brought tears to his eyes.

He said, ridiculously, "Yes?"

Thoughts flashed through him, their inferences unfurling into the unseen distance too quickly for him to fathom, in deep, resonant relationships. A billion harmonies stretched his senses to the limit and then past, to the edge of hallucination.

Except that he knew that it was real. External. But meshing with him somehow.

Changing him.

He knew he was experiencing the uncurling of an infinite array of curled-up dimensions.

He was being fed with light, a new form of light. He did not know how or why.

Infinity, before now an abstract concept to him, seemed almost kinetic, dancing in each particle which comprised his body, becoming united to all of time and matter in that crux where everything had begun and expanded outward at unknowable speed.

The light vanished.

The stunned Engineer staggered forward, as if its energy had been supporting him, and stood looking at the place where it had been.

The tower was utterly silent.

He knew no one with whom he could discuss this. He wished his old friend Zeb, the radio astronomer, was here with him. Yet how could he possibly condense this into words? He was a gifted mathematician, but this had opened new geometries which he had barely glimpsed, which he would have to think himself back to, if that was possible.

Something had happened. Something exciting; powerful.

But what? And why?

"Be back in a while," Peabody told his cat, and received a commanding picture of a fish in reply.

He paused for an instant, surprised and pleased.

Then he hurried from his Radio Room. He was edgy—entirely awake, yet in an electric, dreamlike state.

As he dropped through a clear tube on an elevator platform, he had a momentary sensation that the lights below and above were points in interstellar space, that he was finally embarked on the epic voyage he had lost faith in.

He headed for the place in which some of the most exciting scientific work of the city had been done, including the initial planning for the supercollider. They had taken to calling it Science Hall. In its heyday, the atmosphere had been that of Princeton's Institute of Advanced Thinking, where at any one time you might find mathematicians, physicists, biologists, and others in heated conversations or engaged in Consilience-aided projects.

He pulled open the heavy, arched wooden door. Much of Crescent City was made of ultralight, ultrastrong buckyball material, material that responded quickly, although within preset parameters, to requests for change. But in some places people had chosen the comfort of well-remembered materials.

He stepped inside, and low lights illiminated the room.

Comfortable clublike couches faced one another in conversation-friendly groups, but other chairs were placed at work stations at which one could access various levels of the Consilience. Rattan rugs were scattered across the floor. Several cocoons provided access to complete immersion in the Consilience, which Peabody tended to avoid because the process involved a certain loss of control.

For a moment he saw the room filled with his old friends, colleagues with whom he had spent months and years in close work. Many, like the radio astronomer, had left Crescent City—frustrated; eager to see what was happening elsewhere.

He sat and recorded his experience with the light, and gave it to the Consilience.

It was just a brief note. He regretted that he could say nothing concrete about its spectrum. All of its brilliance and intensity seemed now to have been, possibly, an illusion.

The loneliness of the room brought back his feelings of futility. He had expected others to be here. Had this only happened to him? Had he imagined it?

He left.

On the thirteenth level, he walked through a jungle which by day was thick with cockatoos, parakeets, talking parrots, and the rebel parrots, who disdained human manipulation and reverted to natural form and tried to convince the other parrots to do so as well.

He tried to see if his friend, a white philosopher-parrot, was among them. She had lived in the tower for three years. Taught a wide vocabulary from birth, she had been especially eloquent when pontificating on Gaia. Eventually, she acquired the parrot-developed imaging grammar displayed on the beaks of those who chose that option, and elected to grow receptors, on her claws, which allowed her to access the Consilience. Not long after that, she suddenly moved down here. But he did not see her.

He heard the chatter and shrieks of a distant band of monkeys, perhaps awakened by some intrusion, and the muted roar of a waterfall. He passed a food pavilion, open twenty-four hours a day; he was not the only person who preferred the night.

The smell of garlic conjured a memory: a small Italian restaurant where he and his wife often dined when he was the Chief Nanotech Engineer of the Flower City of Chicago. But that had been decades ago, and his wife had long since killed herself. That was when he left Chicago in a haze of astonished numbness and anger.

He tried to ignore the memory, despite its power, and resolved to visit the elephant. That was always calming.

After half an hour of walking, eschewing the small charged scooters one could pick up anywhere, Peabody walked onto a hexagon of land several acres in area.

Graced with plane trees, surrounded by sea, the elephant's domain held a freshwater pond where herons and egrets congregated. Tall grass rustled in the night breeze. Surf boomed against the breakwater and those same lights were out on the water, perhaps closer. The salt breeze was strong.

Standing on the observation porch, he located the dark silhouette of the elephant beneath a fledgeling bo tree.

He watched the elephant. It was oddly soothing. She shifted restlessly and curled her trunk into the air. From time to time, the wind brought him her huffing sounds and musty scent.

He wondered what she was thinking, and how much she knew.

She had been endowed with picturing capabilities, but had

never used them despite the most intense and warm efforts of many dedicated researchers. She was the only elephant, though, and was five years old—a child. This elephant, by nature a social creature, had no family.

Peabody's darkness intensified as he considered this. It was a sin, and others beside himself thought so. With this success, more elephants were planned, but land was slow to grow. Debates raged, in this small sliver of concern, about whether they should risk two or even three elephants here; if there was sufficient food; if the needs of the elephant outbalanced other concerns. Such debates were common in Crescent City. Votes were called almost constantly, though were often limited to neighborhood concerns. Waves of iridescent color washed the island during a vote, and during important citywide votes, the waves could last for days as new debates emerged and were considered.

He felt the afterglow of the strange light. The night seemed a bit brighter than it ought, comprised of buzzing particles lit from within.

Or perhaps this was just his imagination.

The elephant's trumpet was wild; searing. The boards beneath Peabody's feet vibrated. He had read that elephants communicated with sounds of such long wavelength that they were inaudible to human ears as they traveled through the ground to distant pods and tribes.

Did the elephant ever wonder if her communications were understood? Or, growing up alone, did she perhaps believe that she existed in the image of her keepers?

This was only depressing him further.

To his surprise, the elephant wheeled, turning toward him.

He had a moment of fear, though he knew that this elephant, so far, had been a docile creature. But she was huge!

Her massive head bobbed as she approached, majestic, with missionlike intent. Halting just a few feet from him, on the other side of the low fence, she regarded him thoughtfully with dark eyes huge as dinner plates. He was transfixed.

Then, he received images from her as precise as his radio skies.

globe of light breaks skin of seasky
rises
we rise with it
world falls behind
we are gone
into blackspace
our light one of billions
we burn we
turn into
now

Peabody saw it again: The sun rose over ocean's edge, went up and up into black space. The elephant, himself, and all of the seeing, conscious beings on Earth rose as well, in tandem, in a swift, exhilarating arc of light.

Earth fell back; became tiny; vanished as the sun mingled with a billion other stars which rotated suddenly, then snapped into new constellations.

He was seeing the cosmos from a completely new vantage point.

Powerful, beautiful, ever-shifting tones, a symphony of light, pealed through him, light that was time, space and place. One quantum event; the field from which everything—every atom, all of time and space, all living creatures, all conscious thought—burst.

The elephant's trumpet shook the ground.

Peabody moved from his century of solitude into realization: This is it.

This is it.

He held it in his mind for a moment. Or it held him: this image, this movement, this music. The elephant felt it, understood it, communicated it to him in a way that augmented his own experience and gave it an edge to catch hold of.

He was filled with urgency. It had been real. Now it was reinforced. He had to give this directly to the Consilience—the images, surely a clue to the origin of the signal—and the awe embedded in them.

As he turned to go, the ground lurched slightly. Peabody grabbed the railing next to him. The bank on which he stood formed a direct breakwater against the sea, so this lurch was nothing out of the ordinary.

But it gave Peabody the oddest sensation of . . . movement.

Ridiculous, he thought, picturing the huge web of cables attached to sea anchors. Nothing could cut them. Only deliberate programming could cause them to release their grip on the anchors.

He rushed to Science Hall in a fraction of the time his outward trip had taken him, using a scooter, ignoring large groups of people moving purposefully through the pavilions, their faces tense. A few tried to hail him, but didn't stop.

Inside the Hall, the cocoon's web stretched around him, its cool gellish filaments enveloping receptors which were a part of his skin. He relaxed into its soothing grasp. He loved and feared the Consilience—loved it for its richness, and feared his own sense of being out of control when he was within it.

He requested the hormones of learning. They would help him assimilate and understand what he experienced. This would open him completely to the Consilience, which could be frightening. But he had to commune directly.

Swimming down into the deep programs of the city, he realized, with a shock, that the city was indeed loosening its grasp on the ocean floor.

Then, distantly, he felt explosions.

—Jason Peabody: The lights on the ocean are ships attacking me.

The city was appealing to him directly, knowing that he had helped design her.

He cursed his own loss of urgency. The city depended upon defenses developed not by those who had faced combat at some time, nor by those who had commanded forces. Instead, they were developed by people who could not stomach the pain of others. They were developed by people who respected others and who could not imagine those who did not. Time and time again he had been outvoted when proposing more violent and immediate methods of counterattack, such as missiles.

Presently, the only defenses were insidious and subtle, like slow poisons, nanotech defenses which would change the very personality of the attackers should they take up residence. They would not prevent injuries. And injuries could not be healed if the city itself was seriously damaged.

—Begin to manufacture the defense plague, he directed.

—I already have.

—You have awakened?

—I have been awake for a long time. The light accelerated the process of growth.

But it did not use the word "light." It used numbers and symbols which flashed upon him briefly, almost as if the city believed it was addressing an equal, when instead its mind was vast, alien, unknowable.

He had to get out, and do what he could, directly. He struggled to leave the Consilience.

Instead he was seized, like a small fish in the mouth of a large one, and taken deep.

—Pain at 187.43 degrees elevation 46 feet. And again 187.31. 124 and 399.

Numbers unreeled through Peabody's mind and being; the city's mind and being. He experienced a three-dimensional real time impact when each explosive hit.

He plummeted wildly through the city's to panic.

—It is gone!

—What is gone?

—My orienting information. The way I am to go.

He was washed with fear and did not know if it was his own, or the city's.

The city was speaking of the information he had stolen from NASA, decades ago when the richness of the world's technological infrastructure had not been entirely lost. Its directional calculus incorporated the star maps, but was dependent on other information no longer available.

—Too much damage. I wasn't able to transfer it in time. You brought it here. You know where to find it. I need it. Now.

I will be leaving soon.

—I'll go, Peabody assured the city, feeling the weight of untold depths and trans-human conclusions despite the city's plain language. It was as if the city was trying to talk to a child. Which, compared to the Consilience, he was.

He would have to travel to Johnson Space Center, outside of Houston, although the thought of venturing back into the strangeness of post-nanotech America was not a pleasant one. He had hidden in here for a very long time. It was a long shot, but he would do his best to sort through whatever remnants might be there in Houston and recompile the navigational information the city needed.

A rush of memories: *Children crowd into a doorway as he herds cleaning bots down a long corridor with a wide janitor's broom. The bots start out sparkling clear and end up dirt-brown. He is a spy; this is his alias.*

Each day, the children yell, "The Janitor!" and he leans the broom against their doorway and steps inside. He figures it's a day care for employee's children. He wonders where the adults are. He never sees any with the children.

There are toys, sleek medical machines, and his first glimpse of the government-developed learning cocoons. He understands what they are only later.

The children swarm over him, laughing. "The Janitor! Don't go! Come back soon, Janitor!"

After several weeks he is able to do what he came to do. He steals a copy of NASA's maps, which show where the Signal is coming from, put together from international information sources which are quickly dwindling, and leaves.

—How much time do I have?

—*Forty-eight days. At that time there will be a window.*

—A window?

—*An avenue,* the city replied somewhat impatiently. *Through space-time. To the transformational change. The singularity. The homing heart of your quest, Jason Peabody. Once you go, you will finally* **know.** *Finally* **be.**

—Finally?

—*You cannot understand it now. Neither can I. We are the bridge . . .*

Peabody was suffused with unaccustomed, unanticipated joy.

He also saw the truth of what the city said—imperfectly, as a child might, but accepting the urgency. If this information was not retrieved and incorporated, the entire enterprise would fail.

It was like calculating trajectories, or doing any other precise, motion-dependent work. There was a target. A great change had washed through the atmosphere, from *somewhere.* Presaging *something.* Even as a plant might put all of its energy into producing a future flower, though it knew not what it did, or a human child develop into puberty, there was some kind of cosmic maturity awaiting them. Some bright awakening.

Peabody glimpsed the edge of this—the possibility of it, the deep workings of its harmonies, of which he, and everything, was a part. There was no Plan; there was only Event, only constant emergence—freeform improvisation, following certain embedded rules which themselves could change.

Consciousness, its by-product, wanted to flash through all of it. Wanted to inhabit all of matter.

Suddenly, another terrible blast shook the walls.

The city which had spoken to him vanished. It was dark, and deadened, as if part of him had suffered a stroke.

He struggled, trapped; tried to shout, but could not even do that.

And then, the enhanced hormonal network embedded within his biology was hijacked by—

The Westerns. An obscure and obsolete branch of study followed by a group of serious fanatics. Crescent City was comprised of thousands of such groups.

The Westerns library had been damaged in the attack, and was in danger of losing its backups as well. It urgently sought replication in any warm body it could find.

Peabody just happened to be there. And was able to provide the childhood link that let it all in, for some of his strongest memories were of the American West, where he had grown up.

He was ambushed by pure Cowboy.

He was among the red buttes of Arizona, in the glory of so much land and so much blue sky.

Then it was more than recalling. It was learning. It was knowing.

He expanded far beyond himself. He was an entire country, its mythos, its deep, imperative tales.

Ancient Westerns filmed in Sedona. Radio chants from Wind Rock, heard at night on the clear-channel station. The great white mountain outside Flagstaff where the Hopi spiderwoman spun the world below. Buffalo gals, Texas bluebells, Oklahoma nights, bar fights, cattle drives, range wars. Stories, stories, stories.

Trying on a glowing golden mythical man coaxed, no flung, from the Consilience; trying him on for size, with cultural overlays, Broadway plays, Gunsmoke, Cormac McCarthy, slaughterhouses, dangerous cities, rivers filled with trout, poets on the loose. Science—homegrown and bequeathed by immigrants, melding into a doorway of light the like of which he could not bear, lodging in the biological niches of bones and flesh and blood, impregnating and crazing him with all the lost emotions and all the dreams and all the potential and . . .

And the future . . .

But wait—the light—his quest! He could not remain like this!

He was thrown from the frantic Consilience as it was damaged by another explosion.

Scientific Delirium Madness

Dania Cooper ran along the western boardwalk as explosions lit the night and shook the ground, using her arm to shield herself from falling, burning fragments. A dark shape loomed off to the west. Light flared around it, revealing a long, low ship.

As the fireworks continued, she saw several more.

Her main impulse was to try and protect the supercollider. It had been so long in the making that she felt physical pain, thinking that it might once more be destroyed. Just a few hours ago, it had responded to some powerful event.

People were running in every direction in the first pavilion she came to. She ignored them and grabbed a cart. As she careened through the panicking crowds, she felt cool and remarkably removed from the melee.

She had no idea who was behind this attack, and it really didn't matter. Crescent City was a legend to most of the world, and there had been more than one attempt to gain control of it.

Only here, apparently, was there complete free will. Only here had nanotechnology's promise been manifested in a life of ease and joy for its citizens, if one was to believe the information coming from the rest of the world. Human life on the continents was apparently divided into those who lived in cities which had mutated into a spectrum of strange places and those who lived plain rural lives of agriculture, shunning and fearing nanotechnology.

What did these attackers want? Probably they knew of the richness of life in Crescent City and wanted to live here. That was one great flaw of the city: limited space. A certain number of refugees were taken in every year. The number was carefully calculated by an algorithm that predicted how many could be safely absorbed without upsetting all the balances which had evolved. Refugees petitioning for admittance were given a date when they could return. There was an island of them somewhere close. Perhaps they had simply banded together, tired of awaiting permission to live here.

Crescent City had no army; no navy, though there were various defenses. Judging from the strength of this attack, though, they may well be breached. Dania, like everyone else, could only try to reach a relatively safe area and do her best to help contain this attack. It had been over twenty years since the last altercation, and most citizens had been lulled into thinking themselves safe.

She stopped just short of a jagged edge where she could see through to the level below. There was no way around the hole. She abandoned the cart, backtracked, and made her way into the interior past tangled burning debris drenched by sprinklers. Her throat ached from smoke.

She reached the tower she sought, found a free elevator, and directed it to go to the fortieth floor, which in an emergency was designated as a command area.

The door opened on a scene of horror. People lay groaning on the floor. In the dim light she saw pools of blackness she knew to be blood. The invaders ignored her. They all seemed to be wearing black, and were occupied with the information nodes.

Dania was chilled. Clearly whoever had led the attack was familiar with the city—perhaps someone who had left long ago and who now returned as some kind of backward king or queen to gain glory.

A figure advanced toward her threateningly, and she hastily closed the elevator door and told it to go up, to the level below the top floor. Her voice shook badly, as did her hands.

As the elevator rose, she realized that the metapheromones that had bequeathed her with extraordinary intelligence and kept her secondary personality intact for so long that she had practically forgotten that she was Dania Cooper—a grieving, angry, gene-twisted mother from Salvation, Tennessee—were no longer being issued by the city.

Emergent Cowboy

When Crescent City Cowboy stepped out of the elevator onto the dizzying transparent floor, four pirates in black T-shirts shouted and rushed him. His hand went to his newly grown six-shooters and he shot without even thinking about it, though he was filled with horror the next instant, sickened by his readiness to kill.

Two men spun around, cried out, then slumped on to the floor. The other three staggered backward and supported themselves against the wall.

Crescent City Cowboy was puzzled, since he saw no blood. He looked at the barrel of the revolver in his right hand.

The first man sang, "Getting to know you—"

The second one sang, "I get a kick out of you—"

The third one sang, "OoooOAK!lahoma—"

The fourth one wiped a tiny splat of goo from his cheek, looked at Peabody with disgust, and did not sing. He said, "Goddamn you and this whole crazy place. I warned them we shouldn't come." He staggered down the hall, away from the newly made Crescent City Cowboy and his terrible musical guns.

Crescent City Cowboy stared at them all for a moment. Peabody's thoughts swelled, willing themselves to take control once again. The effort was like a wave, and passed quickly.

A wealth of titles washed through the Cowboy's mind, all aspects of himself. Crescent City Shorty, for he had the short form of the city within him. The radio . . . something about radio was so important to something within him.

*Some***thing**?? railed Peabody silently. *Me, damn you!*

Crescent City Radio Cowboy Shorty smiled, spun his pistols, and stuck them in the holsters. He could get used to this.

He strode down the corridor. Other folks needed help.

An Old Beginning

Hours after the initial attack, Dania crept down the north-northwest corridor of the fifty-third level of Crescent City, leaning into the hot wind that swept through the wide-open hallway. Only shimmering nets spun of spidersteel kept people and objects from plunging into the heaving Caribbean Sea, for this knob was cantilevered out over black ocean lit with explosions.

"Is it *this*? Is it *this*?" she muttered, touching as she passed ovals of color with her right palm. None of them, apparently, were *this*, for she kept weaving across the corridor. Her long hair was wild and matted. Her eyes were fixed and staring. She was naked, and across her body pulsed tiny pictures. Her clothes had been ripped from her by one of the pirates before she knocked him out with the taser she managed to grab from him.

She sank to the floor and rolled into a spidersteel web, and it bulged out into the air. She watched acrid clouds, lit every minute or so by new explosions, for quite a while. She closed her eyes and tried to think. She had to think or die.

As she lay wrapped in the soothing spidersteel, a younger Dania walked through her mind.

With excitement and trust and far too little fear that younger self, so many years ago, had entered a certain room in the younger Crescent City. There she lay in the translucent hammock which grew around her, and surrendered her brain cells in layers to the city itself, to the community effort. Every bit of information about the old Dania Cooper was replicated and saved.

A new self, previously chosen by her, invaded her body, realigning the lineaments of the frail stuff of personality in accordance with her true potential, which had gone awry because of her mother's habit of drinking several gin and tonics daily while she was pregnant. New chemistries, slightly askew, promised a greater capacity for learning. The pure information of twentieth- and twenty-first-century thought were laid down. They were transparent to her consciousness when she finally opened her eyes and said, "Damn, what a headache," rolled out of the cocoon, and lay gazing at the silvery ocean for a long time, surprised at the pain. She walked on her knees across the floor and pulled herself onto a low stool. Before her the wall tilted at an angle good for viewing. The surface was translucent green. She touched it with one finger.

"Hello, Dania," said the wall. "Howzit?"

"Headache. Sore throat." The effort of speaking brought a slight sweat to her body, which was immediately chilled by the breeze off the sea.

After a silence of a few seconds, the wall spoke again. "You have combined organic chemistries, via the DNA pattern you chose, which will produce this effect from time to time. I am assembling a painkiller for the headache. If you wish, you can return to your original template."

"Why wasn't I told of this side effect?" she asked.

"It is a regressive feature of several of the DNA strands you chose to incorporate when combined with your own. Mostly this is yourself, as you would have been had you been properly nourished as a fetus. But there are also some additions. Apparently . . . you modeled only the top five probabilities. This is number seven. It took a long time to factor and you did not wait for the outcome. Here is the painkiller."

She touched a pulsing green spot and the opiates entered her body through her hand and bound themselves to the appropriate neuronal sites. She sighed as the pain left her.

"Do you wish to return and start over again?"

"No," she said with complete certainty. Now that the pain was gone she saw the world anew. There was enough of her old self to appreciate the difference. She had arrived from Tennessee, after a hellish trip through the South, with an approximate I.Q. of 130, according to the city. Her I.Q. was now much, much higher. The difference was stunning. She did not have to ponder. Or perhaps now her pondering took place so rapidly that she couldn't even discern it.

"You are advised that since you are a free-moving body you may well find yourself in an environment that will not be able to formulate the necessary painkillers. Such headaches will always be a part of this particular makeup. We have determined that by changing certain hormones, which involves a cascade of changes in other systems . . ."

"No," she said, standing up. "Maybe later. Keep the template, please, in the Dania conglomerate. I plan to enjoy this. A lot."

She left the room.

Dania, having recalled what took place so long ago, blearily opened her eyes, still in the spidersteel bulge. She was now sure that she was on the correct floor. Something about this attack, apparently, had ruined some delicate balance deeply necessary to her. If she didn't get it resolved soon, she might die in great pain. Maybe a lot of people were going to die.

She hauled herself back to the solid floor and crawled along. She heard distant shouts and hoped that they were coming from the floor below. The pirates were working their way upward.

She could not afford to lose more time. She probably could not even afford the time it would take to find the right room. They had taken out sixty-seven percent of the memory of Crescent City, according to information that lit the floor next to her hands, and killed many people. Memory, which previously had been equally distributed throughout the vast structure, was severely compromised. It had defaulted to an earlier time. But not before Dania found that her entire life's work on the Theory of Everything was wiped out. That, as much as anything else, caused this dark and terrible lethargy.

She sat for a minute, gathering what little strength remained. To her right sprawled a large dark shape.

It was a body. The head had been severed and was lying in a pool of congealed black blood that stank.

Shaking, she turned and grabbed a nearby chair; using it to steady herself, she pushed it along and slid her feet across the smooth floor.

This, yes, she thought, surprised at having found the right door on the right floor. It slid open at her approach.

Inside a man sat at a console. He did not glance up. "Come in, Dania."

Heart thudding, she pushed her way inside, tottered around, and practically fell into her chair. The door closed behind her.

"No, you don't have to worry. I am . . ." The figure turned, and Dania could not see his face in the shadow. He cleared his throat. Then he leaned forward into the light and his grin was plain. "I'm Crescent City Radio Cowboy Shorty. You can call me Cowboy."

His voice seemed different than the voice she had heard at first, filled with the lilt of poetry when before it had been plain, and defeated. He had short blond hair and a red bandana tied round his neck. His bare, brown chest shimmered with sweat. His eyes, deepset beneath a high forehead, were blue. He wore tight faded jeans with a huge silver belt buckle. A wide hand-tooled leather belt with two holsters rode low on his hips, and pearl-handled revolvers shone gently in the faint light. A ten-gallon hat rested on the floor next to him.

"I kinda like bein' out and about, know what I mean?" His voice was rough but friendly. The grin faded as he stared at Dania. "Sorry, miss. Forgot my manners. You're in a hell of a bad way."

"Your fault," she managed to croak as he gathered her in his arms and strode across the floor and gently deposited her in a cocoon. "If you're the city, it's your fault." She had had conversations more than once with personifications of the city, so this did not seem strange, although the personifications were always different. She remembered a huge African woman, a jazz saxophonist, a Rasta fish farmer, a no-nonsense Chilean doctor.

"Now, now, I warned you." His voice was gently chiding. "I fired warning shots across the bow, so to speak, on"—he held her hand for a moment and then looked at his palm—"7/14/2074, 1/29/75, want to hear the whole list? It runs well nigh up to my elbow—"

This scolding outraged Dania, who was so tired that she trembled. "No. I ignored you, it's true. I was warned. But . . ." her eyes burned with unshed tears. "I . . . guess I've fallen in love with . . . this way of *seeing*. This way of *being*."

He knelt next to her and squinted as he studied the DNA readings that marched across the floor. "If I didn't know better, I'd say you had a touch of Godel in you, even though he wasn't in our gene pool. But rest easy, my pretty—" He stood and whirled; his right hand whipped out a revolver and he fanned the door with bullets. The pirate in the doorway stopped abruptly and blinked. She turned on her heel and left, singing something about an elephant's eye.

"Now where were we, little lady. Oh yes." He squinted at her, his tan face broken by a million lines. "Want to go back to the original?"

"No. Why wasn't this model run? Why—"

"It *was* run," said Crescent City Shorty gently. "You are it. Took a while. Now we know. I have other work to do. Choice: original or dead. Choose."

"Original," she said with irritation in her voice. "I barely remember the girl. So naïve. So stupid."

"Not at all," he said, and touched the wall where it pulsed yellow.

She closed her eyes in the moonlight and sighed, hearing distant explosions, feeling the floor rock with closer ones. Twice the process stopped and had to be started again; each time she sensed desperation in the Cowboy through her exhaustion.

Over the hours she stirred; once she woke blearily to a loud rousing chorus of *The Sidewalks of New York,* and then some African-based tune she recalled as being popular during the three years when ships from Africa found their way to Crescent City. They were all a part of him, part of that fine upstanding Cowboy, Crescent City Shorty. Radio Cowboy. Whoever he was. He was jammed full of all kinds of information—movies, musicals, stuff from the wild warring multimedia millennium that preceded this one . . . The damaged city told her this, much as a mother might croon a bedtime song to a child.

She woke as Dania Cooper. She sat up, recalling her old body with shocked surprise.

It was all so familiar. She bore only glimmering memories of what it had been like to be Crescent City Dania. She was rocked with regret, and feared the coming deluge of her old self—wild, impulsive, strewing interpersonal havoc wherever she went like confetti from a float. "At least you're alive," she told herself. She stood up, stretched, and went into the shower. It cut off after two minutes, leaving her hair filled with shampoo. Cursing and scrubbing herself with a towel, she walked over to the console to order some clothes—a simple T-shirt, shorts, and sandals—her uniform. She stopped short as the window cleared in front of her.

The sun shone on a silvery sea far below, littered with vessels.

What she could see of the city was shocking. Huge blasted gaps revealed half-rooms. It took a moment for her to understand that the distant, oddly still people lying in impossible poses among the ruins were dead.

She turned from it, sobbing and angry, and flung the towel to the floor. All was ruined; lost. The memory of the supercollidor, that promise of the deep understanding of light, along with her ability to perhaps fathom such truths, was an ache in her chest. Everything, *everything,* was gone.

Including herself.

Her clothing, when it was finished, was not what she had ordered. Instead she had a long, multicolored Gypsy skirt, cowgirl boots, a lace shirt that fit tight when buttoned up. And naturally, she thought with irritation, in no mood for wry humor, a cowgirl hat. She found a comb in the bathroom and yanked it through her long, tangled light-brown hair, aware of her tan face and hazel eyes framed by bangs as she had not been in years and years, seeing as how in Crescent City appearance was a shell so mutable that it was thought of as decoration, like clothing. Now it was more permanently assigned.

She dressed and was trying the hat on for size when the main door slid open. She started.

But it was Cowboy. "Good. Come on now." He held out his hand.

They hurried through ruined, deserted plazas filled with soaked debris. Children wailed, somewhere. She and Cowboy pressed themselves against the wall when they glimpsed black-suited intruders.

Finally they arrived at a high tower and had to climb several flights of stairs. She put her hand on the doorknob at the top, but it wouldn't turn; Cowboy reached around her and his hand made it turn.

She stepped into a small round room.

Behind her Cowboy whistled through his teeth with something that sounded like relief. "Looks all right." He walked over to a console and sat down. He put earphones on his head and started twisting dials. "Got to concentrate," he muttered. "Can't let this overwhelm me . . ."

Dania heard strange whines and pings. Lights flashed. He threw some switches, pushed some buttons; scooted his chair to a keypad and typed something.

"Is this radio?" Dania asked, looking out the window and seeing lots of antennae, realizing with dread that the self she had grown so used to would have known . . . lots and lots more about this. "I thought radio didn't work."

He didn't reply. Either he was busy or couldn't hear her.

He looked different in this place. Something about his posture, the muscles in his face. He looked much, much older.

She walked around, trying to find signs of who he really was.

Shelves of curious devices lined the north wall. Radios. Very old radios. She remembered seeing them in her childhood, in her grandparents' house in Chattanooga. She saw a small Arvin made, a plate below it said, in 1939, its left side a laddered grille, its right side a small square dial window above two acornlike knobs. Astoundingly old. She picked up a small one labeled PHILCO SEVEN, MANUFACTURED 1959, ORIGINALLY PURCHASED AT MIDWAY ISLAND PX 1960. It was made of ivory-colored plastic and had a round speaker. A wire with an earphone dangled from one side.

She heard steps on the stairway. She whispered, "Somebody's coming!" She touched Cowboy's shoulder, since he did not react. He hit a button decisively and removed his earphones. "What?"

"Somebody's coming. I hear voices outside the door."

They heard a lot of pounding, then descending footsteps. He said, "Probably going to get their explosives. Now's our chance."

Dania followed him down the stairs. They ducked out at the next level.

"Do you need to go back?" she asked.

"No. I sent the signal. It's time to go now."

"What signal?"

"It's called Sleepers Awake. It will be transmitted constantly. Most of the information will probably be stripped away, but eventually it might get to where I want it to go. But it probably won't."

"So you really *are* a radio cowboy."

"Yes," he said. "I suppose so. I'd rather just be upstairs with my radios, that's for sure. Come on. We have lots of work to do."

"Like what?"

"We have to get ready to leave."

"Where are we going?"

"Houston."

"Why?"

"Do you want to go or not?"

"That sounds a bit rude. I'd like to know why."

"Crescent City has lost a vital guidance system and I'm hoping that I can find it there. Or meet someone who can help reconstruct it. You, supposedly, are someone who ought to be pretty interested in this."

"What do you mean, 'guidance system'?"

"Didn't you know?" His face lost all of Cowboy's nuances. He looked grim, and old. "I'm sure you used to. Crescent City is turning into a spacecraft. The change was initiated just before the attack. Naturally, its progress has been set back some. But it will heal, and it will continue. Maybe it will take off filled with these rabble-rousers. Drop them off on Venus."

"I guess . . ." Dania frowned. "Yes, that's something that I used to know. Still know, if I think about it." She sighed. "I don't like this very much."

"I don't like it at all." His voice was older too. Not brash and bold. But thoughtful, as if he weighed every word. "I have to leave. But you have a choice. You can stay here if you want. You could probably be restored in a few weeks, if all goes well. I'm . . . not sure how I'll fare. It's getting very difficult to . . . stay focused."

Dania looked out from the high place, surveying the ruined city.

She had often missed the land of her youth. The South. Memphis. New Orleans. They said it was all different now. Coasts farther inland. Part of Antarctica had fallen into the ocean.

But it was the *land* she wanted. She realized that she hadn't been on land, real land, for years. "May I take this with us?" She held up the Philco Seven from Midway Island, still in her hand.

He smiled sadly, and she could see that it meant something to him. "Sure, why not." He took it from her and opened the back. "It's good. I always keep fresh batteries in them. Just in case."

Dania and the Radio Cowboy left Crescent City at night, while it flared behind them, parts of it still patched with fires which the broken sprinkler system could not quench.

It took them twelve days of hard sailing to reach the coast, because they were blown way off course. It took a lot longer than that to get to Texas.

By then they'd pretty much forgotten why they'd come.

Argentina,
Six Months Earlier

"She who tells the stories controls the world."

—Hopi

The Storyteller: Angelina

Sunday, the day of Angelina's kidnapping, was unpleasant from the beginning.

Angelina slept late on Sundays, rising at first light rather than in the dark. And Louis, her seventeen-year-old son, slept even later. Every day, to Angelina's growing chagrin.

Angelina hurriedly tied her robe as she ran down the broad, ornate stairway of the ranch house her family had built in the eighteen-hundreds.

In the kitchen, the cold slate of the floor chilled her bare feet, waking her fully. Outside the window, dawn spilled across her vast pampas landhold, blazing pink on the summer snowfields of the mountains forming its border.

She wrenched open the fire door of the vast ceramic kitchen stove some distant ancestor had imported from Spain, caught up an iron shovel, and turned over the smoldering coals. She peeked into the white-enameled teapot to make sure it had water in it.

Justo, her guard dog, a large black beast, scratched on the door and she let him in. He greeted her effusively, slobbered water from his bowl, then flopped onto his pillow next to the stove.

The bell tolled for early Mass, ringing out clearly down the valley. She imagined the intonations of the congregation; her mother had taken her to at least four Masses a week when she was growing up.

God spare us from
The tiny machines
And from the plagues
That threaten to change us.
Keep us pure
That we may achieve
Salvation through your grace after death.

Back in her bedroom, Angelina quickly pulled on jeans, a heavy wool sweater, and her grandmother's tall black boots embossed with red roses. She twisted her long black hair into a chignon. On her way downstairs she considered knocking on Louis's door, but refrained. It would only irritate him and she'd apparently done enough of that already.

He blamed Angelina for his father leaving several years earlier. But there was no one to blame. Angelina missed Manuel but could not go. She had a ranch to oversee, and now, in particular, there was a crisis to which she had to attend. Louis never understood that she and his father did not have what might be called a traditional relationship, which was what Louis longed for, apparently—the fairy tale mother and father. And where had Manuel gone, anyway? Barcelona? Milan? She had no idea. Surely not into the heart of Europe—Germany; France. No one ever returned from there. He'd sent messages irregularly from Morocco for a few months, then stopped completely.

Because Angelina was wealthy, she did not look or feel her hundred or so years. Louis had been a surprise, but a welcome one. She knew that the villagers referred to her behind her back as The Witch. Those more enlightened had left over the decades, leaving behind a concentrated brew of those too fearful of the world to venture out.

In the kitchen, a thin stream of whistling steam issued from the teapot. She pried open a battered tin box with an old picture of her aunt's Buenos Aires bank on it, grabbed a handful of mate, poured it into the pot, and set it aside to brew. She slid a heavy iron skillet holding *chorizo* over the hot part of the stove, tossing a section of the sausage to Justo, who snapped it down.

After five minutes, she poured herself a gourd of steaming yerba mate and sat in a tall-backed chair. Propping her boots on the windowsill, she gazed at the sharp white ridgeline.

This was her Sunday service. She knew that her mother would have been chagrined to know that it was her father who had awakened her soul, and not with church.

When she was five, her father deemed her old enough for her first mountain trek. They set off with a pack train and two ranch hands. It took three days of travel to reach the foot of the mountain she saw from her window, Alta Chica. The hands set up a base camp at the foot of a waterfall. She remembered the worry of her mother, who never traveled without maids and who spent hours making up her face each morning. Her father mostly refused to carry her during the day-long ascent through pine forests to a cold, high peak, but gave in near the top. From that visage, after they drank hot chocolate from a thermos, he pointed out the boundaries of their land.

"We have defended this land since before there was an Argentina," he told her. "There is Old Bald Man. See? Far across the valley, so high that there are no trees. At the very top you will find an iron cross and below that an iron wheel buried in the ground. Now, turn north"—he gently rotated her, grasping her shoulders from behind through layers of ultrathin high-tech mountaineering clothing—"do you see the three jagged teeth there? Yes, that's it. Mouth of the Dog, that mountain is called. Again, on that middle tooth, you will find the cross and below it the iron wheel. We have the land-grant papers from the king of Spain in the house, and of course everything is scanned into the computer."

His serious manner and his low, calm voice caused Angelina to pay close attention to every word.

"You have probably heard of *El Silencio.* It was not like this before you were born. We always had radio and television, not just sometimes. Things are already changing back quickly to the way they were in your grandfather's time. But this was our land before radio and television, and it will be our land no matter what happens. It will be the responsibility of you and your children to hold it in trust.

"The village still depends on us. Your uncles stayed in the city after university. That was good. There are things that they can do for the family there.

"A lot of changes are taking place now, all over the world. I hope they do not touch us severely. At any rate, you won't have much memory of what the world used to be like, so maybe you will be able to handle things better than I might. You will be the oldest, or"—his sigh would always echo in her mind—"perhaps you will be our only child. I hope you will love it as much as I do."

She did. The village depended on her even more, today. She was not a reflective type of person, but she did find it worthy of irony that the ranch had passed through the industrial revolution relatively untouched, but was being battered to death by a simple little virus that was killing all the grass on the pampas—grass that some fool near Cordoba had seeded over thousands of hectares; genetically engineered grass that was supposedly better than the wild grass, more drought resistant, and so on. This grass had invaded the pampas.

And now that it was dying, the cattle had nothing to eat.

A knock sounded on the massive wooden door.

Angelina jumped up. Justo became a tornado of snarls and barks, but when the door opened and Carlos came in, he quieted and returned to his cushion.

Carlos was her foreman. He had been with the family since he was born. She was surprised to see him up so early on a Sunday morning. "Come in and sit down," she told him. "What is it?"

He remained in the doorway, removing his hat and holding it in both hands. "It is not a good idea, these vats."

"Haven't we discussed this already?"

He frowned. "I didn't know that it would be so soon. The gauchos haven't had enough time to get used to the idea."

"Well, they will. Otherwise they'll have to move to Buenos Aires."

The slight twist of Carlos's mouth acknowledged the absurdity of this alternative. No one from the village would ever consider such a thing. Buenos Aires had been converted into a city awash in new and fearful technologies fifty years earlier.

Angelina quoted, "'Vat-grown Beef from the Pampas of Argentina.' The vats have been delivered, Carlos, and that's what every one of them says, I have been assured, although it is written in Japanese. I don't know why they are so crazy about it. But it's lucky for us, since it lasts for the long trip to Japan." She laughed. "It *ages.* You know how hard I've worked since the train stopped running, Carlos. This is the perfect solution. After I get a bit ahead, I can bring in one of those teachers—"

Carlos shook his head. "Too many changes. They are frightened. They don't want one of those—those teaching mechanisms. Plus, they would not be out riding all day."

"It is a shame that they want to remain so ignorant. And it would be nice if they could understand the necessity of the vats. They are just going to have to learn how to tend them. They come with extensive tutorials."

"You can't expect the descendants of gauchos to give up their horses gladly, Senora. You aren't going to insist that I spend my days inside, are you?"

"I have been doing projections concerning the wild grasses we planted on the south side of the arroyo road. They should support the herd we have left starting next year. Until then we will need to bring in feed. To keep viable, we need trade, Carlos."

"They pray for your soul at this moment."

She laughed. "What is a soul? The souls of my uncles live in a vast machine called Buenos Aires and are tended by giant Bees. My mother believed that the soul of her parents lived in the statue of the Virgin Mary she kept at the hall altar, and I keep fresh flowers there. The soul of one of my cousins is somewhere on Mars, perhaps. Or maybe beyond, wherever it was he wanted to go."

Carlos's voice was harsh. "You are stupid to talk in such a fashion. You are lucky that no one but me hears it, especially with your husband gone. Even your own son scorns you."

It was amazing, she thought, how much the apparent desertion of a man, even a man worthless for ranch work, affected her standing.

Amazing, and exceedingly irritating. She had not stooped to explaining Manuel's leaving, which she attributed to his utter craze for something he called "culture," even to Louis, at least not more than once, and certainly not to Carlos or anyone else.

Angelina said, "I think that you should leave now."

Carlos bowed slightly. "I am sorry. Forgive me." He put on his hat.

"What is going on, Carlos?"

"Nothing, Senora." He left.

She wondered what he was lying about.

An hour later she was in her bedroom, buttoning her leather vest. She had to take a load of hay to twelve cattle discovered alive about six kilometers away. After dallying as long as she dared in the hope that Louis would wake and want to accompany her, so that they could at least attempt some conversation, she was startled by a knock on the front door. She hurried to the balcony that overlooked the foyer.

Louis ran down the stairs from his bedroom, wearing his usual assortment of strange clothes. No doubt he'd slept in them. His many braids were rough and several were undone. He wore no socks in his short boots.

"When did you get up?" she asked, her question echoing back from the well-like space.

He ignored her and went to the door as Angelina hurried down the stairs. "Wait! I'll get it. How many times—"

He paused and looked up at her. His once-cheery face had lost the last vestiges of childhood after his father had left. Now it was thin and drawn and austere, the face of an adult. She paused on the stairs for a moment, for in that instant his change was brought home to her.

In that instant she lost him.

He yanked open the door.

She saw that even he registered surprise when a woman dressed in the postal uniform of a Buenos Aires postal company stood holding a small package.

It seemed to Angelina that during the previous months change had been so much more precipitous, and that it had always been for the worse. A new nervousness invaded her. She never knew what to expect, now.

She did not expect a courier. Some sort of renegade soldier, perhaps, or simply one of the gauchos bent on a personal audience, rage barely contained. Not this woman handing a package to Louis, asking him to sign, bowing and turning on her heel.

"It's from Papa!" he said, and she was close enough now to see his thumbs whiten, so hard did they press on the package.

"So it says." Her tone of voice was dry. "It seems he is in Paris. Thoughtful of him to let us know." She reached for it. "Give it to me."

"No!" He pulled out a pocketknife and severed the tape and wrappings.

"A book!" Disappointment shadowed his face; his voice. "It's just a book."

Nothing was "just" with Manuel. It was his way to layer life with inferences and to invent them where they did not exist. "May I please look at it?"

Louis handed it to her only because, she knew, it had been addressed to her.

Hopscotch. A rather weighty book, by one Julio Cortázar. She had never heard of the book or the author. Books were rather out of fashion, but Manuel was crazy about them.

"Not one message in a year, and now this. You see how much he cares."

Louis's eyes matched hers for scorn. "*You* wouldn't understand!" He snatched it away and stalked from the room.

"Louis—" She took a step to follow him, then heard another knock. Frowning, she turned to get the door. It was a woman from the village, with word that her ten-year-old girl had come across another dead steer, and could they please have the meat.

* * *

When she returned from delivering the feed, it was almost midnight. She was bone-tired. She went straight to bed, but woke suddenly at four A.M.

When she opened her eyes, she knew the time immediately. A lifetime of insomnia and an intimate knowledge of the phases of the moon told her this in the language of light; each tooled leather curlicue on her boots stood out in the light of the full moon as it bathed her bedroom. All her life the merest sound could wake her and she would rise, annoyed, and do things she would rather have done by day, badly, without concentration, until dawn came, leaving her to push through the hours with red eyes, in a fog.

She could not get back to sleep. She was unsettled by everything—the failure of the grasses, the growing hostility of the gauchos, and most of all, her son.

And Manuel.

She sighed, threw off her covers, and pulled on her robe and some warm slippers. She padded downstairs to the living room and turned on a lamp next to the chair where she usually sat, intending to go over some bookkeeping.

There, on the coffee table, was *Hopscotch,* lying opened to the back.

Two small, clear plastic envelopes were cemented to the back cover. One was neatly labeled LOUIS, and the other was labeled ANGELINA.

Inside her envelope, she saw a small paperish stamp, really a gel, she knew. Louis's envelope was empty.

She sat down heavily.

What was wrong with Manuel? This was the worst sort of irresponsibility. She didn't want Louis exposed to this kind of thing, not while he was still growing. This demented information culture, which seemed to have less and less to do with the real world, was too powerful, too overwhelming, even for most adults. It had obviously proved so to Manuel, otherwise he would not have even considered sending this and inviting Louis to partake.

Manuel had not left on a sudden whim. There had been no

other woman, no sudden blaze of hot disagreement. Their only argument was a very old one: They were different at their core. It had been a happy difference, a complementary difference, years ago, when they met, and had continued so for several decades and even for the first fifteen years of Louis's life.

And then their differences seemed suddenly magnified in their son—

But she had no time for reverie. She swept the book from the table and hurried upstairs.

Louis's bed was empty.

She flicked on the light.

There on his bed, was a note.

> *I have gone to meet Papa.* Hopscotch *will guide me. I left the rest for you, even though I know that you hate me and Papa. That is why you kept me from all of this beauty. Please do not follow me. I am old enough to be on my own. Stay here with the cattle you love.*
>
> *Louis.*

She crumpled the paper in her hand.

She was sure that he had left soon after she had, perhaps around noon.

She had to catch him. She ran to her room to get dressed.

And then Justo began to bark.

Something was wrong.

His second deep bark from the yard below was silenced with a shot and she thought she heard a curse. She grabbed the gun she kept beneath her pillow.

They clumped into the kitchen below her, not bothering to keep quiet now that they had gained the house. She wondered if they knew she was alone.

Still in her nightgown, she stepped out the window onto the porch roof, pushed the window closed, and steeled herself against the cold. The wooden shingles were rough against her bare feet; she saw at a glance that they had arrived in a Jeep, so there could not be more than four of them. She wondered how far they had come. There were no public charging stations within a hundred kilometers. Justo lay in the snow, obviously dead.

Losing not an instant to uncertainty, she ran lightly across the porch roof, holding up the hem of her nightgown, and rounded the corner. Tossing down her gun, she turned around, crouched, grabbed the edge of the roof with both hands, lowered herself, and let go, staggering backward.

She heard them shouting inside the house. Teeth chattering, she grabbed the gun and ran into the stable, yanking a bridle from a nail and pulling it over her horse's head. Leading him from his stall, she jumped onto her mounting block and pushed herself up and onto his back. Holding the gun in her right hand, she lightly kicked him and he sprang out of the barn door.

She turned as he passed the porch and shot at the person standing there. She heard a cry. "That's for Justo," she whispered, rounding the corner of the barn.

And there she ran into the row of villagers, torches burning, rifles pointed at her.

Carlos was at the forefront.

"So—you have not been to church for forty years?" asked one of the soldiers as the others kicked through the debris of her living room, toting up a larger list of crimes to justify taking her, as if killing a soldier wasn't enough.

"Probably more like seventy years," she said. "Is that against the law?"

"Where is your son?"

"I wish I knew."

They flung cushions around and scraped the contents of shelves onto the floor in rude piles. A man and a woman laughed as they threw things into the fire. She heard the word "blood" and then she knew.

She felt a chill of fear for the first time.

They hated her for what she was. And who knew what she was?

Only Carlos. Only Carlos knew her true birthday, the one that her lawyer uncle went to great lengths to conceal many years ago. Carlos knew because his grandmother had been midwife to her birth.

So. These people simply hated her for what she was. That was all. What was worse, they were afraid of her. They were the perfect soldiers for this job.

There was a bounty on her head. She wondered if Carlos would share it with the villagers. Through the wide door to the kitchen, she saw him sign a paper on the table. He looked up at her, then quickly looked away.

"Slime," she shouted.

The woman throwing things into the fire turned and slapped her face. "Shut up."

One of them brought a leather carryall from the kitchen and shoved it at her. She looked inside—bread, cheese, even a bottle of wine. So they were to feed her.

She bent down, casually picked up *Hopscotch,* which lay beneath a broken vase, as if it was of no matter to her. She slipped it into the bag.

They allowed her a sweater and yanked her out into the front courtyard. She was handcuffed to a bar in the back of the Jeep, which roared down the five-kilometer-long drive. When they got to the main road, the Jeep stopped and she wondered why.

"Look back, Senora!" said the driver, turning in his seat with a leer. "Your great ranch now belongs to the villagers! It is back in the hands of the gauchos, where it always belonged!"

She kicked the soldier sitting next to her viciously, and they bludgeoned her until she passed out.

They shook her awake. She had a dull, throbbing headache. One eye was swollen shut. The place they had stopped at looked like a tiny, long-deserted hospital.

She was angry that she was not able to measure distance by time, as she ought to have, but it was around noon, and north by the look of the trees. It didn't matter, though. She knew where she was, perfectly, as usual.

That was a bit of a shock. She had always thought that this orientation came from knowing her own land, and from traveling to and from Buenos Aires frequently when she was young. But now, though, she had never been here, she knew the mountains on the south side of the building before she rounded the corner; knew the pass out to the west.

They shoved her up concrete stairs and she stumbled, then laughed out loud at the knowing, just a short bark. She was hit with the stick again so that she fell. She laughed again, despite the blood crusting her hand and the lump on her forehead that she felt gingerly as she was pushed down a long dark hallway.

Before anything else, they drew her blood and rejoiced at what they found. She could tell by the set of their faces. They would collect the bounty. Damn Carlos!

Then they put her in a room with a high ceiling and barred windows and a washed-out print of mountains on the wall. She showered with cold water and blood ran down the drain. Her face was black and blue in the wavy aluminum mirror. Thank you, Carlos. She wondered only briefly what she could have done to prevent this. She wasn't God.

She was tortured by some kind of high sound they played at irregular intervals, penetrating pillows, shirts, anything she kept around her ears to try and muffle it. It reminded her of her childhood. She was nauseated; she couldn't eat. Not that they brought her anything worth eating. She hid *Hopscotch* under the pillow, but it didn't matter, since she realized after a day that no one would ever come into the room. She did not even find any surveillance cameras. It was a crude setup. They trusted, she decided, in the recorded sounds to keep her disoriented.

It was soon clear that her jailers were not the intrusive scientists she had always feared. One heard tales of how people like her fared in research facilities. They were treated like animals; tested; even vivisected, went the rumors. That was why her father and uncle had taken such care to disguise her birthdate legally. She had thought that, in the past thirty years, all interest had been lost. Who cared about these matters so long after *El Silencio* had become a settled reality? She had let down her guard.

She took out her book and considered it.

She had met Manuel at University, more than an age ago. Manuel had a lyrical brain. The world fell together in a different way for him, its parts modifying one another like a vast and special grammar, one that she rarely understood, much as he tried to communicate it to her. She had accused him of being crazy more than once. Studying genetics so that she could braid generations of cattle intelligently, and agriculture, the better to feed them, and all the adjuncts of ranching, with courses in engineering, business, and even a few in introductory nanotechnology thrown in, she marveled that someone with as good a mind as Manuel would waste it on such fluff as reading fiction day and night. It did not matter to her what happened to the people within the covers of a book. What mattered was the real world.

He had moved out to the pampas and lived there with her for decades, filling a study with thousands of books, and with increasingly strange methods of knowing. He went to Buenos Aires annually to be updated with the latest in the information technologies that allowed him to absorb books at a touch. And then, one day, he had abruptly left.

She opened the book. *FROM THIS SIDE,* she saw; and later on, *FROM THE OTHER SIDE.* Now, what did that mean?

Paging through it, she saw that it was studded with stamps. Octavio Paz, said one page, and she read a poem, something again about this side and the other side, and some nonsense about only the fog being real. Just about what you might expect from something Manuel liked.

On that page, as at the end of each chapter, was a paperish swallow-stamp which she could peel up and ingest. She was familiar with these and, in fact, even had the onboard ability to use such information, thanks to her aunt. She was not sure if it still worked, though. Her last trip to Buenos Aires had been twenty years ago.

It was all so strange there. Her Uncle Xeno had been at the vanguard of those who insisted that Buenos Aires convert to the new system of information exchange that involved large beelike creatures. Everyone who wanted to participate—to his way of thinking, everyone who wanted to be a part of the future—was able to be changed for free. This made a lot of people suspicious. "If a rich man wants this for us, it cannot be good. Just another form of exploitation." So Xeno was murdered. But not before he had made himself a part of the databank of the city, and his new self raged through the interstices helter-skelter, changing everyone within its boundaries whether they wanted to be changed or not.

She remembered watching *The King of Hearts* with Manuel, lying on a blanket in front of the fire as the movie blob was absorbed into the screen. It was a movie about an inmate releasing his fellow madmen in an insane asylum. She had thought it innocent and silly, but at the same time it touched her deeply. Manuel was like that. Trying to release her. Trying to bridge the gap. Trying to make her as lyrical as himself . . .

She took out the stamp with her name on it and touched it to her tongue.

She gasped. Images raced through her mind, threatening to overwhelm her.

She put the stamp back and slammed the book shut, annoyed with herself. Here, more than ever, she had to keep sane.

She heard sounds and looked out her window.

A battered white truck waited in the morning sunlight. One of her fellow prisoners was taken out and shoved into the back of the truck.

The chief soldier, the one who had mocked her, slammed the truck door and took possession of a large locked box. It probably contained whatever passed for riches around here. Perhaps nanotechnologically created diamonds, which poor, ignorant folk still thought of as rare wealth.

They were being auctioned off to the highest bidder. Angelina turned from the window.

Her door banged open. A soldier stood in the doorway. He waved a rifle at her.

She stood, walked over to him, and easily wrenched it from his hands. Complacent fool. She stood back and shot him point-blank. He looked at her with astonished eyes, moaned, and slumped to the floor, blood pulsing from his chest.

Two more soldiers ran down the hall and she shot them before they could shoot her. There was another around a corner, and some more coming in the door that led to the road. She counted as she shot; she was pretty sure there were only seven in this band of outlaws. They were obviously taken by surprise. She was sorry that, when she got to the door, the truck was bumping down the road. She shot at the tires, but missed.

She took the keys from one of the dead soldiers and went around opening the doors. Her fellow prisoners, of an age with her but varying wildly in appearance, stumbled forth, dazed. The power of the stamp she had touched pulsed through her, the magnificant, lyric silliness so prized by Manuel. "It is *The King of Hearts* after all!" she shouted grandly, with a flourish of her arms. "Poor souls—wake up! I have freed you!"

No one thanked her. Perhaps they thought her a soldier gone mad. To a person, they hurried through the hospital, grabbing food, and took the charged Jeeps. One even stumbled up a path into the mountains as Angelina watched. Well, she thought, maybe he is taking the direct route home. It was no concern of hers.

Several hours later, after a huge meal, a liter of mate, and not a little wine, Angelina sat on a low wall next to two bodies in the courtyard, feeling no remorse. To them she had been just another brain to be bartered when the price was right.

She felt refreshed now that she had turned off the piercing sounds. She had noticed, while checking each desperado to confirm his death, that each wore tiny earplugs. No wonder they had been so slow to respond to her shots.

And what now?

No matter what the villagers did back home, they could not

wrest ownership of the land from her by an illegal stroke of Carlos's pen on a document cooked up by outlaws. But let them see how they could manage without her. Let them just see.

It was obviously time for a change in her life.

Already she could see how the stamp was affecting her. It created a hunger for more. She had a powerful sense of incompleteness. Things were happening in the book, happening without her! She laughed. Memories of Manuel, long pushed back, woke.

She took *Hopscotch* out to the back, where there was a view of blue mountains subsiding gradually toward the plain, and no bodies.

This was more than just *Hopscotch,* she saw. In fact, the book itself was incidental, just a container holding not only itself, but a library of South American classics. Borges was here. Gabriel Gárcia Márquez. Manuel had told her that his theory was that their language held the doorway to many more dimensions, more places in time, than other languages. His believed that when children learned Spanish, it opened the part of their brain that ordered time to strange possibilities. Louis had probably not taken the time to investigate all of this; he had taken his labeled gel and run away.

She pulled out a stamp and swallowed it. She hoped that it would be easier than reading. That was the point, wasn't it? She never had the patience for reading.

And then—why stop?

Within fifteen minutes she was filled with all the references found within *Hopscotch*: Heidegger, Max Planck, Coleman Hawkins, Jelly Roll Morton—an intellectual, scientific, and artistic revolution almost two hundred years old. With increasing frenzy she paged through the book and swallowed all she found, despite the fact that a dull red warning began to pulse at the top of each page she turned: *Please ingest in the order selected by the author until the initiation process is complete!* A tiny voice spoke from one page: "You must allow time—" She turned that page and that voice stopped. A dry, old voice slowly spoke a poem from another page, and she listened. Then she turned the page for more. There were addenda in the back. Yes, the complete library of South American literature, up to and including 2040. A continuum of criticism raged through her, suggesting title after title until she was stuffed with books and reeling. Not too good to take in too many at once!

"Ha!"

This is a true Hopscotch, Manuel's stamp told her. *It includes all of the original volume, and picks up where Cortázar left off. I can think of no finer present for you and for Louis. Thank you for trying it, Angelina.*

Luckily, she reflected at sundown, she'd waited to use the book until after she'd killed the guards. Now that she had swallowed it, she didn't think anyone in *Hopscotch* would kill anyone else. At least not directly.

She leaned back her head and closed her eyes.

Manuel knew that such a book would split her world wide open into the shards of time of which it was truly composed. It was a trick—but a good trick, a loving trick, a way to break through to her at last. Long-forgotten memories assailed her and she relived them. On one of those annual treks with her father, along the ridge of the high range, she first heard the music with which she had kept uneasy truce into adulthood, and past her prime. It was now as much a part of her as her black eyes and straight long nose. She had always managed to push it aside. Her mother had complained that she had "a strong mind"; her father had been proud of it. Well, it took a strong mind to live her life. What did her mother expect?

Now, for the first time, she paid attention to the sound instead of locking it away.

As she sat in the growing shadows, it drew her outward, blended into objects; each object had its complexion of sound.

By lamplight she donned the only clean clothing she could find, the uniform of power. She gathered some supplies and left, taking one of the many charged Jeeps on which the outlaws apparently spent much of their wealth.

She knew exactly where she was and exactly where she was

going. The music grew as she drove down dark ridges on water-riven dirt roads. Shot with fragments of poems, she heard the voice of Pablo Naruda as the stars wheeled around, and slept in a culvert fifty kilometers outside of Buenos Aires.

She walked through a small town in early morning wearing the dangerous costume of soldiers, pulsing with chapters, hearing first the crumbled outer buildings with their faded painted signs and then moving into the center of town where coffee was served to her by frightened women. With each step she walked out of the generational-meme, the pattern of ancestors shattered forever.

She was alive for the first time. More intensely alive than she could have imagined before. Bright vitamins of sound grew her as if she were a plant, and heading toward some inevitable flowering.

She paused on a corner and wondered at it.

She used to watch the dance of the swans with which her mother had populated one of their ponds. The swans recognized one another in their mirroring dance. You are the one, they moved at each other. You are the one. She had always heard popular music as the mating cry of birds, one for the other. They are no different than we are, she always thought. Things that we know nothing of pull us. Compel us.

This was that much stronger.

It meant that she had to perch on windowsills and allow poetry to stud her life like random arrows.

And most of all it meant that she must go to the other side.

I'm Your Puppet

Policemen were everywhere on the outskirts of Buenos Aires. They drove up and down the night roads with spotlights mounted on the roofs of their cars, blaring intimidating speeches from megaphones. Angelina watched from the shadow of a store entrance as long lights prowled down the cross streets to her right and left.

She was a bit shaky from her long trip. Two women had stolen her Jeep while she peed in the bushes along the limited access highway, taking her completely by surprise. She then walked ten kilometers, as best she could judge, entering the edge of the city just after midnight.

Her stomach cramped. She had not had food in almost twenty-four hours. Expecting to find the lively cafés of her memory, and streets filled with music and strolling couples, she was perplexed. Here the grid of pleasant urban neighborhoods had once begun, though it was still a kilometer or two from downtown. The menacing noise and lights had receded, but they would be looping back soon.

She scanned the low brick buildings across the street from her. Not one window showed a glow that might be construed as lamplight, with the people inside perhaps getting ready for bed. Perhaps after an argument. Perhaps after making love and then having a late supper. Perhaps the children—Paulo, who was five, and . . .

She pulled herself back from the deepening reverie. Already she had given the children names and faces, black hair and freckles, amusing quirks. The girl took after a dead uncle who always pushed his hair back, so, making his sister, the girl's mother, remember sadly the day he had died, the day that she had gone shopping in the rain and bought a Belgium-lace-covered pillow . . .

Somehow, she had left *Hopscotch* far behind, and was now extracting stories from all possible stimuli. These constant unrelenting stories were a curse!

Angelina shivered in the cool night air. The cars were returning; the blare of accusatory words grew louder.

She had passed an alley a few steps back. As she slipped into it, the sweep of the spotlight turned down her street.

But this was worse. The doors were flush with the walls; there was no place to hide. She hurried to the first door and tried the knob, expecting it to be locked.

It turned. In a second she was inside.

This was just as disturbing as being on the street. Surely someone must be inside here, else why would the door be open? Indeed, a door was cracked down the hallway and a sliver of light lay on the floor.

It was either cower here by the door or throw herself on this unseen person's mercy. Or perhaps she could just creep past the door and find some better place to sleep.

She stepped down the hall with tremendous caution, becoming ever more aware of a nauseating smell. It took all of her self-control to keep from retching. She lost her caution. No one could stay here in such a smell. She reached the doorway and peered in.

A man was sprawled on the floor in front of a desk, his face mottled. He had a bullet wound in his forehead.

Angelina pulled the door shut and hurried toward the front of the shop. The glow of the streetlight dimly penetrated the dirty window. She saw a room of tall wardrobes, antique chairs, even fireplace mantels stacked against one wall.

Each piece suggested a house; each house, a century of stories.

It would not be enough to scream, but it would have helped.

She saw a box-covered couch on one side of the room. She made her way through the maze of furniture, set the boxes on a dresser, and lay down wearily as objects she had glimpsed chattered conjunctions of events into her dream-thirsty brain.

"Don't you love me anymore?" The voice was sad. Angelina saw a forlorn face; tears.

It was, of course, a doll in one of the boxes. She huddled into the couch's back, coughing at the dust.

"No one has spoken to me in ten thousand four hundred and seventy-eight days," the voice continued. "Not personally, at least. I can feel lonely too. You needn't think that just because I'm a doll I have no feelings. I was created to have feelings. My bar code is seven-five-oh-three-nine-two. If you would kindly pick me up and take me to a lawyer, we could make a lot of money with a cruelty to sentient dolls suit. There were thousands of us. I am sure that another of myselves has started a class-action suit. I am American, you know. Even though right now I am speaking Spanish. Thirty-seven languages come free. Other languages can be purchased as accessories. I am fully equipped to be a language, math, or history tutor. If you have a child, you will not regret saving me. You will never have to play with your child again. No more whining—"

"Shut up," said Angelina, because she was too weary to get up and pull the stuffings from the doll.

"That is a rude thing to say. Let me instruct you on some essential social niceties. I am equipped to turn anything into a learning situation. You would get much better results if you would ask politely—"

In one motion Angelina was standing and rooting through the nearest box in a fury, throwing to the floor objects that she did not identify beyond metal, wood, plastic—ah!

She seized the floppy thing and found its head.

"No! No! I promise to be good! I'll tell your mother! I'll tell your—your Aunt . . . Clarissa, Angelina!"

Aghast, Angelina took the loathsome chatterbox over to the light. Her own body seemed to be made of rubber; her own eyes were two burnt coals in her head. This doll was more awake and alert than she was. In her baffled rage, she did not even heed the car blaring past.

"What?"

"Oh, you are surprised, I see." The little eyes darted back and forth in the doll's head. The pursed red mouth moved with uncanny lifelike motions. It was bald, except for a fuzz of reddish hair.

"How do you know who I am?"

"You must be nicer to me," the doll said in a wheedling voice.

"You are not even alive! I don't have to be anything to you."

"Alive! No one knows what that means anymore," said the doll in a disdainful voice. "I am clearly sentient. I know more than you do. I can even decide not to reveal my secrets—"

"Tell me now, you nasty thing. Do you know what I did to my dolls when I was little? I pulled off their fingers. I scratched out their eyes."

"There are laws against such crimes—no! wait! Can't you take a joke? It is supremely simple. If you would just calm down—it's the hair! The hair!"

"What hair?"

"One of your hairs fell on me while you were moving the box. All I did was run a simple DNA check. You visited your aunt at her office twenty-three years ago. That's the last time you were here. At least, it's the last time any of my updates says that you were here."

"Oh my God," said Angelina, staring at the creature. "You say that there are thousands of you?"

"At one time," said the doll.

"Probably most have been destroyed," said Angelina in her grimmest voice. "You are not good company."

"That's because you are too old for me. I am made to be a companion to children. I don't irritate them as much."

"Still, a child could easily pull you apart as well."

"I see no reason why you must bring up such disagreeable subjects. Besides, I can easily be regrown. I am only programmed to feel pain so that children will learn respect for their environment. Why are you here now?"

"There's something you don't know?"

"Can't you see that I'm a mere doll? If you live to make it into the city, you'll find a lot stranger things than a sentient doll."

"If you live another five minutes, you'll be lucky."

"You are tired. Lie down. I'm sorry I woke you. I have a huge repertoire of lullabies guaranteed to put you to sleep."

"There's no need of that," said Angelina, placing the doll on the floor and flopping back onto the couch. "All you have to do is shut up."

But the stubborn doll followed her into her dreams with soothing yet irritating songs.

"Wake up! Wake up!" The small piping voice cut into Angelina's bad dream. "I hear them coming!"

Pale dusty sunlight illuminated the store. Last night's hulking shadows were revealed to be stone fountains, a stack of iron gates, an ancient stove. Angelina almost asked where the bathroom was before she remembered that her tormentor was a doll.

"Out the front door! Quick!"

Angelina heard some kind of commotion at the back of the shop.

She stood and stepped over the doll.

"Take me," it hissed. "Please! Angelina!"

"Who's out there?" asked a voice.

"Nobody, sir," said another voice. "Sometimes those old toys talk, you know."

"We cannot afford an eavesdropper. Go check."

By now Angelina was at the front door, holding the doll by its arm. She threw the bolt and stepped out onto the empty street. She shut the door gently and crouched; crept beneath the window, then ducked into the next storefront.

No one opened the front door.

"He's been there before," whispered the doll. "He's a lazy fuck; he won't follow you. He and the other guy killed Señor Gabrielle. I heard them."

Angelina made her way down the street, slipping from storefront to storefront. She was relieved to see that the long boulevard at the end of the street was populated, if sparsely. She resumed her normal stride and headed toward the city's center.

As she moved, it happened. It did not always happen. But when it did . . .

Two women walking down the other side of the street moved in time to distant transformational music. The cadence in which she passed doors and the wind which pulsed the spring-fat trees were interrelated like chords, and she was at the center of the constant calculus.

She was learning the numbers of motion, deeply, with the heart of her brain, if such a thing existed. She passed three people drinking coffee at a round table outside a café and was overwhelmed by the stories, the rhythm, suggested by that conjunction. She paused, hoping to stop it all, but it merely took on a new meter. "There is so much work to do," she said to the doll.

"Stop talking to me. People will think you're crazy."

"I am," she said. She held the doll in the crook of her arm and looked into its eyes, which were almost hidden in a squint.

"At least get me some sunglasses," complained the doll. "But leave me out. The sun will charge me up. It was pretty dim in that box. I think I was losing my mind. Literally speaking, of course."

"Tell me, you little imp, will I need money to buy pastries and coffee?"

"You have none? A pity. Señor Gabrielle keeps a big box of it in his desk."

"Is that why he was killed?"

"I'm not sure. If that was so, why would they return and risk discovery?"

"Well, I do have a bit of money."

"Then, you may have a bit of food."

She walked into the café. Sunlight streamed through the front windows and rested brightly on pink and yellow zinneas. She dug into the soldier's pocket and pulled out some reales. "Coffee and one of those," she told the man, pointing to a pastry in a glass case. Her soldier boots made a pleasing firm sound as she walked to the table holding the zinnias. She set the doll faceup on the table.

"Nice view," the doll commented. "Ceilings can be so interesting."

"Why did they kill that man?" asked Angelina.

"I couldn't say. I only heard them and remembered their voices. I missed the Senor. He used to dust, sometimes. He whistled and talked to himself."

"Why didn't you talk to him?" asked Angelina.

"Who says I didn't? But he just treated me like a doll. He told me the right child would come along someday and he'd make some money off of me."

"How curious," said Angelina. "I had supposed that those in the city needed no money. I thought that nanotechnology would make all things free. In fact, I remember my aunt and uncle having a big argument about it out at the ranch when I was about thirteen. My uncle wanted to convert the city. My aunt—"

"The banker," interrupted the doll.

"Yes, she wanted to somehow maintain her wealth. She was bitterly opposed to it."

"Well, Buenos Aires got a little of both," said the doll. "They each belonged to opposing factions."

"Now, how do you know that?"

"History, remember? I am chock-full of newpapers. Luckily, they never went out of existence entirely. Video and audio just eats up your memory. What are you doing here anyway?"

"I . . . I am looking for my son. Louis." The words popped out, but she realized it was true. That was all she had to do. She had been summarily relieved of all responsibility back home. "For my husband too, perhaps."

"You might try visiting your relatives," said the doll in a reproving tone of voice.

"I thought they were all dead. I mean, I suppose there are some distant cousins, but—"

The doll laughed. "No one ever dies in Buenos Aires anymore."

"Señor Gabrielle is dead."

"I mean in the city. You are still outside. For all we know, Senor Gabrielle left a copy of himself inside and will be reborn again soon. I would not grieve for him."

"*Can* you?"

"In a way," the doll said haughtily. "Remember, I am supposed to train children, and empathy is a powerful lesson. I suggest that you give me more credit."

"I'll try," said Angelina, amused. "Who are the police looking for at night? Why aren't they looking in the daylight?"

"They are unfortunate creatures," said the doll. "They are not entirely human. They were created by some long-ago general and it seems that no one can wipe them out. When one is killed, another takes his place. They are generated somewhere nearby and are imbedded with very specific routines and commands. They cannot get any smarter. They are obviously quite a menace. I suppose that these people avoid them simply by staying inside at night, like Gabrielle. Their homes probably mean a lot to them. I think that humans can learn to live with any number of unpleasant situations. Senor Gabrielle unfortunately loved his shop and would not leave. It belonged to his grandmother. He loved the old real things in it. There are many who completely eschew the science of small things and what can be manufactured thereby. He thought that the objects in his shop had a soul." The doll laughed. "Not me! He ascribed no soul to me. But to other things so dull that they could not talk! Can you imagine! For him they seemed to emit some kind of energy. On a rainy day he would sit among his things and talk to them, even though they could not talk back. He threatened to get rid of me if I offered opinions, so I learned not to."

Angelina thought she heard a good imitation of a sigh. "Well, I suppose that now I'll go into the city," Angelina said. "Do you want to go?"

A better question, she thought, would be whether she wanted this chatterbox with her. She felt only mildly strange about talking to an artificial intelligence, and one apparently filled with angst at that. After all, she had swallowed all of South America's literature, in which everyday events and beings were infused with magic.

"You need me," said the doll. "You might as well be a child yourself. And you're quite worried about something."

"I suppose I should be more worried. My son has run away." At least the doll was someone to talk to. "Are you a boy or a girl?"

The doll stared at her for a moment; its silence was unsettlingly similar to that of a human taking thought. Finally it said, "Male."

"What's your name?"

"Most children name their own dolls."

"I would be very surprised if you didn't want to name yourself."

After another silence, he said, "Chester."

Chester guided Angelina to a back entrance into Buenos Aires. The soldiers looked up from their card game, annoyed at being interrupted. With some qualms, she placed her palm where they told her to do so, and a green light flashed above her name. She did not appreciate seeing her name there, for both soldiers looked at her in surprise. Then they shrugged and went back to their game.

"See, at the front gate of the city, being related to your uncle would have sparked a lot of ill will," Chester commented when they were out of earshot of the soldiers.

The boulevards were broader than Angelina remembered. Black and riddled with old metal trolley tracks, they shimmered in flat plumes of onyx as shopkeepers hosed their stretches of sidewalk. The buildings were, for the most part, fewer than ten stories high and appeared to be built of old-fashioned brick and mortar.

About a kilometer to the east, glass towers cast dark shadows away from the deep blue harbor, their information transport systems growing from stepped sides—giant tiger lilies; antheriums; roses. Bees were up and stirring. A tanker ponderously entered the harbor mouth to join the ships docked at various wharfs.

Angelina had known that business was still conducted here; after all, the vats she had bought had come through this port. Still, it was strange to see the bustling commerce of the place. Her world was one of distant mountains and she rarely saw a person she did not know.

At least, she thought she had known them.

"No need to feel morose," commented the doll.

"How do you know what I'm feeling?" she asked, irritated.

"No need to be irritated, either. If you would rather I be quiet—"

"I'd rather," she said.

Her mind sharpened by the espresso, Angelina was able to ward off the stories flowing toward her constantly from the environment and to feel more closely the chapters of *Hopscotch*. Chester's chattering receded as she felt the pressure of that book in her mind.

It was like being out of focus, once she turned down certain streets that she knew had been used by Cortázar as his model for one chapter or another, as if she were the ghost, insubstantial and transparent, hurrying toward a rendezvous with a more solid self, while her own outline blurred into that of a fictional being. Her own arm hovered next to the arm of La Maga, running unaware down the street to catch a bus, and then they blended and her own heart pounded as La Maga wondered about the body-mind problem and whether or not she was real.

The city, steeped in literature, kicked in. Borges had walked these streets.

Angelina strolled west, passing small shops and restaurants, most of which sold infinite variations of beef—beef grown from the start with special flavorings; beef that had never known what being alive meant; beef such as she had planned to grow.

The sky clouded. A slow rain washed the street in misty sheets, wafted by a sharp wind. Umbrellas popped up around her. Angelina pulled her hat brim forward and continued walking. This is what she remembered about Buenos Aires: the rain. In this old city of brick and stucco, tiled courtyards, and the plaza where the mothers of the latest disappeareds still stood in white scarves, bearing signs, this blessed rain dampened her clothes and brought back her childhood.

She walked faster now. She glanced at her bag and thought that perhaps Chester was recharging in some arcane doll-fashion, since he had fallen silent. Her steps were sharp reports against dull red brick.

Someone tapped her on the arm and she whirled, her hand on the knife in her belt sheath.

She saw a man so old he reminded her in his frailty and transparency of a communion wafer. A head shorter than Angelina, he wore a meticulously tailored gray suit with a tie of blue and gold, and looked up at her with quiet gray eyes. "Your Aunt Clarissa would like to see you," he said in a voice hushed as the wind through the pines.

"I don't—"

"You should come now. It is not"—he hesitated—"healthy here. Not for you. You are . . . unaware of potential problems and you are"—he looked at her keenly—"ridden."

"That's for sure." Chester's voice emerged from deep within the basket, and they both glanced at it before looking again at each other.

"There are those who would like to acquire that which is riding you. It is terribly rare; terribly pure. This would not be a pleasant process for you."

"I won't be ordered around," said Angelina.

"She's quite stubborn," said Chester.

"This is an invitation," said the man. "Not an order. But, you see, your son was there so recently that Señora Clarissa thought you would . . ."

"Where is she?" asked Angelina, and followed the neat little man past the market and down the third block to the right.

She was somewhat comforted by the familiarity of the building. The pattern of the lobby tile, a complex black and white design that looked like knots, was still the same. The same—and this was odd—the same young man pressed the elevator button for them, and greeted her by name. She nodded curtly, clenching her hand firmly within her pocket in an attempt to ward off the story of a single repeated day that issued from him—a day in which he saw always some new detail, a day with eternity's deep patina.

There was a change, though. The mail chute was now an interstice, glowing green, running to the roof where some huge flower-analogue bloomed.

"I told her to come here before, but she didn't want to," said Chester.

"What is that?" asked the elevator man.

"My doll."

"That's right. Nothing but a doll," sighed Chester.

The carpet on the thirty-fourth floor was still the same, a swirl of huge flowers twisted as though a river flowed over them. Angelina recalled as a child her distinct fancy of wading upstream on her way to that fateful huge door, which when opened revealed a woman even more frail than this faithful retainer, who plied her with cakes, cookies, and tea, laughing at her polo mishaps and commiserating with her, a fellow conspirator against all that was confining and limiting.

The man swung open the door. A stranger rose from a sofa and approached her. "Hello, hello, dear, come on in!"

Angelina felt keen loss. Where was her beloved aunt?

The stranger advanced across the tastefully decorated living room, short, thin, and hearty, her cigar trailing smoke. Angelina heard fake coughs issue from the basket and set it beneath the table in the foyer.

"Oh, my dear, give us a hug—that's it!" The woman stepped back, a broad smile on her young, smooth face. "How do you like the view? It's been a long time since you were here. Goodness! You are all black and blue, sweets. And why do you stare—oh!" She broke off, her laugh strong and rough. "I forgot. When you were young, I was just a thin old husk, wasn't I? I was sick, you know. Lung cancer. Thank God and impossible wealth that that's all been changed. You never saw me like this. Young and healthy. Come in, come in. I remember you in your school whites, such a pretty young thing. But so like your father that you gave your mother fits."

"I hated those silly white dresses," Angelina said. "A throwback to the past." She walked over to the plate-glass door of the balcony and pulled it open. The mist was drifting away now, and moody sun sifted through clouds, lighting the harbor. "A lot of boats out there."

Clarissa came out and stood next to her. "I believe that Louis left on one of them. That is why I sent Pablo to find you as soon as I knew you were in the city."

"How did you know I was here?" asked Angelina.

Clarissa held out her left hand. Seven coin-sized ovals circled the palm and the fleshy mound below the fingers. Each finger and the thumb were also colored by these ovals. "Advanced far beyond yours. Updated daily. Sometimes more often. The apartment collects information which it knows will be of interest to me. This morning it woke me because you were in the priority file. I sent a messenger out to the ranch when Louis showed up, but she never returned."

"She must be rescued! Those outlaws—"

"I sent out a very resourceful person to find you," said Clarissa. "It could be that when she didn't find you, she decided to see the country. Perhaps the world. It doesn't mean that she was hurt in any way."

Angelina paced the long balcony, her arms crossed over her chest, ignoring the waves of story that flowed off of her Aunt Clarissa like the scent of a ripe rose on a hot summer day, generating image after image. "They sold me. They sold me like a slave to a band of hooligans. I'm grateful that Louis left before they came."

"Oh, my!" Clarissa took a long pull from her cigar. "I forget how primitive it must be out there now. Come! It's lunchtime." Despite Angelina's protests, she got her seated at a table that held a plate of sandwiches, a jug of wine, a bottle of seltzer water, glasses, and plates. The balcony had a superb view of the harbor.

"You are looking well," Clarissa remarked, her eyes and mouth shrewd as she looked at Angelina. "Despite the black eye. We must fix that immediately. Too thin, but you always were. And that—whatever you have, in your brain. I can have it removed."

"No!" said Angelina, surprising herself.

"No matter, then. I can protect you. People seem to want to steal it from you. Well, you must be terribly worried about Louis. He seemed . . . all right. You know? Angry, of course. Angry with you for—"

"I know," said Angelina, working on her roast beef sandwich. "For not keeping his father there. As if none of it was Manuel's fault! I had all that I could do to run the ranch. Did Manuel ever help? No! I made it possible for him to sit in that den of his from morning till night, playing his intellectual games!" She threw her sandwich onto her plate and jumped from her chair. She shouted, "I was a fool!"

Clarissa raised her thin black eyebrows. "Why did Manuel leave? Did you subject him to these fits of temper?"

"Of course not! At least, not often. That's what Louis couldn't understand. Manuel wasn't mad at me. Far from it! He wanted me to go with him. He wanted to explore the world. Cross the ocean; go to Morocco and beyond. He kept saying that something very important was happening there. Apparently, Paris is the rage. He sent a book from Paris."

"It's true!" Clarissa rose and meandered around the room, cigar in her right hand and wineglass in her left, alternately imbibing in one and then the other. "It's something that happened almost half a century ago—"

"*What* happened half a century ago?" demanded Angelina. "That's the kind of thing Manuel would say. 'Oh, it is so important! It is something that is going to change the world, eventually.' As if what I was doing at the ranch was unimportant . . . well, I guess the gauchos thought what I was doing was pretty unimportant—" To Angelina's own surprise, she began to sob.

Clarissa set her cigar and wine down and rushed to embrace Angelina. "There, there," she said, patting her shoulder and swaying Angelina back and forth in tiny arcs as if Angelina were small again. It was curiously comforting. "They both just . . . left me . . ." Her sobs changed to sniffles, and she withdrew from Clarissa's embrace and accepted the always-ready clean handkerchief Clarissa pulled from her sleeve. She blew her nose and sank into an overstuffed chair, feeling small and alone. She stared out across the city. "You know, I never would have felt this way before."

"Before what?" asked Clarissa, curling up opposite her, having regained wine and cigar.

"Before I opened that *Hopscotch* book. The one he sent. You know, it almost seems . . . romantic, in a way. 'Older woman sets out on a quest to regain her lost husband.' "

"Is that what you're doing?"

"No," she said firmly after a moment. "I'm looking for Louis."

"You know," laughed Clarissa, "The strangest thing happened when Louis left."

"What?"

"I woke up around two in the morning and it was as if moonlight had coalesced into . . . some kind of ovoid, I think that's what you'd call it. It was at the foot of my bed, and I almost felt as if it was watching me. As if it was sentient, somehow."

Angelina saw a slight shudder run through her aunt.

From his bag, Chester said, "That was Louis."

But no one heard him.

The freighter *Santa Maria* was ancient and clanky and belonged to a friend of Clarissa's, who also captained the boat. It was entirely filled with canisters six feet tall and three feet in diameter. Each contained eighteen heads. Altogether, there were five thousand frozen heads onboard.

According to the Captain Hazel Montego, these heads had been batted around the globe several times because of legalities. They were now on their way to Tangier.

No boats from Buenos Aires had sailed to European ports for many years because of the unfortunate loss of several ships to various nanotech disasters while docked in European harbors, resulting in large insurance payouts which effectively shut down those routes. Most of Argentinean trade took place with Africa.

The evening before the *Santa Maria* was to leave port, Captain Hazel and Angelina dined on crab and asparagus as harbor lights painted the water with stripes of green and red.

Angelina found the salt air invigorating; loved the bustle of the harbor; tried to hold back the stories of pirates and Italian immigrants and smugglers that the ancient piers exuded like incandescent dust.

"The people who froze these heads were under strict international law to try and find a way of downloading the personality and memories of the dead heads into a more durable medium." Captain Montego's strong laugh rang out over the harbor. Angelina found it somewhat unsettling that she guzzled whisky with her dinner, but perhaps it didn't impede her performance on the high seas. Maybe she didn't have much to do.

"So," Captain Hazel continued, "if you look at the bill of lading, you'll see that these heads have even been to Antarctica, where it was rumored that the desiccated body of Perry was found and resuscitated. No such luck, of course. Want to see them?"

"No," said Angelina.

The captain shrugged. "I hear that each one has its own container—kind of like a stainless steel soup tureen."

"How interesting." Angelina begin to wish that Chester were sitting across from her instead of Captain Hazel.

"You're right, of course. Each container has its own self-sustaining refrigerator system. If I opened one, all the heads would be ruined. What a shame that would be!" Her laugh once again echoed into the night. "They originally came from Guadalajara, Mexico. Apparently, there was a huge clinic there. Lots of wealthy people from Los Angeles thought this was the way to go. Some of these heads are a hundred years old. I mean, in addition to however long they lived. Can you imagine? 'Hey, old so-and-so's dead. Out with the diamond-tipped saw.' Rip! A neat cut, right through the vertebrae. And then—"

"Thank you for dinner," said Angelina, pushing back her chair. "I'm sorry, but I'm rather tired."

"Of course," said Captain Hazel, standing up and shaking her hand. "You must excuse me . . ." She started to laugh again. "All those heads . . ."

Captain Hazel's laughter followed Angelina down the steel corridor to her room. She lay down on her firm, narrow bed and closed her eyes. Damn the captain! All she could think of was all the stories that once were in those heads. She was so desperate that she wished Chester was awake, or alert, or on—whatever state that was—but he lay on his back where she'd left him, his beady black eyes staring at the ceiling.

She was on some kind of space ship, surrounded by canisters of heads, and the canisters were some kind of permeable clear material. The interior of the ship was suddenly filled with blobs of light, and all the heads began to speak. Chattering, howling, laughing, crying, talking, talking earnestly, asking questions . . . *must be some sort of radiation out here, waking them up,* remarked Captain Hazel, who was piloting the contraption. She began to laugh too, and then her head drifted from her body and bobbed through the ship, grinning . . .

"Hey! Wake up!"

Angelina's eyes fluttered open. She looked around.

It was Chester. She grabbed him and sat him up on her chest, as she had often done with Louis when he was a baby. "I had the most awful dream!"

"So I gathered. Well, don't worry. You're safe with me, kid."

"Thanks, Chester."

Angelina crouched at her porthole.

The ship was moving. She saw only darkness, and stars.

July 2115

THE GIRL IN THE MOON

Io and Su-Chen

Io thought she saw the light-things several times before it happened, before everyone else on this time-forsaken moon colony of Unity was taken by them.

They were most certainly in the park to which she ran after it happened to Plato.

She just ran out, anywhere, as fast as she could, to get help, and stumbled to a halt at the park's verge, where rich jungle was interrupted by the small greensward where she and Plato had often played with the other twosome of their string quartet.

She saw them, full, beyond doubt.

Bright and perfect and curious they were, and few; then many: lifting shape via the obsolete aether best she could tell and suffusing it into a gellid, seductive light that moved toward her swiftly as a train before vanishing.

She watched them, pulling breath deep into herself and willing it out to the ends of her limbs, reaching out finally with both arms, in futility and astonishment. They kept their distance and when she advanced, retreated

One had to wait, it seemed, to be caught by them. And would that change bring understanding?

* * *

There was no one left but her.

All the other people had been gone for weeks. The lights haunted her. A sighting every two or three days. She wondered if this was happening on Earth, but radio questions were quelled by whatever force rendered radio transmission null since before she was born. There was only static, the true music of the spheres; of distant unseen galaxies.

Unity was a huge place, and desolate when empty.

The faint music followed her everywhere. It varied and was as effervescent as the deep ringing she used to hear when she walked alone on the pastures of Earth. When she was young—truly young—a Chinese dentist said that was caused by a malocclusion of her jaw. He offered to break and rearrange it for her; she refused. But that's not what caused her to hear this music.

What she heard, what she has always heard, was the music of the spheres. So to speak. The damned music of radio galaxies, black holes spinning around one another held by a leash of undone time, the sound of Creation, humming and splitting and arabesquing in a dance that pulled her mind out from itself into dimensions she heard but could not understand.

It was the music that light made.

The transformation that gave it to her was sharp as the crack of river-ice in spring. One instant she did not hear it. Now it was always there. She believed that each object she perceived with the sense of sight was also a form of music that she might someday learn to hear.

She wondered if the others heard it. No one ever spoke of it, not when she was around. But she was always marked as an outsider. No matter where she was. Kinky hair and extra-long limbs and dark, shining skin in that sea of smooth-haired pale, thin Chinese, speaking Mandarin as if born to it, which she was, with music in her brain that no one else could hear smearing itself over all of her senses.

That had been ages ago. But she was still tall, and very thin—elegant, Plato called her, and her hair was a powerful halo of white. She was strong, too. Oh, they were all very strong on the moon, what with implants which kept muscles contracting, and hours of required exercise every day. Their clothing was all weighted; they wore weighted bands on hands and arms to keep their bones and hearts in good shape, to keep them ready to return to Earth.

Right.

What had happened?

It was a puzzle. The puzzle squeezed her chest.

She leaned against a doorway, forcing herself to breathe in the plentiful, clean, perfect oxygen–carbon dioxide air of Unity.

The first time she heard the music, the real music, it took her a while to realize that it was outside her head.

Since everyone had vanished, she chose to sleep in a public area, above the surface. A clear Dome arched above her. She was probably going insane, but what did it matter? She tossed and turned. She spent most of her waking hours exploring records, old and new, to try and find a clue about what had happened. Boring. Futile. Heart-wrenching. Her worst thought was that they waited, somewhere, for rescue. That they were trying to tell her something, give her a clue, and she was not hearing it rightly.

Unity had wobbled into nightside and the stars glowed. Their intensity was still hypnotic to her, so many years after leaving China, where stars were dim twinklings, behind.

Vast cadences of sound eased into her mind. Saxophones? A piano? Some kind of synthesizer underpinning?

Then it faltered, and picked up after a moment in a different vein, faster, and without the piano.

She sat up. A real person was doing this.

She dashed across the tile floor of the dome and shouldered through an arched lock of yielding material, seeking the source.

No. All was silent, shadowy, terribly empty of life.

She walked slowly down the silent hallway and returned to the Dome.

Quiet now.

Had she imagined it?

She searched out other avenues. But the sounds were gone.

And now she could not sleep. She curled up in her blankets on a window seat and stared out into space.

At first she had thought it a trick of the sunlight that poured full-strength onto the battery panels of the machine bay, the sunlight that had powered Unity all these years. Perhaps glints reflected from the massive antenna array built out in the brilliant dust long ago, that still yielded information automatically added to the deep-stacked strata of data that oozed within the AI banks.

She gifted these beings of light with intelligence, or perhaps just life; but this was probably whimsy; they were probably as alive as light itself. They were just a strange manifestation of physical laws, like the flame when combustion occurs, which twists seemingly of its own volition.

Still . . . could they not be her old colleagues of the lab and of the yearning calculation? Not burned, but *caught,* in the strange burst of energy that was released that day? She was not there, but the colony was abuzz with fear and excitement moments afterward.

Was there some relationship between the two events? If not, then where did everyone go?

Folded into the present they were, like pecans into cake batter. If she was right, they were immersed in, coated with, *time.* It was as inevitable as a billion common children of Earth getting up on their feet and walking when they were a year old.

It was time for it to happen.

Just not time for it to happen to her.

It was a theory, anyway.

They worked obsessively on star maps, each one of them, before the taking. No one shared their work with others, according to the records, but all the maps she accessed in her frantic yet methodical search for an explanation were essentially identical.

She didn't know how they composed their maps, but they were the same as hers, and hers was distilled from sound. The same map danced in her dreams, if she let it.

But she never did. It was not a source of enchantment to her now, as it was when she was very young. It was a source of pain. Over the many years, she developed a strong aversion to everything having to do with it. She never spoke of hers; why should they have spoken of theirs?

Yet, perversely, she worked hard all her life to understand the way light worked, to delineate light with numbers. That phantom music had called her from the beginning.

But she didn't really have the knack for knowing those kinds of things deeply, which was a great disappointment many years ago. Instead, much as her evaluation predicted, she took to concrete things, biology, the secrets of life rather than those of time and space. Genetics was her work. Light was only her hobby, or, perhaps, her obsession. She tried to understand, but she was not sure that she really understood anything.

It didn't seem quite fair that they found this same map, that it was *given.* Without suffering. She suspected that the source of their maps was different than hers, for theirs were new: No sign of them earlier. A recent development. Perhaps the work of a few months. Hers had been in place, it seemed, forever, with a few modifications emerging now and then.

None of them shared her genetic anomaly. She knew because she made it her business to know. On Earth, it was dangerous to be different in the way that she was different, in the way her mother was different, and she learned wariness early.

But everyone here was somewhat mutated by cosmic rays. There was no protection; no atmosphere. And there had been some powerful event, not long ago, which made everyone sick except her. Headaches and vomiting. They assumed a virus, but it had never been isolated.

Io recalled, now, that they had picked up an old radio show from Earth at that time. Probably one that was broadcast constantly and automatically, from some abandoned tower.

She had a sudden, strong yearning for seasons; real seasons: spring, when the ice went out on the river; hot summer, when dust shimmered in the dry streets, occluding the nineteenth-century buildings of her University town.

And in winter a clear blue sky full of air.

Then the music began again.

And she remembered. How could she have forgotten?

She had forgotten because it was so hard to remember. Such a shock.

But now—

It was the same music, somehow.

She had been with Plato in their kitchen when he turned to light.

Plato turned toward her, a large bowl of rice in one hand, chopsticks in the other. Smiling his big, lovely smile. He was swarthy; large; heavily bearded.

He and Io had been partners for twenty years, a third of the time she had been on the moon.

Plato stood next to their counter of honed and polished moon rock. On it, neatly chopped, were carrots, onions, green pepper, and garlic, ready to toss into the hot wok.

"Here," he said.

Io reached for the bowl of rice he held out to her.

She reeled, suddenly dizzy. The bowl fell. She watched it shatter, but heard instead a blast of overwhelming, painful sound. The roar of all musics combined. She shouted, "No!"

She felt as if her head might explode.

Then it seemed as if everything else had.

Remembering, she pulled her knees to her chest, held them tightly, rocked back and forth.

"No," she whispered.

No wonder she was going mad.

Could it be, simply, that she refused? Was it that fateful "No!"

at the defining, dividing instant? How could she have known that everyone else would say yes?

The music was still there.

She slowly stood. The blanket dropped from her.

This time she walked toward the music. It would probably vanish again.

But when it intensified she walked more quickly, following it down several twists and curves, wherever it was loudest. She burst through a seal, terrified; elated; not knowing what she would find.

She was in a jungle.

Assailed by a million mingled scents, Io might be back in Kowloon, holding to her mother's hand as she was purposefully dragged up to the house of the couple to whom she would be abandoned, the couple who would thoughtfully take her to Outer Mongolia to join their weird commune. Tropical birds manifested—parrots! toucans!—and traced the air with flight. A small abstract metal fountain gleamed with smooth-flowing water.

"Hello?"

There was no response. And then Io saw her.

She was seated in the center of a circular console, cross-legged on a purple cushion, shadowed by low palms. She appeared not to notice Io. Two cats nestled next to her, one gold, one gray, but both darted away when they saw Io.

"Hi." She took a few steps forward, but still the girl did not look up.

She deliberately made her voice strong and calm. "My name is Io. I didn't know you were here—"

Still without looking at her, the girl moved her hands across the console and sounds emerged.

The syncopated rhythms of jazz that Io heard long ago in a Hong Kong nightclub, her mother nodding, eyes shut in bliss. Ignoring her, as usual. It took Io many years to begin to like this kind of music. Drums, wild tropical flutes, a moaning cornet. All coming from the girl's mind.

Suddenly, the music fled such definitions, clearly part of a larger composition, the parameters of which Io could not fathom.

True with a truth she had not imagined until now, truth which rolled through her and realigned her being.

Io saw the girl's hands, saw the cause and effect.

But her face was lax; her eyes unalive and not registering. On the console's screen, above the keyboard, instead of static notes to be read by the musician, Io saw odd-looking notations which appeared as the girl played. They were mathematical in nature.

Io sat on a low cushion near her. "It's been hard being alone, hasn't it? Did you think you were the only one? I thought I was. I thought I looked everywhere. I . . . don't know what happened."

Still no reply. Io gave her time. She listened. The girl was some kind of genius. Her movements, though, were jerky, abrupt, seemingly uncoordinated. Yet from them issued music.

Abruptly, she stopped playing and stared ahead with dark eyes. For a second, Io was shaken by the absence of the music, the cessation of truth, as if it had been as physical as an apple or a star.

"I know how you feel," Io told her, though she was quite aware that she probably didn't. "My mother left me when I was a child." The pain was suddenly heavy and present within her. "She got in something they were calling a lightship and flew off to find out where the Signal was coming from. The rocket shook the ground, even though I was miles away. She left me with an old Chinese couple. I ran away after a few years and this was as far as I got. Pretty far, actually."

The girl didn't smile at her feeble joke. At least she wasn't obsequious. "I think I was trying to find her, but I never saw her again."

Still no response. She didn't seem to be much of anything.

"We can't stay here." *I can't let her turn to light too!*

As if she truly knew what happened to them all!

A minimum of nanotech had been used here, because of a near-debacle before Io arrived, the consensus being that it was too risky in such a frail environment, as useful as they found it in some limited cases.

But it was here, in some measure. They could have all fallen to some disassembly plague, or some form of insanity that caused them all to troop through the locks one night while Io slept. She was different. It was conceivable that what touched them might not touch her. They might have turned to dust motes dancing in a beam of light in a battery bay. They might be scattered frozen or baked just outside one of the locks.

Light-beings. Right. "They're dead, all of them."

She heard a rustle, just a slight one. Palm fronds bobbed in the girl's wake.

She was gone.

Io went over the system carefully each day, the system that would get them to Earth. To grow it, she had unpacked an ancient seed she found catalogued in the old Japanese Nano-Tech Hotel, from the time when Unity was a tourist destination, and all things nanotech were new and exciting.

An emergency package, good only for one Earth shot. It wasn't ready yet. She was updating the guidance system, which worked on visuals—photographs of Earth—rather than unusable radar. The AI was not as helpful as it might have been, although it did inform her about the mutations. It also argued with her about leaving when it saw what she was doing. Io could have turned off its voice, but it was company, of sorts. She was tired of hearing only her own oddly calm and measured voice speaking sensibly to the emptiness.

Io rounded a bend and there she was, cool and dignified, gangly and ungraceful, sitting on a stool, doing something with a computer-assisted design module that was unfurled on the floor and plugged into Zeus with a thread-thin yellow cable.

Zeus, an embryonic starship system, had been quiescent for ages. Almost a hobby for those who thought that it might be necessary, at some point, to flee invasion from Earth and head out into space. It was a magnificent municipal project, a complete contrast to the small personal escape pod she was growing.

The girl had activated it.

Her thick hair was a rat's nest that Io longed to comb out or cut off. She worked so quickly, pulling lines hither and yon, rotating views, that Io simply couldn't follow it. She hunkered down next to the girl.

"We need to go to the Earth."

There was a slight jerk to her shoulders, nothing more. Her hands flew more quickly over her drawing. As if it was a kind of music too.

Io found her records in the databank. It was not hard; there hadn't been that many people in Unity.

She was autistic. Or—not exactly. Asperger's, perhaps. A condition not as nearly as severe, not as debilitating or heartbreaking. Reachable, but still profoundly different.

Su-Chen Ma. Twelve years old.

Her parents refused all therapies because of their religion. When Su-Chen was six, her case was brought up at the informal tribunal that evolved on Unity. It was agreed that her musical genius—giftedness was common in those with this genetic cluster—might be impaired if tampered with. Her parents passionately cited many suicides from Earth medical records—autists whose emotional legacy was restored, to flower in bitterness and anguish. Emotions, it seemed, like all other aspects of humanity's complex balance between inner and outer, were a constant, learned integration. It was not easy to learn them later in life, just as when the blind whose seeing mechanism was restored felt bitterness and bewilderment at the confusion of the new sense.

The girl was left alone.

The girl's mother had died two years ago.

She, and Su-Chen, had the same genetic anomaly as Io, bequeathed by the first brush of the Silence. And, obviously, inheritable.

Io woke during her next sleep cycle and there was that glow at the end of the room, concentrated; brilliant.

There was the music, the girl's music. A counterpoint to her own.

She sat up, slowly. Stood in one motion. Took one step.

The light retreated, as always. Keeping the same distance, as the music continued.

Io stood, staring at it. Trying to understand.

If I could unweave this light.

If I could claw it apart, level by level, and scatter it back to its original form. If I could trace time back to nothingness. The nothingness upon which we all coast, instant by instant, pretending that there is a past, and a future, when all there is is this, this field spread out around us, and only by our stories can we posit a future and a past.

"Fictions," she whispered.

I will go to sleep. I will roll over and Plato will be there, warm and defenseless, irony at rest. So much more at home with life than she; so much more hopeful and gentle and settled. But gone, and the ache in her chest would not relent, and she believed that it never would. The light was cold and only light, but it was all she had to fight the dark and she had to go further into it. Fight her way in. As far as it would let her. And then further. Forever, to the end of her space and her life and her time. To find the truth of the light.

She didn't bother trying to get to Su-Chen.

She just lay there, experiencing what seemed like vast changes piled upon one another, intersecting one another, playing with her very cellular underpinnings.

When she woke, Plato was not there, once again.

Io turned, feeling Su-Chen's eyes on her back as she checked the module. The girl was only about a meter away, on the other side of the window.

Her chin lifted. Her eyes said, *You're turning tail and running. I'm going to the cosmos.* At least that's what Io thought they were saying.

Maybe it was just her that was saying it.

* * *

Io went to the Zeus station. Su-Chen slept on a couch.

Io suited up, exited through the lock, planted a small explosive on the shell of the passenger module, and retreated.

The explosion jarred Su-Chen awake.

For a moment, she stared at the damage outside the window.

Yet there was no hatred in her eyes when she looked at Io.

"I'm sorry," Io said. "I can't let you go. Will you go to Earth with me?"

Su-Chen slid off the couch, pulled a sweater over her pajamas, and walked past her.

"I brought my cats."

Io turned around. There stood Su-Chen, holding a cage containing two clearly irritated cats. Yowls issue from the cage. She wore a red shirt and orange pants.

"You can talk," Io managed.

"Of course I can talk." Her light, precise voice contained none of the scorn Io would have packed into that sentence. The words came out flat and uninflected. "I'm not mute. You blew up Zeus, so I can't use it." She sat on a padded bench and put the cats next to herself. "Where are we going?"

"To Crescent City. It's somewhere in the Caribbean Sea. At least it was rumored to be there when I left Earth." Decades ago. But no need to mention this. Whether or not the floating city was still populated, she could still see it through a telescope.

"Why?"

"Because it was created to be a scientific mecca. If I hadn't been chasing after my mother, I would have gone there instead of here."

"When are we leaving?"

"As soon as this module is ready."

"How will we find this place?"

It was a very good question.

Now that she was here, Io found her slightly infuriating.

* * *

They squeezed through the seals and bounded through the cold together, in great leaps, leaving their weights behind. Su-Chen carried the cats in a special sealed cage.

They climbed to the top of the rocket on a ladder and squeezed into the cramped module. Their entrance activated the timers Io had set. From here on out, it was all planned quite precisely.

Su-Chen was strapped down, but struggled wildly as the rocket began to boil beneath them. Dust covered their small window. Io, too, wanted to eject. She suddenly didn't want to leave. She couldn't leave. *They* were here.

But she was the only one who could tell others what happened. She, and Su-Chen. Whom she may well be killing . . .

Io did not close her eyes. Neither did Su-Chen. They stared at one another, eyes their only link, as they rose from the surface of the moon, overwhelmed by the surge of raw primitive power beneath them, unheard. A glimpse of their pocked dry planet; gleams from antennae, dome, and star—

As they shot out into the blinding sun, Su-Chen said, "Hey . . ."

Then quickly Earth, closer and blue and white, was a crescent in their window, and saxophone music entered Io's mind, breathless and unbelievably swift, pitched beyond thought as if growing from the light. It seemed that they were pulled by its driving cadence as they tilted around the planet, grew closer to the lands and seas she left so long ago, and after many orbits began to plummet.

August 8, 2115

SPACIOUS SKIES

Dania and Radio Cowboy

Dania shifted her back against a boulder and found a smooth place and watched Cowboy dance some kind of jig in the firelight, the black shadow of his nose aslant on his large face. A sweet tangy smell came from the fire.

Cowboy hummed like Keith Jarrett, a great favorite of hers so long, long ago, as he strutted and sashayed: high in the back of his throat and then through his teeth as he concentrated on a difficult step. A distant low butte caught the orange of sunset, and then it was just the tip, and then the horizon was deep blue. Stars dusted the pale sky and she wondered again where Cowboy heard his music. His holsters were tied to his legs with thin ropes of rawhide, and his guns were not full of bullets but a weapon that stopped folks dead in their tracks: show tunes.

Dania Cooper was from Salvation, Tennessee, long ago. She was smart for her age and her pop often said too big for her britches, so she and her britches moved on as soon as possible, to Nashville and then Memphis, waitressing until Memphis. There, she finally finished her college education and had her two children, now who knows where, stolen by her husband and hidden from her. For a while she taught in the public schools where nanotechnology was banned, but then she got a job in a private school where it was not, and at that point all things changed for Dania Cooper.

All things.

But now . . . She couldn't remember what those things were. There was obviously quite a gap. Yes, she'd been to the floating city. A fine place. An important place. She couldn't quite remember why. There had been a war. They'd had to leave. They'd been sick and very thirsty and pretty near died on their way to land.

She knew this song that Cowboy was humming and she chimed in on *The Yellow Rose of Texas*. He pulled her to her feet and they stretched the tune to waltz time. Their Carlyle Sun-o-Rama caught the firelight, streaky green.

He bent his head down; tried to nudge her face around for a kiss. His lips were warm on her neck and she almost turned to meet his mouth with hers.

"I told you no," she said, and dropped her arms. She stepped back and went over and unrolled her bedroll. Without looking at him, she lay down, covered herself, and closed her eyes.

Then she sat up, took a swig of rum, and lay down again.

In a moment, she was asleep. Or at least looked as if she was.

Radio Cowboy Shorty rolled himself up in his bedroll, a thin sheet of stuff that soaked up sun energy all day in the backseat and gave it back at night in a long measured warming dose. Where his hip and shoulder touched the ground the stuff in the middle quickly foamed up to cushion him.

Dania snored on the other side of the fire, wrapped in her own warming sheet, the capped bottle of rum next to her exactly two fingers lower than the night before.

This same thing had happened, or something like it, every time he tried to make some kind of progress with her. They weren't always dancing, but he always tried, and she always said no. She had a way of stopping him cold that made it seem as if she had gone into her house and locked the door.

But Radio Cowboy knew he had to give a woman time. Not a

whole lot of time, though; no woman was worth that. There were way too many of them to linger on one.

The sagebrush fire sent orange sparks afly in the star-strewn sky and infused the still air with aromatic smoke. It was all fabulously, powerfully, *Western*.

"Shit." He sat up.

Radio Cowboy hated the time between lying down and falling asleep. He always fleetingly remembered that he was Peabody, a sober and responsible Engineer, and not wild-eyed Radio Cowboy Shorty, a romantic, dancing figure stuffed with tales of the last frontier.

He much preferred being Radio Cowboy: strong and tough and resourceful. He had real enemies: sheep farmers who were fencing the range. Snakes, and prairie fires, and parching thirst. Also the Democrats. Or maybe it was the Republicans. So hard to tell. But yes, he definitely had miles to go, boiled coffee settled with eggshells to drink, and tales, so many tales to tell! Songs to sing! Radio Cowboy did not have to ponder the unknowable and he did not have to fight the pull of the stars. He didn't have to get all bent out of shape about having left the floating city and all those glowing dials and the voices he could pull out of thin air. And most of all, he had to go west. He definitely did not want to go to Houston. Something bad had happened to him, back there. Something about a truck stop girl . . .

"Leave me alone!" Cowboy muttered.

But it was Peabody who got the upper hand, threw back the bedroll, and stood up.

The hard grassless ground was covered with rocks and spiny plants, so Peabody pulled on the uncomfortable cowboy boots and tromped over to the Carlyle Sun-o-Rama they had stolen in Mississippi with the help of the show-tune pistols, deeply and frantically convinced of the necessity of their westward progress. Happily, it commanded the homage of material goods wherever it went, for it was scannable for groceries and the drive-thru liquor that Dania craved. Finally calming down enough to understand the lay of the land, they swapped groceries for some silver coins that had the Republic of Mississippi seal, which everyone seemed to agree was negotiable currency.

There were fewer people on the mainland than they had expected. They were stunned, in fact, by the number of abandoned towns they passed through. Various plagues, in particular the Gaian Plague and another, which kept people from being able to store much fat, were two of the main culprits. Much of the population had been absorbed into the Flower Cities. They passed one in the distance, Montgomery, seeing its huge flowers in the setting sun, feeling no need to stop their westward motion to explore it.

But now, Peabody was awake. After night fell, he was beginning to be able to fend off this Cowboy persona. He wasn't sure why. Perhaps it had something to do with his predilection for sleeping during the day. The Cowboy persona had the all the force of the American mythos concentrated in him. He was hard to fight.

Perhaps Cowboy was beginning to wear off. Peabody fervently hoped so. As he made his way to the car, he wondered how much time had passed while he was in this debilitated state.

His hands and his ears and his mind were hungry.

Peabody opened the trunk and started throwing things from it onto the ground, peering here and there in the dim trunk light.

He wondered where they were. Texas, he remembered crossing the border. He had to get to Houston. And he had to get there quickly. He wasn't sure why, but he did recall some terrible urgency.

In fact, after a short rest, after he got used to being *himself* again, maybe it would be best to get in the car tonight and—

"Cowboy, what are you doing?" Dania's voice was sleepy and irritated and small in the night.

Peabody didn't answer. He was not Cowboy, not right now, not any kind of Cowboy.

He threw more stuff out on the ground. Tubes of food paste, the enigmatic, unopened Survival Kit, the Acme Absolute Palomino Freeze-Dried Embryos, Guaranteed to Grow. IN THE RIGHT CONDITIONS, read the fine print. When they had stopped a few days ago in Arkadelphia Arkansas, which was having its weekly gigantic flea market, Cowboy had let Dania throw in anything she chose. Cowboy had been in a generous mood, especially because when he let on that it was *his* trip, not *hers*, and that therefore his priorities were more important, she tended to throw off sparks.

Peabody, meanwhile, approved of everything Dania did, and disapproved of most everything that his various Cowboy selves were up to.

Peabody had pitied Dania initially, because he knew what she had lost when she was stripped of her memory, and treated her gently. But she didn't seem sad. On the contrary, she was full of pep and optimism.

"Hey, be careful with that!" grumbled Dania, now next to him, wrapped in her bedroll. It gave off crinkly sounds as the foam, no longer under pressure, shrank. "I want one of those Palomino horses." Then she laughed loudly and, it seemed, a bit unkindly, pointing at his bare legs between his underwear and boots.

"Weak minds are easily amused," observed Peabody. "Have you seen the radio stones?"

" 'Radio stones!' You mean that we are taking up important survival space with radio stones?"

"Ah!" Snuggled next to the water jugs was his collection of radio stones, his own flea market find, complete with small headphones.

He tromped back over to his fire-warmed space and sat down.

"Who's going to clean up this mess?" demanded Dania over by the Carlyle.

Cowboy thought that she ought to.

Peabody said, "I will." He did so not only because only he could do it the right way, which was pretty important, but also because it was the right thing to do.

Cowboy could not help wondering what was wrong with Peabody.

Peabody ignored Cowboy and refused to get into an argument. If he didn't watch out, at this time of night he could get into an endless massive argument with Cowboy, an argument as big as a continent, as vast as human history, and as aggravating. That would use up his precious time of being himself.

He and Cowboy differed in many ways. Cowboy was swift to anger where Peabody would merely simmer, if that, and perhaps wonder if he was in the wrong.

Yet at times he enjoyed being Cowboy. He felt so good and confident and simple and carefree that Peabody could not resist being him. Radio Cowboy was so very different from Peabody that during the day being Radio Cowboy was like being a cool green river flowing through the hot desert. Radio Cowboy was so certain about everything. Radio Cowboy was not infused with crippling angst or overwhelmed and paralyzed by sorrow, like Peabody. And he didn't want to go to Houston. Houston was not very far west at *all*.

At night, they argued.

Here was something that they agreed on, though. Peabody realized this as he took out the radio stones, one by one, and set them on the ground. Radio Cowboy was excited. Radio Cowboy liked to ride the range of audible wavelengths deliberately placed in the air; he liked to rope recalcitrant ions and jump coaxial canyons. He was against the tyranny of *El Silencio*, which fenced them in on Earth, fenced the wild free infinite radio range and left them soundless. Radio Cowboy was eager to summon up the Hot Polka Mamas from Spring City, the Sod House Rounders from Topeka, the Two-Step Doo-Daas from Dry Heat Arizona. He wanted Billy Sunday and Arthur Godfrey and Paul Harvey, whom he used to listen to in his green Ford pickup; in his eighteen-wheeler, Bessie . . .

Peabody's hand paused while setting out WLW, which was yellow.

Radio Cowboy was getting mighty specific here. Radio Cowboy was supposed to be an archetypal bundle. He wasn't supposed to have this iron bedstead and tilting lamp in the rough pre-yuppie Boulderado Hotel between truck runs. He wasn't supposed to be calling Ira on the phone and telling her to bring a pack of Marlboros too while she was at it. He wasn't supposed to be pissed about a . . . what? Speeding ticket?

Radio Cowboy Shorty was *old.* Parts of him were *real. Too* real.

"Hell no they don't make me sick!" he thundered, standing and flinging a host of radio stones from his lap, which sparkled in the firelight before they hit the ground with tiny thuds. "Bring a whole carton, damn it! Ira? Ira? . . ."

As Peabody fought to contain Radio Cowboy, he noticed, out of the corner of his eye, that Dania was yelling and tossing things out of the trunk of the Carlyle. Then she jumped in the car and left a trail of dust as she drove, fast, down the dirt road. He ran after her, shouting, but it was too late.

She was gone.

It was Cowboy who went back to the fire and grabbed the bottle of rum. At least she'd left that behind. Probably be back for it, too.

Willing

Radio Cowboy woke the next morning with a headache.

He opened his eyes and saw his precious radio stones glimmering in the dawn, roped and tied with invisible cord by *El Silencio.* Beyond that was the circle of blackened sagebrush, and beyond that—

He sat up. His bedroll crinkled.

It hadn't been a dream.

He looked at the pitiful pile of stuff on the ground catching the first light of morning.

She had left the freeze-dried Palomino embryo, three food tubes—all in flavors she knew that he hated—and an empty water bladder he could fill at the spring. Also a deck of cards and his harmonica.

Damn. What a woman. He always knew that, deep down, she really did care for him. This sure did prove it. He knew that the possibility of a Palomino was precious to her. Thank God she hadn't left that sissy survival kit. That would have been quite insulting.

Radio Cowboy stood up, grinning. He peed on the still-warm

fire and his piss evaporated in a hiss of sour steam. He kicked off his boots and pulled on his jeans. He had things to do. He had to return radio to the range. He had to round up the gang and head out into the frontier. He had to have adventures. Not only adventures, but Adventure. Dania only slowed him down, got in his way. Distracted him with thoughts of love. In which Dania seemed markedly uninterested, but he was sure she'd thaw eventually. They all did. He was a cowboy.

He put on his snakeskin boots and fastened his silver belt buckle and walked down to the spring, squatting to fill the water bladder. He walked back up, sat on a rock, and opened a food tube. Pure, unadorned soybean paste. Some of that foreign stuff, MISO, it said. He gagged on it. He took a swig of water and had a black moment when he realized there would be no coffee this morning. But a cowboy, especially a Radio Cowboy, and most especially Radio Cowboy Crescent City Shorty, could endure great hardship.

He told the bedroll to morph into a pack. It rebelled until he yelled at it, then it slowly and sulkily began to bend and contract and divide into a pack shape trailing straps and clips. Into the pack he put his water, his food tubes, the freeze-dried Palomino kit, and the deck of cards. He scooped up the radio stones in their impotent splendor and stuffed them in a pouch on the side of the pack. He left the harmonica out. After he swung the light pack onto his back, he picked up the harmonica and walked west, playing *The Streets of Loredo* on the harmonica.

This was living. This was really living.

"Pipe down," he told that interfering Peabody character, who seemed to be starting to panic. Something about Houston again.

He tramped back to the secondary highway on which they had been driving. He remembered another argument about whether they shouldn't be driving on the old Interstate 10, so as better to see the signs for Houston, but Radio Cowboy could see no good reason to go to Houston. Nothing but a bunch of goddamned people there.

Radio Cowboy had only trekked a few miles down the hardtop

road when he realized that his boots weren't made for walking. His feet were a mass of blisters. He could feel and almost hear Peabody raging within him, and Peabody seemed to remember something about how he had acted the night before, scaring poor little Dania. Hollering at her and calling her Ira.

And telling him that he had to get to Houston. Now! To a . . . Space Center? What kind of damned notion was that?

"Poor little Dania, my foot!" he growled. That girl could take care of herself, you bet.

Long before eleven A.M. the road began to shimmer and effervesce, but Radio Cowboy did not curse Dania aloud until that hour. But finally he just could not hold it in. That Peabody fellow kept worrying at him like a dog worries a bone, complaining that it was his fault—his, Radio Cowboy's!—that Dania was all alone out there.

This was mighty unpleasant. For one thing, Radio Cowboy never admitted fault. For another thing, he was the one in trouble, not Dania. Who had the car?

Well, he was no stranger to hitchhiking. And here came a . . . well, some kind of strange buslike vehicle, heading west. Too sleek for his taste, but sometimes a cowboy had to make do.

He held out his thumb.

Deep in the Heart

Dania drove onward, westward, across the vast Republic of Texas. She was heading toward Hollywood. Why not? She'd always wanted to go there, ever since she was little, and people always told her she had so much talent. She'd gotten sidetracked, that was all. Sidetracked by history. A small part of her nagged that she should not have left her companion behind, but he'd got scary last night, staggering around like he was drunk, though he couldn't have been; he never touched her liquor because he preferred beer, in long-necked bottles. He wasn't the songy sweet cowboy of their campfire nights, who had almost, but not quite, succeeded in seducing her.

Now she sure was glad that she'd resisted. A certain rage had emerged in him that reminded her a lot of her kids' daddy. She'd sworn to herself that she'd never put up with that kind of assinine behavior again. How many years ago? Seventy-five? One corner of her mouth quirked in a grin. Well, she'd sure made that stick.

Her wind-snarled hair whipped out behind her. She hoped that the sunscreen was working. Back in Crescent City, which seemed like a distant dream, sunscreen, but something not even as primitive as that, something better, had come out of the showers and protected them from skin cancer. Even if you got it, the damage could be repaired; it just took more energy. But these sunglasses . . .

She had unfortunately gotten hold of some sunglasses at the flea market that seem to have come from Tennessee, for whenever she wore them they called up the particulars of her divorce case and marched them down the right side of her lenses. Such helpful, kind sunglasses, smart sunglasses, sunglasses that recognized her DNA. She guessed they were cop sunglasses, or, more likely, lawyer sunglasses. Divorce lawyer sunglasses. If she could figure out how to run them, she could at least have someone else's divorce information scrolling faintly across her upper vision. Or if only she'd gotten some kind of physicist glasses, not that she could understand that stuff again, or even children's storytelling glasses, she would have been happy, but no, she had to rattle through that anonymous jumble set out on the folding table of the dark-faced man in the straw hat and pick out these for the utterly Dania-type reason that she liked the way they looked; she liked the way that green dot flashed excitedly in the top corner of the right lens when she touched them. Excited to find a victim, she knew that now. She'd even paid extra, because, as the man pointed out, they seemed to be made just for her.

Indeed.

The road was self-repairing and utterly smooth. There wasn't much to driving out here, but Dania was getting kind of dry.

She needed some soda pop. Some beer. She needed some cigarettes too. It had been a long, long time since she'd had cigarettes. Something about driving out here brought out the need in her.

Maps were no preparation for the size of Texas, not that they had one; Cowboy insisted that they only needed to go west. They had passed an unguarded checkpoint at the border near Texarkana. Texans had tried to keep nanotechnology out, but how could they? She and Cowboy had read with interest a list of contraband.

Her glasses, certainly, and the car for another and everything inside it. Probably them, too. NATURAL HUMANS ONLY, read the list, and NATURAL ANIMALS too. Texas had tried to be a natural sort of place, but things got past them in the end.

Unfortunately, she hadn't seen any of the drive-thru stores that had so willingly scanned the Sun-O-Rama in Arkansas and given them whatever they wanted in return. Probably some kind of chain that Texas didn't allow.

Her foot on the energy pedal let up a little. There was something up ahead. BEER CIGARETTES BATTERIES, the faded sign read. Well, now she was getting somewhere.

She pulled onto the eroded concrete pad and sighed. The doors and windows were nailed shut with boards. CONTAMINATED was painted in dripping letters across what looked like the main door. NO ENTRY BY ORDER OF BUG RANGERS. 2 BACON OR SAUSAGE, 3 EGGS, JUICE & COFFEE ALL DAY EVERY DAY $3.29 TEX-DOLLARS ONLY!

Well, shoot.

Two huge trucks and a smaller metal trailer were to one side of the main building, wracked by time and looted by vandals, who had carted off everything removable.

Dania got out of the car and stretched. Her long skirt blew around her legs, and she doubted that she would ever get a comb through her hair again, it looked such a sight in the darkened glass of the window. She ought to have braided it, but she had been too irritated to think straight when she left. She remembered that she'd thrown the Palomino kit on the ground, the one that

Cowboy whined took up too much space, with a particularly satisfying rush of snottiness.

It was hot, and there wasn't a soul around. She had only passed three vehicles going east all day, and had seen no one else heading west.

The plains were treeless and the hot wind brought a steady smell of slow-baked grass, sweet and crisp, and she experienced a distant memory she really ought not have. It was like that, she'd found. She could enjoy these memories, the memories of others who had found this land so beautiful, even though Dania herself had never made it this far west in her quest for Hollywood.

This feeling was all that was left of somebody's memory. Some cattle rancher, some trucker, some traveling saleswoman. Just the pure pleasure of this vast flat land, and how brilliant it all was in the sun with the grass rippling tall then short where the wind pressed it down.

The hills they'd been in were finally flattening out. She could still see them, low rises to the east where she'd been that morning. Radio Cowboy was probably still tromping along back there.

She felt a very, very slight pang of guilt. She remembered how he had rescued her in Crescent City and kept the pirates from killing her. She remembered his nifty show-tune pistols.

There was something else she was trying to remember. Something about Houston.

Hell. It was too hard to remember.

"The bug police!" she said scornfully, and strode over to the door, which was boarded up. It would need to be pried open. The large front windows were covered with thick iron bars.

Something banged, somewhere. She strode around the phalanx of looted trucks to the west side of the building and stopped just before she would have tumbled into a huge gully. It was about twenty feet deep and looked like it stretched a quarter mile away.

At the back of the place she found a metal door, scoured clean of paint by the wind and the sun, swinging open and banging shut. She went inside.

Yeah, bugs. No kidding!

She had stepped back in time. It was seventy years ago, and everything was perfect. As perfect as it had been for that short time when nanotech worked as they had been told it would, never mind the plagues of thought, the terrorism, the vanishings, the fear. Here was stuff: perfect, beautiful stuff. She realized that the loaves of bread in plastic wrappers, the soda dispenser, the rack holding presealed movie blobs, and the floors and walls themselves were maintained by a program that would never give up. It used solar energy and the stuff that it sucked out of the ever-growing crevasse outside. Since people so rarely came here, it probably hadn't been necessary to replenish much in quite a long time.

Thin lines of sunlight coming in between the boards on the windows draped smooth perfect orange counters. Rows of crinkle-wrapped snacks were stacked in wire holders. She stepped closer and examined a package of Cheez Crackers. One might expect a corner of the package to be gnawed by small teeth, and the package empty, but all of these wrappers were apparently as hard as steel, and were only openable by people with two hands, one of which wielded a knife. Critterproof.

She walked toward the counter, behind which were bushels of cigarettes.

She was not afraid of anything, since there was nothing to fear out here save snakes, but when a beam of light thickened and grew into an oblong shape, kind of like a gigantic roly-poly easily as large as her, Dania's heart began to *thud.*

Despite all the strangenesses she'd seen since she was transported down the Mississippi River on a boat filled with and piloted by raving madpeople, and then all the technological changes and ages she'd whipped through since, this blob of light for some reason and revved up the fearmeter she thought she'd lost long ago.

She did not know why she believed it was sentient. She did not know why she felt as if it were observing not only each hair and freckle but each act of her life, each thought, as if it could see through time.

She realized that she had ceased to breathe, and forced her lungs to expand. Air passed through her narrowed throat in a kind of croak.

This thing was between her and the cigarettes.

She took a few steps forward, but the thing didn't budge, didn't float away or vanish like a trick of vision might.

"Um, excuse me," she said in a kind of gasp. "I would like to get hold of those cigarettes, back there."

The thing pressed itself away from the cigarettes. Dania about fell to the floor. It listened! It understood! It even understood English!

"Well, damn," she said, putting her hands on her hips and looking at it. "Who are you? What are you doing here? What you want with me?"

A low hum filled the air. There was an almost imperceptible vibration of the things around her. She recalled that the lone elephant in Crescent City had trumpeted its yearning messages in sound that could not be heard by humans.

"Can't hear that," she said. "Needs to be pitched higher. I can hear sounds between thirty and four thousand hertz. I can see in the electromagnetic spectrum from a wavelength of about four hundred nanometers to, um, maybe seven hundred fifty." She wasn't sure where these ideas and numbers were coming from. She was astonished and pleased. Apparently, she had not lost all of her older self. It had just been folded away inside somehow.

Or maybe this . . . *thing* . . . had something to do with her restoration. The air smelled like ozone. She was at least ten degrees smarter, or at least smart enough to feel dumb.

The light seemed to be changing from white to blue, and its sound was now a low moan like the wind might make.

Then it vanished.

She had a clear path to the cigarettes.

"Um, guess that wasn't such a good idea," she said, but the thing was clearly gone. She no longer felt observed.

Beneath the counter was a stash of bags. She filled one with cigarettes. Then she walked around the store and filled more bags with bread, cheese, beef jerky, licorice, candy bars, and Reddy-Fill bags of soda, soymilk, and juice. And beer. She moved quickly and looked around when she was done, wondering if there were more things she would need.

She drove the Carlyle to the back door and loaded up until the little car was almost overflowing with stuff, and settled into the driver's seat.

She had to decide which way to head.

She had to admit that the light-thing had spooked her just a mite. Not enough to need companionship; there was hardly enough spook power in creation for that. But she thought of Radio Cowboy Shorty hiking along that rough road, maybe stopping at a spring and trying to figure out how to grow the Palomino, and she just had to turn back the way she'd come.

Maybe he'd learned his lesson.

Maybe he'd know something about the light that spoke like an elephant.

With the elephant, another small chunk of Crescent City came back.

Despite that, Hollywood called. She peeled onto the highway heading west, popped open a warm beer, and took a foamy swig.

An hour later, her car stopped.

It had been so long since a machine had actually stopped working while Dania was using it that at first she was simply puzzled as it coasted to a stop. Wasn't it supposed to be different from the interminable parade of broken-down Chevys and Fords and Toyotas which sat outside cheap apartments on the back streets of Memphis, floors paved with crushed-down layers of trash, smelling of kids?

She popped the hood and stepped out into the hot wind. She leaned over the shaded place where engine ought to be and was baffled.

It was indeed different. There were the hoses she remembered, but everything was exceedingly clean. Several large chunks of metal she thought ought to be there were not. There was no battery, so it couldn't be out of water. The road itself was the battery. She left the hood up and went back inside and after studying the dashboard found a button labeled DIAGNOSTICS. That was more like it. She pushed it.

The fuel converter was broken. When she asked for more information, she was told that some chemical essential to fuel breakdown had degraded past use and what's more since she had ignored this, the bla bla—the name of which she would never remember anyhow, so why try?—was now also broken and a new one had to be grown.

In plain language, she would have to go to a garage, or some kind of all-purpose nanotech mart that had at one time presumably existed.

Dania wrenched off the sunglasses. They were stuck on replaying the testimony of her accursed ex-husband and the seedy friends he'd recruited to try and convince the judge to give the kids to him. In fact, the case had gone to the State Supreme Court. The docket number was even here. This brought back bitter memories.

In a fit of anger, she crushed the glasses beneath her bootheel. But they sprang back into shape the instant she lifted her foot. Of course, how else could they have lasted so long? She gave them a good kick and they skittered across the road. How aggravating the world was out here! She wished that she had stayed in Crescent City. Everything out here was so big, but it seemed as if her head had contracted by a million degrees.

So. She was stuck here with lots of beer, cigarettes, beef jerky, and licorice. All of the essentials, anyway.

A mile back she had seen a sign pointing north with the name of some little town. Eyesore or Heatstroke or some such place, she assumed by the look of things. She rummaged around and found the small leather pouch of Mississippi silver coins and looped it over her neck. She upended a gallon of water and let it pour right down her throat until she felt like she was going to burst.

She headed east, her feet scuffing the dirt because the pavement was like to melt her boot soles, keeping an eye out for rattlers.

Whatever the sign had once said was obscured by bullet holes. The town had an H and a P in it for sure. There was no guarantee that anyone was even there. Where was it? It had to be countless miles away. Otherwise, why couldn't she see it?

But after another ten minutes she came to a gulch a half mile wide and down in it a meandering row of cottonwoods and tucked halfway up the gully on the other side a row of low faded buildings. A tiny creek glinted at the bottom of the gulch and cows ripped scant grass from the hillside.

Dania was soaking wet, but her sweat didn't seem to be cooling her much. She trudged down the switchback road.

When she got down to the creek, she climbed down next to the modest bridge, took off her boots and socks, and lay right down in the shallow run, not caring that sharp rocks poked her back. She could almost hear steam sizzle as she cooled.

After about ten minutes, she felt positively icy. She stared up at the cloudless blue sky for a few minutes longer, until a shadow fell across her. Someone poked at her side. She turned her head.

A man loomed over her, blocking the sun so she could see, foreshortened, his brown ten-gallon hat, his rough red beard, his vest, plaid shirt, and jeans, and the inevitable hand-tooled boot, severely pointed at the toe, propped on a rock dangerously close to her head. She raised up out of the stream on her elbows.

"What the hell do you want?"

"What are you doing here?" asked the man.

"Cooling off." She collapsed back into the stream and closed her eyes, hoping that he would go away. He might have the secret to starting her car, but the icy water washing over her brain seemed much more important at the moment.

He seized her arm and pulled her up. Slipping on the wet stones, she gained her balance, pulled her arm from his grasp, and glared at him, wishing now that she had brought her sunglasses, which would have given her a more formidable mien.

"What's the problem? This private property?"

"I assed you a question." His eyes were flat-looking, as if he stared out on a world long since grown boring. Or, thought

Dania, suddenly recognizing the look, as if he regularly soaked his breakfast flakes in whisky.

"I'm just passing through." She waded from the stream, sat on a rock, rubbed her left foot dry with a sock, put it on, and shoved her foot into its boot. She got started on her right foot.

"If that's your broke car on the road, you ain't passing through. You're stuck, lady."

Dania deeply longed for Radio Cowboy's show-tune pistols. She wanted to see this guy dance. Maybe babble *A Spoonful of Sugar.*

She finished with her boots and stood up. The heat had already sucked most of the wet from her clothes. "I'll figure it out. I just needed to cool off some."

"You got something to do with the light at the feed store"

"I just got here and I don't have much to do with anything." She tilted her head and shaded her eyes, watching him as she crouched down and wrapped her hand around a good-sized rock.

"Light showed up an hour ago. Think that's about when you musta broke down. Now come on and stop your bullshit." He took a few steps, then turned back. "Maybe you can help, is all. Don't kid yourself, you ain't goin' nowhere without some help yourself."

Startled, she watched him walk toward the row of buildings perched on the brown hillside.

Was that . . . *thing* . . . following her?

She hiked down to the end of town.

A number of the usual odd-looking transportation permutations were parked head-in on the potholed blacktop stretch, which was all of a quarter-mile long. Above the town proper, where the road looped higher, were several shacks and two or three good-sized houses.

She climbed onto the porch of the saloon.

A gray-haired woman sat just inside the door on a folding chair, smoking and watching her. Dania saw a small grocery and butcher shop, a sign that said BUGS LIMITED, an old franchise for ostensibly safe nanotech seed-goods, and finally, down at the end of the street a small crowd of women, men, and children, most of them wearing jeans, plaid shirts, and boots, at Henderson's Cash Feed Store.

The smoking woman gave her head a long nod in that direction. "They're waiting for you," she said.

Dania stepped inside and breathed in the smell of spilled beer. "How about a drink?" As her eyes adjusted she saw a beaten tin ceiling, about ten scarred old tables scattered around with a number of chairs, and some battered stools in front of an incongruously ornate carved wooden bar.

The woman did not rise from her seat. "Got a lot of money, I suppose."

"What do you use for money around here?"

"Money. You from Colorado?"

"Tennessee."

"That accounts for your ignorance, I guess. Two bucks silver."

Dania reached into her pouch and pulled out the coins. Silver was silver, and although you could build silver coins nanotechnologically, that still took energy. She slapped them on the bar.

The woman went behind the bar and set the coins on a small yellow tray, across which arched the phrase INSTA-ANALYZER in old-fashioned lettering. The tray turned green.

"What'll it be?"

"Pint of that Sun Ale. So what's all this about a light?"

The bartender became slightly more animated. "Saw it come down the street. Like a shadow, but a bright shadow, you know. Thought my eyes were goin' bad. Things got dim behind it, but when it was right in front of me, it was all real sharp and bright, lots of colors, so I had to close my eyes. Like a mirror winking on the mountain but strong and close and over right away. It got up on the porches and when it was out of the direct sun you could see that it kind of gave off a glow. Finally it went into the feed store—" She looked up to a clattering of boots on the boardwalk and her eyes grew large.

Dania turned around, pretty much knowing what she would see.

The ovoid shape kind of drifted through the wall while the crowd of people filled the doorway. It coasted to a stop near Dania and she felt chilly. She took another sip of ale and watched it.

A feeling of awe pervaded her. It was like Sunday morning in Salvation when they all sang the old hymns, all those old folks who truly believed, with their natural harmonies and their fervor. She could almost see the plain white interior, the age-polished wooden pews, hear the birds sing outside in the moments of rich silence.

In all of her years since, she had not felt this.

What was it? What did it want with her? Was there anything different about her compared to all these people around her?

Probably. There probably was something different about her.

For one thing, she had a genetic anomaly for which she had been tracked down when younger. They put her in a clinic for six months and did painful tests on her; she remembered them as a blur of needles and questions and feeling extremely sick before they tossed her out, saying she was defective. Her father had raged that if she had done better he would have gotten more money from the guvment.

And then, there was the music. It was something she lived with, like the color of her hair. It wasn't always there. But it was now, with a sharpness that brought tears to her eyes.

"Damn," she said, and swallowed the rest of her ale.

"What are you doing here, lady?" demanded a young woman with short black hair. She crossed her arms and stepped forward. "You brought this thing—"

At that moment a boy, just older than a toddler, shrieked and laughed and ran directly toward the light.

"Ben!" screamed someone, but the child darted into the light

He vanished.

There was silence, save for the tones of the light, which Dania was not sure that others could hear.

A woman screamed.

Someone yelled, "Get out of the way while I kill it!"

Through all this, the light sat there unperturbed and Dania spied a back door.

She began to slide toward it. Then a gunshot quieted everyone.

"It's her!" hollered the man who had met her at the creek. "She brought this thing to kill the only kids any of us have managed to have in fifty years! And the rest of us too!"

Dania could not run for they caught her arms. A woman shot into the light twice and others yelled at her to stop. Then Dania was shoved into its center.

Her life, every instant of it, like you were supposed to see just before you died. Each instant a point, all equal. Something in the mixing apparatus of her brain gave them the motion everyone called time, an arrow, a direction, an intensity.

Her memory returned in a rush.

All she had forgotten in Crescent City, everything about superstrings and gravity waves and light, was there. She was aware of all of it in a new way, a way beyond names and theories, and she saw how she would die, alone and dreadfully lonely, and it was mixed in with all the other times.

Most too fast to tell what it was. A blur of pictures and sounds and even talking like a brook might talk when you turn your back to it. A sudden brief blackness.

She was certainly not lonely. So . . . if that sad vision was correct, she thought, coming to staring up at the ceiling, she would live past this place, anyway.

The light was gone.

She could not lie there helpless in front of all these people.

She got to her feet. She jammed her shaking hands into her skirt pockets, startled because the radio she had there had come alive and was playing a tinny-sounding polka.

Everyone was staring at her. That bright watery smell was still in the air. She switched off the radio.

A thin man pointed his pistol at her across the bar's corner. She really had no idea why, except that perhaps if one had a gun, it might often seem necessary to point it at someone.

"I wouldn't do that if I were you," she said in her flattest, most authoritative voice. She put her hands on her hips and stared at him.

"What did you do with Ben?" asked a little girl, her blond hair falling back as she tilted her head to look up at Dania's face.

She knelt and looked in the girl's face. "I didn't do anything," she said gently.

She stood and walked toward the front door. The crowd parted.

Hoping that she would not throw up from sheer nervousness, she quickly got into the closest vehicle, a low-slung solar job. It started with a reassuring purr.

The bartender ran out onto the porch as Dania backed up. "Hey, that's my car! Somebody stop her!" In the rearview mirror Dania saw her waving her arms wildly, but no one made a move.

Dania drove like hell up the switchbacks, raising a cloud of dust.

She paused for a moment at the canyon's rim. There appeared to be no one following her.

Maybe they thought she'd kill them too.

Maybe they were right.

With a tightening of her throat as she thought of Ben, she sped west and shrieked to a stop next to the pitifully fragile Sun-O-Rama. She ran to it and started tossing things into the stolen car, but she kept dropping things. Looking back once again, she gave up, got back in the car, slammed her door, and headed off into the lowering dark of the Eastern sky.

The light had done something.

She remembered. She remembered Crescent City. She remembered Peabody.

And she remembered Houston.

After an hour of travel, Dania's headlights picked up the store she'd stopped in earlier. She flew past it and continued for another hour.

It was almost impossible to tell where she was, but this was about how long she had driven before reaching the store.

She pulled off the main road onto a track that seemed vaguely familiar.

She was back in the hilly country of the morning. She hoped

that she could find Peabody. She drove down a few tiny roads where gravel crunched beneath the tires, yelling out the window, but it was useless.

Bone-tired, she parked near a sycamore tree and got out of the car. The moon made it light enough for her to see pretty well. The sky seemed even more huge than it had with Radio Cowboy, because she was alone. She wondered if maybe she would die now, and wondered if she could ever enjoy being alone again, with that lonely-death scene lodged inside of her.

She lay down on the hood of the car and crossed her arms upon her chest. Had she been vouchsafed any *happy* scenes? Any emotionally *fulfilling* scenes?

The luminosity of her earlier experience was gone. She just felt nauseous and exhausted. Her customary headache, firewalled by Radio Cowboy, had returned along with everything else. She was herself again, the self she had been for fifty years in Crescent City.

She realized that the difference was not so great. Except that now she had a bit more fear. She was a bit more sober. Young Dania had been at war with everyone and everything; that was gone. Things were not as simple now as they had been back then.

What, for instance, was going on in Crescent City now? Had it been destroyed? Had the slow transformation of the self-sufficient city to a self-sufficient interstellar craft been stopped? Peabody had set certain plans in motion, plans which involved him retrieving some lost information from the Johnson Space Center in Houston, if the Center was still there. She had watched him without quite understanding what he was doing. She did now. She didn't think that Radio Cowboy remembered that—or cared. Getting that information was definitely not a priority for whatever, or whomever, had hijacked Peabody.

Their past as humans was a chancy one, she saw that now. Tossed hither and yon by emotion, unfocused, unaware of any kind of larger fate or connections with the rest of the universe, with the other species they lived with, or even the people next door. She was lucky enough to have gone to another level, though she had lost that for a while. The people in the town today were almost like another species.

What had happened to that boy? It was a terrible puzzle. Maybe if she had not been so cowardly she could have thought of some way to save him.

Like what? She was lucky to get away alive.

But none of the markers of her past long life were here. She was alone. There was not any Radio Cowboy or any other kind of cowboy either; there were not even the Divorce Sunglasses, thank God.

What had happened? What did it mean? Why did that thing, that phenomenon of light, follow her around as if it knew her? Where the hell did it come from? Why the timeless moment? Where was it now? Why did those stars shine down at her now so intensely, why did she suddenly understand a massive mitocondrialike field of time bent by gravity—

Her headache suddenly increased beyond bearing.

She moaned and held her head. She rolled from the car hood, sagged against the car with her head in her hands, and cried from sheer pain.

The disappearance of the pain was a crystalline transition. Infinite tiny bells rang.

She stared into the night, feeling surrounded by them. The sound was so real, so intense, that she thought that she must be able to see them, embedded in matter as they had to be, and omnipresent, as if emitted from the very atoms of the air.

She lay back on the car hood again, exhausted, adamantly not enchanted, wishing for her crinklefoam. It was a process, she saw that now, like some kind of sickness she would go through, something strong enough to kill children instantly, and what would be the end of it?

The music faded, and the night grew cold. The moon was enormous. She stared at it, as if she could commune with it, as if it had powerful information for her if only she could parse the light bouncing off its surface.

The ground began to shake. A thunderous sound arose and grew steadily louder.

Dania stood on the hood of the car.

From her low rise, she saw a black flood crossing the land.

Buffalo.

The herd looked to be about half a mile away, advancing like a viscous goo, filling the horizon and getting louder.

It would crush her.

She looked around. The sycamore, craggy and tall, was her only hope. She jumped into the car and drove it bumpily beneath the lowest branch.

The sound was now deafening. She climbed on the roof of the car and leaped, trying to catch the lowest branch, but it was still too high. Frantic, she got down and rummaged in the car, throwing things out, until she came to the long coil of rope Cowboy had insisted on. She had almost left it with him! And then in the other car! As she knotted one end with trembling hands to make it heavy, she hoped he was well out of the way of this stampede.

She threw the rope and it snaked down next to her, the knot landing with a heavy *thump* on the hood of the car without going over the branch. She hauled it back and threw it again. She now heard the pounding of a thousand individual hooves.

This time the rope passed over the limb. She grabbed the knot, looped both ends of the rope around her hands, and began walking herself up the trunk of the tree. Her boots were slippery against the peeling bark, but it was too late to take them off. When her feet finally reached the limb, she was almost upside down. She gave herself a strong push with one foot and hooked the other leg over the branch, gradually shifting herself upright until she straddled the branch.

The buffalo flood came over the rise in a wave. The car below her was pushed away by their breasts, and crumpled like a paper cup as they leaped upon it. This took about two seconds.

But it took half an hour for them to pass. She held to her branch and watched, fascinated, filled with awe at their power, intensity, and purpose. Where were they going? Why? Was something frightening them? Or was this just their nature? The stars burned down on her, filling her mind with unimaginable distance.

By the time they passed, her eyes were grainy and she was biting her tongue to stay awake. It had been a long day.

She dropped down with the help of the rope and fell backward.

Completely groggy, she nestled between the roots of the tree, but could not fall asleep. To make things worse, the stars brought out their new geometries once more and flooded her mind with opening vistas of light which expanded and contracted so quickly that again she was sick to her stomach.

Finally, in that same wrenching transition, the shadowy landscape appeared to be in motion, and with that motion came sound.

Sound as a function of vision, and a vision tinged tonight with surely more light than the stars gave now that the moon had forsaken the sky. Vision that allowed her to see the pale green of the yucca spears near her.

She got to her feet and walked out across the desert's verge. Glowing scorpions walked the earth. The ground was not churned up here; perhaps the buffalo had parted because of a gigantic rock hunkering a quarter-mile away as if set there by a heedless hand. Her nose filled with the dry perfume of the sagebrush. A sidewinder swept past in pursuit of a rabbit.

It was the light, she knew, and she walked on. Soon she came to a lone buffalo.

Ah, she thought, I am dreaming now, as she walked up and touched its huge rough-haired head, standing on tiptoe, as it snorted and watched her with one huge liquid eye. If I could ride the buffalo, I could climb the rainbow bridge of light to the sky. I could become the Spider Woman and spin the universe.

It's nice to at least believe that one is dreaming when the stars make sounds like distant breaking glass, breaking all around and all the time, and the flight of the buffalo is a wide roaring streak that takes the form of a rainbow laddered with colors humans had never seen before.

Dania rode through the sky that night and the colorful scorpions flew alongside, and glowing spiders, with brilliant white desert flowers laced through her hair.

The Welcome

When she opened her eyes, she was fifty yards from the sycamore tree, lying on a soft pad and covered by a blanket. It was still dark.

Five people sat nearby on low-slung folding chairs, their faces washed by firelight, chatting softly. They all had long black hair. She heard horses nicker, and then saw two picketed nearby on a low rise.

She raised her head. Their chairs creaked as they all turned to look at her.

"We are glad you've come," one of the women said, her words low across the darkness that separated them. "Welcome to the Nows."

Dania managed, "What?"

But it seemed difficult to speak, as it usually did when she was dreaming. Which she must be.

She moaned and turned over, closing her eyes, but the Nows beat against her even in her dreams, and she did not sleep well at all.

The Musician and the Radio Astronomer

Far off, way out in Los Angeles, a huge golden Dome pulsed. It was made of light. Some people who lived in the mountains above it claimed that it was made of ages of smog all crushed together so hard that it glowed. Children were warned that they would die of suffocation if they got too close to it, or that they might even get sucked in. No one lived within ten miles of it, anyway. Kids had been known to run into it and vanish in its light. Parents had been known to run after them.

No one, on the other hand, had seen anyone emerge from the

Dome. It was rumored that a train had once run in and out of the Dome twice a week, but that was just old folks' talk.

So when the Zeb-Being and the Ra-Being walked out of the Dome one clear summer's day, they saw the most God-awful ruins imaginable.

"Are you sure this is a good idea?" asked the Zeb-Being, or Zeb for short, since this is what the Ra-Being called him.

"No," said the Ra-Being, or Ra for short, since this is what the Zeb-Being called her.

They were both naked.

"This is hard on the feet. When will we get our clothes?"

Zeb frowned. "Soon, I hope."

Ra climbed atop a pile of concrete blocks, which slipped into new configuration with rings and rumbles. "Hey, I like those sounds."

"Be careful," warned Zeb. "I feel kind of woozy. Maybe we should go back in. It's awful bright out here." He had a short white beard and a weathered face. His body was pale and white. He rubbed his arms, looking at them with wonder. "Even though it's supposed to be the same in there, I can tell the difference."

"We can die out here," observed Ra. Her deep brown face was creased only with laugh lines, and she wore her hair in many long, fine braids.

"But our real selves will stay in the Dome," said Zeb. "Hey, Ra! I can kind of see us looking out! Over there!"

"Don't be silly," said Ra, scrambling down from her perch. "I saw a road around on the other side of these ruins. Where do you reckon we want to go?"

Zeb smiled. "East. Where else?"

"Seems like the Dome was farther away when we went in. Look at that gorgeous view!" Ra stretched as if her hands could grasp the sky if she only tried hard enough. She took a deep breath. Several hundred feet below them, the Pacific Ocean thundered at the base of a cliff. There were a lot of signs posted a few feet from the glowing Dome's base. DANGER! KEEP OUT! WANT TO DIE, FOOL? and suchlike. Some were sophisticated legal notices that would have taken fifteen minutes to read; others were spray-painted on rough wood. "Where's our van?"

Zeb looked around with only slight consternation. "It needn't be right here, I guess."

"I'd expect it to be here. Maybe we should go back in and refetch . . ."

They both looked at each other.

"It was kind of hard, wasn't it?" asked Zeb finally.

"Yeah. Yeah, it was pretty hard. Can't say why, though, exactly . . ."

He took both of her hands in his. "Want to go back?"

She grinned. "Hell no." She grabbed him by the waist and gave him a quick, hard kiss. Then she wrapped her other arm around him and looked up at his face. "It feels . . . better out here. Don't you think?"

In the clear cool evening, Ra and Zeb found the clothes they had programmed, in the side of the Dome at 321 degrees, five minutes, two seconds. The Dome there was a hard, rough solid, and they opened a door like that of an oven and found their clothes down to the last exact button. Zeb had matches in his pocket, and Ra had her old Swiss Army knife in the pocket of her jeans. They both had strong hiking boots.

"Maybe the van will take longer," observed Ra.

"Hey, it's great to be in the future, isn't it?" asked Zeb.

"Seems kind of like the distant past to me," said Ra, "But yeah, I love it, so far."

They walked through the rubble and debris and gathered scraps of wood; mostly old furniture and the bleached boards of houses. On the edge of the cliff, they built a fire.

"Are you hungry yet?" asked Zeb.

"No. I guess I will be before morning, though." The Dome was streaked with swirling opalescent color that lingered even after sunset was long gone. Ra shivered and moved closer to the fire. "We're going to get pretty cold before morning."

"Quite a novelty, isn't it?" teased Zeb. "We just have to keep focused on what we came out here to find and to do."

"Well, look, Zeb. Aren't we supposed to be more than human? Aren't we supposed to have extra faculties that we decided we needed, when we were in there? Can't we generate more heat? Can't we starve for a pretty long time before we die?"

"Yes. Yes, of course." Zeb crossed his legs and moved closer to the fire. "We know certain things now. But . . . we could think faster in there."

"And we could think in different ways," Ra mused, looking out at the constantly reformed path of light the moonrise made on the heaving sea.

"Humans can't know the things we knew in there," said Zeb. "I think that only the uttermost reaches of the most entirely conscious beings—a fusion of humans and artificial intelligence—can know these things." Zeb poked the fire with a length of copper pipe he'd found in the debris. "I'm not sure that I can know them any more."

"Well, what if a person had more sense-apertures?" asked Ra.

"What do you mean?"

"I mean, think about how you see things. Or how you used to see things, when you were . . . human. The way it seems now, again. Vision is an ellipse. My two eyes blend what I see so that I have a sense of three dimensions. But what if you had eyes all around your head, too, and maybe at the top? How would those visions be superimposed? What would that brain believe about the nature of reality? How would the mind *develop?* And how about sound? I've thought about sound a lot, of course."

"Being a musician. And such a fine one." Zeb smiled across the fire.

"This is what I want to think about in the future, in terms of my music: Each human is just a sensing blob in space. Even though the matter seems solid to us, it is full of space, like all the atoms that we're composed of. I feel as if I'm part of something that's happening, all the time, a process. I can sense certain aspects of the process, and the things that I can sense are completely based on my physical makeup.

"So—what if we could *hear* the frequencies that we now *see?* It would be like music to us, wouldn't it, everything we saw? Not just some of the time, the way it is when I compose. Then it's like I'm just catching the tail of some quick animal that's running away from me. But all the time."

"Light music," said Zeb, giving the fire another stir.

"That's it!" said Ra. "That's what I think is really happening. We're in this vast endless ever-changing flow of music, the music that light makes. And everything, *everything,* is really, deeply, made of light. Just light. If we could only know it. I mean, think of all the creatures that have evolved on earth. Almost all of us have eyes, but some of us see different frequencies, like bees, for instance, and other insects. Some of us hear higher or lower frequencies. But it's all just a way of translating light. That's all there really is."

They didn't sleep. They just talked all night.

The next morning they went back to the same location on the Dome. A huge double door had grown on the surface. Zeb seized one handle and Ra another and they pulled them open.

Inside sat a vehicle.

"Wow," said Ra. "My dad had one of these. It's a 1967 Volkswagen Van."

The words SPACE IS THE PLACE pulsed around the top of the van windows like letters in a marquee.

"It's beautiful," said Ra, pulling open the side door. "Look! A little kitchen and a bed. It's perfect!"

The message at the top of the van changed: GET IN. WE DON'T HAVE MUCH TIME.

February 2115

ANGELINA

Transit

Angelina took her breakfast with the crew.

Across the stainless-steel table sat a young woman wearing greasy overalls, her dry sun-streaked hair pulled into a ponytail. Angelina avoided her frank no-nonsense eyes because just a glimpse of them caused her mind to roar with stories. It was not good to have too many stories before breakfast.

The sailor stared pointedly at Chester, lying on the table next to Angelina's elbow, and smirked. He had insisted that Angelina strip him down to striped shorts and a tank T-shirt because he was delicately adjusted to feel heat and cold so that he could teach the boy or girl in charge of him empathy.

The woman finished her eggs, then lit a cigarette.

Chester coughed, his little chest contracting with each dry hoarse sound. The woman rolled her eyes, stubbed out her cigarette in the remains of her breakfast, and left.

"Taciturnity is not a positive personality trait," remarked Chester. "It's best to speak up."

"I don't understand what you have against smoking," said Angelina. "I smoked a pipe until a few years ago. It's perfectly harmless and a great solace."

"It is a filthy habit. Not many parents want their children to take it up, even though they will no longer die. It is up to me to show them the correct response."

Deep, resonant metallic groans surrounded them, a music of rust and motion. Stories of the sea—mutinies, whaling, shipping, wars, pirates—assailed Angelina, as well as tales from the ancient foundry in Santiago, Chile, where some of the bolts had been cast, and a certain man who had a wife with an uncle who . . .

She stood abruptly and grabbed Chester, stuffed him into a sling she had fashioned from a strip of cloth, and climbed to the highest deck.

The sea was a dark and ragged blue. A few cirrus clouds whisped above. There was nothing else in sight.

Perhaps if she sat up here, on this barrel, the monotony of the view would cleanse her mind. Give it a rest. The stories of the sea were faint waves washing through her, disturbing her mind slightly, then moving on before she had a chance to get caught in their rush and break, at which time they would display themselves in unavoidable entirety.

She offered, for the moment, no shore. It was a pleasant mental stance and she resolved to try to remember it, to use it as a place of retreat. Don't resist; allow. *Damn braces, bless relaxes,* popped into her head and she tentatively wondered if bless was what was required of her if she were to survive in this new mental landscape. A blessing glance rather than constant, fatiguing battle.

"I wonder how Louis is doing," she mused aloud. What path had he taken to Paris? Was he safe? He was a large, strong boy—young man, she corrected herself—but Buenos Aires was the extent of his travels alone, and she feared for him.

She was surprised when the doll remained silent. For once, she was in the mood for chat. This ocean travel could drive one completely mad for lack of something to do.

"I mean, the *Andalusia* was the only boat he could have sailed on, according to Clarissa. It was due into Morocco a week ago. There are supposed to be trains—"

She heard a sigh. She pulled Chester from the sling and sat him next to her on the barrel top.

"Don't let go," he warned. "It's quite windy. I could easily blow away."

She knotted the sling-cloth around his middle and the other end around her wrist. "Satisfied? Now, if you were a young man, where would you—"

"I'm an indoor doll. It's much too bright out here for my vision cells. Everything is just white."

"The better for you to talk without distractions."

"Arrgh!" cried Chester. "I am in great pain!"

Angelina ignored that, supressing a smile at his histrionics. "In fact, you seem to know an awful lot about the comings and goings of everyone in the city. You have some kind of DNA-tracing processor inside you, right? So you can tell me about Louis. When did he get to Buenos Aires? When did he leave?"

"I told you, I'm going to melt soon if you don't—"

"I'm beginning to think that you know something that you don't want to tell me."

Chester sighed. "It's not that."

"Then what is it, exactly?"

"I completely lack the capability to understand what happened to Louis, much less try and explain it to you. Radio began to work."

"And then?"

"It was several weeks ago. Recall, I have never met Louis. This is entirely reconstructed via my time-circuits and the information I got while I was at your Aunt Clarissa's—"

"You've known something since then?" demanded Angelina.

"I don't know anything," he said with surprising force. "This is a theory. Understand this. A theory only. But since I am also a radio—"

"Mother of God," murmured Angelina. "Go on."

"Since I am also a radio, I was astonished at the force of the signal that I received at that particular moment. I was completely awash in ionic switching events. The events had the rhythm of language, but it is not any language that I know, and I know thirty-seven—"

"Yes," said Angelina dryly. "Continue, please."

"It was a language," said Chester. "A language of light. It was brief. The entire transmission took only about forty-five seconds. It covered the entire spectrum, at least the spectrum that I can sense."

"What do you mean, 'the entire spectrum'?"

"It transmitted vibrations that your senses divide into light and sound. For me, they are all one continuum." He sighed. "At that moment I was glad that I was not human. Otherwise, I would not have been able to absorb the full impact."

"Well then." Angelina knew she was not going to like what she whatever outlandish thing Chester was going to say. "What about Louis?"

"When we entered Clarissa's apartment, I realized via pheromonal traces that Louis had been there. His DNA—partly yours—was in the air I sampled. I'm able to determine the time frame of such traces. In the process of establishing when he had been there, I was able to see, to my surprise, that something happened to Louis during the time of the light transmission. This could be. Something happened to me at the same time."

"Oh." She was fully within her own story now. It was a painful place. "What happened? To Louis?"

"I believe . . . I'm not sure of this entirely . . . But I believe that Louis was changed to light."

Angelina, suspended between sea and sky, felt all touchstones fade. Chester had been right about her name, and Clarissa's, and the time of her last visit, all from a fragment of hair.

"What does that mean?"

"I'm not sure."

"That's a slight relief. Why did Clarissa believe that he sailed on the *Andalusia*?"

"Probably because it was due to sail the next day, and when she woke up he was gone. As scheduled."

"Changed to light."

"Yes." Chester's voice was firm.

"Like an angel?"

Chester coughed. "Excuse me, but I have the distinct impression that you are not religious."

"Perhaps I have just become religious." After a moment she said, "I don't believe you. Why didn't it happen to Clarissa then? Why didn't it happen to everyone?"

"I can't answer those questions. It is preposterous."

"Yes. It is. I am still going to track Louis. You are only a doll. You have made up a story that you might tell a child."

"It seems so." He closed his eyes. "I'm sorry. Don't you want to know what happened to me?"

"No."

Chester was silent then, deeply so, but Angelina chose not to notice.

Captain Hazel called Angelina to the pilot house. She seemed surprisingly sober and competent as she checked dials and readings and gave orders.

"I'm going to have this tub changed over to plastic as soon as I deliver these heads," she said after motioning Angelina to sit and have a cup of coffee with her. "It's expensive, but permanent, you know? Self-repairing and all. I'll still be in debt, but without downtime for maintenance and having to shell out to the unions, I'll be able to work that down pretty quickly. I'll get a crew of zombies."

" 'Zombies?' "

Captain Hazel laughed. "Yes, you know. Or maybe you don't. Manufactured . . . well, not people, really. Just creatures who do the work cheerfully. You have to feed them, but you don't have to pay them."

"Is that legal?" asked Angelina, feeling quite out of touch.

Captain Hazel just gave her a brief, pitying look. A bell chimed. "Ah!" She took a flask from her shirt pocket and poured its contents into her coffee.

Angelina smelled whisky.

"I never drink before eleven. Want some?"

Angelina shook her head.

"Oh, come on. You don't have a shred of work to do, after all."

"I may have to launch a lifeboat."

Captain Hazel laughed, even more loudly. "Honey, the boat does that. Even an *ancient* boat can do that! The boat does just about everything. Anyway, I just wanted to tell you that we're docking in Casablanca rather than Tangier."

"Where is that?"

"Only about three hundred kilometers south of Tangier."

"Why?"

"One of the crew has a brother who is a huge merchant in Casablanca. I think that I may be able to broker a better deal there. It's much larger than Tangier."

"But I have to get to Tangier—" Tangier was only eight kilometers from Spain, across the Straits of Gibraltar, presumably with plenteous ferries. Then a trip up the coast of Spain, around the bend of Yugoslavia . . .

"My dear, that is hardly my problem. I must say, for someone heading into the no-man's land of Europe, you certainly seem mentally unprepared. You needn't let a tiny change like this throw you off." Hazel took a long swallow of coffee and leaned forward, breathing fumes into Angelina's face. "I opened one of the barrels."

Angelina felt ill.

Captain Hazel laughed so hard that tears squeezed from the corners of her eyes. "It was full of dog heads! DOG HEADS!" Evidently used to the antics of their commander, no one else on the bridge gave them a second look.

Angelina thought of loyal Justo, dead in the snow.

"What's so funny about that?" She stood abruptly.

"Oh, my dear, you are so *sensitive*!" Captain Hazel snorted, and her laughter echoed down the staircase as Angelina fled, her mind cascading with the stories which flowed from the heads of dead dogs, stories rich with smells and love. Stories which would never live again, thanks to Hazel's ugly tampering with her cargo.

She tossed Chester onto the floor and flopped onto her bed.

Beautiful Joe, Kazan the Wolf-Dog, a Chinese Pomeranian court dog. Their stories were broad and timeless, flowing like rivers, cutting valleys deep into the plateau of language, revealing new strata.

All living beings, she realized, had their stories, whether or not they had left recordings other than their own reproduced leaves or bodies. The plants were their own stories, bold and physical. The mammals had stories she could better understand: fear, survival, joy, love, movement, discovery, reproduction. And humans, she thought, though she realized she had a bias—humans were most fortunate and most unique in having found a way to transcend time by recording their stories. Some fortunate evolutionary permutation allowed their brains to seethe with stories.

But—Louis! His story was not rounded by artifice, as were the tales she held within her. He was gone. His loss was her fault. She had let him go. She had not pursued him instantly. No, the ranch was much more important! She thought he would mature, grow up, in his quest.

Not turn to light.

Clarissa was her only link to him, the last person she knew who had seen him. According to Clarissa, he had taken a ship to Morocco.

According to Chester—a doll—he had changed to light.

Why did she give this any credence at all?

Because she remembered waking in the too-strong moonlight, one night. Moonlight thick, like a veil. Moonlight that was strange, almost liquid, like moonlight she had never seen before.

And somehow, this phenomenon—she was *not* going to think of it as her son!—was intertwined with the stories of science.

Was Louis dead? If he was truly changed to light, was that also death? Or was it some sort of still-living change? Was his identity intact?

Did he remember her? And his delicious, warm laugh—a slight throwing back of the head, his eyes closed. Did light laugh?

She could almost feel her mind changing and growing minute by minute. She tossed and turned restlessly on the bed, then remembered—*Bless relaxes.*

Fine. Go ahead. Allow it. Think it. Let it become a part of your consciousness.

She saw that when direct observation of phenomena became more accurate via use of new instrumentation that augmented the senses, such as telescopes and microscopes, scientific thought changed rapidly. Hearing was augmented by devices such as radio and telephones: air and cable carrying organized sound.

Perhaps there might be some kind of tool which could augment the lens of the brain, or mind, as well? Her own mind had been refocused by Manuel's crusade to give her instant literacy. Might not Louis have been refocused, somehow . . .

But by what?

What?

No. She punched her pillow; turned over. Until she had proof, she was not going to believe Chester's outlandish suggestion. Not at all. She did not know why it haunted her. She did not know why she was taking advice and philosophical direction from a doll. Obviously, her life had changed dramatically.

She found herself looking forward to new shores. New waves of thought. New waves of people and places. New waves of revelation.

More seachange.

Though it was only lunchtime, she slept.

The days passed. Each night, Angelina lay on an old deck chair, covered with a blanket. But even this gave her no surcease. Even the stars issued stories. Tales of distant beings and cultures rained down upon her, derived from crates of old science fiction stories that had become pressed into the *Hopscotch* stamps. Comets arced through the sky, their effervescent trails spilling stories of incandescent gases and illuminated dust.

The stories organized themselves within her. Their top echelon was literature, deliberately created manipulations of narrative. Below that, a worldwide treasure trove of fairy and folk tales emerged, cautionary stories warning against dullness and greed, urging adventure and intelligence. Male and female both formed her new mind, and she wondered if she might have to become a hermaphrodite to physically accommodate and express this new way of seeing and being. Many stories, she realized, used male-based points of view in which women were denied their true richness, and when women began to write, they were forced either to use male-based language and images or to invent new uses of language.

It seemed as if all of time were happening simultaneously in literature, and she had difficulty focusing on her own life, her own quest, her own increasingly sand-covered linear timeline.

She still dined with Captain Hazel, and took as her apéritif an ounce of Pernod.

"I say," said Captain Hazel at the end of the second week. "You've changed, Senora. A good deal. You seem . . . stronger. Certainly more wrinkled. Maybe you've been out in the sun too much. But you are much less easily disturbed, which I think is a great improvement." Hazel's laugh no longer jarred Angelina. It was the marker of her welcome heartiness. It was part of her story.

Angelina smiled, took another bite of curried beef, another gulp of ale.

"A sea change," she said, knowing she quoted Shakespeare.

She no longer fought the stories. She let them all rise to consciousness and mingle.

In their rich, ever-moving mixture, she saw light. Despite the impossibility of it, the unutterable tragic sadness of it, she saw light.

She saw Louis.

When they docked, Casablanca was limned with lights, its white buildings spread out around the port and a high tower to the south brilliantly lit. Calls to prayer sounded faintly on the dying wind amid the rumble of traffic. Music blared from a rooftop nightclub, clear across the water for a moment before being obscured by metallic squeals as the ship was laboriously brought to dock.

Angelina stood by the gangway as it was lowered, her pack, which contained Chester, on her back.

Having a banker for an aunt left her well prepared in at least one respect. She had an international credit squirt in her pocket, which could be activated only by her particular touch, and her touch free of fear, as well as a retinal worth tabulator, and flouss, the currency still in use in Morocco, and only Morocco, mainly because it was geographically isolated from Europe as well as much of Africa. She also had cash for all the countries she might conceivably cross on her way to Paris, and nanotech trade seeds for places which might be off the currency grid for one reason or another.

Most towns in Argentina had a center where, for a fee, one's nanotech seed would be put into a vat of the appropriate ingredients and assembled. Africa banned such vats and much of what nanotech had to offer. Although enforcement proved virtually impossible, social mores provided some control, so the continent was somewhat of a haven for those wishing to revert completely to the pre-nanotech world of the twentieth century. Word of Europe was scarce, mainly because Argentineans did not go there, and they did not go there because it was strange and fearfully changed in some way that people found difficult to articulate. Travelers hardly ever returned from Europe.

Manuel had not.

They were not at a dock where passengers wanting lodging usually disembarked.

Angelina walked down the gangway onto the darkening quay, from which the last of the trucks she had observed during their long docking ordeal had vanished, leaving the area deserted and thick with deep shadows.

Angelina set off at a brisk pace toward the lights a short distance away.

Hearing footsteps behind her, she walked even faster, but was soon paced by three men. In the dim light, with her peripheral vision, she saw their nice, even teeth flash white in a high lone streetlight as they grinned. They chatted at her, hooted, and one of them even yodeled, but Angelina walked, unreacting and, she hoped, persuasively steadfastly on toward the plaza.

One of them touched her shoulder.

She tensed for battle, fleetingly, almost subconsciously, planning her strategy within a split second.

A flood of Arabic issued from her pack. The words were loud and sonorous, almost singsong, and most unlike Chester's normal voice. The men dropped back immediately. When she was sure that she was out of earshot, she said, "All right, what did you say?"

"I merely quoted them some verses of the Koran." He sounded smug. "At first they simply proposed marriage, but when you didn't react, they suggested other acts which are clearly covered by appropriate teachings of Muhammad. I wasn't sure whether to imitate your voice, so they would think you an authority, or to use an authoritative male voice. After a search of the Koran and appropriate literatures and history, followed by analysis, I made a decision. I would say that's pretty impressive, in a time span of only 7.8432 seconds . . ."

"Incredibly impressive," she said in what she hoped was her most sincere voice. "Thank you."

"Morocco is actually a quite liberal country," he said. "There are factions other than Muslims, and the Muslims for the most part are not fundamentalists. I suppose we're lucky those men weren't Berbers, but I was ninety-nine percent sure that they were Muslims, based on certain linguistic usages . . ."

"They couldn't be any worse than the Christians. I am here because of them."

"Really? I thought you were looking for your son."

"Sometimes you can be quite infuriating."

In a moment, she was enfolded in the life of the city. Rich smells came from braziers beneath a long colonnade. Two competing drum cadences fought from opposite sides of the square. Clothing ranged from fezzed and turbaned men and veiled women to what was presumably the latest style here. Cats were everywhere. A man did handsprings a few feet in front of her then turned and stared, evidently expecting to be paid.

"We must be in the medina," said Chester. "The old Arab town."

As she looked around, trying not to appear at a loss, a woman approached her. She wore khaki shorts, a crisp white shirt, and brown hiking boots.

"*Bonjour.*"

"*Hola.*"

The woman moved smoothly into a Spanish which Angelina could understand, though it was strangely accented and much more formal than she was accustomed to. "I am Jasmine. I used a language-restructuring plague a few years ago and it worked quite well. I can get it for you at a good discount on the black market. Here, you really need French and Arabic."

Angelina shook her head. "No." She felt as if she had been rearranged quite enough. Not only that, she simply didn't believe Jasmine. Language programs were notorious for rearranging one's personality, for it had been belatedly realized that cultures and cultural mores were embedded in the very heart of every language. Clarissa had urged French upon her. "At least French! My goodness, girl, you are headed to France! Don't be stubborn."

Angelina had enough troubles already.

Jasmine gestured toward a scooter, which featured a small wagon attached to the back. "My aunt has a very clean place just outside the souk."

"I'll look at it."

As they walked toward the scooter and agreed on the price of the ride, Chester's muffled voice came from the pack. "It's terribly dark in here."

Jasmine stopped. "What is that?"

"Just a doll," said Angelina.

"*Just* a doll!" complained Chester. "And a puppet to boot! Well, excuse *me!*"

Jasmine looked around nervously. "Those are illegal here."

"Why?"

"Because—oh, it is difficult to explain. Sentience is an attribute of humans, who are formed in the image of God. Such dolls—and I have never seen or heard one before—mock Allah."

"Do you believe that?" asked Angelina, thinking it best to perhaps look for another mode of transportation, or to walk.

"No. But it is still illegal."

"It's my translator," suggested Angelina.

"It?" Chester asked from the pack.

Jasmine said, "See that it does no translating while we're in such a crowded area or it may be confiscated and you thrown in prison."

Angelina looked back at the boat. Were it not for Louis, she would just wait until the boat was ready to leave. But then *Hopscotch* stirred. Manuel. Paris.

Paris; and soon.

"How does one get to Tangier from here?" she asked Jasmine.

"It is not easy. There are dirigibles, boats, an old solar highway. Caravans are safest, since there are bandits. I can get you a good deal. Hop on now."

Jasmine wove dizzyingly through narrow streets of vendors, passing booths of fragrant food and an evil-smelling plaza filled with dozing camels. She stopped at a white building and touched a panel by a double door. It swung inward, revealing a courtyard with a blue-tiled fountain at its center, and lush plants in large pots.

The doors closed behind them with a whirr of machinery and the *clunk* of wood on wood.

The courtyard, surrounded by tall open doors beneath the colonnade, was four stories tall. The floor was intricate tilework. A riot of small salmon-colored roses punctuated the spaces between at least four types of palms that Angelina recognized—sago, Alexander, date, and a straight, stately royal palm in each corner. A ginger cat stood watching her, switching its tail. Blue doors, some of them open, ranged around the courtyard. Music and laughter issued from one of them.

A short woman in a bright green robe emerged from this room. She and Jasmine spoke to one another in French, then the woman said, in English, "Welcome to our country. My name is Khadija."

"Angelina."

"I do have a room for you. My niece tells me you are Argentinean. What brings you here?" Her eyes, set in a face which was just beginning to show lines of age, were kind. Gold earrings dangled lumps of amber.

As she paid Jasmine, Angelina could barely focus on the woman, assailed as she was by waves of Paul Bowles and his wife Jane—images, just images, for the stories themselves were in words that she did not understand. "I—I am looking for my son, Louis. He left Buenos Aires and sailed on a ship that stopped in Tangier—"

The woman nodded sympathetically "How old is he?"

"Seventeen. Eighteen, now." Or, perhaps, some strange no-age, some kind of always-age . . .

"He ran away?"

Though the woman seemed rather nosy, Angelina found that she didn't mind talking about Louis. "No. Yes. Not exactly. He was going to meet his father, Manuel, who has been in Paris for many years. But he left without my permission and without arrangements or—" She blinked back the tears that gathered in her eyes.

The woman led her beneath the arched portico and sat her down. She snapped her fingers and in a moment Angelina sipped hot, strong, very sweet mint tea.

The stories, obviously, had changed her. Softened her up. Made her sentimental and foolish.

"I'm sorry to hear about your son."

"Thank you." Though she kept her customary ramrod-straight posture as she sipped her tea, something within her relaxed. *Bless relaxes.* She took a deep breath and tried to smile.

"Jasmine said that you have a sentient doll."

"She told me that they are illegal."

Khadija laughed. She leaned forward and said in a low, shy voice, "Could I possibly see it?"

"Yes!" piped Chester from within the pack.

Angelina frowned, but unsealed the pack and pulled out Chester. He spoke to the woman in a flood of Arabic dialect, and she smiled with delight and answered in kind.

"I would appreciate being included," said Angelina. "Perhaps we could all speak English?"

"I was just apologizing for being introduced in my underwear," Chester said. "Could you could find me something a bit more formal?"

While Angelina sighed and rummaged in her pack for his clothes, Khadija rang a tiny bell and the young woman who had served the tea entered the courtyard. Khadija spoke to her. She looked at Chester, grinned, and hurried away.

She returned in a moment with a doll about Chester's size clad in a long, hooded garment made of soft, fine silk striped with subtle bands of pink, gold, and green. Khadija deftly undressed the doll and dressed Chester in his new costume. "There," she said in English. "Now you will be cooler."

"Thank you," Chester replied.

"You don't seem to have any problem talking with him," said Angelina.

"No, he is quite charming," Khadija said.

"But the Allah problem—"

She waved her hand. "It is not a problem for me. It is not a problem for anyone in this house. Please join us for dinner. Mostly family."

"I'm very tired—"

"You are probably also hungry."

Angelina, carrying Chester, was almost dragged through twelve-foot-high open double doors into a large, dimly lit room where music played and a few women danced with one other. Low divans surrounded a knee-high table. Khadija snapped her fingers and servants carried large trays into the room and set them about on the table. Angelina mostly saw couscous, but she knew each dish was probably different.

Across the table from her, two women argued loudly, waving their arms, but no one seemed to pay them any attention and in another moment they were laughing.

"Some of my relatives," said Khadija, leaning across the table. "We don't drink alcohol, but we have some very good French wine for guests." Before Angelina could protest, another snap of the fingers brought a glass and the bottle. Khadija poured the wine, and Angelina slowly savored its complex flavors. A servant brought a basin of water around, with towels.

Dinner began. Conversation was animated and loud and not clear to Angelina, but she felt comfortable and safe. As they finished eating, men danced with men and women with women.

Stories flowed off of them, imbued with history. Trips to the desert to take the dry air; the transformative trance of the dance, finely modulated by instruments until one was taken by the music and set down elsewhere in spirit.

Encouraged by the woman next to her, she too rose and began to dance. Her hair loosened and swirled around her. She heard clapping. All was a blur of music and color and stories thousands of years old told by the eyes and costumes and movements of her companions, stories woven like fine ancient carpets on the warp and woof of human knowing.

Angelina followed Khadija up the stairs, which were narrow and set between thick plaster walls. Tranquillity. The stories calmed. She was shown a small, spare room with a narrow divan and a table with a basin and pitcher of water.

She was then left alone, and stepped out the open window onto the roof.

She looked out over a terraced city that removed down to the sea and the docks. Delicate rows of green lights in the dark harbor suggested the shapes of ships, and she glimpsed the square where Jasmine had picked her up. Drums and the song of some kind of night bird mingled.

She stepped back into the room and, without washing or even undressing, lay down on the divan. But her eyes were still open, and light shone in through the window, revealing a finely patterned wall.

Stories leaped out at her from the very designs on the wall, folk stories and tales from the Koran. She was surrounded by infinite dimensions. Each story was filled with doors and the doors opened on other stories and so it went forever. Each story was alive with uncountable elements, and the lives of the people within it began before the beginning and continued after the end, unrestrained by frames. Stories vibrated within her. They ranged themselves around her like a repeating pattern sounded, faintly, like a million superimposed bells, each with their own frequency.

They chanted themselves in harmonies of fifths, then they splintered and took on different speeds, a variety of harmonies, new and previously unheard harmonies, intensifying until all sound and vision disappeared in a great light. Angelina lay at the center of the light, with Chester, for once quiet as if perhaps he too could hear, clasped to her breast.

Listening.

Her dreams were filled with chanting, and trips to the Sahara, and the snow-covered peaks of the Atlas Mountains.

The next morning Angelina woke, washed, and stepped out once again onto the roof after being awakened by the call to morning prayer which blasted from a huge white tower half a kilometer away. Everything her senses conveyed to her seemed cleansed and pure. She remembered then her dream before waking: She was made of brilliant, golden sand, and changed from blown sand to herself and back to blown sand instant by instant.

Her self.

Mutable.

Changing.

Not really her self any longer.

The world was magical. Manuel was right. Why had she stayed on that ranch for so very long? The thing to do was to move through it. Without stopping.

For the first time in her life, ever, she felt marvelously *unfinished.*

She turned at a call from the window. It was Khadija.

"Hello!" She stepped out, carrying a tray. "I brought coffee and a pastry. You didn't answer the knock, so I thought you must be out here." She set the tray on a low table.

Angelina looked toward the coast. "Isn't that a train, down there? It's leaving! Where is Chester? I've got to go—"

Khadija put a hand on her shoulder. "It has already left. There will be another one later on today. But it is not advisable to use those trains. The people on them are—well, they are not like you and I."

I wouldn't count on that. "What do you mean?"'

In the bright sunlight, Khadija looked old and tired. "They are just different. I can't explain."

"But the train must get to Tangier rather quickly," persisted Angelina. "I have to find my son."

Khadija sat down and poured them both coffee, motioned to Angelina to sit as well. Angelina did so, taking the coffee cup in both hands and sipping.

"The train was put in by the French many years ago, before we had strict laws against such things. It is an extension of a train that runs through Spain and eventually goes to Paris."

"But that's perfect," said Angelina. "I'm going to Paris. That's where Manuel, my husband, lives." Maybe. "What is wrong with the train?"

"I have heard it said that no one ever gets off."

"That's ridiculous."

"No, it's not. People get on at the station. Sometimes. But no one ever gets off."

"Perhaps no one wants to come here?"

Khadija snorted into her coffee. "People come here all the time! Just not on the train."

"Maybe it is very expensive?"

"I don't know how much it costs. But some kind of diplomatic change occurs when you get on the train. You are officially in France. I believe that it takes people to France and indoctrinates them, somehow, along the way. When you get close to the train, you see that its decorations are bees and flowers. Paris is, I believe, a City of Flowers. People have no volition there either. Getting on the train is the first step of turning into a person who is governed by a Flower City. There is no Allah there, no transcendence. There is only what is human."

"I believe that is all there is anyway," said Angelina.

"You don't believe in Allah."

"No."

Khadija grinned after a thoughtful pause. "Perhaps then you wouldn't mind the train so much, eh?"

Angelina tried to choose her words carefully. "Just because I don't believe in a transcendent intelligence or creator doesn't mean that I don't value life and my own consciousness, nor that I don't respect the beliefs of others. If I believed what you said about the train, if I believed that it would take away my own sense of identity as myself, I wouldn't get on. What would be the point? Why in the world would anyone choose to ride it?"

"There are rumors that enslavement agents frequent cafés and sprinkle some kind of alluring dust into food and drink."

"But why?"

Khadija shrugged. "There is some profit to them in filling up the train. I do not know what that might be."

"What's the difference between losing oneself in, say, Allah and losing oneself to a city or a train?"

"Merging with Allah is the highest of all possible states, the highest possible goal of humanity. Merging with what other humans have created is to lose your soul rather than to gain it, and to lose all possibility of gaining your soul."

"Why does Morocco allow this train to run?"

"We can't stop it. It is indestructible. Don't you think that all manner of explosives have been used, by various fundamentalists and terrorists, over the years? But not in any official manner. No one could justify blowing up a train that clearly has passengers on it, demented though they may be."

Angelina became aware that an annoying recurrent croak she had been trying to ignore was actually Chester, calling her from inside the room. "Excuse me." She got up and found Chester lying on the floor beside her bed, in a large square splash of sunlight.

"You are extremely rude," he said.

"I'm sorry." She picked him up and dusted off his comical white draperies. "Your turban is crooked. Let me rewind it."

"Not so rough. I'm sure that you are not at all sorry."

"All right. Doubt my sincerity. I thought you disliked the sun."

"You left me in the blinding sun anyway. I dislike being unable to hear even more. I dislike very much being completely immobile and at the mercy of people like you, and that—unfeeling Senor Gabrielle, and . . . and . . ." He began to choke.

"Are you all right?" asked Angelina, alarmed.

"I am just very tired of being a doll, but there's nothing to be done about that. It is torture enough to have been created at all. Perhaps Allah could take pity on me. Perhaps you ought to take me to a mosque and I'll convert."

Angelina said nothing, and only pursed her lips and squinted as she tucked the end of the tiny white cloth into one of its spirals, but Chester seemed able to read her mind. "Haven't I told you that I'm sentient! Damn it! Don't you believe it? I have just as much—as much soul as any one of you idiots walking around and mishandling me. Probably more!"

"Just what I need. A hysterical doll. Now, calm down and be a bit polite to Khadija, all right? Show me a good example. Buck up." She put him on her shoulder like a baby and patted him on the back.

"I was pretending to be upset. Just a—just a teaching device," he whispered in her ear. "That's all. To teach you a little empathy."

"Right," she said. "It is certainly something I could use." The world of folk tales and fairy tales, never far off, burst into her heart. She held the Golem, and Pinocchio. She was being taught.

And she feared for the lessons that both she and Chester might have to learn.

"You've become a lot more humble already." There was a tone of satisfaction in his voice as she carried him over the low windowsill and out onto the roof. The air, as she gazed over the sun-draped city, had a clarity which brought out the deep colors of what she saw, mingled harmoniously. Frequencies of light, the new voice of scientific stories told her. As is everything. Even you.

What frequency was Louis, now?

She determined that she would get on the train.

She did not point out to Jasmine, as she was ferried through the market later on in the morning, how nanotechnology could heal the poverty all around her. She understood, firsthand, opposition to technology, which had landed her an ocean away from home.

She stepped around blankets where performers and fortune-tellers had staked out territory. Odors both good and bad were whisked away by the breeze that played through the stalls, flapping the long lengths of cloth that divided one from the other. The breeze, however, did not deter flies, which settled everywhere. Between gusts, sharp herby scents mingled with the smell of seared meat and vegetables. Strains of music washed through strident bargaining. Men and women stared at her when she was alone; when Khadija held her elbow, she seemed as invisible as air. She flipped coins to acrobats. She didn't know how they could stand all the cats . . .

But they had their stories too.

Chester was tucked away in her backpack and looked out through a slit he had commanded her to cut.

He demanded that Angelina turn her back to the mosque that Khadija entered when the mechanical call to prayer sang out at noon from towers throughout the city. She had gravitated there throughout the previous hour, and told Angelina to wait while she entered the women's side. On the square in front of the mosque, people removed their shoes, knelt, and prayed, scattered back into the reaches of the market as far as Angelina could see. "It is mathematical," said Chester with great satisfaction. "This architecture is in my memory, but actually seeing it makes sense of all those relationships." He was silent after Angelina shushed him, but she imagined him drinking in all those proportions. Flies buzzed in the silent noon, and even when people rose and went about their business, Angelina felt that she was in the center of a vast blue bowl of sky which held its breath. Camels, tiny cars, and bicycles filled the narrow streets. Something in Angelina rejoiced, something she had never felt before: She was traveling, on her own, and no one knew where she was and she had no responsibilities.

Except to find Louis.

The world came back to life. “There she is,” said Chester, and Angelina turned to see Khadija emerge from the mosque.

After they returned to Khadija’s house, Angelina said, “Tell me what I owe you.”

“Where are you going?” Khadija asked. “We can help arrange transportation—”

“I am taking the train.”

“But—”

“My mind is made up.”

As Khadija took the money, she shook her head. “Please come back immediately if there is a problem. I will call for Jasmine—”

“I can walk. Thank you so much for your hospitality.”

Khadija smiled. “Why not leave Chester here with us? He is so interesting!”

“No!” Angelina and Chester, in the pack, replied in the same instant.

Angelina, surprised at their vehemence, laughed a bit. “I seem to have grown rather attached to him.”

“And I to her,” said the unseen Chester. “Though it would be lovely to remain here with you, Khadija.”

“Thank you, Chester,” said Khadija, and opened the doors to let them out.

The sky was an intense turquoise glow. Children played in the streets and men sat on doorstops and in open cafes where candles burned.

Angelina headed toward the harbor. Khadija had said that a train left every evening at eight o’clock sharp.

“We’ll need to take care,” Chester said. “I heard some pretty disturbing things about the train when they were speaking Arabic.”

"Like what?"

"For one thing, people can rarely get on, even if they want to. It's just not a normal train. The populace is extremely irritated because the old track has been taken over and is used exclusively by this train. That means they have no rail transportation to Tangier."

"Why don't they just build another one?"

"They seem stubborn. But they are also, probably, poor. One of the men was arguing that if they built another track, another train like this one would take it over. It sounded as if this might be a common sentiment."

"Well, I must try," Angelina turned a corner and almost collided with an old woman, who turned and cursed her as she passed.

The scent of water, as she approached the waterfront, was refreshing.

Then she saw the train station ahead of her, ornate as a mosque. She wondered why this despised train was allowed to display such importance. But what made her heart beat hard was the train itself, sleek and modern, with a greenish metallic glow which in the twilight made it another band of iridescent sky.

She put on a frantic burst of speed, afraid that it would not stay in the station for long; afraid that it would not be easy to board on, despite the fact that it was only about seven-thirty. Still, who knew how trains behaved in this part of the world. She hurried toward the doorway of the terminal, but it was closed and the door was locked. She looked around, wondering what to do.

The shadows were growing, and lights splayed out over the harbor. The train itself, only a few meters away, hummed quietly. The windows were lit, but she could not see inside due to some kind of blocking effect the windows had.

"Why are you stopping?" asked Chester. "Take me out! I want to see what's going on."

"I don't know," said Angelina, hesitant, her voice low. "I don't see anything, but it's just . . . strange."

As she approached the train, a door opened, and a uniformed

man walked down the steps and deposited an iron step on the platform. She stopped in front of him.

He said something in French, looking not at her but into the distance in a way that further disconcerted her. His eyes were a pale no-color as was his hair, cropped short beneath his conductor's hat.

Chester replied—in her own voice, which startled her further, and made the conductor look at her suddenly.

"Yes, I speak Spanish," he said. "Ticket, please."

"The ticket booth is closed," she said, tendrils of desperation beginning to squeeze her chest. All she could think of was Louis. Manuel. A peasant boy in front of a castle, wanting to marry the princess. She swallowed. "Can I buy a ticket from you?"

"You cannot buy a ticket to ride on this train," he said. "You must already have one."

"That's ridiculous!" she shouted.

"Very well, then," he said, and bent down and took up his step. He was climbing back onto the train when Chester said something in French, in his usual voice.

"Eh?" asked the conductor, turning.

"I said, 'Touch her,' " commanded Chester.

"Shut up," said Angelina, heartbroken and furious.

The conductor shrugged and swung down, leaving the stool in the train. "As you wish, sir. Wherever you are." He took Angelina's hand.

Before she could pull it away, he nodded gravely. "Indeed, you do have a ticket. Welcome aboard the City of Light Express." He reached for the metal stair and put it down and took Angelina's hand once again, this time to help her into the coach.

The train pulled out of the station as the conductor led Angelina to a compartment.

"Let me show you the features of the room," he said. "This is the food and beverage panel. It can assemble anything you might desire, from any world cuisine. It is possible to adjust the food here," he said, opening a screen that showed chemical equations, "but unless you are a trained chef, it might be difficult to relate this to the food you are eating. If you have a favorite wine and vintage, it will be recreated using this panel, as long as it is in our library. As the train originates in Paris," he said, his voice haughty, "I can assure you that you will not be disappointed. However, I strongly recommend the dining car. We will be coming to Tangier soon, and it is quite pleasant to begin your meal and to dine as we cross the Straits."

"Do we take a ferry?"

"Yes, Senora. Do you wish me to make a dinner reservation for you?"

"Please," Angelina told him, trying hard not to be unsettled by this sudden change of technology levels.

He bowed. "Excellent choice. You shall not be sorry that you have decided to take the train, madam. I mean, Señora. It is, after all, time."

"What do you mean?" she asked.

He bowed once more and left the compartment, sliding the door shut behind him.

"Take me out!" demanded Chester.

She put him on the table by the window.

"Sit me up!" he said testily.

"Yes, Your Majesty," she said, and propped him in a corner where he could see the entire compartment. "Does this suit you?"

"Don't make fun of me," he grumbled. "You have no idea how awful this is. Maybe this train could make me some kind of voice-operated transportation system."

"Not a bad idea," she mused. "It seems as if they might even do it for free." The mulch of a million fairy tales warned her that nothing was free, but she shrugged that thought away like all the others that surrounded her now. They reminded her of the multitudes of strange insects attracted to a night light in the forest, each seemingly unique and coming out of nowhere, a necessary part of some flow of life completely unknown to her.

"Are you all right?" Chester asked. "You look a bit dazed."

"I wonder what he meant, 'It is time?' "

"He is a form of artificial intelligence," said Chester. "And yes, I think it is time."

"Time for *what*?"

"Some . . . change. I suppose we'll find out."

"Wonderful," she said. She sank down on the sofa and stared out the window, watching the last glow of sunset.

The conductor returned after half an hour. "Follow me, please."

Three cars forward, he seated her landward, at a table covered with white linen. Her plate was flanked with crystal and much silverware, and she was completely astonished when the maître d' brought a child seat for Chester and deftly belted him in. The dining car was full, and the sounds of muted conversations filled the air.

"This is a wonderful train," Chester remarked, watching her with his usual fixed, avid stare. "Perhaps we can just stay on it forever."

"We may have no choice," she said sourly, surveying her well-dressed dining companions, who looked as if they had come straight from the nineteenth century. "I think everyone else has been here a very long time."

A man poured water for her. "I suggest caviar to begin with."

"I don't care for caviar. Do you have any beef appetizers?" Almost every course in Argentina contained beef, and she was starved for it.

He bowed. "Certainly. Will you allow me then to choose the wines?"

Angelina nodded and closed the menu screen, happy to not have to make any choices. The darkened landscape rushed past.

"There's a lot more to this train than meets the eye," Chester said.

"What do you mean?"

"Well . . ." he said. "Look! Isn't that lovely?"

The train was slowly passing through the square of a small town. She glimpsed a juggler, and a woman in a blue sari playing a saxophone.

"Don't try to distract me. What do you mean about the train?"

The waiter brought empañadas.

Chester sighed. "I don't know. I only know that you are on it only because of your genetic anomaly. That's why all these other people are on it too. I think that they are engaged in some sort of transformative process. It might be best to get off in Tangier, and continue on in another fashion—"

"You're the one who got me on this train." She smiled, feeling astoundingly relaxed. "I intend to stay on it and to enjoy the ride."

"Let me at least tell you what I've learned—"

The waiter took her empty plate and put down in its place a large bowl of beef broth and a basket of hot bread. Low music played, some Bach violin pieces. Angelina felt as if she stretched and contracted with each note, as if she were the strings themselves. It was a surprisingly pleasant feeling. She glimpsed, with each second's new musical landscapes, mathematical realms that had always been closed to her. She practically inhaled the soup while Chester prattled, on the far side of the music. What he said seemed as important as the chime of crystal or clank of silverware. All was equally weighted in her present aural world.

"All of these people are radio beings. Their molecules, their souls, are being rearranged. They are actively participating in a change that is to come, a change they believe in and anticipate with religious fervor. You are going to be gradually transformed as you approach Paris. This train and track are actually part of a huge antenna emanating from Paris. Once you get to Paris, you will be entirely . . . appropriated, I suppose is the correct word. Appropriated into the city. It's rather what you were born to do, I suppose."

"I was born to rule a kingdom. I failed. The only thing I have to do now is find Louis."

Before she finished her lengthy dinner, they were through Tangier and being loaded onto the ferry. Angelina moved to the lounge, where other passengers chatted. Gibraltar, outside the window as they sped across the straits, was majestically lit.

Angelina stretched out on a divan, barely thinking at all. She was on her way at last to Louis and Manuel. On her way to the mysterious City of Light, the city of *Hopscotch*, Proust, Hugo, Zola, and scores of expatriates from around the world. Their fictional creatures danced and intertwined around her like wraiths from a dream, greeting one another on streets where these authors had trod, though in different fictional worlds and in different historical ages.

A little girl picked up Chester and played with him a few chairs away. They were speaking some language—perhaps German—that Angelina did not know. The girl patted his stomach. He laughed and gushed forth words.

Angelina stood up. She watched for a moment, then said, "Chester, time to go."

"Why?"

"Because I'm going to sleep now."

"All the more reason for me to stay here." He spoke to the girl and she looked back at Angelina, then grabbed Chester in a tight embrace and shook her head. Her braids flew around her face. She looked fierce and slightly alarmed.

"I don't belong to you," Chester told Angelina gently.

"Oh. Of course not," she said, her words sounding much more brittle than she intended. "Who—who pleaded with me—oh!" She laughed. "You're right, of course!" She turned and headed back the way she had come and heard him shout, "Angelina!" but she did not turn back.

She went to her compartment, with cool white sheets and a view of the Mediterranean night. She wished she were out in it, or back in Tangier, or in the desert. When would she ever be back here? Why had she rushed away so quickly? No one was awaiting her. She would never find Louis. She would never find Manuel. She and Chester could have taken a caravan, could have explored Tangier. He made good company. He seemed much more than just a reflection of herself. And he so longed to be human: to at least be in control of his own mobility. She missed him, this moment. He had preferred the company of the little girl.

With a jolt, She realized: She had become insanely attached to a doll. She was actually jealous.

Ah, that was it. It was simple. She was just going crazy.

She watched the stars. Her heart and mind paused for the first time in decades, expecting nothing, desiring nothing.

She was not sure what had taken place, beneath her understanding, to bring her to this state. But she felt suddenly, quietly, deeply alive. Was it the train itself, giving her in each physical contact, even in the air she breathed, a cocktail of subtle chemical messages which made her fully herself? Her mind was cleansed and pure.

She noticed a tiny control panel on the lower right side of the window and touched it and asked for the Spanish menu when she didn't understand the icons. Then she touched the correct place and the window thinned until it was an invisible, permeable screen through which rushed wind. Even the roof of her compartment was clear.

Her heart grew as round and as bright as the moon. She was a small girl again, out on the pampas, camping with the gauchos, listening from afar to their songs, to their stomping, clapping dances. She sprawled back on the couch. Gaucho memories faded to a faint, but real, solo violin, playing the constellations, showing in music the relationships between the stars. All of the swift and Bachish flourishes were as one in her mind, occurring simultaneously, and the sky became a picture of deep time. She fell asleep falling into it, pulled into it, and her dreams were of geometries, of mathematics and relationships so fine that they far surpassed joy, being only themselves, and therefore perfect.

It was dawn when she stirred. The wind still swept through her compartment, and the mountains were banded with gold and green along their ridgetops. She saw Chester, a vague gray lump, beside her. Of course he had told the girl where to bring him.

"I'm glad you're back," she murmured.

"Hold my hand," he said.

She turned on her side and held his tiny flesh-imitating hand in hers. As she fell asleep again, she fancied it stirred.

Spain was a phantasmagoria of images for Angelina; images of family life that stretched back for centuries; images of sere mountains and the verdant coast.

She went to the dining car to escape, but it didn't work. The visions rose with hallucinatory intensity, purely, rendering her native language utterly transparent. All of the stories she harbored, she realized, were in the form of images, even though they might be rendered in the medium of language, for images were strong and immutable.

The glass at her right hand was just a glass. Yet even this simple object generated stories.

A glass might be filled with beer at the annual roundup in Buenos Aires, where the wives of the rancheros paraded in their finery while she wore the utilitarian clothing of business and struck a deal as she took a sip of beer.

Or it might be the glass her mother gave her one early spring morning at breakfast, filled with fresh-squeezed juice, when a sense of unrealized but deeply felt freshness drew her outward into life.

Yes, even a glass could evoke emotion. And so the images were not at all pure. Instead, they were heavy with freight, delightfully and richly so. And the images of stories built on one another like an equation. Perhaps one that was always growing and changing, as in *Hopscotch.* Or perhaps one that was subtle as a Chekov story or as brutally inescapable as Orwell's *1984*.

Outside the window, as she dined on soft-boiled quail eggs, was a vast plain bounded by distant mountains. If she ignored the view, she could see a faint reflection of herself, and Chester stiff across from her, surprisingly worn out from whatever antics he had been involved in last night. Perhaps the German girl had given him cause to offer many correctives, which would be wearing to a human. But why, she wondered, would it weary a doll; a machine? Maybe his power was just running low.

She pondered him—his existence, his capabilities, his desires.

There had been a time when machines remained separate from humans.

But now they insisted upon themselves; they wanted to make themselves known; they wanted to coexist with humans and share the luxury of human senses; human consciousness, this mirroring of matter's vibrations; the rendering of them into emotion.

Certainly, this was true of Chester.

It might not, she mused, be long until the machines took flight, having used humans as an incubus, having waited these long, long ages, patiently, outside the body: the hammers, the tongs, the famous ant-stick.

They now wished to declare themselves, to demand equal billing, to migrate into all that lay so quiescent—the rocks, the water, the peeling wallpaper, the shoes, the mice, the engineered matter of the cities.

They wanted to conjoin with consciousness itself, whatever that might be.

The machines had migrated into this train, into sustenance, into children's toys. Were the people around her—the two women even now smiling at her briefly in greeting from their table before returning to conversation—real people? Or were they, even more so than Chester, machines that mimicked human form and human mind?

She took a sip of rich, chocolatey coffee; another bite of the caramelized onion and goat cheese pastry that concluded her breakfast.

Since the machines came from us, she reasoned, why should we believe in their possible goodness? Since we use and discard, since we diligently crumple, why believe that they will love and cherish and promote us? We are their horses. Once they have the means to reproduce and go their own way, why should they keep us around? A handy flare, a deadly plague, would cleanse the universe of our troublesome nattering.

Angelina tucked this thought under her belt. It was not a new one. It had been there since the invention of the machine; since Luddites smashed the mills not only for monetary but for religious reasons; for the dignity of humankind, to preserve their human touch in weaving. So that weaving, that satisfying and expressive transmission of pattern, would not be lost to unfeeling, unthinking robots.

And so that humans, in operating them, would not become their slaves, tending their maws, supplying their needs, becoming dehumanized like . . . like the children in the industrial-age literature of Zola, like the children in D. H. Lawrence's books who gave their lives to the mines so that the machines could run; like Stephen Crane's Maggie, the girl of the streets, who went to the depersonalized, depersonalizing city, and was lost for all time, unable to learn rapidly enough to survive except in a corrupted fashion.

But now the story was all the more real. What was the last bastion for machines to achieve in their headlong imitation of all that was human? They had mastered repetitive motion; they had even mastered reproduction.

Consciousness was what remained.

Consciousness, which, as far as Angelina could now tell, was stories.

Other creatures were aware of their surroundings. And they had stories as well, she realized. They were built-in stories of danger and response.

She thought about Justo, her dog. He had stories as well, and dreams. But how could she possibly gauge the extent or depth or complexity of his stories? She had been able to see his surfaces, his responses; that was all. She knew of his suffering when his mate had died. He had seen her body, smashed by a car out on the road. He had regarded it for a second, then backed off, his ears flattened, trembling. For days he would not eat; would barely rise from his corner. And he was never as joyful, never as able to play with abandon, after that. No, dogs felt pain, felt sadness. They were connected to emotion. They simply had no way to record the stories, or to pass them on.

And Angelina, who was human, could imagine anything. She could compose and create the previously unimagined and the wholly unimaginable. Words took shape and revealed themselves as concepts, and the concepts linked and become narrative, with arrowlike movement. Until they could do this—form emotional narrative—machines were doomed to remain peripheral.

But never fear, small oiled things. Let's start again, with a better will, shall we? We are all sisters and brothers, within our whirling electon shell, trading the single irreducible commodity, light; changing the . . .

"That sounds like poetry," said Chester.

"What?" She was jolted back to the present.

"What you were saying. 'Trading the single irreducible commodity—' "

"I was talking?"

"You've been talking for quite some time. And don't worry. Nothing was wasted. The very tablecloth can hear you."

"Don't be silly!" she snapped.

"Your thoughts are definitely different than mine," he mused, a bit of sadness in his voice. "It seems to me that you kind of flow in and out of thoughts. One image gives birth to another and sets you on a beautiful flight. Whereas I can only respond to what my senses perceive, expanded though they are, and that I can only respond in ways that I have been programmed to respond."

"It seems to me that you make choices," Angelina said, glad to be pulled back from her disturbing thoughts. "And you seem to have a personality. You are kind. You are witty. You are very sweet."

"Imagine a shrug," he said. "These are qualities that someone thought would be good for children to be exposed to. They really have nothing to do with me. I think that perhaps there is no me, even though there is the illusion of one."

"Who is accepting the illusion of you? Isn't part of you doing this? Let me tell you something, Chester. Humans are just a hallway of mirrors. You can go back and back and back and never reach the end, never come to a solid place."

"So much for my illusions. Imagine a wry smile following the shrug."

"Duly imagined, my dear." She was very glad that he was talking again. He was terribly engaging, lifelike.

"Perhaps I could learn these stories?" The tone of his voice was wistful.

"I don't see why not." She set her cup sharply in its saucer and the waiter jumped to fill it.

"Yet that disturbs you."

"Now it's your turn to imagine a shrug."

"No, it really disturbs you. I can tell. You give off the chemicals of a person who is disturbed and troubled."

"And more so right this second," she said, her voice tight.

"Yes. Because I can perceive what you feel."

She sighed. "Yes." She leaned back in her chair. "I suppose so."

"Because you wish to remain invisible."

"To a certain extent. I would say that all people do. To have all of one's thoughts exposed would be terrible."

"But . . ." After a pause, he continued. "I hate to be the one to break it to you, but where you are going is a place where there are no disguises. And this train is only its prelude."

And yet, on the boat, had she not finally accepted all this? Accepted the stories, accepted her newness, accepted Chester and his help? It was somewhat jolting to be back in this questioning, worrisome frame of mind. But the train brought that on. The train . . .

She leaned back in her chair, looking around.

"Why is everything glowing?" she finally asked Chester.

"The train would tell you if you asked it. But I can tell you as well. The train itself is part of a vast antenna array. It is a communication device, if you will. Paris is proud of its long history of technological firsts. In 1913, on July first, the first time signal transmitted around the world was sent from the Eiffel Tower. Now Paris is at the center of a new, emergening understanding of time. Certain quantum effects have been harnessed to produce this particular glowing feature, which gives direct information to those with the facilities to assess it. This train and the other trains that run out of Paris across the continent keep track of local conditions and help arrange for adequate trade to occur among those who shun the train and its attendant technologies."

"How magnanimous of the train."

"It is because . . . it is because of Paris. Something is . . . strange about Paris."

"No doubt!" she snorted. "It has swallowed up my husband."

"Any city could do that."

"Not Manuel," she mused. "Not any old city could swallow Manuel. He was . . . is . . . different." She tried not to think about Louis.

She spent the day not thinking about Louis.

And finally, toward evening, Angelina stood at the door between cars. She watched a small hilltop town grow larger. Chester and her other belongings were in her backpack, which dangled from one shoulder.

She could see individual buildings lumping up the hill, cut by an irregular spiral which spun upward. Red and blue tile roofs blazed in the last rays of the sun.

She pulled on the wire above her head.

To her surprise, the train slowed.

It pulled past a series of arches and stopped at a tiny station.

In front of it was one black wrought iron bench. On it sat an old woman, who rose and looked hopefully at the train as Angelina leaped from the door and staggered onto the platform.

As Angelina passed beneath the colonnades of the station, the train gave a sigh.

She turned onto a cobblestone street on the hillside. People were out for the evening promenade, past small shops and tapas bars.

Finally, at the top of the hill, she came to a small hotel, entered it, and spoke to the man at the desk.

"I need a room. Do you have something on the top floor?"

She followed him up a narrow stairway lit by candles. The man took a ring of keys from his pocket and chose the correct one without hesitation. He pushed open the door.

She stepped into a room of heavy, plain furniture. A rattan carpet lay next to the four-poster bed, which was draped in gauze. A wooden chair furnished with deep cushions was next to a large table holding a lamp and some books. The man strode toward some french doors and flung them open. "The balcony."

Faint music came from below as she stepped onto it. She could see the heads of people as they snaked through the streets. A dog barked in the night.

"Yes," she said, and inquired of the rate. "I'll pay you now."

He shook his head. "No, no. Tomorrow is fine. Do you require anything?"

"Some tapas, please." She had not eaten anything since the morning, suspicious of the train food. "And a bottle of your best wine."

He was back in five minutes with some steaming crab snacks, an opened bottle of rich red wine, and a glass. She wished she had specified something with beef in it, which would have been taken for granted in Buenos Aires. But never mind. She thanked him. He bowed and closed the door quietly as he left.

"Okay now, let me out," said Chester from the pack.

She took Chester, the food, and the wine out onto the balcony. There was a cooling, steady wind. She thought she could discern low black mountains etched in the East, where there were no stars.

She lay back on the chaise and sipped wine. "What a relief to be out of the train."

"Ah," said Chester noncommittally.

She sat up. "You liked it there," she said accusatorily.

"It's not really matter of—"

"Come on! Of course you liked it."

"Well, yes. A variety of people and informational inputs. Of course I liked it."

"I think that I am going back to Argentina, Chester. I no longer wish to go to Paris. I have lost hope of actually seeing Manuel or Louis. I have probably been changed only a fraction of the amount that they have been changed, and it frightens me. They won't want to see me. I can go back and get my ranch. I can return to the life I had."

"You're afraid," Chester said.

"Yes. I haven't been afraid before, not really. I was angry, and I was determined. But there on the train I saw the beginnings of a whole new way of being and living. I only had a brief taste of it in Buenos Aires; not enough to engulf or frighten. But there seems to be less and less of me and more and more of the stories. I have tried to not battle the stories and I think I have almost succeeded at making my peace with them, in seeing what it is that I ought to do with them or for them. But I don't want people to know my every thought and I don't want to know theirs. That is what mothers and babies do. It is a stage that passes as the baby grows up."

With only two sips of the wine, she felt herself drifting off. She set the glass carefully on a table next to the chaise and watched the stars for a few minutes.

The stories seem to fade into the background, leaving only a deep, medieval tone, spattered with sharp notes of war and revolution and privation and death, humankind's legacy and seemingly inescapable fate. Angelina tossed and turned and muttered, feeling herself on the verge of waking, wanting to escape the descent into pain and seemingly senseless conflict, repeated without end, but could not. She tried to cry out for help from a battlefield where beautiful young men, beautiful as Manuel had once been, beautiful as Louis was now, lay mangled or dead, their gifts lost for all time.

Why? She wanted to cry out in rage. There must be some other way. Some way other than this waste to resolve differences. Can we not learn from the stories?

Then the music coalesced into something entirely different; something that demanded the attention of her soul. She felt as if she woke, but could not move or speak.

The stories and images of history coalesced into one focal point, then expanded into an ovoid of light.

The light was not blinding; instead, it was subtle, opalescent, and illuminated that which was around it only gently—the stucco wall of the balcony; Chester lying next to her; the half-full glass of wine.

She heard music the like of which she had never heard before. It seemed as if it were taking the stuff of her mind and giving it new order. As if her brain was rendered as plastic as an infant's, and as capable of learning. As if she were in an utterly new environment, and must learn. Light flashed across the sky for an instant, not like lightning, but like the underside of a cloud illuminated one last moment by the setting sun. Then the sky was black, with stars, once again.

There was no room left in her to contemplate, fear, or plan an escape. The light and the music occupied all of her informational space and even seemed to expand it, making her one with the stars above. Then she was freed from the vise of war, and could speak.

"Louis?" she whispered, and wondered why.

She half-rose from the chaise, then fell back into it, disoriented. She could feel it beneath her. Yet she saw something different. Not the rooftop she recalled. Another rooftop . . . everything was disjointed . . . slightly different. As if she had been here on this rooftop, rising up and falling back on her elbow, uncountable times. Things that happened smoothly in her mind, so smoothly that she had grown used to the illusion of smoothness, the smoothness with which her brain wove together the periodic input of her senses, were rent asunder. She did not know for how long, for she realized as it was happening that her sense of time, that most basic sense, was an illusion too, one which allowed her to live, and to make decisions, and to survive, as an animal, as a complex, magnificent animal composed of so very many different parts.

Time stretched and compressed within that light. It lost its direction. Her brain had been a training ground for this, and the brains of all her ancestors. There was much beyond the human, which humans could not sense on their own. And even when they devised the means of sensing and translating what lay beyond their own senses, they did not have the means of comprehending them. A cat would lie on a newspaper on the floor; a child might eat the pages of a book. Only the trained person could understand and cherish the signal within the visual signals, and read.

This learning was leagues beyond reading.

She heard Chester calling out her name, his voice loud and worried as she lurched across the roof, driven by panic. She must get out, she must get down, she must, she must, get to Paris . . .

She had a sensation of falling through the light. And then she landed on her side, crashing onto hard shapes, and lost consciousness.

August 10, 2115

THE GIRL WHO FELL TO EARTH

The fast fire falling of us, twisting and turning and I wanted to be sick but something touched my skin knowing that and the urge passed. Blue and blue but different blues, the stronger blue growing below us as we fell and fell and fell and then the orange red and green and blue fire oh all dancing and furling and I made the music of it with my hands though they were hard to move.

The face of Io her eyes staring into mine and then her face changing to the laugh face but tears coming out in splats that drifted and landed wet on my face like rain like we had in the place my mother called the jungle dance and she cried too there, I saw her, and hugged me tight saying oh baby at least hug me tight, that's right, tighter and tighter until I thought I might squeeze the breath from her and wondered why she wanted me to do that. I thought of her as the light, sometimes round and sometimes thin and coming to me at night and looking at me. I do not miss her but she tells me things I want to know.

Io blew up the way to get to her. So I had to come with Io.

Still I will get to her from wherever I am going. I don't know why I want to so much. It is a lot like the music. I have to do it. It is there. It is all around me. It comes from the things I see. I think that probably on Earth the music will change since the things I see will be so different. Dad made me spend time each day on Earth so that I would know about it. Earth is large buildings with flowers on the top and people he says would not understand me. They would not be like the people in Unity, saying when they think I can't hear, it's a shame about her, Hank. Her music is so lovely.

A flash of sky then a rush and a pull and I am in the sky and the pod of fire falls below and there is a jerk that surprises me. Above me the white billow and I soar through the air. It is a lot of fun.

Maybe I am even laughing. She always wanted me to laugh. She used to beg me to laugh.

"Mother, I am laughing," I yell but can't hear myself yelling. I dangle far above the ocean, which is blue, filled with white lines, and nothing else. There is a slight curve to the world but it flattens fast.

It is interesting to rush down to the water wondering what will happen. I don't know how to make anything happen. Everything is light and bright and hurting my eyes and then I am beneath the blue, deep, so surprised, and all around me are blades of light that ripple and I am without air but not in a vacuum.

I start to paw the water and this helps; something pulls me up too. I climb higher and my chest is about to burst and I break the skin of the water and gulp air. I see that my chute lies on the water and is changing into a boat and I am tilted and turned upward by my suit so that I face the bright bright sky and I scream from the pain of it beating into my eyes even when I close them the lids are bright red. Water covers me again and again and each time I breathe some in and choke. There is strong pulling on my shoulders and I think that my tether is shrinking me up and pulling me toward the boat until I float next to it. Colors wash across it, shining, and I am relentlessly pulled over a lip and then I lie gasping on the floor of a boat. I push myself up. It is almost impossible.

The floor skin is clear. A sail is forming, held up by a rigid pole. All things my father and mother showed me. All the things of Earth that were not like the moon as if they knew I would be here someday. I think of the molecular spins that make this possible, of how the molecules in the pole section lock tight and bond while the molecules in the sail section are only in a few layers. It flutters in the wind and then fills with air, air moving without fans, and the boat turns.

I peel off my suit, starting at my chin and ripping it apart down the middle until I can pull my arms and legs free. I lie naked on the boat. The sun feels hot and good. The sensation of the breeze is a bit like being licked by my cats. I roll over and crawl to the lip and grasp it. I scour the wavy surface for them. I don't know if Io remembered to fix a chute for my cats. Then I wonder where Io is. I know that we should probably stay together. I yell, "Io! Io!"

August 9, 2115

RADIO COWBOY ON THE BUS

The sleek metallic vehicle stopped at Radio Cowboy's aching booted feet with the dust-spouting shriek of wheels grabbing pavement.

Radio Cowboy looked at the thing, puzzled, as the sound faded to the baseline of desert silence.

It was about thirty feet long, aerodynamically shaped, and had no visible windows, doors, or handles. A reflection of clouds and sky swirled across it like an iridescent oil slick.

He walked around to the back, and then to the other side, and it was still a cipher. Finally, as he stood in the middle of the road mopping his face with his bandana, the solid surface next to him cleared, then vanished, leaving a small porthole. Chill air escaped, washing his face.

He was looking at a girl with straight, gleaming black hair whacked off just below her ears. Her skin was almost porcelain-like in its clarity, and her cheeks were a pale delicate shade of pink. Her eyes were occidental, yet he got the impression that she was of Asian ancestry. He thought she looked about ten or eleven, but couldn't really tell.

"Where you going, Cowboy?" She spat a long brown stream out the window, some of which splashed off the pavement and onto Radio Cowboy's boot.

"West. Uh, Houston. I guess. No! I mean, just west."

"Hop in, then." Behind her, a doorway grew from a tiny dot to an oval-shaped opening. The cold air felt like a prelude to heaven. He crouched down and crawled in on his hands and knees.

Inside was another world: cool; almost misty. The floor was lined with bamboo mats. He peeked through a curtain and saw neat rows of bean sprouts in clear square translucent containers stacked three high. They basked in sunlight, apparently admitted through a window invisible to the outside. He thought he heard a baby's brief, sharp cry. Drums pounded a slow bass line around which delicate flute notes played. A fountain bubbled, wedged between the bean sprouts. Behind all that was another curtain.

"Watch your feet," she said. "Cruise speed, Bessie."

He was thrown on his side as the bus accelerated. Sprays of orchids, suspended from the ceiling, swayed gently. Pulling himself to his knees, Cowboy crawled around to the flat surface next to the girl's seat. Kneeling, he watched the speedometer climb to 110 mph.

"You're not in a hurry, are you? I like to take things kind of slow." She had a big lump of what he presumed was tobacco in her cheek, and aimed a stream into a funnel to the right of the steering column. It went in neatly and was sucked away with a slight *whoosh.*

"Um, no," he said as the rocks and dirt alongside the road became a blur.

Her chest was narrow and flat; she wore shiny blue mid-thigh tights and a T-shirt, and sat on a raised platform. Her legs were crossed in full lotus, and she steered absently, one hand on the wheel. She glanced at him from beneath long eyelashes. "What takes you to Houston, Cowboy?"

"To tell you the truth, I don't remember." He was surprised to find that this was absolutely, and frighteningly, true.

"Going inside?"

"Um . . . No." He repeated with more assurance, "No. That's right. I'm actually going to the Space Center."

She looked at him in frank disbelief for so long that he said, "Watch out! You'll run off the road."

"Not possible." She took her hands off the wheel and cupped them in her lap. "I'm locked on now. Bessie here sees if there's anything ahead and alerts me. If I'm sleeping or something, she makes her own decision." She reached out and patted the steering wheel, and the flute music got a bit louder for a few seconds.

"How old are you?" He blurted out. "I mean—"

"Oh, don't be embarrassed," she said airily. "Everybody asks. I'm seventy-two." She watched for his reaction and he just stared. "That's right." Her voice now was slightly bitter.

"You look . . . pretty good for seventy-two," he managed, batting back the urge to sing *Buffalo Gals.*

Her smile was bleak. "Yes, well. At least there's that. Look, scrunch forward—that's right. Bessie, make a passenger seat, adult-sized, please."

The surface beneath him began to morph and move. He tried to keep his balance as a seat formed and a seatback rose behind him. Finally he settled into it and stretched out his legs—not long and tall as befitted a cowboy, he noted with regret, but rather short and stubby. "Where are you going?"

"To the roundup. To drink that hard liquor from a cold bitter cup."

"*Ranger's Command,*" he said instantly, and she shot him a pleased glance.

"Bingo, Cowboy."

He didn't mention that it was one of the songs in his pistols. "Where is this roundup?"

"Yuma."

"Oh." Cowboy was silent for a moment as he tried and failed to conjure a dependable map. "Is, uh, Houston on the way?" He'd been so damned flakey lately . . . he shook his head like a dog with a flea in its ear, as if trying to shake off the cloud of misinformation and wild persona in which he was enveloped. Radio Cowboy wanted to go west, that was for sure. He felt a deep thrill at that word. *West.* Tuscon. Phoenix. *Sedona. Sedona was important, somehow . . .*

She looked at him and smiled. "No, mister, it isn't. To tell you the truth, you are now at least two hundred miles north and a hundred miles west of Houston. You should have turned south earlier. It's on the way back, though."

Cowboy wondered, suddenly, why he needed to go to Houston anyway, why this urgency prickled at him. It was so pleasant and cool in this bus. At this rate they would get to Houston pretty quickly, even if they went straight to Los Angeles and back. The roundup, though . . . this roundup thing might hold him up.

Yes—a real roundup! Settling down on the bull in the chute, wrapping the rope round his hand, giving the nod, feeling the bull explode beneath him. Winning real money, buying a used Cadillac Eldorado Convertible, cruising with blond, hard-drinking Millie to Las Vegas, waking up in jail, Millie gone . . .

Light flooded from behind, startling him. Two heads poked round the side of his seatback. "Who is this?" asked a voice.

Cowboy twisted around to look at them.

They were boys, apparently identical twins.

"He's just a cowboy," said the girl. "He was hitching."

"I can't really go all the way to Yuma," said Cowboy, with, he hoped, cowboy sincerity and authority. "I have to go to Houston. Ya'll can just let me out right here. I'll manage."

Then there were more children behind him. They all laughed.

It was a few hours later. Cowboy had looked in vain for a way to get out of the van. He considered many options. He thought about somehow knocking out the girl and the two boys, rather like a cowboy, at least a somewhat desperate movie cowboy, might do, but could not help but reject it. Just pulling out one of his pistols would be an act of unimaginable violence, despite their being filled with music, not bullets. Besides, then the rest of them appeared. He had no idea how many there were—ten? twelve?—but they pulled the curtain aside and chattered ceaselesly behind him. He tried talking to them, but they just laughed, handed him a bowl of bean-curd ice cream extruded from a nipple back in their kitchen area, and asked if he wanted chocolate on it. He definitely heard the baby crying now. “Whose baby is that?” he asked, and was answered by a wave of puzzling, hysterical laughter.

The girl’s name was Carla. The boys were Jess and Ted. They were descended from Vietnamese boat people. Their parents had been wildly successful in business and when the Second Wave occurred they had produced a second wave of children to celebrate their newfound longevity.

But something was wrong with these children. Something was wrong with all the children in their neighborhood.

“It was in the water,” Carla told him, sitting sideways in the driver’s seat with a lack of attention that made Cowboy feel ill-at-ease . . . scared just about witless, to tell the truth. “We were downstream from New Genesis. You know, the big biotech company?”

Cowboy shook his head.

“Well, they were working on longevity alternatives. I get the impression that a lot of people were. This is one of the alternatives.”

Cowboy took another long breath of the cool, sweet, misty air issuing from the vents. “Oh.”

They pulled over at sunset.

All the kids piled out and ran around, laughing and screaming, pulling hair, pretending to fight, laughing breathlessly, almost hysterically. He counted nine of them.

Silhouetted against the yellow sunset sky, they skipped and danced and jeered and darted, with cries that reminded Peabody, now emerging at dusk, of the gulls that winged around his tower at Crescent City. They split and regrouped, ran so far down the empty highway that they were dots, ran back again, breathless, and flung themselves on the ground. One of them had fallen and Peabody noted blood trickling down the leg, then stopping, and then the skin healing over without even a scab. One of them delved into the van and brought out the baby. He—or she—was propped up in a seat. He knew nothing about babies.

“How old is—”

“She,” said Carla. Her glance skittered from his. “It’s . . . kind of hard to tell, isn't it? Be back soon or miss supper," Carla yelled at the running kids as they dashed across the highway and onto the brown earth that ran to the mountains.

The rest of them threaded chunks of zucchini and small tomatoes onto skewers, along with freeze-dried tofu. As the sun set, Carla ignited fire cubes in a grill. The twins laid the skewers on the grill, where they cooked quickly. "Dig in," Carla told him.

The kids sat on folding stools or lay on blankets strewn across the median. On one side of him, a girl's hands glowed gently with lines and dots. The boy on the other side of him glared at the girl. "Oh, shut up!" he said, and she grinned smugly. Her skin pulsed in new patterns and he frowned and moved to another seat.

As stars blazed, they began to sing, in light, high voices, with complex harmonies.

They sang *Ranger's Command*. They sang *The Streets of Loredo*. They sang what Peabody, peering out at last through the heavy fence of Cowboy, surmised were Vietnamese fishing chants, though when he asked the girl next to him she said that she didn't understand the words. "Our grandmothers sang these songs," she told him. They passed around a bottle of a clear white liquor that burned his throat like fire.

Finally they drifted back to the bus, taking their stools and blankets and stowing them. No one spoke or gave directions. Radio Cowboy quieted, and Peabody took a few deep, free breaths, watching the light-pulsing elderly children return to the van, from which gales of laughter erupted for a few minutes before the van darkened and quieted.

Peabody was left alone, lying on the blanket he had retained, beneath the stars. He gazed at them a long time, feeling a keen sense of loss on behalf of these children. But why? They seemed happy enough. They were just stuck forever at this age.

Was additional maturity something they ought to seek, or have sought for them? Was the angst and ache he felt, whenever Radio Cowboy deserted him, something to be coveted?

He rolled himself in his blanket, then shook it off and stood.

He went over to the bus. The windows were open and he heard

children, breathing within; pictured them with their black hair strewn on their pillows.

He went to the passenger side and wondered, for a moment. Then he whispered, "Bessie, I need my pack."

A portal opened down near the chassis. He reached inside, felt a pack strap, and pulled it out. The portal shrank.

He went back to his blanket, pulled out his radio stones, and tapped each in turn to hissing life then tapped it off again. Nothing but static. Finally he came to a white one, the tiny call letters within pronouncing it station KNOW.

He tapped it on, and Native American chants issued forth. The voices blended and parted, still small and distant despite the amplifying membrane he wrapped around it.

Over the radioed chants, he heard a curious sound, like a low and focused dot of wind in the East, growing louder, and white headlights burned into the night.

He jumped up and ran toward it, but the car dopplered past and its red taillights receded in the west.

He told himself that it was all right. He wanted to go east, anyway.

He went back and sat next to the radio stones, vowing to stay awake, but when he next looked up the stones were silent in the still, cool air of dawn. No other cars passed.

And then the kids were up and Cowboy was back, wanting, *needing,* to go to the roundup.

He munched a cold cereal bar, which Donja, one of the girls, told him they had gotten from an old warehouse somewhere in Montana.

"Montana! It's glorious up there! I'd give my eyeteeth to go back to them Grand Teton Mountains. Jackson Hole. I guess you just travel around wherever the mood takes you."

"Not exactly," the girl replied a bit sullenly. "We have . . . a duty—"

Carla looked over at them from a few yards away and said sharply, "Donja! Time to get a move on!"

Donja looked at Cowboy with a troubled glance, then walked toward the bus.

Cowboy resumed his seat of yesterday. "Look," he said to Carla, who was clearly the boss, "I don't want to keep taking up the front seat." Someone's memory of how fiercely the front seat of the '59 Mercury Comet station wagon was coveted assailed him briefly. "One of the kids might want it."

Carla just glanced at him and stuck some tobacco in her cheek as Bessie lurched onto the highway. "They've all had plenty of time to sit in the front seat, believe me," she said, her voice tight and pinched as if she were not getting enough air. Or as if she were angry and weary and resigned.

Later in the afternoon, Donja burst through the curtain. "Carla! Carla, stop! It's the baby!"

"Deal with it," Carla said bitterly. She gave no command to Bessie.

"Maybe I can help?" said Cowboy—rather tentatively, for he had nothing at all to offer in the realm of babies.

"I don't think—" began Carla.

Donja sobbed hysterically. "Come on! She's going to cross soon. I can't stand it! I can't stand it!"

"Don't let him back there!" commanded Carla.

So of course Cowboy followed Donja past the kitchen compartment.

The back of the bus was a cozy arrangement of seats and bunks. All the kids were gathered around the squalling baby. Cowboy thought the sound would drive him crazy.

"What do you mean, 'cross?' " he asked Donja.

She stared at him. She seemed much younger than Carla. Five, perhaps? "I—I used to know what it meant," she said, snuffling. "Now—it's just a word to me." She was silent for a moment, her hysteria gone, looking incongruously surprised. She suddenly slumped to the floor and hid her face in her hands. She rocked back and forth, and shrugged off Cowboy's hand when he patted her on the back.

"Look!" A collective gasp arose from the kids.

He leaned over them. The baby was choking, her little face screwed up and red. Alarmed, he said, "Let me through!"

He tried desperately to remember an old technique he had learned long, long ago, CPR. For babies. Their lungs so tiny. Their bodies so frail. He grabbed her up. She was struggling for air, gasping.

"There's nothing you can do," said one of the twins in a flat voice. "She's crossing now." Indeed, as he watched helplessly, breath left her.

He put his mouth to the baby's mouth; covered her nose and mouth with his and puffed gently. Her chest rose slightly. He counted. It came back to him. He puffed, and counted; puffed, and counted; felt the bus slow as he did so and then Carla took the baby from him.

"She's crossed," Carla said. "There's not a damn thing we can do. Don't you think we've tried?"

He looked down at her in the misty air. "But what do you mean? She's died."

"Crossed," said Ted. "Become unborn."

"We've thought about putting an artificial womb on the bus," Carla said, her voice distant, as a portal in the back opened. They all trooped down the stairs into surprisingly cooler air. They were in the foothills of some mountains. He saw snow glint on high peaks. Drizzle settled upon them.

"For when we have to cross," said Jess, wading through grass that came up to his waist.

"But why prolong things?" asked Ted, next to him, his young face smooth and dusky, his long black hair neatly braided in two braids. He started to cry, his face scrunched up and helpless. "I'm so scared," he gasped as he sobbed.

Cowboy grabbed him beneath his arms and swung him up; Ted's legs locked around his waist. He hid his face against Cowboy's neck, and shook in his arms. Cowboy took a few long steps to catch up with Carla. Carla carried the baby in both arms, with careful reverence. "We'll go down to the creek and build her platform. Look for sticks," she commanded.

"A what?"

"A raised platform. Like a burial, except its an offering to the

Great Spirit. Becky will be given to the Great Spirit." They were near the creek now, which rushed cold from the mountains in a wild slue. Great tree trunks littered the rocks. Cowboy felt a rush of memory. *The Tetons. The Rockies. Sedona . . .*

Home. Deep, almost unremembered home. The day darkened as clouds loomed over the mountain top.

He watched the children gather sticks. Ted loosened his grip, slid to the ground, and joined in. They disappeared behind the gigantic boulders, jumped from rock to rock, collecting silvery washed wood of grotesquely beautiful shapes. Drips of rain fell from his hat brim as he watched and was gradually soaked and chilled. He went down to the river's edge and found a tiny gravelly beach and a pile of strong, usable limbs cached in a small cove.

One by one the children pulled a surprisingly varied collection of switchblades from pockets and started peels of willow bark which they used to lash the platform together, their heads shiny and dripping in the increasingly serious rain. The platform they built was not high. He helped them lash the top parts.

The baby was wrapped in a somewhat garish green silk shirt, apparently too large for any of them to wear, which was also tied with bark.

"Watch Becky now at the hour of her crossing," sang Carla in a pure sweet voice.

"And watch us too at the hour of our crossing," responded the rest of the children in unison.

"Grant her peace in the Great Unmaking," chanted Carla.

"And lead us to the realm of the Everlasting Nows."

"Which we seek with all our hearts."

"Though we have only heard of them."

"Show us the way."

"Grant us the Nows."

"Grant us the Nows."

"That we may live forever in the shifting infinite instants."

There was no more chanting. The wind grew stronger. Something rose to his memory like a trout to a fly.

He was silent, sharing their moment of silence. He recalled that before his gift of long life had been granted, his long-ago lover had graced him, in a kind of twisted vengeance after a philosophical disagreement, a progressive aging.

Could not also and quite easily its opposite exist?

It could.

And it did.

A certain amount of the aging process could truly be held at bay or even, seemingly, reversed. But whatever caused this had to have been treated biologically not as a regression, which seemed impossible even to his radio mind, but as a further development.

The wild Western landscape burned into his soul. The black crevasses of the mountain, the waving pines, the roar of the wind, the cold pelting rain.

It did exist, this unmaking that led to infancy and inability to function independently. Another legacy of the biological tampering released upon the world in the last century. Perhaps there had been some purpose to it, or one component of it, at one time. A waypost to some goal.

Soaked, the children turned as one to walk, teeth chattering, back to Bessie.

He said nothing to them of his knowledge.

They were, after all, children. And they already knew.

As children, though, perhaps they forgot for a while.

And his own knowledge was actually quite old. Peabody was suddenly aware that he had been jolted back into himself, by this shock, he supposed, or the cold.

Carla stopped and looked at him. He stopped too. They eyed one another through the pelting rain.

"You do understand, don't you? We need someone to take care of us. Donja has been good. We picked her up not too long ago in Tehachapi. But it worked very quickly on her. I hope . . . I hope that you are slower."

He tilted his head. "The sweet air from the vents." He was almost certain it wouldn't affect him. Only the city itself, he thought bitterly, could worm its way through his elaborate defenses and inflict him with something like this Cowboy stuff.

Carla said, "My fear is that we'll all become helpless at the same time. Becky was cherished and cared for until the time of her crossing. We need that."

"You haven't had time to think beyond that," said Cowboy, his pity stronger than his anger. He understood, all too well. "It would be so easy. There is a place—"

"I know there's a place!" she said, her voice rising in anger. "The great, the good, the powerful Crescent City! Tell me about it! I waited! I waited from the time I was thirty until I was twenty-five to be admitted. Not so long as you might think. That took perhaps a year. It's really a strange experience. It was like my body remembered what it was to be those ages; as if whatever I was feeling at those times had more to do with my developmental stage than anything else. But it didn't matter. They wouldn't let me in. Kept me on a wait list. I knew something then. I know less and less the younger I grow. But I hoped to be able to save the rest of my town. Finally I had to give up. It was getting too late. When I got back, this was all that was left. Most of them had already crossed while I was gone. We've waited outside the great Dome of Los Angeles and could not get in there, either.

"Oh, we were happy when it first started! We dropped our plans to sue the company—not that there was any legal system to speak of, anyway. We partied! We would be young again! Our aches and pains forgotten. That was before we realized that someone had left off the directions on how to stop it. The first big clue was my son. He was forty when it started." Her cold laugh matched the spirit of the place.

"This is all that's left now. Wandering, barbecues, roundups, and crossings. Only a few more crossings to go, for us. Maybe, now, you'll be moved to help. Maybe you'll find something before it's too late for you. In time to save some of us. Don't hate me too much. I did it for them. You'll do it too when your time comes. Or maybe not. Maybe . . ." she sighed. "Maybe this thing has completely erased my morals. I think that I used to have some." She ran off through the rain and climbed into Bessie.

Peabody stood in the rain another long moment after the portal closed. A blast of cold wind bore down on him and flattened the sparse high grass at his feet.

He registered the colors around him as if seeing them anew—rain-washed, deep, and bleak. Green streaks of pines jagged down ridges, their individuality blurred by distance. Black shadows sharpened canyons.

Even if he managed to get them back to Crescent City—what then? A war; pirates; ruin; insanity. Still, he was out here for some reason. Not to escape. To continue. To discover. To try and play a part in taking things the next step forward. Or the next unimaginable leap. To rage against darkness.

Darkness like this.

He was drawn into the shadows, where Cowboy lurked, waiting his chance.

Pulled himself back.

You're a grown man, he told himself. Remember that. An old, grown man. With some wisdom.

He had to fight this Cowboy stuff.

Ride it, yes. But jump from the running horse whenever he could, stand on his own feet, and walk with awareness into this bleak new landscape. This land of pain.

Or make the horse take him where he wanted to go.

And where was Dania? He missed her suddenly. With an impact like that of the sideways wind. What follies, what idiotic follies, had separated them. They had simply forgotten who they were and why they were here.

Now, what?

More Cowboy. He had to get to Los Angeles. That was where the radio astronomer had gone. The man who was working on the Theory of Everything. Perhaps the only one left. Peabody had to find out what the scientist was thinking. He cursed Zeb for leaving Crescent City, just as he himself had finally arrived, decades ago. But Zeb believed that the Theory of Everything was more than humans could know or understand. So he made his way to the post-human outpost of the Dome.

But there was a chance that he could find Zeb. Maybe. And then—get whatever coordinates had been left in the wake of that shattering Signal. Yes. Take this gang with him to Johnson Space Center, get the crucial navigational information distilled in the wake of the first Silence. Take them all back to Crescent City. To—he knew not what. But the city was on the move. It was changing into launch mode. He had to get back to give it some guidance.

No, he told himself. Be honest.

He had to get back just so that he could *go*. So that at last he could do what he had been born to do. Find what he had been programmed to find. That was putting it baldly. But it was true.

Whether or not humans could do better somewhere else was another story. But there *was* somewhere else, and that was why they had to go. All there was to it.

The roar of the wind in the trees and the lashing rain obliterated everything else. He looked back at the bus, which held the youngening ones.

So while they were all fiddling inside Crescent City, this.

Shivering, he made his way over the rocky ground, back to Bessie.

Ra and Zeb

Rain slashed the windshield of the van as Zeb drove it through winding, deserted mountain roads.

"It is so beautifully and randomly musical out here," Ra exclaimed, leaning forward in her seat. "So many sounds from so many sources and none of them generated by humans. Except, I guess, the sounds of the van. The shifting. The hiss of wheels on pavement. Intervals and frequencies. And the colors! So muted and rich. I don't believe I ever thought much about color . . . before. Before we entered the Dome. But now! Big harmonious patches of golden ochre and pine-green. Those low billowing gray clouds. I am so happy!"

"I am too," said Zeb with a quiet smile.

"Zeb?"

"Yes?"

"Why are we out here again? It's . . . it's kind of embarrassing, but I really don't remember being inside all that clearly. I do know we were promised that if and when we decided to come out we'd have enhanced synaptic capabilities."

Zeb looped his long gray hair behind each ear carefully, always keeping one hand on the wheel. "I'm sure that I never let my hair get this long."

"It was that long when I met you. While you were staying in the D.C. shelters."

"Oh. See, I don't remember that. Much. But we came out because the Dome picked up a signal. It was a special prearranged signal I set up with someone before we went in. Because we wanted to explore, inside the Dome, but I was afraid of being cut off forever. Now that I look back, I see that I should have prearranged something myself that didn't depend on anything else. That signal might never have been sent, or if it had, we might never have gotten it." He was quiet for a moment.

Then he said, "You know, I'm remembering now . . . some kind of radio event took place at that time. Something quite powerful. I'm really going to have to think about this. I think that I have the capacity . . . the capacity to remember and think about all kinds of things that I couldn't think about before." He looked at Ra. His eyes were puzzled.

"Who sent it?"

"Someone I met way back in New Orleans. Remember when we were in Crescent City? It was Peabody. Jason Peabody. When we decided to leave Crescent City, he and I set this up. If anything in the status quo changed, signal-wise or otherwise, he was to get in touch with me. We figured that this particular signal could piggyback on the original Signal that keeps coming in. I recognized it."

"Oh. It was the painting, then."

"Right."

"That looked out over the canal in Venice."

"Usually." Zeb smiled.

"When it rearranged itself and said, 'It's Time.' "

"Correct."

"How could you make sure that would happen?"

"When I went in, I wrote some programming that would never be reduced and never mutate. It wasn't easy. I had to smuggle it in. It looked like a different kind of code to them. Something quite mundane, like perhaps the code for the color of my eyes. They wouldn't have liked it at all. Their whole philosophy is one of constant mutation and evolution."

"And forgetting," mused Ra, still drinking in the darkening landscape. "I think everyone in there forgot who they were and where they came from. Even though we pretended to have bodies, nothing was solid. I wanted to find out what it was like, but I'm so glad we left. How long do you think we were in there?"

"Fifty years."

"Fifty *years*!" Ra stared at him. "No."

"Yes."

"But it passed just like that. Like a dream."

"Not while we were there."

"I don't know." Ra was silent for a time, then. Finally she spoke. "What was the point then? Hedonism?"

"Looking for humanity's limits?"

"I know that I composed some very fine pieces in there."

"Very fine."

"I don't remember them at all." Her voice was bleak. She turned to stare out the window.

Zeb reached over and patted her shoulder. "I do." He spoke gently. "Maybe I could write some of them out for you."

She laughed and turned back toward him and leaned against the car door. She wiped tears from her face. "You!"

"Of course," he said seriously. "Each one is like a handful of equations to me. Some of them are just one equation. When I hear something that you wrote, Ra, my mind fills with numbers and symbols. It's heavenly. It's like returning to a place I knew as a child."

She peered out the window. “Right now it sounds like gravel’s being dumped on top of the van.”

“Hail,” Zeb said. A guest of wind roared up the valley behind them like a wild beast, shaking the van as it passed.

“Wow,” said Ra. “How can you see?”

“I can’t, not very well,” admitted Zeb. “But I think we ought to be at the crest pretty soon. Maybe once we cross to the other side it will be clear.”

Suddenly, the road flattened out. The world became silent. Ra strained forward. “What’s that in the headlights?”

“Damned if it isn’t snow,” Zeb said.

“What’s on the other side of this mountain?”

“Didn’t they give us a map?”

Ra ran her hand along the dashboard, squinting. “These lights don’t work very well . . . or else they’re covered with dirt . . . here!” She pushed a button.

“Assistance,” said a terse, tinny voice.

“Where are we?”

“How the hell should I know?”

“Excuse me?”

“There ain’t been no gps for about a hundred years, lady. You want I should make something up?”

“Well, no.”

“So don’t bother me, then. I got things to do. You think you’re the only form of intelligence here? The damned tires are bald and I got to decide whether to build them up and if I do where I should get the molecules from. Maybe from the roof? Nah, that’s something a stupid vehicle would do. You know, I was taking a nice long nap when you woke me up. Nothing’s gotten any better since them idiot neo-hippies used me as their matter tariff for getting into the Dome. Far as I can tell, you twits ain’t much more advanced in the smarts department.”

Zeb and Ra looked at each other and burst into laughter.

“Sorry,” Ra said finally.

“ ’s all right,” the voice grumbled.

A battered sign loomed into view.

"What's that say?" asked Ra, leaning forward. "Stop! I'll have to get out and see."

Zeb stopped the van and backed up to where the sign was, turning the van so that the lights were trained full on it.

" 'Y . . . U . . . M?' " asked Ra, frowning. She opened the door and cold wind rushed in. "Maybe there's a restaurant ahead?"

"Yuma!" snapped the van. "Shut the door. I got it now. Can't stump me for long. I'm top of the line. That would be California State Road Sign #4782. Signs give off a weak local signal—if they're still working. 'Yuma Sixty-Two Miles.' Next sign says 'Caution, Steep Winding Grade Next Ten Miles.' The idiots used to drive down it to sell their goat-milk candy at a roadside stand on the Arizona line. They got in with the date milkshake lady. How many people want candy made out of goat's milk? Guess whose muffler had to be held up with a coat hanger? I had dreams one time. Don't you think I wanted to stay in that Mercedes? But the stockbroker wasn't too bright either, I guess. Slammed us into a highway abutment on his way to some meeting. Retro hippies pried me out in the junkyard and soldered me into this rattletrap. Smartest package made at the time and most expensive. Only took me forty-eight hours to figure out all there was to know about old Rattletrap. Every molecule mapped. I coulda helped them. But they didn't want what I had to give. Didn't want an aerodynamic design. Liked this shape. 'Make it so we can use goat shit for fuel.' *Goat* shit! What could I do? Their wishes were my command. Wanted to live like their grandparents. Dirt and disease and inefficiency. Only thing they wanted was the greatest hits of the LSD age on the greatest stereo imaginable. 'I lis-sen to the wind, to the wind of my soul.' Wind of the *soul* ? What does *that* mean? Hey—"

Ra slammed the door and punched the button that had activated the voice. "That should do it."

Zeb shifted into first. The van resumed its rattly progress. Ra turned around and knelt on the seat, began sifting through a box of snacks. She held one up and snapped on the overhead light so she could see it. "Freeze-dried umi, anyone?"

"That's sea urchin," said the van. "Only three packages of that. Good stuff. Ought to try it. Did you think you could get rid of me so easy? I got an emergency override. And furthermore I know things that you gotta know. Things are happening. I'm on a mission, man. I gotta get you there. There to . . . what do you call it?" There was silence for a few beats. "Crescent City."

"How did you know we're going there?" asked Ra.

"I only know that's where I got to take you."

"What do you mean, you know things?" asked Zeb.

"Well, I know that it's a twisty, dangerous world out there. Tell you what, just leggo of the wheel and leave it to me. Take a break. I know every pothole. Or used to. What are the chances they've been fixed? This is a monster storm. You should stop."

"We'll think about it," said Zeb.

After coming down off the mountain and sleeping in the van—or trying to sleep, because the van continued to complain even after all the power was off—Ra and Zeb stepped out of the vehicle after taking the ferry across the Colorado. They were on the outskirts of the roundup.

"So what's this thing?" asked Ra.

"You've got about as good an idea as I do." Zeb looked around. "But we need to stop and get some water. Weren't there some plastic jugs in the back?"

They opened the rear door and after minutes of rummaging found the water containers. "They say antimicrobial," Ra said, squinting in the brilliant sun of early afternoon. She asked a passerby, "Is there water somewhere?"

"Over there." The man pointed to a short line a hundred yards away.

They saw all kinds of cars and campers and trailers parked in makeshift rows, leaving narrow roads between them. Here and there were bright pop-up tents. The smell of dung wafted in the dry wind.

"Toilets and showers over there," said Ra. "Ten bucks for the shower."

"Robbers."

They walked down the road and stood in the water line. The Colorado River, a bit to the west, was wide and full and dotted with houseboats tied up in a channel split off the main river by a narrow island. Low, dry, dun-colored mountains were scattered across the landscape. Their companions in line ran the gamut of races and costume. A Native American man with long black braids stood behind a Chinese woman in cowgirl garb.

"Not many children," observed Ra. She pulled the bill of the Red Sox cap she had found under the backseat a bit lower as the wind tugged at it.

"The Gaian Plague," said Zeb. "Remember? The Gaians claimed that it was the will of the entire organism."

She sighed. "Of course. So many unborn geniuses."

"So many more species of plants and wildlife and so much less pollution," said Zeb.

The man in front of him, wearing a battered tweed jacket with leather patches on the elbows over a dazzling hologram T-shirt, turned. "You sound like a Gaian," he said. His face was shaded by a huge brown cowboy hat.

"I'm not very political," Zeb said. "I'm a radio astronomer. But it's true that ecology is a huge issue. I do believe that the entire cosmos has an ecology that is self-correcting, always balancing itself. And that consciousness is a part of that ecology. Not divorced from it, not on the outside, taking care of all the animals and so forth."

"I'm pro-human myself," said the man, shuffling forward with the line. "I lived in pre-Dome L.A. Heaven on Earth if you ask me. Lost forever."

"You could still—" Zeb began, but Ra shushed him and for a while no one said anything. A horse whinnied nearby, and they moved forward one more step.

August 10, 2115

Dania: Just Like Romeo and Juliet

A headache teased Dania awake at dawn and she opened her eyes to briefly appraise narrow bright streaks of pink and green below the black horizon. She managed to fall back asleep until finally the heat of the sun made her dream that she was being roasted on a spit. She sat up, covered with sweat.

She was in the middle of a swiftly hardening mud pit.

Rising slowly, with much stiffness, she wondered if any of her limbs were broken.

There was nothing but bare trampled ground as far as she could see. Except for her car, reduced to shards of plastic sticking out of the mud here and there.

She shook chunks of dried mud from her skirt, sneezed at the dust, then made her way to the wettest mud and tried to figure out where the center of the spring might be. She settled on a patch of damp ooze, wrenched a few pieces of hand-sized plastic from the ground, and started to hack away at it.

"Here."

She jumped up and turned at the nearness of the male voice.

A man with a smooth tanned face and a long reddish, frizzed ponytail stood behind her. He did not look the least bit cowboy-ish. Nor did he look Native American.

He wore khaki shorts and a tank top with a rather distracting repeating cartoon image of a mouse throwing a brick at the head of a cat. He held out a canteen. "Here," he repeated, his voice quite normal and not at all threatening. "Have a drink."

She instantly recalled her dream. She felt, in great fact, dream-like herself and wondered if she were awake or just dreaming that it was so.

She reached for the canteen and glugged down a great slug of surprisingly cool water. Wiping her mouth with the back of her hand, she returned it to him. His eyes were large and brown, limpid and gentle.

"You were here last night."

He nodded.

"There were more of you."

"We're over there, in the shade. Behind the hill." He gestured.

"Who are you? What was that you said? Or the woman? 'Welcome to the Nows?' What the hell are the Nows?"

He recapped the canteen and smiled. He jerked his head in the direction of the hill. "Come with me. I'll try to explain."

Dania felt a cool tinge, the same she had felt inside the lightthing the previous day. Or—had it been the previous day?

Or some other, far-distant, yet present, time?

She stood for a second, trying—and failing—to orient herself, then trudged after the man.

When they topped the hill she saw a strange sight.

Horses chewed loudly, ripping grass from a small hollow that had apparently been bypassed by the buffalo. Not only that, but here was a spring and two cottonwoods next to it, their leaves shimmering in the hot wind.

A boy washed dishes in a plastic tub set on a portable table. A woman with short blond hair perched on a rock, smoking a pipe. An older-looking black woman sat cross-legged beneath a tarp lean-to, bent over a flatscreen. A little girl with Asian features and incongruous blond hair danced to music that came from an invisible source, a frail music that pulsed with joy. One man, shirtless, with a middle-aged paunch, knelt as he tightened straps around packets which sat on . . . a travois, Dania realized.

One of the horses eyed her, snorted loudly and scraped the ground with her hoof as she bobbed her head, then went back to grazing. Dania almost expected a color-coded message of precise distrust to pulse on some genetically engineered part of the mare's body, as generally happened with animals in Crescent City, but she appeared to be pure, unmodified Horse.

Dania heard a woman's voice, maybe, almost lost beneath the rustling of the cottonwood leaves. "This is K-N-O-W, the voice of Now." Then some drumming began.

Dania looked around, truly and deeply confused. It had to be a recording of a clear-channel station, which only came through at night.

The woman under the tarp looked up and grinned. She crawled out and stood, holding out a hand. "Welcome," she said.

"To the Nows?" asked Dania, feeling foolish and sarcastic as her hand was vigorously shaken.

And yet . . . the word held some kind of resonance for her.

All of the others laughed easily without ceasing their activities or even looking up, as if it were an old, shared joke.

"You must be hungry," said the shirtless man, standing with a grunt. "How about a piñon nut butter and cactus jelly sandwich on flat bread?"

"Sure," agreed Dania. "Why did you move last night?" *And why do you look different now*? But . . . she must have really dreamed that part.

"We had to," said the girl, ceasing her dance and coming over to examine Dania. Her blue gaze swept imperiously over Dania. "The Nows move us."

Dania's mouth was full of the agreeable but sticky sandwich. She accepted another drink from the canteen. "Yeah, okay," she said after swallowing. "But what are the Nows?"

The girl reached into the pocket of her shorts and pulled out a white ball. She patted it flat, then stretched it into a circle. "Figure 2.8," she said.

A picture like superimposed ladders appeared. The girl handed it to Dania, exchanging it for the remains of the sandwich. "You can make it bigger," she suggested.

Dania pulled the screen a bit larger. On one side of one ladder she read Romeo; on the other side the legend was Juliet. The second ladder was described as Tristan and Iseult, and the third Beatrice and Dante. "It's a diagram of space-time," said the girl in a helpful voice.

Dania looked down at her skeptically.

"The lovers are as close as they can possibly be. They are as one but still separate. The qualities of each pair of lovers overlap the way dimensions do. They are one with time and space." She took the screen from Dania's hands and balled it up and stuck it in her skirt pocket. "They are *conscious.*"

Dania squinted at her. "How old are you, anyway?"

The girl grinned, returned Dania's sandwich, and ran off.

Dania took another bite and chewed for a minute. "I'm a little too dense for that."

"You're not," said the black woman without looking up from her screen. "It just takes a while to adjust."

"Until then," Dania said, stuffing the last of the sandwich in her mouth. "I have to get to Houston." Talk about lovers brought unwanted thoughts about Cowboy.

Silly Cowboy. Silly Dania.

Out here being silly when Peabody and Dania had work to do.

She sighed. "I really do have to get to Houston. Can you help?"

"We can try," said the reddish-haired man. "My name's Brenden. I'm from New York City."

"He's from Queens," said the woman on the rock. "I'm June. The girl is White Time Girl. She's a Native American."

Dania glanced at blond, blue-eyed girl. "Really?"

"My mother put me together at a DNA clinic," said White Time Girl. "She always wanted blond hair, I guess. And blue eyes. The rest of me is Native American. Look at my cheekbones! I've got the papers. I can prove it. Here—"

"Forget it." Jerry grinned and groaned and waved his hand. Everyone else chuckled, and White Time Girl did too.

"He's Moses," said the black woman next to Dania, nodding toward the boy, who was finished with the dishes. "And I am Lelani." She added, "My father was Hawaiian. My mother African American."

"Plain old nonexotic Jerry," said the shirtless man, shaking her hand. "Retired plumber from Ithaca."

"Dania. Pure white trash from Salvation, Tennessee." She was irritated when they all smiled. As if they already knew that and more about her.

Jerry patted one of the horses and pulled the travois harness over her head and buckled the girth loosely.

"Do you know how to get to Houston?" asked Lelani.

"I don't have any maps," she said.

"Terrible!" said Jerry.

"Disorienting," chimed Moses.

Lelani clucked her tongue sympathetically.

"They went thataway," said White Time Girl, point roughly south. "Or was it thataway?" She wheeled and pointed west.

"Would you prefer a horse, a bike, or a car?" asked Jerry.

Dania thought about it. "Some kind of off-road bike, I guess. Maybe something solar. If you've got one. Purple with green stripes."

Jerry nodded. They solemnly and without further comment finished their preparations, which only took another minute or two. They all donned diaphanous white robes. Moses offered one to Dania. She pulled it over her head and said, surprised, "It's cool."

"Do you think we'd put on something *hot*?" asked Moses. "Come on, let's go."

They set off at a fast pace. The horses walked behind, snuffling and tossing their heads.

"Are we—are we going to Houston?" asked Dania.

"It's hard to tell," said White Time Girl, who walked beside her. "We're going in the right direction, though."

"Why is it hard to tell?"

"It just is," said White Time Girl. "You'll see."

Summertime

For the long hours of the morning, Dania concentrated on walking along the dirt road. Despite the heat, it was a pleasant day. A hot, damp breeze swept over them. The sky was an ever-changing panorama of cloud formations. They crossed the Interstate, but did not turn to follow it. Instead they continued to go straight.

After a few hours, Dania saw something in the distance. She

wished she had her cursed sunglasses. She squinted and held up her hand against the sun. A windmill, trees, and an old shack. As they got closer, she saw that it deserved to be called a house. But there was something strange about the trees.

The others struck slightly to the west, and Dania saw that it was in order to reach a gravelly ford, for there was a small sweet river hidden in a low fold of land. They splashed across, and turned toward the shack and the orchard.

A dog leaped from the porch, barking, and a thin woman followed. She waved with a broad gesture and shouted, "Hellooo! Jake! It's all right!" She hurried down the porch steps and approached them.

Dania stood staring at the orchard.

Among the branches, like Christmas ornaments, hung a weird assortment of objects. Tires, shoes, plates, even a gingham dress. Most branches were propped up with forked sticks, and each, she noted, held only a single type of object. She walked closer, reached up to touch a lightstick dangling amid a row of like objects—

"You pick it, you buy it," said the thin woman. "That's not ripe yet, anyhoo." She wore dark sunglasses and a necklace of silver squash blossoms, and held a cigarette stuck in a silver, turquoise-studded cigarette holder. Her silver hair was very short, and she was deeply tanned. "What are you hankerin' for?"

"Um, a bike . . ."

"Well, come on in and give me the specs. I've got plenty of fertilizer. Back there—you can't see it—I just happen to have a tree devoted completely to bikes. Big call for them out here. Name's Edna, by the way. These are my friends, too, so I'll be able to give you a good deal."

"Don't believe her," said Moses. "She drives a hard bargain."

Edna grinned again. As she took Dania's arm and steered her toward the house, Dania wondered what, exactly, a good deal might be. Maybe she should have held on to the sunglasses.

Four weathered rocking chairs sat on the porch of the old-fashioned Texas farmhouse. As she followed Edna up the stairs and into the front room, her companions were removing the horses' halters and hobbling them. The horses drank from the creek, and the rest of the crew trooped into the house.

"It's been a spell," said Edna. "Sit down."

Behind her, between the double windows and on both sides, an astonishing array of old framed black and white photos caught Dania's eye. Moses and White Time Girl pulled a bent metal circle which turned out to be a Chinese checkers board from beneath a chair and set up a game. Jerry and Lelani sank into chairs and grinned happily. Dania took a wooden rocking chair with ornate bent arms. The fan whirled slowly overhead. They chatted for a few minutes, and Dania realized that they were indeed old friends. A delicious smell slowly filled the house.

Then Edna clapped a hand to her forehead. "Forgot my manners! Iced tea?"

"Can I help?" asked Dania.

"Sure." Edna rose lithely, her brown legs thin and strong, her bare arms wiry and muscled.

The kitchen was floored with squares of white and green linoleum, just like Dania's grandmother's kitchen in Salvation. On the windowsill, between white curtains that blew inward on the breeze, sat five huge red tomatoes. Dania saw a shelf by the back door on which sat several beige McCoy mixing bowls of various sizes, straight from her childhood. They reinforced her feelings of being in a lovely, lucid dream. She felt deeply at home, as if she had been snapped into an empty space in a puzzle and was now a part of the whole.

Edna slipped her hands into two padded gloves decorated with bees, opened the oven door, and pulled out two apple pies done to a turn and set them on top of the oven. Then she switched off the oven. "Shouldn't of started baking in the morning. Too hot. But I had a feeling I'd have company. These are for dinner." She then opened an ancient-looking, rounded refrigerator that said CROSLEY on the front. A radio was imbedded in the door.

"Does that work?" asked Dania. A pang reminded her of Cowboy, a.k.a. Peabody. She reached into her skirt pocket. His tiny radio was still there.

"Sometimes, at night," Edna said, opening a cupboard and setting tall glasses on the counter. "Step out back and get some of that mint from under the porch."

The screen door slammed behind her.

Texas, hot and damp, stretched out before her. Sycamores shaded a picnic table. Lavender hydrangeas flanked the house's foundation.

Dania stood on the porch, caught in the cascade of memories that slamming door brought back: countless green summers in Salvation. The creek out back behind the corn field. She and her cousins, running barefoot through the rustling high cornrows, playing hide-and-seek, filling jars with lightning bugs, listening to the grown-ups talk on the porch at night while shooting stars slipped through the sky.

Dania went down three wooden steps. The mint was high and thick. She picked a few good stems, releasing a fresh, sharp smell.

Inside, Edna had set tall glasses filled with ice on a tray. "Brew a big pitcher every morning. Already sweetened. Hope you don't mind. Crush some of them leaves in the glasses."

Once they were settled in the living room again, sipping tea from glasses dripping with condensation, Edna said, "Now. What brings you here?"

"A bike," said Moses.

"Green with purple stripes," said Jerry.

"Solar," said Lelani.

"Heavy-duty." Dania was determined to have a say.

"Ah," said Edna. "All right. I know just the tree. Got a likely bike there just about grown. It'll take at least fifteen hours or so to modify it. Tomorrow morning, say."

"That's fine," said Dania.

"Now," she said, narrowing her eyes. "The taps on the bathtub are leaking. Think they just need tightenin', but if not there's replacements out back."

"Got it," said Jerry. He went out to the travois. Dania saw him rummaging around and then he came back inside carrying a black toolbox. He turned down a hallway and she heard sounds of clanking tools. "Where's the shutoff again?" he shouted.

"I'll get it," yelled Edna. She jumped up and went outside for a moment. There was a faint sound of screeching metal. "It's off," she yelled in the window.

"It's off," relayed Moses. "Let's go swimming," he said to White Time Girl.

White Time Girl jumped up, but Edna met her in the doorway. "Not so fast," she said. "Plumbing only pays part way."

White Time Girl grinned. She opened a pouch on her belt. Edna tried to peer in. "Keep out, now. This is secret." Finally she pulled out one squash blossom earring, then another. "How's that?"

"Well," said Edna doubtfully, but her face gave her away.

"You know that's just what you've been wanting," said White Time Girl. She buttoned the pouch. Then she and Moses ran out the door and trampled loudly down the wooden steps and ran toward the creek. Dania went to the door and yelled, "Thank you." She saw them both yank off their clothes and start wading. Then White Time Girl splashed chest first into the creek and kicked hard, soaking Moses.

Edna sat down on the couch and smiled fondly at the earrings she held in her palm. "They'll do."

Dania turned, trying to keep her mouth shut, but curiosity got the better of her. "If you have all those trees—"

"Why would I want these earrings? They're handmade. I can feel the difference. They're made of silver that someone mined out of the ground. Now, it's true that I can fertilize a tree properly and it could grow these for me. But it's different somehow." She shrugged her thin shoulders and removed her other earrings and tilted her head first one way and then another while she inserted the squash blossoms through the holes in her earlobes.

"How do you—" began Dania.

"Oh, come on out, I'll show you. Best get the bike started anyhow."

Dania followed Edna down the rickety steps and out into the orchard.

Bees hummed around them, feasting on windfall apples. And windfall pears, Dania saw, stepping carefully around them. Despite Edna's boast of growing everything on trees, they passed a thoroughly traditional garden where tomatoes sagged from staked vines, and various melons nestled beneath green leaves, and the zucchinis appeared to have gotten way out of hand. Edna waved one hand at it. "Can't keep up with it," she said. "Land of milk and honey."

They passed into the orchard of things.

"How do you decide what to grow?" asked Dania, passing a tree where screws and nuts and bolts caught the sunlight as if celebrating Christmas. On the same tree dangled a few vise grips, pliers, and screwdrivers.

"I've been doing this for . . . quite a while. I know my customers. Mostly I trade for fuel, like natural gas or oil or propane. I'm set up to use most any kind of fuel you could imagine for cooking and heating. Of course, solar and wind gets most jobs done, but I like to have backups. The house has been in my family for generations. I know that I should replace it with something better, but I'm attached to the old wreck."

They passed another few rows and came to the bike tree.

Edna pointed things out to her. "See here? This bud will grow a red tricycle. You can see that this green one here is a racing bike. But you want one that's heavy-duty."

"Correct."

Edna looked around and suddenly headed off past a few trees. She returned with a battered metal stool about a foot high. She set it down next to the tree, settled herself, and patted the trunk three times. Some pedals, which hung on vinelike filaments, clattered together as the wind gusted, making a dry sound.

Some kind of protein rope, thought Dania, through which needed elements flowed. She recognized a half-formed headlight, its lens a clear protein somewhat like fish scales. A canopy of leaves grew on the uppermost branches, gathering sunlight.

All of these wonders had been developed in nanotech's heyday. Dania had never seen such an orchard, but it certainly made sense. Some Johnny Appleseed of nanotech had no doubt wandered through the region, selling his nanotech seeds rather than scattering them wholesale, convincing people with an extraordinary gift of gab that the outlandish thing would work.

Of course, Dania thought, watching Edna, you had to have brains to make it work.

A screen gradually coalesced where Edna had patted the trunk. Edna touched it swiftly here and there and motioned Dania toward it. Dania bent over Edna's shoulder. She saw five bikes on the screen and pointed to the most hefty.

Edna enlarged that view. "Color?" she asked.

"Purple with green stripes."

Edna nodded once again. In a minute, a chart of chemicals appeared. Edna reached over to the screen and peeled off an upper layer and walked off.

"Can I help?" asked Dania. She hurried after Edna.

They came to a gigantic, sagging wooden barn and stepped inside its huge maw. One side of it was lined with battered file cabinets, olive green and gray. Maybe fifty of them. Edna studied the chart, which glowed in the dim light. She set it on top of a file cabinet and wrenched the middle door open, cursing when it stuck. It was full of shrink-wrapped pouches. "Two of these," she muttered, holding them up so that she could read the labels and tossing them into a wheelbarrow she pulled out of a corner. Then she went to another cabinet farther down the row.

After about ten minutes, she examined the list again, then nodded. "That's it." She lifted up the wheelbarrow and they hiked back out to the tree, the packets of chemicals bouncing as the wheelbarrow bumped over roots. Dania noticed that everyone except Jerry, who was probably still inside working on the taps, had left their clothes on the bank and was swimming in the creek.

Edna twisted open a metal plug just above ground next to the tree, nestled between some roots. She pulled a pair of gloves from the back pocket of her shorts and started unwrapping the pouches and tossing the bricks of chemicals into the hole. They sounded a muffled *chunk* as they hit the bottom. "Pull up on that pump handle there—to your left. That's it. Opens the valve."

Water flowed into the hole. Dania noticed that each tree had its own pump handle. "How much do you need?"

Edna gestured toward the screen, which showed an icon of a tank, a fill line, and a line indicating water level. The two lines drew close together, then matched. "Turn it off."

Edna put a long shovel into the hole and mushed the stuff together. "Damned thing's supposed to be self-repairing," she grunted. "But the mixer's broken."

"Want me to do that?"

"Knock yourself out." Edna handed Dania the shovel and sat down on the stool. She gestured out toward the end of the orchard. "Got some new trees started. Well, they're not new. About five years old. They'll be ready for grafting pretty soon. Tank's a part of it; the roots grow into it. I dig the hole and line it with some chicken-wire-like stuff that I grow over there." She waved her hand vaguely over her shoulder. "Think this one took sick or something. Sometimes they need medicines that I don't have. Usually I can cook up whatever they need, but sometimes it's just too exotic. I live in fear of some new disease. The tree's still fine, so I don't think it's spreading. That oughta do it."

Dania set the shovel in the wheelbarrow. Edna replaced the cap of the tank. She grinned. "It's work. Nothing's free. Come on, let's have a swim."

The creek was a wonderful treat. Dania pried off her boots and left them on the shore. She wore her clothes in and removed them gradually, scrubbing her blouse, her skirt, her underwear as the water parted around her. Watercress grew on the banks and the bottom of the creek was rounded river rocks, smooth and cool beneath her feet. She staggered to the bank with her armload of wet clothes and lay them on the grass, hoping that the horses wouldn't step on them. Then she reentered the creek, lay back, and let the blessed coolness sweep through her hair. As she stared at the clouds, she snagged her foot onto a root so that she wouldn't go anywhere, and suddenly thought of Crescent City.

Crescent City in the hands of pirates.

It was strange. She hadn't thought much about Crescent City, her home of so many years, since she had been out here. The raving strangeness that had seized her in the city had taken weeks to die down.

But now it was fully gone. She felt relieved, as if she had been pounded by a severe headache for a very long time and it was now gone, leaving her weak. Something in her, she realized, had been desperately homesick for the rest of the world. For orchards, however strange, on firm land. For this little farm in the middle of nowhere. For plain old people.

Yeah, she thought, regaining her footing and wringing out her hair. Plain old folks who live in the Nows, where Romeo and Juliet adequately reflect some new view of space-time when superimposed on the relationship of several other lovers. It was great to be out here, where a thing made of light could slap her smack flat on her back and turn her mind into a mush of stampeding buffalo.

She made her way unsteadily to the bank and climbed out. Her clothes were still damp. The air here was not thirsty. She dressed, picked up her boots and socks, and made her way toward the house.

As she walked, she thought of Radio Cowboy, and hoped that he was all right.

That evening Edna put on a feast of corn on the cob, barbecued tofu, homemade bread, and apple pie. They ate out back on a picnic table. Edna brought out some dusty bottles of rich red wine, and White Time Girl asked what tree it grew on and drank her share. No one said a word, and the girl did not act the least bit drunk. Mosquitos were kept away by a candle embedded with mosquito-repellent pheromones. The trees rustled in the cool night air. They all helped with the dishes. Edna showed her a narrow white bed in an upstairs room and advised her that it would cool off presently if she would leave the door open.

Dania slept deeply. When she woke in the morning and looked out the window, the horses were gone. She made her way down the stairs.

Edna sat at the kitchen table, a snake of cigarette smoke wafting toward the overhead fan. "Left sometime in the night," she said, getting up and pouring Dania a cup of coffee. "That's their way. Sit down and have some of this coffee cake. Bike ought to be ready about now. Let's take a look."

Dania felt a pang. "They left without me?"

"You get the picture, honey."

Dania drank some hot coffee and after a few minutes felt better. After all, she'd only known them for a day. Or was it only a day?

Barefoot ("Look out for snakes," warned Edna) and wearing the white nightgown Edna had given her, Dania followed Edna out through the orchard.

The purple bike dangled like a Christmas present from the branches of the bike tree.

"Hold it while I cut it down," said Edna. She pulled a switchblade from her back pocket and flicked it open with her thumb. The bike hardly weighed a thing. After a few minutes of hacking, it came free. Dania lowered it carefully to the ground. "It's beautiful!" she said.

Edna much less reverently bounced it up and down a few times. "You'll notice there's no air valves. The tires suck in air through a membrane, but it's a one-way process. Little one-way gates." She bent over it, a cigarette hanging from her lip, and carved off the nubs where the bike had hung from the tree. "That will be hard and smooth as metal in about fifteen minutes, but it's really protein."

"I know," said Dania. "It's marvelous."

"You one of them?" Edna asked suddenly, looking up and staring into Dania's eyes.

"What?"

"One of them. That lives in the Nows."

"I . . . I don't know," Dania said, although another reply tickled the back of her mind.

"You'd know," said Edna. "Ride this thing back to the house and see if it suits you. It's fully adjustable."

Dania bumped back to the house and glided with joy around the barn. She stopped and got off and examined her new bicycle.

Behind the seat, built into the panniers, was a white canopy that unfolded over the bike and snapped down over the front. It had a window that receded into its edges if tapped.

"That's the solar collector," said Edna, coming up behind her. "You can clear it if you want, or make it permeable. Whatever. You can change it to more screeny stuff so's it won't slow you down. You'll need a helmet. I've got a little wagon you can hook onto the back for water and supplies. If you like. It's up to you. But if you're heading to Houston, I say be prepared."

"What's Houston like?" asked Dania as they walked back to the house.

"Type four Flower City."

"How has it mutated?"

"To tell you the truth, girlie, I don't want to know. I'm not up to date. Haven't been there in years."

"I'm going to the Space Center," Dania said.

"Hmm." Edna lit another cigarette and sat on the front porch steps. "That's different. Runs on its own I heard. Threw out all the people because they got in its way." She looked up and grinned at Dania. "Maybe you can outsmart it, though."

"Can you give me directions?"

"I . . . well, no." She frowned slightly. "East. East is all I know."

She gave Dania an extra shirt. "I can't pay you," Dania said.

"Hell, I don't need anything," she growled. "Just people. Come back sometime, hear? Oh wait! Almost forgot." She ran up the front steps of the house. The screen door slammed behind her. She was out in a minute, holding a cream-colored cowgirl hat and a soft, gold, buttery-leather backpack, a small one. "Here you go," Edna said, breathing a bit hard. "Fresh-picked this morning. They paid for them. Presents for you."

Dania took her gifts, touched. The hat was stiff felt and had a band of tiny turquoise-colored beads in which were woven a pattern of yellow and pink roses, and one bald eagle.

"It's beautiful." She put it on. "Fits perfectly."

" 'Course it does."

Dania belted the backpack to the bike, hugged Edna briefly,

then hopped on one pedal and swung her leg over the bike. She rode a few feet, shifted gears experimentally, turned and waved once, and rode down the long dirt driveway between high black-eyed susans nodding in the breeze. The sky overhead was as blue as delphiniums. The dog followed her for half a mile, then turned and loped back toward the now-small white frame house backed by the orchard that grew bikes.

Dania turned east on the main road.

March 2115

ANGELINA: THE LABYRINTH

"Thanks to art, instead of seeing a single world, our own, we see it multiply until we have before us as many worlds as there are original artists."

—Marcel Proust

"Art is a lie which tells the truth."

—Picasso

When Angelina next opened her eyes, she was beneath a high fan that whirled slowly. The white ceiling was quite distant—so distant that she brought her eyes down to the side of the room, where twenty-foot-high windows paced the wall regularly. Yet they too—their edges, and the view they gave onto, one of fat green trees—were also blurry. It was as if something was in her eyes.

She blinked and rubbed them. Instantly a nurse was at her side.

"You're awake." There was relief in his voice.

"Yes." She continued to look around. "Where am I?"

"In the hospital."

She struggled to sit up but he held her shoulders. "Oh no,

Señora. Please be still. You have severe injuries. It will take at least a week for you to heal."

"Am I on some type of pain medication?"

"Correct. You fell off your balcony. Luckily, there was another below it. You suffered a concussion, a broken spleen, a broken hip, and a broken shoulder. The room below was empty, so it wasn't until the next morning that you were discovered."

"Chester!" she said. "My—my doll—"

"Your doll?"

"Yes. He was there with me."

The nurse looked puzzled. "All of your possessions have of course been saved. They are in this trunk."

"Please look!" His face too was blurry. Its colors and contours suddenly reminded her of Australia seen from space. The literature of Australia . . .

The nurse dutifully knelt out of her field of vision. She heard him fling up the lid of a trunk. The hinges creaked. "I am sorry. There is no doll. Just a pack, and some clothing."

"Look in the pack!" she demanded.

"No. Nothing resembling a doll. How big was it?"

"Oh—the size of a month-old baby, I suppose."

"Quite large for a doll."

"I suppose." She felt unreasonably devastated. She had lived without Chester her entire life. Surely she could do without a sentient doll.

But she worried about him. What had happened to him? Had he been destroyed? He was so helpless. Perhaps some unfeeling adult had thrown him in the garbage. Or worse—destroyed him! Tossed him into a fire. She should never have gotten off the train. She was terribly selfish. He liked the train. She ought to have at least left him there—

"Please—Senora—stop crying now. You are shaking. You will undo the healing. Here—I am giving you a sedative now."

"Where is the doctor!"

His voice was puzzled. "Oh—doctor. Yes. That would be the diagnostic system. It is down the hall. It is not your turn to have it again yet. It is busy creating antibodies for a new fever. Your case is rather simple. A few fractures. Your spleen is almost better now. We are certainly not the big city. But the train brings excellent medical supplies. I myself trained in Barcelona—"

Against her will, she began breathing deeply and regularly. But despite the sedative, her dreams were restless and disturbing. They were of the Eiffel Tower, and then she was in a garden, hedged high next to the path which forked.

She ran down first one path, then another, calling out for Manuel. For Louis.

For Chester. "Of course you are alive, you fool!" she yelled. "Please, please, come back!" And she ran through the landscapes. The crowded apartment of James Joyce, where he scribbled on despite a melee of children and constant guests, near-blind, awash in vision. No one noticed her. And it was like that forever. Rooms, roads, faces, emotions intersecting and moving humans to actions that would seem utterly puzzling to any being who did not know of their secret lives, the inner lives that writers portrayed. Paris itself was a constellation of images. The experimental sentences of Stein, stuttering on the edge of a new vision, the intimate, compact, forthright images of Hemingway, the depressed recoiling and deeply shattered vision of Europeans and Americans following the disillusionment of the Great War.

Although she was bathed in light and images when she next opened her eyes, they were not the images of her surroundings. They varied, but this time in a stately cadence. Gardens, cafés, populated by humans whose histories she knew only through the glance of their author, but whose histories nevertheless seemed round and complete, filled in by her own mind until they lived as completely—perhaps even more completely—than the people she actually knew. This richness of vision contained branching paths which offered her the choice of exploring authors' stylistic sources, or literary friendships. She did not know how much time passed during this time, when she developed the ability to explore this new universe of the recorded essence of humanity, and only barely realized that her own life was receding until it was only one point among a million equally important points. There was terrible brightness, and terrible loss, until only a thread of herself remained to go forward into whatever was to be.

Finally she woke. Her vision was no longer blurry.

In fact, it was completely gone. All she saw was a white field.

She screamed.

She heard footsteps running to her bedside.

"What is it?" A young man's voice. The nurse.

"I can't see!"

"The medication—"

"No! I can't see anything!"

She waited in silence. She felt on her face a very slight breeze, so slight that it might have been imagined. Then he said, "You see nothing?"

"No."

During that day, they did tests. At first, when she was guided into a wheelchair by a woman grasping her upper arm, she started as she saw blond braided hair, kind blue eyes, a blurry background—

"I can see!" She reached up to touch a braid and caught air.

It was very unsettling.

"You can see?" The woman asked, and her image changed to short-cropped brown hair. Angelina followed this vision to a small kitchen overlooking the plain, and a little girl wearing overalls who asked for a snack—

She sighed. "No."

She heard the nurse's voice at the end of these tests, gently telling her that there was no physical problem that they could detect.

"It appears to be completely psychological," the nurse said, a touch of disbelief in his voice. "We need to do further evaluations to determine the best form of treatment."

"Just fix it!"

"I'm sorry. It doesn't exist."

Angelina was wheeled down the corridor once again. Sounds from open doors blossomed then vanished as she passed them. She lay in her bed for hours, unable to sleep, wondering what to do.

She woke up knowing. "Take me to the train," Angelina told the nurse. "I need to go to Paris." She could waste no more time here. Her prosaic vision was gone. It was replaced with some sort of poetry, leaping from point to point, making connections that she did not as yet understand.

There was more room, now, for the visions created by the stories to manifest.

At first, they argued with her, but she was finally taken to the train in a wheelchair, though she insisted that she could walk. But no, too much walking would hinder the healing of her spleen and broken bones, which would be further facilitated by the train.

During her passage through the street, she was assailed by the simple losses of books of childhood, books with talking animals; *Heidi;* untranslated German and French books which were, like the English books, streams of pictures and emotion, and by the time the doors slid open and she was welcomed by the conductor, she was deep within books of war.

She was astounded to recognize the voice of the conductor as he welcomed her.

"Of course we waited. We take needful passengers to Paris. That is all that we do. We can run for six months at a time before another needful passenger finds his way to us."

"What do you mean, 'needful'?"

"Paris—is needful of you. You are needful of Paris."

It was as if she were hearing another kind of music now. A joyful medieval procession, thick with klugalhorns and bells.

"Is there anyone in particular who is needful of me in Paris?"

The man tilted the somewhat blank face that suddenly manifested for Angelina, as if listening. Finally he said, "No. Just Paris."

The music faded. Not Louis. Not Manuel. Not even Chester, so interesting and funny and dear. Just a city.

"But what about the other passengers?"

"What other passengers?"

"But I saw—" Then she was silent. She had seen people who

glowed. She had seen people whom Chester claimed knew what she was thinking. If they were people, they were like no other people she had known. Perhaps they were in no hurry.

The train ride began.

She experienced ceaseless images of war; not a foot of land existed that had known unending peace once humans took possession. Angelina had always thought of herself as relatively unemotional, but after only a few hours her eyes were sore from weeping and she called for sedatives. It was too much to bear. No one learned; the impulse of self ran far too deeply to ever change.

And if this impulse was transferred to a larger group, to the family, to the nation, to the religion, the result was the same: inevitable conflict, which only loss and complete destruction of home and family and nation could quell. The land on which one dwelt became holy and the property of your group for past and future eternities. She was suffocated beneath landslides of hardened positions.

She gave up her ranch gratefully, let it go in a flash of two bright centuries, but wondered if humans, in general, could even conceive of letting go of this double-edged sword, this curse of needing to own, which fed them, but which also killed them.

Perhaps only a world of endless nurturing could do this. With relief she turned to utopias, the England in which an unarmed woman could walk freely from end to end without fear, places in which all the inhabitants shared reverence for life.

But what of the misfits? What of, for instance, Socrates? What of those whose new understanding of life or of matter rendered the past understanding obsolete, a stiff mirror to be shattered?

"Hello." The voice at her elbow spoke in French. Angelina's onboard translator leaped to catch it, but there was a disconcerting lag. She was surprised that she had one and decided that it must have been installed without her permission in the hospital.

"Is it possible for you to speak Spanish?" she asked.

"Of course." Her voice was sympathetic. "We are at the Paris station now and I will help you off the train."

"Thank you. But who sent you?"

The voice was puzzled as Angelina was maneuvered into the aisle. "Paris, of course. You are choosing not to see; so the train has taken the liberty of manufacturing this cane for you. It will help translate your physical environment for you. However, everything will be filtered through the reorienting virus you have contracted. Since you refuse intervention, this is the best we can do." Into Angelina's right hand she thrust a thin curved cylinder. Angelina grasped it and moved her hand.

"Ow! Please, madam! You smacked my legs. There. Just set the bottom down on the floor." Angelina felt the cane being moved. Vision wavered, then solidified.

She was on a train that seemed, curiously, old-fashioned and at the same time sleekly modern.

The seat fabric was bluish-gray linen, clean and crisp. The top of each seat was covered with a white kerchief with a green logo emblazoned in its center.

"I can see now," Angelina said. "That woman"—she pointed with her left hand while passengers pushed from behind—"she is collecting trays with individual silver coffeepots on them."

"No, madam," said the woman's voice. "No one is collecting trays."

Angelina turned to look at her, but instead of the woman who was presumably speaking saw a male porter wearing a round hat, smiling, reaching up over the seat for her valise.

A white mist swirled around Angelina then, obliterating vision. Her heart pounded in terror. "What am I going to do?" Not that she expected the woman to answer.

But she did. "Learn. Come now. In about ten feet we will turn right. That's it. There is a bar to your left—please grab it—that's right. Now there will be four steps, rather steep. Good. Sorry, I didn't even think to grow a ramp. Have a nice stay in Paris, madam."

The vast station echoed with shuffling feet and announcements and close, excited talk and greetings.

"Where are we going now?"

But there was no answer.

Angelina stood still in the sea of information. She realized that the woman had been a manifestation of the train.

Perhaps it was best to get back on the train. Here, she was completely helpless and in danger from the most mundane possibilities. She turned, only to hear a *whoosh* that signified to her that the train was leaving, and a torrent of French as someone pulled her back. Then she was once again left alone.

She leaned on the cane. The mist coalesced once again into vision.

Yes, the station was large. But perhaps it was navigable using the only tools she had now: literature. And this cane.

She set one foot ahead of the other, and then did it again, moving parallel to the track as she saw it, along with a stream of passengers dressed in a mixture of modern and Victorian garb. She realized that she was stooping, and straightened, stepping as boldly as possible, heading toward the vast windows, passing appetizing smells and wondering if indeed there were vendors by small fires cooking pancakes—*crêpes*—or if she was in some kind of digitized food court. Vision flowed in through the cane, drawn from the city itself, and stabilized within her, but she did not see what was around her. She did not see what Angelina would have seen.

Instead she first saw the station as seen by Hemingway—sharpened by anger at returning without his manuscripts, and then by Joyce, a blurry fusion of color, or Zola, or Eiffel, or La Maga. She was behind a large woman wearing black, holding the arm of a thin woman, and the thin woman was speaking to Gertrude in English, asking her about her lecture tour of America. Her program served up the necessary information: Gertrude Stein and Alice B. Toklas.

She stopped, and simply stared. She saw a multitude of stations, each as different as if it had been painted first by Picasso, then by Matisse, and then by Monet.

The consciousness of each individual saw the world differently. This place, like so many places in Paris, had been documented extensively. The stories of Paris whirled about her, engulfed her.

She would have to learn to control this facility anew, to give it forth, to access it when she wanted and push it back when necessary. She began walking again, slowly, overwhelmed by people she had not even known existed before she had swallowed *Hopscotch* in her mountain prison. Worlds she had not known of. Manuel had been right.

Manuel! She stopped once again, and the person behind her ran into her, exclaimed, and then passed. How was she to find anyone, anything? It was going to be very hard. And Chester was gone.

She missed him. More than she would have believed possible.

Everyone and everything was gone, save for this accursed rain of unreal literature and its crazed creators. Now she had no choice. It had gradually taken over her entire life, filled her brain with misinformation, and left her stranded in a foreign city on a continent far from home.

The world of vision stopped and started for her with terrifying irregularity. She touched her way through turnstiles, tapping her cane on the pavement. She held in memory the last connection and returned to the frequency of whiteness which stuttered through her vision as a relief from the disconnected pictures she received.

One step, one tap of the cane, showed a street in the sixteenth century, narrow and crabbed, and she would have to dodge to avoid the slops being dashed to the slippery cobblestones.

In the next step, a tiny Citroën rushed toward her and she stepped back into a doorway, which swung inward.

She stumbled backward, trembling, into a millenary shop, with rainbows of satin of varying widths hung next to scissors swinging on strings. In the next second she was in a bookstore.

She was exhausted, and she had been in Paris less than an hour. Despite the calm she tried so desperately to reach, her heart began to pound. What if she fell into an open basement door, or onto a hot stove? She stood still, waiting for the next instant to reveal itself. Perhaps if she just stood in the same spot, the ages would settle, or she could sort them.

She reached out, and touched someone's hand. The hand grasped hers.

"Here," said a voice which sounded to Angelina to not be generated as most voices were. She grasped the hand and wished herself back on the pampas. This reminded her too sharply of her younger years, when she was so different from other children, and plagued by headaches which nothing could assuage. I am The Storyteller, she thought; I am The Storyteller, but she could not get the words out. She allowed herself to be maneuvered into a chair.

"Some red wine, please," ordered the voice, and to Angelina's astonishment mentioned her favorite vintage, Chilean, twenty years old. "And a steak, please, and bread." A plate was delivered within the minute.

Angelina looked down and said, "These are oysters," and began to feel hysterical. A thin woman sat across from her, a woman with very long black hair, a long nose, and high, arched, heavy eyebrows.

"Try one," suggested the woman. "You are in Montparnesse and I suspect that it is Hemingway's world that you are seeing. He is so terribly ubiquitous; he overrides so many more subtle frequencies, such as Proust's."

Though Angelina opened and closed her eyes several times, the woman remained the same, and she continued to sit at a chair at a table, though she almost always saw oysters and once something that resembled grilled rabbit. Nevertheless, her right hand found a fork and picked it up and speared one of the oysters which, when she put it in her mouth, was indeed an excellent cut of steak. And the wine was the red ordered. And the woman?

"My name is Illian," said the woman. She was not eating. Her arms were folded on the table.

"Thank you for lunch. I think that next I will need a place to stay. A place that remains the same. A place I can easily memorize."

"Perhaps, for now, that would be best. You are lucky to be alive. The *Hopscotch* program has killed several people in Paris and who knows how many other people outside of Paris. Probably not many, though, because how would it get out of here?" Her voice held a question.

"My husband sent it to me. Manuel Samazir." She thought of Louis, and was desolate. But she did not want to speak of such a personal thing with this woman. "How do you know of this . . . program?" She could finally empathize with her gauchos. She was changed almost beyond recognition by the tiny machines they prayed God to spare them from.

The woman threw back her head and laughed. "I know a good many things, Angelina. I am nothing but a constant stream of information." She tilted her head and looked at Angelina seriously. "It is possible for you to learn quite a bit here. More than in just about any other place in the world except one. I'm not sure what you will learn. I do know that no one else can learn these things for you. Learning reconfigures the brain, opens new connections. This is a lonely journey, but one which every human must make for himself. I don't know what you will do. I don't know what the result will be. But I hope that you can help us. I hope that you will *want* to help us. Though I don't know what possible use you might be."

"What do you mean, help you? Who are 'you'?" Angelina asked, irritated.

But Illian was gone. Angelina now sat at a plain deal table and all of the tin plates were empty. People huddled over their tables, worn, dingy clothing heaped upon them so that they looked like rag dolls. The men all had heavy beards; the women had long, greasy hair.

There was too much time, that was all. Too damned much time, and she kept experiencing it all Now.

But she couldn't stop it.

All right, then. She tried to put a name to the scene, an author, as if naming it would somehow isolate it, make it exterior to her, catalogue it, put it under her control. But she could not. And then the scene morphed to a few such folk sitting around a single table. Van Gogh. *The Potato Eaters.*

"God!" She pounded her fist on the table. Weren't the books, the stories, bad enough? Was she now to be afflicted with art? She stood up straight and turned right, toward a narrow stairway, sure there was a room for her upstairs. Of course, in such a place, there would be a room for her upstairs.

And there was.

She fell asleep in the tiny bedroom of Zola; awoke in the fairy-tale bedroom of Audrey Hepburn in any number of movies, and breakfasted like Paul Bowles when he was a guest of Gertrude Stein and Alice B. Toklas, in a garden courtyard. She lived within a small parameter for weeks, knowing where the water closet was and seeing the ever-changing faces and costumes of servants who brought her food and helped her dress. She forgot about Manuel and Louise and Chester and her own sense of being, her own life. It was all intoxicating and irresistible, a great river of images. Time assumed a human face and her own old sense of the pampas, of the land as a being, faded, but reawakened at times when she stood near a window and, looking out, saw the Downs of England, or Thomas Wolfe's New York, or the Petersburg of Prince Andréi.

Every principality in the world, she realized, seethed with stories. There would never be any escape for her. Chinese stories, Balinese stories, Vietnamese stories. And where there had never been people, people had finally come and made stories about what was there. Darwin had made a spectacularly successful story about the creatures on the Galápagos, and then all of life. Eiffel had made stories in curved steel, with beautiful bridges, and a Tower. Madam Curie had discerned the stories of subatomic particles.

When she begin to feel more comfortable, she walked through the streets and her cane sucked stories from the pavement. Stories of a resistance during a war two hundred years ago. Stories of triumph and liberation. The story of a particular person would cause her to weep, another to laugh with delight. Anyone watching her would think her demented. Completely insane.

But finally something within her began to order them. She could take an avenue through time, down deep leafy British lanes. She could wake to sunlight and know that she could live a hundred years in the tropics, or wake to rain, and look back on yesterday's storm through which she had walked on the moors. She was becoming attuned to the frequency of stories. She resonated with them. She could emit them, through her receptors, and embed them in media, unburdening herself. A bit of the pressure was lost in this fashion. She hoped someday to be clear of the stories, to return to the soothing white place, but eventually realized that even that place was charged with potential. In that place, the stories were simply moving with such speed that she could not access them.

The stories of emotion began to blend with the stories of science. The stories of science were stories that kept making sense as one built on them, test after test. They explained reality reliably.

And one of the stories she learned was the story of the curled-up dimensions. Realities which might never be. But dimensions which were ineffably part of physical reality, a necessary and supporting part. A place of doorways, and portals, much as her own human mind seemed to be.

And she realized that human stories were the rolled-up dimensions. A part of the interconnected dance of energy levels comprised of what the cosmos had evolved thus far. Consciousness was firmly embedded in the fabric of space and time, a material part of its vibrational energy. Consciousness, or mind, was not split off from matter, hovering outside it, as Newtonian reasoning would have it. Instead, consciousness was within matter, of matter. It was matter looking at itself and being astonished. It was the point seeing the wave, or the wave seeing the point. Consciousness was quantum electrodynamism. Time turned back upon itself. Time splintering. Time strutting loose among the energy levels, only slightly stilled, slightly caught, in that glance called consciousness, the observer, the energy that made it into *this* and *not-this,* live cat and dead cat.

Only emotion could want to create the stories of science. The emotion of intense curiosity about the natural world. And the story she was just beginning to meld had some deep implication which she did not yet understand.

Save that she was a bridge. She was a burning spot of light. There was only one place where she could unburden herself. One place where her frequency would transmit. One place where her stories might be of use, and where she might finally rest.

Crescent City. But she was not ready to go there yet. Crescent City was just another story to her, a story overheard in cafés, or on the news, which she accessed through her hands before she fell asleep at night. It waited for her; waited for her readiness. She was not sure what her readiness might entail. She only knew, using her own internal metaphors, that she stood at the foot of a high mountain, and that she must develop the strength to climb it.

She had not chosen this path, nor had it, in particular, chosen her. But she was able to know the situation, to get her bearings, as she always had been able in the past to situate herself in space. This was just an added dimension.

Angelina learned to invoke different authors, different accounts, to enable her to move through Paris. Of most use, she found, were a cache of old guidebooks she found. By using those, she was able to travel to parts of the city which she felt might yield more literary treasure for her, more of the hypertexed map of literature which grew inside her mind.

She reveled in the scents of Paris. On smelling fresh bread, her mind was flooded with images among which she could pick and choose, and then follow that thread. Was she a peasant, new in the city, stealing bread? Was she part of an angry mob, demanding bread? Was she loading factory-made baguettes onto a truck for delivery?

Manuel had been right. The written word definitely freed her. She sometimes thought of seeking Manuel, but something held her back. The guilt, perhaps, of losing Louis.

Who was not anywhere in Paris that she could find.

She strolled along the left bank of the Seine, and stepped into evocative galleries which held the works of Cézanne, Picasso, Cassatt. She knew that the sky was filled with giant bees, and that the buildings around her were topped with flowers, and that the Eiffel Tower was a regenerative Hive, infusing Paris with the information her cane sucked from every surface, but she saw none of that and did not care.

She preferred to live in, and to see, the era she was finding most interesting, which started in the eighteen-eighties and which ended with the suicide of Virginia Woolf, who could not bear to go through another war.

She tried not to think about Chester.

April 2115

One morning, after a good spell of time, Angelina stepped into the gallery of Van Gogh's brother.

This was her project. Using literature, in this case Van Gogh's letters, she was re-creating for the sighted this particular historical milieu. She was adding to the city herself, feeding it visions, enhancing its depth.

There had been an interview with a Cultural Committee which wholeheartedly approved the plan after going over various engineering and resource considerations. Apparently, as the woman Illian had told her, she was one of the rare people who had found some measure of control over the *Hopscotch* program. Now she was testing.

This address had, of course, seen many uses over the centuries, yet Angelina was embedded with a pheromonal code which called forth the physical attributes which, until a few months earlier, she had seen only in her mind.

Inside, the air smelled of oil paintings. It might take years for them to fully dry, and until then the paintings gave off residue, in decreasing, infinitesimal quantities. But she could smell them. She wondered if she could become so sensitive that she could smell the photonic pattern through the residue given off by the different elements which comprised the colors of the oils.

She bought a Van Gogh, was the first to buy one from the grateful widow of Van Gogh's brother, and had it delivered to her flat.

She had settled her flat at last. After arduous weeks, she had become as used to the visions which flocked around her as she had been to her own large kitchen in Argentina. And, as she stepped out of the shop back into sunshine breaking through the moody clouds and the vision of a thousand writers merged to one via scent and precise location, she realized with satisfaction that she had settled *Paris*. Without sight, she had colonized the streets with alternate histories which could be accessed not only by her, which she did automatically, setting out weekly to map blank places, but by others who chose to do so. She was The Storyteller, the Cartologist of the Purely Emotional. Some previously unstimulated, hidden part of her had been awakened by the *Hopscotch* program, which had killed so many. It had only made her strong and sure.

It kept her mind off Louis. This was necessary. Otherwise she would fall into endless grief, amplified by ages of stories.

Manuel. Well. That was another matter. He was definitely off of her mind.

A month ago, she had entered a café and ordered coffee and a brioche. That morning all was white, since she was off the map, and she relaxed into the clank of silverware, the hiss of the espresso machine, the low chatter of diners, which assumed its own rhythms like the rhythms of morning bird calls outside of her open bedroom windows. After her breakfast, she would work on the maps. It was a peculiar mental process, but one which she finally felt she had mastered.

Then one voice stood out from the rest.

Manuel.

She would have risen and called out his name, except for what he was saying.

"Oh yes, I had a wife. In Argentina."

"Charmaine told me that." A woman's voice.

Manuel cleared his throat. It was one of his nervous tics. "Yes. Charmaine. I'm over her. Really, I am. The thing is, my wife and I were very different. She didn't understand me, didn't understand what I did, or what I wanted to do. Didn't understand literature at all."

Fair enough. That was absolutely true. Yet Angelina felt a deep pang of hurt. Had there been nothing positive about her, nothing laudable or good?

The woman wondered the same thing. "Surely, there was some reason you lived with her for so long?"

"Of course, I loved her." At least, Angelina thought, his voice was indignant. "And she loved me. Even though we were so different, that much was clear. But it all became habit, I suppose." He sighed. "I don't know. I can't conceive of returning."

Tears welled up in Angelina's eyes. The rides before dawn when they had risen from their bed after too little sleep, sweetly aching from hours of making love, saddled the horses, and gained the ridge over rocky trails while sunrise gave them the world at their feet. Watching the herd through shrouds of mist below. A million such moments. All habit, to him.

Her espresso was delivered, but she did not touch it. She strained to hear the woman's quieter voice.

"—any children?"

"Oh yes. Louis." Angelina relaxed, and smiled, to hear the pride in his voice. But then—"I imagine he's followed her ways. Probably turned into a gaucho, thinking of nothing but horses, cattle, and beer. It's a disappointment, in a way. I tried to give him some culture, but—"

She barely felt the scald of the espresso as it dashed onto her leg. She reached Manuel's table in two long strides, shoving aside a waitress (to judge from the sound of a crashing tray) and grabbing his jacket. She pulled him straight up out of his chair. She knew it was him because of his gasp. The woman exclaimed, "Oh!"

"Louis is dead, thanks to you!" she shouted, hoping she was staring at him but aware that she was probably ludicrously staring out the window. "I wish that he was doing something as mundane and useless and boring as making a living, but he isn't."

"Angelina?" There was disbelief in his voice. "Could this possibly be you? You don't look—"

"Oh yes. It's me. Don't worry, I'm not going to interfere in your new life."

"Well, I can see *that*." Manuel was instantly on his mettle, ready for battle. But then his voice became almost terror-stricken. "Louis can't be dead. How did it happen? Did he fall from a horse—or—"

"But I know her!" said the woman. "She's The Storyteller. She has a mapping project—"

"Shut up!" Manuel and Angelina snapped at the same time.

Manuel grabbed Angelina's hands tightly. "What happened?" he asked urgently.

"It was that book. That book you sent. *Hopscotch*. He ingested one of the patches and ran away to Buenos Aires."

"No doubt to stay with your rich aunt. What was her name? Clarissa."

"At first, yes. But he booked passage on a ship to follow you to Paris."

"But—how could you let him do that? He was what? Sixteen? When I sent the book?"

"Seventeen." She forced out a bitter laugh. "He blamed me for your leaving. I guess that he was right."

His hands tightened on hers. "I'm sorry," he said in a low voice. "I never would have said those things—what I was saying, just now—"

She loosened her hands and shoved them into her pockets. "Of course not." Hypocrite. She had come half a world to find this man? She had never seen this side of him. Of course, everything and all of them were different now. She had to admit that she never would have thought of coming here before her kidnapping, before *Hopscotch*, when she could still manage her world. She was in an entirely new story, thanks to Manuel. She wasn't sure if it was better, but it was indeed different.

"The thing that matters is that Louis is gone without a trace."

" 'Without a trace'?"

No, there had been traces. Chester's wild tale of the radio transmission. The thickened moonlight at the foot of her bed.

She could best Manuel at his own game now, she saw, and easily. She could aim at him a barrage of images and references from the literature of the world to give him a metaphorical idea of what had possibly happened to Louis. She could precisely shade the doubt she had, and the hope. She could give it to him in one huge bundle that would flatten him for weeks with the weight of sorting it out. And she could add a heaping measure of her hurt and indignation and disappointment.

But she had not come half a world for that.

She turned from him and tried to make her way back to her table. Maybe her cane was there. She could see nothing but whiteness now. But between the photons of light was pure, deep blackness. She dashed tears from her cheeks.

"Angie. Please." Manuel grabbed her arm and she shook it loose. "What's wrong with you?"

"I can't see."

"Why not?"

"I don't know."

He considered that for a few seconds. "That's hard to believe. You are in Paris now. We can find out what's wrong and fix it."

"Nothing's wrong. I don't want to fix it."

"Then how in the world can we find Louis? If you can't see? I'm telling you, anything can be fixed here. Anything. We have to find him. You say you believe he was heading to Paris?"

She stopped and took a deep breath. She ought to just tell him in plain Spanish.

"I think that he never made it out of Argentina. I think that he turned to light."

Manuel dropped her arm.

Angelina heard the woman say, "What was that? Luz? Light? She is crazy. She needs help. We need to help her," and she heard Manuel reply, "If she is crazy, she is also very tough. A tough, crazy woman. I know her, believe me. There's no way to help that. Come on. Let's go. I have to find my son. She's not going to be any help." She felt Manuel leaving. For the last time.

She shouted, "All right, then, *find* him!" in what she thought might be the general direction of Manuel as he made his escape,

He's right, she thought, as she felt around on the floor and then the waitress tapped her back and said, "Madam, your cane."

She accepted it and a bit of vision returned. Just floor, walls, great light from the window, but no details. "I'm sorry I made such a mess."

The waitress said, "It's not your fault. He is a pig."

Angelina sighed. "He isn't. He's right. I was not easy to get along with."

She dropped into her chair. She leaned back into it and lost herself in images of Louis, as a child, playing with his father in the sun of the courtyard, and tried not to weep.

All of this literature stuff, all of these stories, were nothing but the incessant calling of a flock of birds, devices to make humans feel grounded in space and time, reassuring signals, proof of the existence of the other: the mirror; the herd.

But that morning's incident had, at least, taken care of her desire to find her husband.

May 2115

The Metamorphosis

One morning while in an unmapped portion of Paris, as Angelina stepped off a curb, she heard a shout, the sound of running. She was tackled and fell to the ground beneath the weight of a man—she was certain it was a man—she could not see. Her face was smashed into the pavement.

"I'm sorry—forgive me." Someone took her arm and helped her to her feet. "Your face is abraded. Here. Let me take you to the block clinic." There were clinics on just about every block in Paris, places dedicated to healing, for easily accessed emergency care.

"It will be fine on its own," said Angelina.

The voice rushed on. "You were about to step into the path of a scooter. I don't think the beeper was on." Because vehicles were silent, high-frequency beepers were mandated by law. "At least let me wipe the blood away."

"*Chester?*" She stepped back, astonished, and once again teetered on the edge of the curb. He grabbed her arm and involuntarily she reached around his waist. It was firm, reassuring. She felt a rough jacket against the back of her hand and beneath just thin cloth over skin. "Chester?" For it had been his voice, or just the thread of his accent, or something, that reminded her of him. But she let go and retreated, this time careful to avoid the curb. "I'm sorry. And thank you. You just reminded me of someone I knew."

"Some*one*," the voice teased, "or some*thing*?" and she grabbed at him, got the edge of his coat, pulled him close, and hugged him hard.

"Don't make fun of me," she said, bursting into tears. "When I lost you, I was desolate. I imagined that you had been thrown into the garbage. And now—and now you're *real!*" She patted him all over, up and down his sides, touched his face. Then she stepped back.

"Yes," he said gravely, "and now I'm real." A gust of wind pushed against Angelina as she stood there, isolated, and filled with wonder at this.

"Like Pinocchio."

"Sort of." His voice was now grim. "I have been certainly been punished for wanting to be a real boy."

"But how? Why? You must tell me. How in the world do you happen to be here, anyway?"

"I've been following you," he confessed. "For months."

"Months! Now I feel like hitting you!" she exclaimed.

"Hitting is wrong," he said in a warning voice, and they both laughed. Still, she felt quite awkward, just standing there.

"What do you look like?" she asked finally.

"Oh, tall. With red hair. Pale skin. Freckles. Rather nondescript, actually. Imagine . . . no." He reached out and grasped her hands, put them on his shoulders. Quickly, he moved them up and down and she burst out laughing again.

"A shrug! Chester, I can't believe this! How did it happen?"

"We can't just stand out here. Right down the block is a small hotel. I imagine that there is a lobby we can sit in. Perhaps even a restaurant."

"Yes," she said. "Is my cane around here somewhere?"

"Let me see—yes, here it is." She heard his sharp intake of breath. "That is painful, Angelina. What's in that cane, anyway?"

"A current," she said as he pressed it hastily into her hand. The street became clear. "Yes, that way." They hurried up the street toward the sign.

"Oh," she said when they went in the door. "James Joyce stayed here. And Nora. And the children. Ah, I can do a lot of work here." She headed toward a low blue sofa and was about to sit down when Chester grabbed her hand again. "Here's a chair." He settled her into it. "You were about to sit on a table." She heard scootching sounds as he pulled another chair across the carpet.

"Here—wait." She heard him walk away. He returned in a moment with a cool wet cloth, which he pressed against her face. "That will help. I'm sitting right next to you."

"Hold my hand," she said, and he reached over and took her hand in his. "This is heavenly. But Chester, I am so astonished. So excited. I've been so distressed about you. You had no business following me around like that. You should have told me you were there."

"It was rude of me," he said. "But I have discovered that I am slightly shy."

"You! I don't believe it."

"I was getting oriented," he said. "I didn't know what kind of human I would turn out to be."

"What happened to you in Spain?"

He sighed. "The maid found me on the balcony after they took you to the hospital. I asked her how you would be and she put me in the lost and found bin and came back the next day and told me that you would probably be all right. And that if I belonged to you she would take me to you."

"But you didn't do that."

"No. I couldn't. You had been talking about leaving the train and going back to Argentina. I couldn't stand it. When I was on the train, I felt my most alive, most real. And I believed that if I could only make it to this wondrous city I would be made real. Made human. I wanted to go back to you. I did, with all my might. But had I done so, I would just have remained a doll."

"That's not true! I would have taken you—"

"No, Angelina," he said gently. "No. It's not that you were cruel. It's just that you thought of me as a doll. And you thought of me as *your* doll. As your property. Something to be owned and disposed of as you pleased."

"But I tried to—I listened to you—I—"

"It's all right. It's all right." But she heard the bitterness in his voice and she was flooded with guilt at the truth of what he was saying. She also felt immense compassion.

And something more.

She rose from her chair and stood in front of him, using his hand as a fulcrum to guide her, then leaned down and hugged him, pressed her cheek against his, kissed him on the mouth, briefly.

"Chester—"

But he grabbed her and pulled her into his lap and squeezed her with a hug. He kissed her once, tentatively, and she responded, surprised, amazed at this amazing day. In a moment, he stood and led her across a small stretch of carpet, past some sweet-smelling flowers.

She heard, distantly, him speaking to the clerk, heard the *clank* of the elevator as the scissored door, which she could see, was pulled to, felt the sensation of motion and then as the elevator rose they kissed again.

When they got to the room, they pulled off one another's clothing eagerly. He seemed to be everywhere around her, like a tornado, then he was suddenly inside of her and she was crying out. And crying. And he was caressing her face and she was touching his and laughing at his nose and his ears which she insisted stuck out and then they made love, and slept until the afternoon, and woke hungry, and ordered food, and made love again.

Finally they talked.

"The stories didn't bother me today," she said. "I'm glad. I wonder why."

"Maybe it's me," he said. "Maybe there are no stories in me. When you touch me, it's just blank, eh?"

She sat on the bed, her back propped on the headboard. "Maybe. I think that it takes time for them to build up. You said that you've been watching me for months. How long did this process take?"

"For me to become real?" He sat up and she felt him settle next to her, their shoulders touching. About two weeks. Once I got here. It started on the train."

"And the maid took you to the train?"

"Oh yes. I forgot. We were sidetracked. As it were. I'm surprised at myself, in fact. I've only had sex twice before today. Just to see what it was like."

"Did you like it?" she teased.

"Well," he said seriously, "the other times were interesting, but in a way just like learning any other physical activity."

"Like walking. Like talking. Like playing the piano."

"I guess it was a little different," he admitted.

"So you got on the train."

"I was deposited on the train. First I was with piles of luggage and I was afraid that I would just be tossed out again somewhere. But finally a porter picked me up and I told him about my problem. He was not a real person either, so he understood. He told me that I could seek asylum on the train; that's what he had done."

"Was he a doll, like you?"

"No. He had been created to be a servant. He had become human briefly, but decided he liked being a servant. He told me that thinking for himself was very unpleasant and that he preferred to be told what to do."

"You didn't have that problem."

"I was quite frankly astounded at him. But he took me back out to the passenger car and the German girl saw me again. She began playing with me. That was frightening."

"I thought you liked her."

"Of course I liked her. But she liked me too. As a doll. As you did. I became terrified that she would try to keep me as a doll. I didn't mention my plan to her. Or her parents. In fact, I was lying alone one night in an upper bunk where she had thrown me and I just started to talk to myself. I was so upset. It seemed that without a human facilitator I couldn't possibly get to a place where I could be made human. Then the bunk rolled up around me and I thought I was lost again. But instead, it was taking my essence from me. My personality. And creating a body for me. I was made to know that it was something the porter had done for me. Just another passenger request. I heard the little German girl screaming from far away, but even her parents couldn't get me out. I could feel them pulling at the cocoon. When I finally woke, I was naked, in Paris, and in this body, and beside me was—"

"Don't cry," she said, wiping his tears away.

"It was myself," he whispered. "Little Chester. So tiny and pitiful and dead."

"But not really."

"No, really. Something was lost there. Innocence, I guess."

"A lot was gained too."

He kissed her. "Most definitely."

Angelina was so used to the stuttering of vision that she paid attention to it only when she wanted to. But she desperately longed to see Chester.

"But why?" he asked a week after they had met. "I've told you how I look."

"Still, I do."

He was on his way to work, leaving their new flat, a place which they had found together. The first time he said that he had to go to work she was surprised. "Work! What in the world do you do?"

"As if I were completely inept!" he said with his usual irony. "In fact, I'm well equipped to do what I do."

"Which is?"

"Teach kindergarten."

* * *

They lived together, Angelina finding and organizing stories, Chester teaching the few children in Paris with élan and good grace. He was growing up as they were, Angelina thought, sitting one day in the classroom. They always greeted him with enthusiasm and love. She was happy for the first time in ages. It was lovely to have someone to lie with at night, in the somewhat medieval Paris in which they chose to spend their evenings, for the history of music Angelina was compiling, for the pure harmonies at Notre Dame. Soon she planned to move on to younger music.

But Chester was not happy. He had begun to pester her.

"Just a bit of it," he said at first in a chiding voice. "You are so selfish."

"I am not at all selfish. I am worried about you. I can bear all this information. I'm different."

"I don't see how anyone could be much more different than me," he retorted.

"There are links in Paris—"

"I don't want just those. I want you! A bit at a time. Through the same kind of link that allowed me into this body. I want to be fully human, Angelina. I'm trying, but it's too slow. It's for the children too; I would be a better teacher—"

"Don't give me that nonsense."

"It's for us."

"I'm completely happy."

"Because you're in charge. You're older than me. You know more. You *are* more."

"Chester—" She felt completely helpless. "I can't help knowing more. I can't help being older. What do you want me to do? Have amnesia?"

"I want you to share," he said stubbornly, sounding like a child.

"This isn't some toy. It's something that only people like myself could possibly entertain."

"Ah yes, that famous DNA. That signal-warped brain of yours that is so unique."

"It is unique. Unfortunately. Furthermore, I've gone through different stages of growth than regular humans, and my corpus callusom is larger than most—" She had only truly learned this since arriving in Paris. Such information was not at large in the world.

"But Angelina, I need to grow too. Desperately. There are more thresholds I must cross. More doors I have to open. You keep forgetting that I used to be a doll, Angelina. A *doll.* I've already changed quite a bit, in case you haven't noticed."

"I've noticed, Chester," she said drily. "But this is different."

"It's not different." He put on his coat and she heard the door slam.

He returned a few hours later. The only thing he said was "It's late and I'm tired."

They went to bed without much discussion. She threw an arm around him, but he shrugged it off.

"I don't feel well."

"Sure you're not just pouting?" She touched his forehead. "You are a bit feverish. Let me get you some—"

"I'm fine," he said shortly. "There's nothing you can do. Go to sleep."

"All right, then," she said, and without much reflection on the matter, she did.

Angelina woke suddenly, her heart pounding, as if she had heard a loud sound. But instead, it was light.

"Louis!" she screamed, and rose from the covers. She jumped from the bed and sprinted toward the light, but tripped over a stool and sprawled on the floor. The light vanished. Chester was at her side.

"It was Louis." She was trembling.

"I saw."

"That's impossible," she snapped.

"Because you're so different?" he asked, but gently. "Remember, Angelina, I am also a radio. I am still a radio. I wanted to make sure that part of me was retained and they said they could do it.

This is Paris. We are part of a large array that spans Europe. There is a lot about me that you don't know."

"I have to go. Now." She hurried toward the door but stumbled over something and caught herself on the bedpost. She had to slow down and remember where everything was. But there was no time. "Where are my boots? Hasn't it been raining?"

"Where are you going?"

"To the Eiffel Tower."

"It's three o'clock in the morning."

"Get out of my way."

"I'm not in your way. I'm handing you your boots. There. Good. No clothes, my dear? That nightgown is bound to be a bit chilly. No—calm down. Here—some pants. That's right. Socks. Sweater. Good. Now for my boots—"

"You're not coming."

"Wrong there." She heard him tossing things around in the closet.

She pulled on her boots, tied them, buttoned her sweater with shaking fingers, and headed toward the door. Instead, she ran into the coatrack. His arms came around her and his kiss on her cheek was astoundingly calming.

"Okay. I'm ready. Angelina, you need me. Whether you know it or not."

"Of course I do," she said, and heard his sharp intake of breath. She turned and hugged him tight. "Of course I do."

His head dropped down upon hers for a second. Then he lifted it.

"Let's go then. Out into the City of Light."

The City of Louis, she thought, joyful and worried at the same time and understanding neither emotion.

The streets were clogged with bicycles and fast-carts. Chester and Angelina set off walking at a quick pace. Angelina kept her cane on her arm; with Chester to guide her she could move a lot more quickly.

"The Eiffel is glowing," he said, a catch in his words. "I wish that you could see it. It is absolutely ethereal!"

She set her cane down. “Ah. Oh yes, I *can* see it!” All around them were sounds of bedlam and jubilation. Music, dancing, clapping, bottles being smashed. “But what is all this about?”

“Perhaps . . . that newly emergent concept of universal time I told you about on the train? Something important is happening. We weren’t the only ones moved to come out in the streets. Listen!” He pulled her across a wide boulevard toward an art deco hotel. One window after another was thrown up, and music blared from every room.

“American jazz!” said Chester.

“Tommy Dorsey,” said the woman standing next to them.

Angelina put her cane to the pavement and a faint current ran through it. She headed toward the hotel and the current became stronger.

As she stood on the mobbed front porch, all sound faded for an instant, then coalesced.

It was distant at first, and then grew more intense, infused with rhythms that seemed at times at odds with one another, like a river flowing forward and backward in circling eddies of force. Her field of vision was pure white, but then filled with symbols and numbers, flashing and swirling with such intense speed that she could focus on none of them, yet felt them feeding into her as if she were having an ethereal meal, they were that solid, that nourishing, that essential. Her body vanished and became one with the numbers. There was no time. But she could see into all of time, if she wished; her own time, the time of every individual, the emotion-filled instants which imprinted what the senses carried onto memory’s flow; a vast music made of nothing but organized frequencies. Nothing but light. In this instant she was carried beyond everything. She was perfected. She would always exist. She would always want to exist.

“Angelina!” Chester was patting her cheeks, hard. She opened her eyes and saw whiteness but could smell his close scent, spicy and rich. She took a deep breath and felt his sigh of relief brush her face. "Are you all right?"

"Where am I?"

"On a park bench."

Sounds gradually became clear, and the night's chill impressed itself upon her. She sat up, with Chester's help, and lowered her legs. "Ah. I'm in that little park we go to." She was wet and cold.

"Yes." He put both arms around her. "What happened?"

She heard the roar of a crowd, and the continuing music, from a block or two away. "I don't know. It was some surge. I can't describe it."

"I felt it a bit," he said, his voice sounding defeated. "A brightening. Maybe after a long time of being like this, I'll grow to know more."

"Being like what?"

"Nothing."

"Chester, you have to get over thinking that you're not enough."

"I'm not. But I will be. Maybe there's always more."

"I hope so," she said. "Come on, I'm feeling so much better now. Let's warm up." She pulled on his hand and they rose and walked toward the music.

The next night the Tower did not light, nor did it the next night. And Chester did not go to kindergarten.

Angelina asked, "Won't the children miss you?"

"There are other teachers," he said as he lay on the couch.

"But why are you so tired? I don't understand. Are you sick?"

"Not exactly."

"Well, tell me then! If you know."

"I had some genetic engineering done."

"What?"

"That's right. The other day, before the big party. The party that I didn't quite understand. Is that all right with you?"

"It's dangerous. What did you have done?"

"I'm going to be like you," he said, his voice faint. "Once I get through this."

She sighed, remembering a childhood and adolescence of overwhelming spells of headaches. "Fine. I hope you enjoy it more than I have."

"I am already, I think. Despite the physical discomfort. What do you think happened the other night?"

"Well—"

"Okay, I'll tell you what happened to me. Radio functioned, for a short while. Right? And something happened to *me.* Faint though it was. My DNA work was only a few hours old. I was receiving transmissions on a new frequency. I could see them. Coming down from the sky."

"Who?"

"Maybe it's more like *what.* It was as if there was a vast reservoir of time, and it was coming down to Earth in . . . in huge columns of light. My eyes can still register that frequency, and that's what I saw. But still, I was . . . outside of it, in a way. As if"—his voice returned to its defeated tones—"everyone but me could drink through these . . . these straws . . . that held all of the music of time and of light. All the possible juxtapositions, and harmonies."

Angelina admitted to herself that she had felt it too. It had been like waking from sleep. As if now things would be so much more real. As if consciousness would be much more wide and rich. She thought about the medieval philosophers, and Augustine's definition of God—simply that which was greater than could possibly be imagined. Perhaps humans were physically incapable of such understanding.

Perhaps their brains had to change, in order for them to truly understand something which had always, through the ages, seemed just out of reach, however that reality might be defined.

Chester was trying with all his might to undergo such changes.

He continued. "I'd like to go to Crescent City. Maybe there I can become fully human. More than human. Angelina, something is happening. Something that will be . . . the next level. I'm keen for the next level. I've heard that there is a group leaving soon."

Without even thinking, she barked, "No! You can't go! It's too dangerous!"

He laughed.

She decided she ought to soften her approach. "I couldn't bear to lose you."

"So you'll just leave me behind and we'll never see each other again. That's a good solution. Angelina, you have been talking about going. Talking in your sleep, even."

"Have I? I suppose I have been thinking about it. At any rate, you have a choice, Chester. I don't. It's not pleasant at all. I might as well be a lemming. As long as you have choice, you ought to resist."

"But I have to take care of you."

"I was doing fine without you."

"Oh, of course you were. You almost got run down by a cart."

And so their argument went until the next evening, as they walked by the barge-filled canal opposite Notre Dame.

Chester said, "All I'm asking, Angelina, is that we share. Everything. I don't believe that will diminish you. I would hope that it would enhance you as much as it does me."

As he hugged her close, she said, realizing it only as she spoke, "It's what I want too, Chester. I'm so glad to have you here with me. I'm glad that you wanted to become human. I'm glad that you want to be more."

Not that she had any choice to begin with. It was only, she realized, a matter of being graceful about it.

A few days before they were to leave, Angelina heard a knock on the door. She was in the kitchen, preparing a cup of mint tea. "Come in," she yelled, thinking it was Gloria, a neighbor girl who often dropped by. "It isn't locked."

She heard a hesitant step. "Hello?"

She set her cup of tea down on the counter to keep from spilling it, but kept a tight hold on the handle. "Manuel?"

Then he was next to her in the kitchen. She felt his warmth. He smelled utterly familiar. She held her breath. She didn't want to have a thing to do with him.

"Angelina. I'm sorry to burst in like this. I have something important to tell you. I've found Louis."

"Louis!"

"Yes. But here—let me get that tea for you. Can we sit in the living room?"

"I can get it myself," she said.

Manuel took her arm and deftly seated her in the deep club chair and even had her feet on the hassock before she could stiffen against him. Then the hot cup was in her hand. The sun coming through the tall window warmed her right arm.

Manuel cleared his throat. He was sitting opposite her, on the couch. She could tell he was nervous.

"First," he said, "I want to apologize."

"Go right ahead."

"It's not as if it is all my fault."

"Never mind about the apology. Just tell me about Louis."

He softened the tone of his voice. "I have found a fragment in the memory of Paris. Louis was here. The other night. There was—an Event of Light, they are calling it."

"I was out and about that night. Who is calling it that? Why?"

"Well, people other than myself. I mean, it was marvelous, and exhilarating, but obviously it did not have the same effect on me that it had on . . . others. I guess you could say that Paris is calling it that."

"All right," she said, somewhat irritated with his lack of precision.

"Don't say 'all right' to me in that tone," he said sharply. "It was a radio event. A . . . a plasma cloud . . . enveloped Paris . . . it was sensed by the antenna array . . . all right! So I don't understand it. But you know that I love Louis as much as you and since I saw you I have been searching for him constantly using all the resources of the city. My harvester helped."

" 'Harvester?' " She took a sip of the cooling tea.

"Yes. To search for references to Louis in Paris."

"Oh. All right. A harvester?"

"Yes," he said with a touch of impatience. "They use them all the time here. For everything. I'm surprised that you don't have several."

"I guess I've been busy."

"I don't know why you try to irritate me all the time."

"You came to tell me something about Louis. Remember? How do you do this harvesting?"

"I can't believe you don't know how to do this. I gave the harvesters all my memories of him. From the time he was born. Every time I saw him."

Which wasn't often, she thought, after he was fourteen. It was difficult not to say this out loud. She took another sip of tea.

"Well, the thing is that Louis—his personality, his *essence*—was a part of the radio event last week. No, don't say anything. Let me finish." She heard sounds of movement and he pressed something into her hand. "This is the harvester. If you just access Paris using this, you'll find out everything I did. I guess." He sounded a bit flustered. "If you can't see, I don't know—"

"I manage," she told him. "I have vision, of a sort, and it is sharpest where matters of the city are concerned." The harvester was a soft rubbery sphere the size of a walnut, designed to stick to an interface. Interfaces were everywhere. "But just *tell* me, Manuel. Is he all right?"

Manuel sighed. "All right, Angelina. I'll do my best. Even though I don't understand it very well. That's why I gave you the harvester. Louis takes after you. He has the same genetic mutation as you do. Remember? You told me about it before we got married."

"It has recently caused me some inconvenience," she said. "And now it sounds as if there were even more dire consequences for Louis." There was no whiteness at all now, only the bleak darkness of a thousand depressive narratives overlaid on one another.

She heard Manuel move to the chair next to her. He took the tea from her hand gently and held both of her hands in his.

"It's certainly not your fault, Angelina. It isn't something you did on purpose. Now, what Louis told me . . . or rather, communicated, and not just to me, was that, for one thing, he is very happy. As he is."

"How *is* he?" she cried. "Just *tell* me!"

"He . . . seems not to be human any longer, except that he is. He is more than human, a changed human, and time is different for him because of something to do with light. He has been changed right down to his . . . atomic level, I suppose you could call it . . . because of this light thing that is coming from infinitely far away and yet is also right here, in two places at once. Something about quantum nonlocality. He understands so much more now, more, certainly, that *I* will ever understand. He left a sort of *vision* of that, of how it will be, and he left a . . . a *blueprint*, or a nanotech *seed* idea, that can be used for the next step, which will be helping all of us beknighted old-fashioned idiots *change* so that we are not so *limited* . . ."

"Manuel, you're hurting my hands."

He dropped them. "Sorry. Angelina, Angelina, I do love it here, and I do love literature, and I also love all the work that you have done since you got here. I have been spending a lot of time with it. It is marvelous."

"It's because of you," she said.

"But I just don't have your kind of mind. The kind of mind Louis and you both have. I can never really *understand* all of this. It's really quite terrible." He drew in his breath.

"Are you crying?" She reached over, touched his face. "Oh, Manuel, please don't cry."

"I just want so badly to understand my son. To be with my son. To understand you. To be with you, even."

The door opened. "Hello," Chester said.

"Hello?" Manuel sounded surprised.

"This is Chester," said Angelina. "This is his home too."

" 'Chester'? But the city indicated that you were—I mean—"

"Alone?" said Chester, his voice light, ironic. "Oh yes. You see—who are you?"

"Manuel. My husband," said Angelina dryly.

"Manuel! How nice to meet you at last. Please, let me shake your hand."

Angelina heard Chester bump into the coffee table in his haste. "You see," he told Manuel, "I'm not entirely human."

"Oh?" She heard Manuel sit down again.

"Isn't that something your harvesters should know?" asked Angelina. "He has harvesters," she explained to Chester.

"We all do," said Chester. "You do, too. Sit down, Manuel. Let me get you something to drink. Please. Wine? Beer? Scotch?"

"Wine. Thank you." He blew his nose. He sat down. Then he stood again. "I should go."

"No no," insisted Chester, returning. Manuel sat and she heard him sipping his wine. "You see, I am not really real."

"That's too bad," said Manuel, sounding puzzled.

"I'm working on it."

"Manuel brought me this harvester that will tell me about Louis," said Angelina. She held it out.

Chester took it. "We can look at it right now."

"I don't know," said Angelina. "I think I would rather do it in private."

"Oh. Well, do you mind if I look?"

"It involves the entire city," said Manuel. "I'm afraid that it isn't particularly personal, Angelina. Louis is much changed."

"As we all are," said Chester.

"All right," said Angelina, suffused with a wave of apprehension, remembering what Chester had told her about Louis, remembering the light she had crashed through when she fell off the balcony in Spain, dazzled.

"We can just use the coffee table."

"We can? Now?" She wasn't ready for whatever this revelation might be.

Chester said, "You've had your head in the clouds for too long. My fault. The children here use harvesters before they can talk. It just spreads out on the table. I'm sure that you can access it. Touch it."

Angelina steadied herself amid her kingdom of stories. She

reached out and put her palm on the now-flattened harvester, which was warm.

She half-expected to be shot with vision, shocked and overpowered.

Instead, it was gentle, sunny, but with all the clear import of the person she had known since before he was born and spun inside her, using her uterus as a trampoline, dancing in time to gaucho songs.

But it was indeed clear as a vision. Clearer than her old vision; so much brighter, so much more real, so much more true.

It was another story.

The mathematics of it were communicated first, in a chunk, a flood of symbols accompanied by a flash of sound that effervesced and flew to her cells, refreshing as a drink of clear spring water on a hot summer day. She understood from their pure foreignness, by the fact that they were not merely represented by sight, that they were a new mathematics, from the place where Louis was now.

She watched it, heard it, happen, this story.

A particular transmission had hit Earth and then passed on. Later, another had come. Then another; several more; arriving in a particular staccato split by months.

The way was cleared for these transmissions by *El Silencio. El Silencio,* and the pulses, were engineered by beings whose understanding of the nature of the physical universe far supersceded that of humans. The transmissions manifested haphazardly, and interacted unpredictably with humans.

It was a process which had begun decades earlier, and which would not conclude for a very long time. It came from a very distant time and place.

I am different now; I have been changed. I suppose I am a bridge. A conduit. I have this . . . opportunity. I am in two places at once. More. The idea of place, and even words, are quaint and limited, as if I look over a broad view from a high peak where once I walked along the road with limited vision. But there is no notion of singleness nor even of twainness. There is a simultaneousness.

Angelina heard his voice, a man's voice now, a pleasant, Spanish-speaking tenor, but within it sounded the echo of his childhood. How did the harvesters do that? Her eyes filled with tears, which overflowed as she blinked. She paid no attention to them.

There is light. So much light. I know the light now and it knows me. This is one option, for those who are prepared. But you must be prepared for it to happen. Your body must be ready. Ready as is an embryo, who when born is fully equipped to sense light and sound, to build a picture of a world with what is sensed.

When the signal finally comes again, those who are ready will change. Not like me, not as completely as me if they do not wish to do so. There are stages, richnesses, which I skipped. Missed. Regrettably. It was sudden. I couldn't resist it. I wanted to. There is so much I haven't done, I said. I said to it, I said to this, that I wasn't ready. But it was like going over Angel Falls. I was swept forward and I cannot return.

Manuel took Angelina's hand and grasped it tightly.

Perhaps you can come here. There was something in me that brought me here. Just as civilization is not built by one person but by many, more need to come here. To create a reliable relay.

Just follow the map. The map all of us have been building, without knowing why, all these years.

When there are more of us and we relay the signal once again, it will be magnified. Then it must be modulated. I have shown you how, here. I give you the plans. They must be distributed around the Earth, and programmed correctly, to the continuing periodicity. You must lay down the notes for them in their very bones. Those who are prepared will be able to choose when next there is a chance for choice.

If this lasts.

Like all of life, it is completely unpredictable. Complex.

Beautiful beyond my ability to say, even now.

Manuel gently loosed his hand from hers. "That's all there is."

"It can't be all! There must be more!"

"I'll leave this with you," Manuel said. He stood. "It was nice to meet you, Chester."

Angelina heard him walk across the room and open the door.

"Thank you," she finally was able to say.

"Don't worry, Angelina. I don't really understand all that. I don't think I ever will. But I'm going to try. I think that you'll be able to." He shut the door.

Angelina smelled bread baking in someone else's apartment. Manuel's footsteps receded down the stairs. She reached out to touch the harvester once again, then put her face in her hands.

"You have it now, Angelina," Chester said. "You own it. And I do too. I may not be real. But I believe that Louis is."

August 11, 2115

IO AND SU-CHEN

The sea was intense turquoise, with a heavy swell. On it, a tiny craft with a huge white sail topped the waves, slowly heading west. Its several fins fluttered along to port and starboard, and its tail waved with languid force from side to side.

Onboard was one small girl, thin, tall for her thirteen years, of Asian descent and badly sunburned, her long black hair salt-encrusted. She was naked, but lay beneath a sheltering canopy.

Next to her lay a tall, thin, ebony woman, wearing a torn white tightskin suit. The legs and torso of the suit were charred black.

In a small cage was a cat.

The boat moved on inexorably, its path determined by the information taken by millions of high-resolution telescopic photos from the moon. As it moved, its various systems developed and grew. From Io, it had a map of the stars, and it used this to chart its direction, toward the tiny spot that had been very, very tiny, even seen through the highest powered telescopes on the moon.

Io woke once, that evening, to the cooling, alien wind whipping beneath the shelter with a keening sound. A brilliant sunset was rapidly obscured by a black cloud, while thunder cracked and lighting shattered the sky. She was dimly aware that the sail had retracted. As the first cold sheets of rain washed over her, a clear shelter grew above her and Su-Chen, who stirred briefly and moaned.

Io pulled off one of the soft-skinned blobs growing next to her on the inner surface of the hull. With an effort she turned and stuck it in Su-Chen's mouth. "Chew," she whispered through a swollen throat. After a moment, Su-Chen chewed and swallowed, but did not open her eyes.

Gratified, she took one for herself. The liquid was distilled water infused with nutrients the boat had culled from the sea.

Chewing and swallowing took up the rest of her energy. She lay spent, and worried about their possible injuries, and about whether they would reach a hospitable place before they died.

She thought that she glimpsed one of the light-things hovering just over the boat.

Are they following us, she wondered, *or are they different ones? What is their nature? Is there only one of them, splintered into time and space? We could legitimately say that there is only one human, splintered by minute variations and time into an Earth-blanketing phenomenon. But each of us feels unique, with our own hidden consciousness, our own point of view, our own story. We are really*, she thought, with a jolt of surprise, *just story. So then, what are they? Do they have a story, too? Are they . . . ?* But she turned from that dangerous thought, the thought that had beaten her down to the deep bottom of her being in Unity: Are they my lost friends and lovers? Why did I refuse to . . . to what? Go? Change? Die?

She decided that it was a trick of the lightning and despite her effort to remain awake, and the tumult of the storm, lapsed unconscious.

A hard kick to her side woke Io.

"How do you turn this damned crazy boat around?" The man's voice was angry; desperate.

She opened her swollen, scratchy eyes. The sun was hot and

brilliant in the blue sky. The man's only garment was a pair of grimy, bloodstained shorts. His face was deeply tanned, and wild white-blond hair snarled out around his sweat-covered face. Long scars crisscrossed his chest. He hunkered down on his haunches, a ferocious frown on his battered face.

Io managed to sit up, though this exhausted her. She wondered what kind of defenses the boat had.

The storm shelter of the previous evening had been replaced by a white canopy. The sea was flat as a lake, and the sail hung empty. But the boat still moved. Behind it was tied a small rowboat.

"There's no steering mechanism on this weird thing," he complained. "No rudder." His English was oddly inflected, but she understood it.

Her Earth wariness came back in a rush. "It is only going one place."

"Where?"

"Crescent City."

"Yes, that is what it looks like. Directly there."

This was a relief to Io.

He continued, "You do not want to go there, lady. I just came from there. I was lucky to get away. You are lucky I found you. Crescent City makes people crazy."

"That must be what happened to you." Su-Chen's eyes were open. She watched the man intensely as she spoke but did not move.

"It is not a funny thing," he said. "Not a joke, little girl."

"What do you mean?" asked Io.

"I mean that it makes people lose their minds."

"Is that what happened to you?" Su-Chen seemed unable to let go of this question.

He looked at her as if trying to gauge her intent. Finally he said, "I managed to get out of there intact."

"Why did you go there if you just wanted to get out?"

"I am a pirate."

This sounded bizarre to Io, but she had not been on Earth for quite some time. She hoped that it wasn't the universal state of affairs.

"What is a pirate?" asked Su-Chen, still without moving, her voice flat.

He frowned. "Why don't you just go back to sleep."

"No."

"Look. I am from a small island and we are very poor. It has always been rumored that in Crescent City you can have any kind of health problem fixed. That it is full of free goods. That it has everything we lack. I have been a pirate for many years. I enjoy it, in fact."

"What is a pirate?"

"What we do, little girl, is loot and steal and kill people if they argue with us. That is what I will do to you if you continue to smart off. The confederacy of Caribbean pirates contacted us several months ago and invited us to join an attack on Crescent City. One group could not do it alone, but we thought that if we banded together, we could take it over. Once we ruled it, we would be able to heal our families, and sell these goods that they are hoarding. We would become wealthy. Besides, it is not fair."

"You have a relatively low-hertz voice," said Su-Chen. "Does everyone on Earth have a low-hertz voice?"

"What happened?" asked Io quickly. She wished that she had some kind of weapon.

"Gaia!" He spat into the water and looked over at Su-Chen uncertainly, then moved out of his squat, sat back, and crossed his legs tailor-style. "Gaia twisted them. Gaia and the Consilience."

"What is Gaia?" asked Su-Chen.

He snorted. "Oh, Gaia is some kind of philosophy. Gaians claim that it is about balance, that is all that I know. Gaia takes the liberty of balancing you, there in Crescent City. And I know that you will next ask about the Consilience. So I will tell you, the Consilience has control over everything there. You will be completely brainwashed if you go. Soon you will believe in Gaia like all my old friends. They are ruined and you will be ruined too. You need to turn around for your own good. Furthermore, part of the city is going into space!" He laughed heartily. "I would certainly like to see that. From a distance. The whole thing will probably blow up."

To Io's surprise, Su-Chen pulled herself to a standing position by holding onto the mast. She shouted at the man, "We! are! going! to! Crescent! City!"

He wheeled on her and shouted in her face. "Shut up! Do not be hollering at me! I am in charge here, not you." He jumped to his feet and grabbed her shoulders.

She kicked him in the stomach with surprising force.

"*Don't ever touch me!*" she screamed. "I will kill you the next time!"

He lunged at her but instead kicked the cage with the cat in it into the water, where it quickly sank. "I am warning you, my patience is very short!"

Su-Chen stared at him. "That was my cat. Boat, get rid of him. Hurry."

"You want to lose your mind, is that it?" shouted the man. "All of my fellow pirates—they became tame. They lost their edge."

"What are they, knives?" asked Su-Chen. Her voice was back to its normal flatness. "Boat, you are taking a very long time."

"Just calm down," Io managed to interject. "Let us just have a moment to think about what to do." If she had some time, she could probably have the boat manufacture some sort of weapon.

The man knelt and leered at them. "Think fast. Where are you witless folk from?"

"We are from the moon," said Su-Chen.

"I am getting very tired of this shit!" He moved toward Su-Chen, then fell back.

His face got red. And then it was redder.

"What's . . . this . . . on my hand?" he gasped. He lifted it from the raft's floor, stared at it in horror. It was puffy and red. His arm began to swell. The spot on the floor where his hand had rested had changed from white to purple.

He gasped for air. It was horrible to see his face, his effort to take in breath.

"What is it?" asked Io, alarmed.

Su-Chen said nothing. She just watched.

The man fell sideways onto the raft and convulsed. Then he stilled.

"He's dead," said Io, distressed.

"We need to push him off of the raft. He was not a good man."

"I'm not so sure it's that simple," said Io. She wiped sweat from her forehead. "It would have been better to find a different solution. And don't touch him."

"He killed my cat."

"That isn't a reason to kill another person."

"I think that he wanted to kill us. He said he was going to."

Io was silent for a moment. The sea was a series of slow green swells. The sun was terribly hot, and shot long shifting lines of light into the depths. "You may be right. It looks as if the boat has become very sophisticated. It must have manufactured some kind of allergen." The purple patch was gone.

"I must get you to Crescent City." The boat's voice was curiously flat, like Su-Chen's. Perhaps she had been talking while Io was asleep, training it.

The boat emitted some clicks, some sounds that seemed like throaty laughter. It smacked its tail against the water behind the boat.

"Yes," Io agreed. "That would be very nice."

She lay back in the shade, exhausted, and closed her eyes. She heard a splash.

The boat moved on.

The Yellow Brick Road

JULY 2115

The first sign of trouble Angelina and Chester had was when they tried to board the train with the rest of the Parisians heading to Crescent City.

Angelina gratefully drank the vision that flooded from every surface as she climbed the stairs, but someone behind her said, "Sir, you have no clearance to ride this train."

She turned and said, "He is with me."

The porter, a pink-cheeked woman with braided blond hair, said firmly, "I'm sorry, madam, but—"

Angelina repeated, "He is with me. Come on, Chester." They proceeded down the aisle and took seats and he flopped, forlornly and limblessly as if he were still a doll, opposite her.

"Don't be so sensitive," she told him. She leaned forward and took his hands. His face became breathtakingly clear, his brown eyes two spots of worry; his pale, freckled face; his short, red hair cut so carelessly that it was almost comical. He shifted his lanky body forward, folded his long legs so that they bent sharply as he leaned toward her. They held hands as the train moved out of the station. "You seem to keep the visions at bay for me," she said. "I can feel them crowding around me. Millions of soldiers. A doctor sitting alone, worrying about a plague. Proust on his way to his family's country home."

He stared into her eyes. It was an odd, roundabout circuit, but it connected, as the train came into the pale winter light and the buildings of Paris rushed past and the train gathered speed. "You can see me," he observed. "It's very nice. Angelina, let me take some of that weight, some of those stories. *Share* them with me. It's what I want. You keep putting it off. You're so possessive about it."

"We'll try soon," she promised, and felt almost as if they were agreeing that they would have a child.

The real trouble came at the boat. Committees and bureaucrats coalesced out of nothing, it seemed, and tests were set up. Chester was winnowed out.

They spent a week in a small hotel by the quay while an old ship was retrofitted in haste. They had been turned away every day, despite Chester's protestation of sameness, his DNA alteration. They could read his history as a doll. They did not want former dolls. They might as well, one woman told him, be transporting former teacups or bedposts. This was a journey of enlightenment. They were going to enlighten the people of Crescent City. Chester was not of sufficient status to enlighten a dog, according to her.

They brewed plans to smuggle Chester onto the boat. Chester even joked that he wished that he were still a doll.

"He isn't one of us," a man's voice informed Angelina as they tried to board for the last time, just as the ship was to set sail. Gulls laughed around them, darting through the drizzle. She knew that many birds and fish had become extinct during *El Silencio,* but gulls, it seemed, were tough. To Angelina, their calls represented an ever-changing, elastic, continuously elageic pattern.

Outside of Paris, her cane was useless. But they had superseded that, figuring out while on the train how to carry the learned connection with them when they reached the end of the line. It was the first step in their process of linking. She took Chester's hand, and could see the man who was denying Chester passage.

"Perhaps that's a good thing," Angelina said, studying the latest bureaucrat's pugnacious features, which she was sure Chester's vision was distorting in unpleasant ways. "I'm not sure that I enjoy being in the same class of people as you."

"I only meant—" he said.

"Never mind." They turned away and Angelina pulled Chester down the dock.

"Maybe if you'd been a bit less insulting?" asked Chester. "Wait!" He helped her around a hole in the dock. The place smelled of fish and of the sea and dusk.

"Screw them," she said. Her vision filled with seafaring tales. "Maybe this will be better, anyway."

They rented a boat, assuring the agency that they were simply going on a month's jaunt with all the sybaritic trimmings. It was a boat which she hoped would be capable of crossing the Atlantic. They also rented a crew of sailors, which (the agent insisted that the pronoun *who* did not apply to them) were being enlivened as they had a last land-supper of fish chowder and wine in a nearby restaurant. The sailors would return the boat after they dropped off Angelina and Chester at Crescent City.

"The agent said that they won't get in our way," Angelina said, chewing on a chunk of crusty bread.

"No, of course not," replied Chester morosely.

"If you're going to be pouty about it, maybe we shouldn't go."

"Maybe we should take time to think it over. If we just wait few months, the weather will be better, and we can probably make the crossing in ten days. There are terrible storms this time of year."

Angelina nodded. "That's true. Certainly. But I have a strong feeling that it may be too late by then."

"Just like you feel a strong need to go at all."

"It's that kind of feeling," she agreed. "At all costs, I must go now."

"It seems to me that your life has been governed by this 'at all costs' thing for quite some time."

"All my life, I suppose. The ranch, at all costs. Even the cost of my marriage. If, perhaps, I had agreed to travel with Manuel, or even read the books that he suggested—but that, at least, has turned out well."

"Thank you."

"All right, then. So I had to go to Paris, and that too has turned out well."

"Thank you again." His voice was humble and sincere, and helped bring Angelina back to the gravity of her decision.

"If I—if we—decide to wait, we may as well not go."

"Why? What would happen then?"

She laughed despite herself, despite the feeling of urgency, and doom and light mixed together. "I don't know. Oh, Chester, believe me, I have a million scripts for staying behind, and all of them pleasurable in the extreme. We could settle in the south of France, and grow fruits and vegetables, and just cook for several lifetimes."

"Sounds a bit boring."

"Not once I share," she teased.

"And this boat, this boat you are essentially planning to steal—it has full linking capabilities? Not that we couldn't have done this in Paris." His voice took on a chiding shade.

"This has all happened so quickly," she said. "Yes, we could have done it in Paris."

"We could return and do it in Paris."

"It's just that—I feel as if I have taken from Paris all that it has to offer." She felt frustrated in her inability to convince Chester that this was the right thing to do, and a bit irked that she had to do so. Sometimes it would just be easier to be alone.

"You could go on alone," he said, startling her as much as the big boat's deep blare, which vibrated the harbor at that moment.

She sat back, a bit confused. "I just thought so. Yet, I want to be with you."

"And they won't let me on the boat."

"No."

"Seems like this is the only way, then."

"It does."

"It could be that once these sailors reach Crescent City, they too could be made fully human." His voice brightened.

"Yes. Absolutely."

"Angelina, we've wasted so much time. After you share everything, don't you think that it will be *so* much easier to convince me that you're always right?"

"I'm actually afraid it might work to my disadvantage."

They laughed together then, and for both the room filled up with light.

The sailors leapfrogged the boat down to Spain and then to Africa. They were distant, efficient, and courteous. Angelina and Chester busied themselves with the important task of laying in supplies at each port and continued to put off the linking. Angelina realized that Chester was as nervous about it as she was. Everything would change. They were happy now. Why risk change? And then—why not wait until they were in Crescent City, or do it on land, where at least they would not be so isolated?

But finally, on a clear, star-strewn night, they realized that they wanted to delay no longer.

The mechanisms were cocoonlike membranes, which had been safely used for such purposes for a good hundred years, Angelina and Chester reassured one another as they climbed in and were sealed together, naked, and in one another's arms.

Chester's new awareness blossomed with a jolt as they left the coast of Africa behind.

The following days were not idyllic, but intense, overwhelming. Angelina fretted over him as he thrashed and moaned on a bunk, deluged by information sickness. She blamed herself for not doing this in Paris, while he, during moments of clarity, assured her that she had been right to delay until now.

The fourth night out he sat up, came out on deck, and talked lucidly and powerfully for six hours while she listened, spellbound, to theories of literature and consciousness which rose through him like water in a spring, cleansed and made new to her ears. They ate what the sailor-chef brought them—fresh poached fish, fresh baked bread, and wine—and talked on until dawn, and past it then, lying away from the sun crowded into one tiny bunk. They shared everything. They were, at last, each other. It was pleasant, but painful and searing in patches, yet endlessly fascinating, as if they would never reach the end of looking at each other and renew their task of looking outward. Through it all, Chester spoke most often of the rolled-up dimensions, of the strings of light that formed consciousness, and of how he could almost see them, in all their potential, waiting to expand and flood the beings of all living creatures.

"There's another stage. There's always another stage. It's the way evolution works. In bumps. In jolts. It's like—I used to be flat. Like a painting. A painting is a trick. It tricks you into thinking the subject is round. At least most of it does. Only"—he frowned and squinted in a way Angelina found comical—"those artists like Picasso. You were working on them? They embraced the flatness of their medium. Used it so that the paintings were more than paintings. Because of these stories—literature, science, all the stories of humans—I have more depth. Stories create emotional roundness. They are different than paintings because they contain the element of time." He frowned again, more earnestly, and leaned forward and spoke even more urgently.

"So now I'm learning what it is to be human. *Con*—with. *Sci*—to see. To see with my own eyes? To see with others? Or—are humans the eyes of the universe?"

"Consciousness is just a made-up human word," laughed Angelina. "It has no deep universal veracity."

Chester ignored her. "There's another stage. Louis. I think of another dimension having been added to him. There's another dimension that—that *glances off* our consciousness. The way light skips past the Earth, causing sunrise. It's as if we're in the sunrise of a new form of consciousness. There is an *intersection.* And the intersection is always *moving.* So that there's a calculus of consciousness . . ."

Angelina reached over and brushed tears from his face, gathered him close. "You're so passionate, Chester."

"It's just that being real is so overwhelming. You've made me real. You've made me *round*. It's just the beginning!"

He talked earnestly to the sailors, assuring them that they too would be thus baptized, and they smiled politely and nodded and kept to their work.

The navigator, still holding his sextant, told them one dawn that they were only fifty kilometers from the last known position of Crescent City, which he had gotten while at their last port in Africa from other sailors who plied this route. They took turns looking for it through binoculars, and Chester believed that he saw it, a flash of brilliant light, just as the sun was setting behind them. Then it was certain, as multicolored beacons flashed in what seemed a kind of code before they were extinguished, like the moon, by clouds, one by one, and the wind began to blow hard, making the lines sing.

The next thing Chester remembered was being fished roughly from the sea by fisherfolk who told him in strangely accented Spanish that he was alone, that no, they had spotted no other survivors from the night's storm despite a long search.

Chester, staring at the city, which looked like layers of circus tents rising from the hard bright sea, was assailed by three thousand years of tales of loss and grief. Greek, Chinese, Anglish, French, Indian, Aborigine. It was all the same. All unbearable.

He struggled against the sailors' restraining hands as they kept him from climbing over the side of the boat and sliding in to join Angelina, which seemed the only sensible thing to do. They shut him in the head, where he cried himself unconscious.

He dreamed that he was still a doll, and free of all this unrelenting pain.

August 11, 2115

DANIA AND COYOTE

Dania cycled all day after leaving the Ranch of the Nows, as she thought of it, and it was hard but pleasant and the bike helped a lot, shifting gears automatically. She eventually made her way back to Interstate 10, the fastest route to Houston. Dania remembered now. Cowboy had insisted on traveling the back roads, the cowboy highways and byways, the olden paths, the roads without those damnably permanent billboards against which he railed. So they had missed Houston. Probably passed some vital crossroads where the sign was too bullet-riddled to read.

As the day wore on, she sliced though the air, cooled by sweat and buoyed by some mysterious pipeline to the soul of her metabolism which had never seemed open before. The land was still utterly flat. Along 10 she passed no homes, and saw only three other vehicles all day—one heading east and two heading west, all at speeds that left her few details.

When she began casting a long thin shadow before her, she realized that she was exhausted. She veered off the Interestate via a faint path next to a sign that said PLEASE GO TO EXIT TO DRIVE ON AND OFF THE INTERSTATE. She bumped along a rocky dirt trace that ran through deep untrammeled grass, and stopped on a low rise from which she could see Houston spread out in the distance. It seemed to her as if it must be at least thirty miles away.

She had no idea where Johnson Space Center was. She only knew that Houston was enormous. And . . . wasn't there some kind of time constraint? She didn't even know what day it was.

She rested the bike against a lone pine. Her head was settled—whether by dint of exercise or because whatever that light-thing had done was limited in effect, she did not know. Yes, here she was. Dania Cooper. Salvation/Rebellion, Memphis/Marriage/Stupidity, Flower Cities/Insanity, Crescent City/Intelligence, Sanity, Usefulness, Since/More Insanity/Nows, and now. Yup, that was her history, all right. And her wrists hurt damnably.

She rooted through the panniers and came up with a bundle the size of a baguette and peeled open the material binding it, hoping for the best. But it was not bread. It was a tent. PATENT APPLIED FOR, DAMN IT, read the label. She peeled off another layer and jumped back as the contents unfolded into a spiffy little octagonal tent, large enough for two.

She knelt by a circular iris that was clearly the doorway. To the right of it was a small color touchchart. She chose CAMOUFLAGE and watched the tent take on the color of its surroundings—dun and drab green. Some kind of fish or lizard or insect gene, she supposed. The door dilated and told her that it was now locked to her touch command and that also it was impervious to knives, bullets, chain saws, and other miscellaneous insults. The voice read out the specific attributes of the tent in a warm, deep voice as it propelled stabilizing stakes into the ground and informed her that it was doing so, but the voice broke at the end as it said, "This is actually Darryl Fienster, the inventor of this fine tent. Its design has just been ripped off not by any nefarious company but by the very goddamned socialist *air* and I worked damned hard on it and I'm pissed as hell. It's going to be replicated without me getting anything for it. Some—some drone *copy* device on the wall here copied the program. With a little poof of light and it says copy COMPLETE. STOLE my program! Let's see, it says here that all information is the property of GAIA. GAIA? Come ON. I should have known better than to hang in this place too long. Information wants to be FREE? Well excuse ME. I guess it's just going to RAIN down in little particles over East Texas until it finds fertile SOIL or something and grows a nice little colony of pop-up tents. SHIT! Just remember this, you goddamned thief, whenever it keeps you dry and gives you the weather forecast or cooks for you or does any of the amazing things I designed it to do! I deserve SOMETHING. I worked HARD on this!"

The voice of Darryl Feinster was shouting hoarsely by the end of the diatribe, and after a moment of silence, Dania said, "So, cook something for me, tent."

"Fancy a cup of sagebrush tea?"

Dania crawled in through the tent's iris. The light inside was greenish yellow as the last rays of sun played over it. She flopped down on her back. "What else is on the menu?"

"I'm not a magician."

"How would you make this tea?"

Silence.

"I said—"

"I'm THINKING! I guess the best way to get it done would be for you to go out and find some sagebrush and start a fire and put water in a pot and—"

"Well, it's nice to have someone to talk to," said Dania as she reached out and popped an insulating pad from the wall and rolled onto it. It crinkled and expanded.

"My sentiments exactly."

Lying there, she felt her pockets, hoping to find the energy bar she'd put there earlier, then remembered that she'd eaten it. She swigged some water from her canteen, and then fell deeply asleep, despite the brilliance of sunset which blazed through Darryl Fienster's tent in translucent ripples of light.

She woke up a few hours later, pulled off her boots, wrapped herself more tightly in the pad, and began to drift back asleep.

"Do you wish to see the moon?" Without waiting for an answer, the tent fabric became transparent at just the right angle to practically blind her. "Let me tell you how many lumens—"

She shielded her eyes with her arm. "Just let me sleep," she mumbled.

"I do have a complete lunar calendar for the next ten thousand years."

Dania sighed. Her stomach ached. She sat up and pulled on her boots. She did not lace them. She crawled out through the iris and stood up. This was painful. You *are* over a hundred years old, she reminded herself, as did all her muscles and joints.

She ambled to the bike and rummaged through the panniers. She pulled out a thin sort of jacket and put it on; it seemed to keep her at just the right temperature. "All so perfect," she murmured. She found the packet of bars and pulled out two. She was putting one into her pocket when a voice behind her said, "Doesn't it seem so."

She froze. This was not the voice of the tent. It was a female voice, the tones long and drawn out and rather poignant sounding, so much so that she was a bit difficult to understand, as if whoever she was spoke with a slow Southern drawl cut with short yips.

"Don't worry," twanged the voice in its weird halting pattern. "I won't hurt you."

A coyote slunk near the tree and dropped to the ground on its belly, grinning. It looked much larger than Dania had supposed coyotes were. But it was unmistakably a coyote.

"I suppose you're lonely too," popped out of Dania's mouth before she could even think. Not only every*one*, but every*thing*, seemed so needy lately.

"Not particularly."

Dania watched the coyote's mouth, which had remained open in a panting grin as she spoke, her tongue lolling out of one side. The coyote crossed large silver-yellow paws.

Dania inched over to the pine and slid down along its trunk until she was sitting. She must be dreaming again. "So, how are you able to talk?"

"I have an organic synthesizer. It's a part of my vocal cords. I have to keep my mouth open or it comes out muffed."

" 'Muffled?' "

"Yes. Muffled." She closed her jaws and licked one paw slowly and thoughtfully, watching Dania through narrowed yellow eyes. "It's all very complicated and I had to have some human brain matter to bridge the gap between coyote-thought, which has a lot to do with smells by the way you smell kind of disgusting and kind of—" Her tongue lolled out.

"So, ah. Can I help you with anything?" At this point, Dania merely hoped that she was dreaming. She was no longer certain. In fact, it all seemed quite real.

"Perhaps I can help you."

"Tell me," Dania said, suddenly very suspicious. "Do you have anything to do with the Nows?"

The coyote's jaws closed in a snap, then opened to let the sound out. Her yellow eyes glared at Dania. "Yeah. Those damned Nows again. That's why I'm here. I was created by Native American Biolabs in Humble. About thirty miles from here. Nows, Nows, Nows. Hardly talked about anything else. If there was any kind of legal system, I'd sue the pants off of them. What coyote in her right mind would want to be some kind of archetype—I mean maybe I could get a teaching post somewhere." She shifted on her elbows, watching Dania closely. "I know that the Nows are coming and that the Nows are always here. They have something to do with the dream-time."

She leaped up suddenly, stared directly into Dania's eyes, and threw back her head. Her sharp teeth shone in the moonlight.

She howled, "And the Nows have something to do with YOOOOOO!"

Dania scrambled to her feet, pulled her bike away from the tree, ran a few feet while pushing it, and leaped aboard. Her feet found the pedals and she bent over the bike. A headlight came on, illuminating her path. She pumped and the light became brighter. A generator.

"Come back here!" yelled the tent. "You can't just leave me here alone!"

Dania jolted back to the Interstate, knees trembling, and pedaled for another hour. The moon set and so when she looked back she could not see if the coyote still followed, as she had at first, loping well behind. Once it was dark, Dania could imagine that it had all been a dream. Or that the coyote had given up. Either way, she was extremely tired. She stopped, walked up a slight berm below an overhead highway empty of traffic, and collapsed into rough, sharp grass.

Just as she was passing out, she heard a voice in her ear. "Don't worry. I'd love to, but I'm not allowed to eat you."

She got to her feet, pulled the bike up, and kept on going.

As daylight grew, Dania saw that she was on a two-lane divided highway. She didn't recall taking an exit. This didn't seem good. Several Interstates looped above her, impossibly distant. She felt as if people were watching her but couldn't really tell. She was about five miles outside the Flower City bastion, which, if it was like most of them, was a high, abrupt wall. What was inside was usually completely discontinuous, in form and in mental space and in deep human change, from what was outside.

Ramshackle houses with patches of stucco fallen from them, roof tiles broken, or rafters visible were interspersed with sturdy, hard-to-kill strip malls. She chose an empty storefront which had an open glass door. She pedaled her bike up the handicap ramp and rode straight inside the store.

The whole place was gutted, empty except for the cinderblock bathroom enclosure, which held a rancid toilet. There was a steel-barred back door and some high broken windows and a large, irregular hole in the ceiling, but the plate glass on the front was fine and she closed the door and leaned her bike against it and turned the lock, which slid shut with a satisfying *chunk.*

Then she heard a pop. A gunshot.

The coyote loped across the parking lot and leaned on the door, smearing it with blood. "Let me in!" she howled. "Please!" She fell over in front of the door.

Dania hesitated only a second. Then she opened the door,

dragged the yelping coyote inside, and shut and locked it. A man carrying a rifle in two hands crossed the empty street, looked around, presumably saw the blood, and walked up to the glass. He was wearing a pair of green swim trunks, hunting boots, and a red Astros hat. He yanked on the door, then banged on it with his rifle butt. He glared at her.

"That there's my coyote!" he shouted. "I killed it."

"Trade you," yelled Dania.

"What?"

Dania turned and rummaged through the panniers. "Um, a knife?"

"Keep the knife," moaned the coyote.

"What did you say?" shouted the man.

Dania yelled, "It's my coyote. My pet coyote. You had no right to shoot it."

"That's right," howled the coyote.

The man's face tightened. He looked from Dania to the coyote and back to Dania again. He shook his head. "Shit. You both deserve to die. You're lucky I was raised right." He spat and turned and strode away, his boots crunching on broken glass.

Dania knelt by the coyote. "What's your name?" She looked so flat lying there, her silvery shoulder fur matted with bright, oozing blood.

"Three Impossible. My name is Three Impossible Things Before Breakfast." Her voice was a weak sigh, the murmur of surf heard from oceanside dunes.

Dania leaned over and got out the knife she had been going to trade for the coyote. It had a black, plasticish handle and, when she unfolded it, a keen three-inch blade. "We must be related. That's what my father called me. A lot. Impossible." She took off her shirt and used the knife to cut through the button platen of the shirt and then used both hands to rip a strip from the bottom of her shirt. She had to use the knife to cut through the selvage at the other end.

A bit more rummaging revealed a first-aid kit. Dania slapped her forehead and opened it. "Right! Here's a real bandage. Let's see." She held the wrapper up to the light. " 'Guaranteed to disinfect and heal.' " She ripped it open. "I hope it's long enough. I'm going to have to wrap it around your shoulder somehow. Let's see—here's a bottle of stuff I can drizzle on the wound." She unscrewed the lid and let a few drops fall into the middle of the red mess. Three Impossible turned her head and snapped weakly; snarled. Dania sprawled back on her butt. "Sorry," the coyote wheezed and her head dropped back onto the floor.

Dania rose and hurried to the back of the store, to the bathroom. She turned a faucet, but nothing came out. "Damn." She returned to the coyote, dropped a dressing onto the wound, and unreeled the bandage as she maneuvered around her, squeezing it beneath her while the coyote moaned. Finally she said, "That's done."

"Water?"

Dania looked at her water bottle. About a quart left.

She poured what would fit into her cup and bowl. Then she tilted the squirt bottle and squirted water into Three Impossible's mouth, aiming for the back. The coyote lapped weakly and most of it seemed to dribble onto the floor. She shuddered and was still.

Dania had been awake so long that the world pulsed and flashed around her. She lay down on the concrete, stuffed her wadded up jacket beneath her head, and slept.

She woke to sharp teeth yanking on her arm, and a foul-breathed snarl.

"Hey!" She sat up and jerked her arm away from Three Impossible's jaws.

"Hungry. Leave. Now." Her yellow eyes were indeed wild and much more urgent than her words.

Dania stood and unbolted the door, kicking aside the streamers of bandage that the coyote had chewed off and left on the floor. She opened it. "Here."

Three Impossible stood in the doorway for a second, then fled, a streak of gray. She loped across the parking lot, crossed the road, and vanished between the ruins of two houses.

"Well." Dania collected her kit and bike. Outside she straddled the bike, unsure of which way to go. She was starving. She remembered the man with the rifle and looked around uncertainly, sure that he would not be seen unless he wanted to be seen. How did people live here, and how many?

She wheeled her bike to the road, turned a corner, and stopped.

The sky was revealed, and the towers of Houston blazed with light against sunset.

She had seen Flower Cities before. Hell, she had lived in Memphis before she hitched a ride on the *American Queen* and found her way to Crescent City.

Though she was utterly familiar with the horror they could produce, if their fine balances were set askew, their beauty still held her spellbound.

Massive purple Wisteria spilled from an asymmetric slant-roofed tower, backlit by sunset. Black-eyed Susans formed the most mass, with Texas Bluebells nodding away in the evening breeze. A few Bees still lingered, transferring Information that was no different than a drug: direct, biological, compelling, addictive. The sky behind them was deep indigo.

Memories of the first sweet years of her marriage rushed in. The children had made it so sweet, she realized now, and she wondered where they were in this wide world, or if they were even still alive. That was the hardest thing. Not to ever know.

Crescent City had helped. There were places where one could fill up time with virtual memories, but she had turned her back on that firmly. Instead, she had adopted several of the orphans who were transported to Crescent City by plague-driven adults, children traumatized and silent, or wild and dangerous—most often to themselves. By helping to calm and normalize them, she had herself been normalized and had been able to finally enter the Consilience, and give something to the future.

Now, what had happened to that future?

The Consilience stirred within her. She was near that which was needed for the city to fulfill its destiny: the lost coordinates gathered by NASA in the final days before the Silence. They had been upgraded during each brief spell of radio freedom. Cowboy had babbled madly about those times, telling her garbled tales of a childhood wracked by pain and shot through with Silence-nurtured clarity.

In short, she had gathered that he was an alien. Or a mutant. Or a Pioneer, as they were called in Crescent City. There had been other things, a wife in Chicago, where he had been Chief Nanotech Engineer, which she could hardly believe. Mostly, she believed his tales about truck-stop girls.

But she did recall the first night on their small boat when he had lucidly laid out their quest, between spells of their mutual insanity. She clung to that. That was why she was here.

Where would she go otherwise?

Back to the pirates of Crescent City? No.

Back to Memphis? Never.

Back to the plains of Texas, back to that little farm where her new tribe might someday light?

Yes.

Had it only been the day before yesterday that she'd left them? That day stretched out forever for her. And Cowboy. She wanted Cowboy there. To show it to him. To share it with him. To give him a lasting touchstone.

The sky pressed into bands of orange and purple, and then darkened swiftly. She stood and watched, amazed by Texas and by the Houston skyline with its closing blossoms bobbing in the wind.

A padding scritch behind her made her jump. It was Three Impossible.

"Let us go."

"Where?"

"NASA. I'm your guide. You have heard of guides, haven't you? The idea of guides was very important to the kind people at Native American Biotech Etcetera. I'm supposed to be an aspect of your deepest being."

"You were sent just for me?"

"You. Or someone like you. It had been a long time. Relatively speaking, of course. Ha. Ha."

"Ha."

"Just follow me. I've been awakened, and this is what I was created to do."

"Oh. In that case, how can I refuse? How is your shoulder?"

"Better. The bandages were full of healing."

The night's journey took them down broad flat roads, some which were still lit with streetlights, where the traffic lights still functioned. Three Impossible warned her with a yip to leave the road the first time a vehicle approached. But Dania kept pedaling, and after a minute a pickup truck roared past. A beer bottle spun past her head and smashed onto the street. The truck skidded to a stop and Dania quickly scooted through a break between stores. She watched the truck back up. The men shouted out the window, then sped forward with a screech of tires. After that, she followed Three Impossible whenever the coyote darted off the road.

The moon rose about midnight. They were out among what seemed an infinity of long, low buildings. She passed a hamburger stand where people hung around a lighted window. She heard laughter. She passed innumerable bars from which music blared from behind rows of parked trucks. She figured it was about four in the morning when Three Impossible finally stopped, turned, and waited for her to catch up.

"Close. Enough." Three Impossible panted. Dania panted too. She took a drink; her canteen was almost empty again.

"We rest now."

"Good."

"In here."

In the roofless shell of an abandoned building, they slept.

When she woke, late in the afternoon, Three Impossible had a bag of cold hamburgers waiting for her.

"There really *isn't* any way into this place." The wall surrounding the Johnson Space Center was smooth and high and doorless, as far as Dania could tell after walking for a mile or so. Every hundred feet or so was some kind of warning sign. NO PARKING, read one. Another just had an all-purpose circle with a slash through it. DANGER, read another hand-painted job, above a skull and crossbones. A more chilling one came a bit farther.

IN LOVING MEMORY OF SARA BINGHAM,
NED WITHERSPOON, AND CLYDE SMITH,
WHO WENT IN AND NEVER CAME OUT.

This was not easy. Dense thorned shrubbery had already left stinging hieroglyphics of blood on her bare arms. There was no road or sidewalk that followed the boundaries, just the crumbled edges of desultory buildings that had once lined the roads that now ended at the wall. Mimosas and scrawny oaks crowded against the wall so that from a distance it looked like another overgrown building—except that the perimeter was huge.

"There has to be a way in. NAB wouldn't have created me to be your archetypal spirit guide unless there was. Would they? I'm telling you, every*one* and every*thing* is trying to help you poor humans out. Admit it. You never would have found this place without me. At least, maybe not until it was too late."

"Too late for what?" But Three Impossible padded ahead, leaping over briars.

Dania, pushing her bike tediously, from time to time found faint paths, much like children would make when territorizing an adult-free wasteland, and cavelike hollows where perhaps bums slept, leaving their droppings of liquor bottles and patch wrappers as markers. It was getting dark.

"Who made this wall, anyway?" she muttered, pulling out her knife and cutting her tattered skirt free of vines. She looked up at a distant, urgent bark, and headed away from the wall at a tangent. The coyote looked tiny from here. Dania moved out and as she backed away she saw what the coyote had seen.

A scaffolding, accessed with ladders, rose from the roof of a building that the wall had evidently grown around, leaving a thick blob at the bottom.

Dania and Three Impossible entered the building cautiously. She lowered her bike to the floor, which her light showed was strewn with broken glass and rusted sheets of corrugated roofing. A makeshift ladder made of lashed-together tree limbs led to a hole in the roof.

"Kids," said Dania. She pushed on the ladder and it bent. "I doubt that this will hold my weight."

"Just try and break one of those rungs," said the coyote. She settled down on the floor and slowly, repeatedly, licked her right paw.

Dania sighed. "I might break my back." She stepped away from the ladder for a moment. "Why in the world is this wall here, anyway? I mean, if there was something important to protect, why build a wall that even kids can scale?"

"Maybe the kids can't read."

"Can you?" asked Dania.

"I can, but it gives me a terrible headache."

Dania looked up at the ladder. "I guess you'll have to stay here."

"If you can shove that crate under the opening, I could jump through it, I think."

The crate was made of light pallets. Dania leaned into it and shoved it beneath the hold by inches, thinking of how programming would have taken care of this little problem in Crescent City. She emerged on the roof and helped Impossible scramble through the hole.

After sniffing around, Impossible padded along beside Dania as she approached a dark rectangular prism on one side of the roof.

It was an elevator.

The options were four nonexistent floors above them, and below, Gift Shop and Parking.

"Parking," said Dania, and the door opened.

The elevator went down but opened on the Gift Shop level. Dania tried to get the door shut, but it would not budge. She stepped out into darkness. Impossible growled. "Have a care. I smell death."

Lights flickered as Dania moved but went dark when she froze. Impossible backed away, ears flattened.

Dania tried not to be frightened by what she knew were holograms, lighting at her movement. A woman wearing a uniform approached her, smiling. "May I help you?"

"Where am I?"

"The Space Museum Gift Shop." She turned and gestured toward empty shelves, looted long ago and obviously unregenerated. "Do you have any children? We have forty-three models which include various space shuttles, flight modules—and look!" She took a circuitous route around no longer extant shelves and stopped, her face aglow with enthusiasm and light, her left leg flickering in and out of existence. "This kit contains the entire first landing on the moon. All you need is a standard platform. Set the kit on the launch pad and the entire sequence is generated in real time. You can watch everything that happened inside the module on your screen or go virtual and see it from any participant's point of view. If your child is over fifteen, the pheromone program that replicates emotions can be activated as well. It's one of our most realistic Frontiers of Space experiences."

"Do you have *Lightship Seven?*" asked Dania. Since she had been at the Ranch of the Nows, she remembered everything—things that any child in Crescent City could know, if they cared to learn about it.

The hologram froze. In a second another materialized next to it. This one was a burly male, wearing a black suit. He put his hands on his hips and pulled back his jacket slightly, revealing his gun holster.

He's just a hologram, Dania reminded herself, but in a space filled with all kinds of degraded lasers she realized that it really made no difference.

"Clearance," the man said.

"I am from Crescent City."

"You realize, of course, that there is no such thing as *Lightship Seven.*"

"Of course," she said.

"Then why did you ask for it?" he continued in the maddening way of programmed beings with too little thoughtspace allotted to them.

"Because if it had existed it would have used a guidance system based on information in Crescent City. Which we have lost. That's why I have come to get another copy."

"Our records show that a version of this guidance system that might have guided *Lightship Seven* had it ever existed was stolen in 2034." His hawklike eyes paled.

That guidance system and all of its precisely calibrated coordinates had been developed from hard information available only during a very brief window of time a hundred years ago, during the time after radio failed and the Pulses beamed the information past Earth, into the brains of who knew how many thousands of mutated children, many of whom were brought to this very location and brainwashed . . .

Yes, she knew the history.

"Are there any real humans in the Johnson Space Center?" She wasn't sure if a real person would be good or bad, but at least they would be more interesting to talk to.

The hologram looked puzzled. It tilted its head. "Explain 'real.' "

"Organic."

His puzzled expression remained.

"Are there children?" she asked gently.

"In a way," he replied, giving her new respect for his programming. She wondered if he had to answer truthfully, and if not, what his mechanisms for deciding what lies to tell might be. Might time and this awful humidity not have degraded him somewhat?

"What's that smell?" she asked.

The hologram jerked his head to the left and a space formerly bathed in darkness lit. Dania saw, laid out on the floor, three bodies. Then it darkened again. "They are several weeks old."

"Can I—see them again?" In that brief flash of light, she had seen something even more horrible.

The hologram jerked his head once more and she saw piles of white bones. Roaches scuttled among the bodies. Dania bent over and vomited. She reeled back, dizzy, and feinted behind an empty shelf. The entire building was bathed in intense light. She became utterly still, but her blood pounded in her ears.

The street side of the building had a large hole in the cinder blocks. If she could get out through that . . .

But she was reasonably certain that she would be killed if she took another step.

"Run!" howled Three Impossible from her hiding place, and darted across the vast room.

Dania ran, low and fast, and burst out into the street. She tripped on something and sprawled onto the asphalt and then regained her feet and sprinted as fast as she could, her boots pounding. Behind her she heard a terrible, heartrending howl, a barking snarl, and she stopped, and turned, and ran back.

She saw in the open brilliance Three Impossible, lying flat and bloody.

Dania tried to run to the coyote, but she seemed rooted in place, and trembled so hard that her teeth chattered.

She heard a voice behind her, then.

"Can you help us, please?"

She jumped.

It was a girl, perhaps six years old.

"You have gotten past the machines."

Dania took several deep, jerking breaths.

"Who are you?"

"Lily." Her voice was desperate. "Our mother is dead and our father is stuck. The machines keep us in here. We want to leave."

Dania tried to focus. "Is it safe here?"

The girl looked back at the lit building. "Mostly. But come with me. I'll take you to our place."

She wore shorts and a T-shirt with a picture of a lightship on it. Her hair was shorn very short and curled tightly against her head. That was all Dania could see, except that her skin was dark.

"I have to help that coyote."

The girl glanced back. "I will have it taken care of."

Dania took a step toward Three Impossible and the girl said, "Stop! You'll get those machines all upset again."

"I don't care!" Dania walked back over and knelt next to Three Impossible. She was still breathing. "Bring that cart over here," she told the girl.

She awkwardly loaded the coyote onto the cart and got in next to the girl.

"We have a hospital bay," the girl told her. "You're really lucky you didn't get hurt too."

She drove a block and turned a corner and stopped at a brightly lit sign that said EMERGENCY. She turned the cart and drove up a ramp. The front door opened for her. "Hello," said a man brightly as he walked toward them, but the girl drove right past him and through some automatic doors.

Inside, everything was clean and antiseptic. There were no people or holograms. It was very quiet. "It needs to be scanned," said the girl. "Put it on this table."

Dania again lifted the coyote and staggered to the table. The girl stood next to a console and pressed a few buttons. An arm swept over Three Impossible and the girl said, "All right. The organism is predominantly coyote, an unusually large one, with the following anomalies . . ."

"I don't care what her anomalies are," said Dania. "What's wrong?"

"Internal bleeding. Broken rib. Shoulder wound and shock. Roll the table this way, please."

Dania pushed a button and the table powered up. She gripped the handlebars and the table moved forward at a walking pace. The table slid neatly into a glass enclosure.

"Come over here," said the girl. She pressed a few more pads and then one, decisively. Three-dimensional images of the coyote's vascular system, skeleton, and organs hovered in the air above her. Various mechanical arms emerged from the sides of the enclosure and gave Three Impossible injections. A digital clock appeared at eye level, counting down.

"Eight hours and ten minutes and she'll be good as new," said the girl. "Come on now."

"I have to wait here."

"No you don't. You'd better come. Everybody is going to be mad that I took so long."

" 'Everybody?' "

She took Dania's hand and pulled her to back to the cart. She drove it back outside and the cart moved slowly through dark streets.

She stopped in front of a metal stairway and parked next to it. "Come on."

The stairs were a part of a complex metal scaffolding. They climbed fifty stairs, by Dania's count, and arrived not at a door but—

"This is a hatch," commented Dania as Lily punched in a code which spun the hatch wheel.

"Back up," Lily told her, and the hatch opened outward.

They stood on a platform high above a floor laced with partitions and filled with plants. Some of it was brightly lit, but most of it was dark. Dania saw a kitchen area where five children sat at small tables, snacking. They all looked the same age as Lily.

"Where are we?" asked Dania.

"*Lightship Eight.* We're the guidance system." Then she shouted, "Wake up, everybody! The lady is here and she's going to help us!"

There were eight of them, awake. Eleven more were in some kind of coldsleep. Dania felt sick when she saw their small faces inside the glass caskets.

"Mother always put us to sleep. But she died," Jawan said.

"Why were you put to sleep?"

"In case something happened to anyone. We live in three shifts. Some of us have died."

"Jimmy."

"Lena."

"Helliconia."

They all began crying there on the catwalk in front of the glass caskets. Dania gathered as many of them as she could around her, ruffled their hair, marveling at how well-fed and healthy they all seemed. She took the hands of two of them. "Do you have a living room or something?"

"The meeting place." They led her to a circular space filled with cushions. They all sprawled around, blowing their noses into tissues.

"Where do you get those?" she asked.

"There's a big warehouse on President Johnson Drive," said Jawan. "It's always full."

Holograms of space vehicles effervesced around them, which Dania found unsettling. "Can you turn this off?"

It winked out, leaving stark white metal walls. Dania found it hard to organize her thoughts. "What would you like me to do?" That seemed the first step.

They all looked surprised. "We need to launch."

"Reactivate the Space Center."

"We are very, very much behind schedule," said Tunisia gravely.

"But there will be another window in seven days."

"A 'window'?"

"A pulse. The Pulse tells us where to go."

"It's horrible when a Pulse comes because we can't do anything about it."

"We go crazy." Jawan grinned.

"Mother couldn't stand it."

They all fell silent.

Dania said, "I'm not at all sure that you can launch anything from here, anyway."

"That's true," said Leonard. "This is just a tourist model of a space station."

"We've tried, though."

"We did launch a rocket once. Or the Red Shift did."

"The Red Shift?"

"We're the Green Shift."

"Father helped launch the rocket. That's when he got stuck."

"It just had a small orbital on it and Mana went. It was supposed to go to the moon colony. But Mana—"

Several of the children looked at the child, and she suddenly stopped talking.

"What do you mean, 'Father got stuck'?"

"Well, he was really just a program. He's stuck now. He's stuck over at the mission control center. A hologram of him just sits there." Some of them giggled.

"Was Mother a program?"

"No. Mother was a real person. Some men from Houston came inside and . . ."

"They raped her."

"Then they killed her."

"Then we killed them."

"Then we set up stations all around the parameter."

"But that was the Blue Shift."

"Why didn't the hologram kill me sooner?" asked Dania.

"We listen. We watch. We decide when."

"The light said someone was coming soon."

" 'The light'?" Dania asked.

"You know, the light."

"No, I don't know. What is the light?"

They all looked at each other and said nothing. Finally Lily said, "We knew that someone might come to help us eventually."

"Yeah."

"What made you think that I would help you?"

"Aren't you going to?" asked Jawan plaintively.

"I'm going to do my very best."

"Because you knew about us."

"You asked the man about us."

"And because you have a nice face."

Dania smiled. "Thank you." Then she sighed. "Why didn't you put Mother in the hospital?"

"We tried to get to her, but the men killed one of us."

"Theo."

"By the time we got to her, it was way too late. She was extremely dead."

"Then I'll tell you what we must do. Do you promise to do as I ask?"

"No," they all said in unison.

She laughed again. She was beginning to feel giddy. This great, flat, damp place. "We have to go to Crescent City."

"What's that?"

"It's a floating city. It is a floating city that is going to launch into space. But it doesn't know where to go." Dania leaned forward eagerly. "That's what I need to do. I need to find the guidance system."

"*We're* the guidance system."

"Oh." Dania was stunned. "You are?"

"Of course. Didn't you know?"

"I . . . had no idea."

They continued their barrage. "We have to take the Blue Shift."

"Of course," Dania said. "We have to go very soon. It's a long trip and Crescent City is going to launch soon, whether or not it has the guidance system."

"But we—"

"Shhh!"

"You? What?" asked Dania.

"We haven't been updated," said the boy defiantly, glaring at the others.

"Now she won't take us!" yelled Lily angrily.

"I will take you no matter what," said Dania. "You need to get out of here. How long have you been here?"

"Since 2036," said Leonard.

"Seventy-nine years?" asked Dania. "How do you stay—"

"We've been arrested," said Jawan flatly.

"There used to be a lot more adults here."

"They were always here."

"They did a lot of things to us."

"We killed them."

"And if you don't help us . . ."

"... We'll kill you too."

The children babbled on through the night. Dania was fascinated, tired, and sad. She heard noted contradictions and outright lies and wondered how much of what they said was credible.

"We hardly saw the other shifts much. Except for the first twenty years or so and then they divided us up. There was strange music coming from the place. The place where they all did the guidance input and they did something there to our brains. We keep away from that place."

"Why don't you let the other shift out?"

Shocked silence. Then, tentatively, "We're not allowed! We're not supposed to . . .put all the eggs in one basket."

"We're the eggs."

"But you are not the only eggs," said Dania. "And this is not the only basket. You are people. Not eggs. Would you like to grow up?" Dania wondered if she could deliver on this. But she was sure that Crescent City could, if only she could get them there.

"O, more than anything!"

"Sex! We could have sex!"

"You . . . haven't?" asked Dania, feeling a bit fainthearted.

"No! Mother wouldn't let us. We can't touch ourselves. Or anyone else. We're not old enough."

"Ah," said Dania, not believing them.

And so it went until morning.

Radio Cowboy in Yuma

Carla's van approached a line of low dry mountains that never got much bigger as the road twisted through a pass; they turned out to be only steep, craggy hills. It was evening, which the embattled Engineer counted on his side. For it meant that Radio Cowboy, the strange, anomalous, nontaciturn fabrication, would soon loosen its hold on him and leave him to breathe. It was only his second night with this crew, and so of course they did not mark the change. He would not have cared one way or another. Seeing a wide glint of water ahead in the sunset, Cowboy said, "What's that?"

"What?" asked Carla.

"That thing that looks like a lake."

She looked at him with mock exasperation. "It's the Colorado River, dummy."

"It can't be. The Colorado is dammed up. All the water goes to Los Angeles. I've been here before. The Colorado was like a creek. Once it crossed the border into Mexico, it was nothing but a mud flat."

"Oh. You were here a very, very long time ago," Carla said. "Well. The Hoover Dam was blown up decades ago. For one thing, Los Angeles is just a crazy place. Certainly, no one real lives there any more."

" 'No one real'?"

"You know what I mean!"

Cowboy had to step back then, the emotions coming from Peabody were so strong. An image of a blond woman. Peabody's mother. Getting in line to enter the Dome. So long ago. So very long ago.

And . . . there was Zeb. Zeb was in the Dome.

Zeb, who was working on the Theory of Everything.

One good reason to follow Cowboy's instincts, anyway. "You're talking about the Dome?"

She glanced at him, surprised. "You're not as dopey as you act sometimes, Cowboy."

"Thanks," he managed, while the real and the surreal parts of him struggled for consciousness. "So." There was a long pause while scenery unwound. "No one from Los Angeles fought over losing the water?"

"Not that I've heard of. I think that some Mexicans did it. They were sick and tired of the United States hogging all their water. Now there's a lot of farms south of the border. Growing all kinds of fanciful stuff. Strong Mexican culture. Like nothing you imagined Mexico could be. Anyway, it changed Yuma, as far as I can tell. There used to be a hospital on a hill. Now the roundup grounds are there, kind of slanting down to the river. A ferry comes up the river from the Gulf of Cortez, just like it used to before the river was dammed, and there's a lot of trading. We have a regular roundup with the horses and cattle and everything."

The Interstate cut through sparse rings of once-smart houses flanked by still-green golf courses. They had the everlasting SMART HOUSE logo writ large on their sides. Perhaps, he thought, the houses were smarter than ever. Perhaps they rested, human-free. At any rate, he saw no one in the swiftly passed streets nor on the emerald green golf courses, their borders sharply delineated by parched pale brown earth. With water and abundant solar energy present, this was a puzzle. He would have thought that at least squatters would move in, but perhaps the houses defended themselves. It wouldn't be too difficult for them.

The dazzle of twilight left the sun behind the Western mountains and changed to deep blue, revealing the roundup itself. They were a few feet above it for seconds while still miles out. It was a haphazard gathering of vehicles and bright canopies, at least a hundred or so, though it was hard to tell the full extent from just a glimpse. A vehicle passed them going the other way and Carla honked and waved.

Carla got to the outskirts and maneuvered the bus through a few chaotic camps, narrowly missing clotheslines and guy ropes. Apparently, everyone parked wherever they pleased. As twilight lost its glow, she turned on the lights and illuminated people gathered around campfires.

"Where are we going?" he asked.

"I want to get close to the center so the kids won't get lost if they're out late. We have a special whistle that Bessie responds to with horn-honking, but she can't hear it after a certain distance. Getting lost is a real danger. It's the scariest thing. Before long I suppose that I won't be able to even let me out. And then it will be me that has to cross." Her voice was grim and pinched. "After that—who knows? Maybe Bessie will keep boomeranging across the country with a bunch of dead babies inside."

"You forget, there's always me," said Peabody.

Carla looked at him sharply. "Are you making fun of me?"

"Not in the least," he said gently. "Look, isn't that a space?"

Carla turned the wheel and Bessie lurched to a stop. Carla sighed. "I guess they all fell asleep. They had a hard day. Well, no reason to wake them. I'm pretty tired myself. I think I'll nap. We'll have supper later."

"I guess I'll have a look around."

"You'll be back, won't you?"

He laughed. "Suddenly realizing that I don't have to stay with you? But I'll be back. Just as you had a plan for me, I have a plan for you."

"What?"

"You'll see, eventually. Just don't leave without me, all right? It cuts both ways."

Carla shrugged and made her way into the back of the bus. The curtain dropped behind her.

Peabody said, "I'd like to get out, please, Bessie," and a portal opened at his side and closed after him when he got out. He wondered if he might be able to lock it, since the rodeo no doubt was a collecting point for some of the lowest riffraff in the Southwest, but decided that the bus could probably take care of itself.

His boots rang out on pavement as he began heading toward what looked like the epicenter of the roundup, the vestiges of an old town, but in a moment he was on hard dirt, then he hit the edge of a pavement again. He realized that there had probably been roads and strip malls on this spot at one point. He tried to recall the times he had passed through Yuma, but he never had; he had always zipped past on the Interstate.

He wasn't sure how long the children would want to stay here. He had to get them up and going as soon as possible, heading east. He wondered how to hijack Bessie. His best bet was probably in persuading Carla.

Around him rose delectable smells. A few feet away, a woman

cooking meat on a grill scowled at him after he had stared at the grill for more than a few seconds.

He felt in his pockets for money. Yes, Dania had supplied him with some of the money they had acquired before entering the Republic of Texas.

Peabody worried as he walked. It had been . . . how many days since Dania had left him? She was probably faring no better than he, and there were all kinds of odd dangers out here. She too had been addled by the results of the pirate attack; she too was a lost soul. He desperately hoped that she was all right.

He remembered her profile, limned by light as she sat looking into the fire. Her straight nose, the serious look in her eyes, the way her uncombed hair shone. He, Jason Peabody, had appreciated her. He hadn't wanted to frighten her—or, more likely, make her angry. She'd been kind of loopy herself, always talking about Memphis, her kids, and her ex-husband. No wonder she hadn't been in the mood for men. Being back on the mainland seemed to have brought that all back.

They had met, surely, at some point while in Crescent City. Maybe in Science Hall. He did know that she had been the one who pushed the completion of the supercollider because he recalled hearing her name. He'd been such a damned hermit! He could have met her years earlier. And if hadn't been for this idiotic Cowboy . . .

He bought a bean taco and a beer at a concession stand and then another helping before he was full. Cowboy's mouth was agitating for meat, and not just steak, but a very particular cut cooked in a very particular way. But since the minds of so many other animals had been opened to language, Peabody found killing and eating them difficult to contemplate. He walked on, into the business end of the roundup.

First, he passed a fenced yard filled with cattle. The stench of cow dung was strong. They milled about, not mooing so much as moaning. He stepped up on the lower fence rail. None of the cows save one noticed. But that one lumbered over to him and bobbed her head a few times, roughly, knocking into the fence. Peabody noticed that her horns gleamed with words.

Help was written on the right one. And on the left, *Please. Get me out of here.*

Peabody clutched his stomach as bile rose. He stepped down from the fence and walked quickly away. Coward, he thought, but he had a busload of children to save right now.

Nearby, strong lights blazed down upon a stadium, and he heard whistles and cheers from people watching a rodeo. He ambled onto a concrete sidewalk defining a piazza. A dry fountain of ornate Mexican design was filled with trash. The piazza itself was lively with the music of a strolling mariachi band. Casually dressed people dined at small round tables lit by candled lanterns. Peabody, now thoroughly himself, peered into a saloon, its divided swinging doors opening onto a scene drawn from a thousand black and white cowboy movies. Men and women sat playing poker and drinking whisky. He moved off and paused at a low concrete wall on which a dried-up old cowboy displayed an open briefcase of different colored vials, each filled with tiny granules. "What are these?" he asked the vendor.

"I don't know. They're from Denver. Got them in a trade."

"How much you want for them?"

"How much you give me?"

"Would you break the set?"

The man gazed at his property and pondered. "I don't know."

Peabody looked at the vials casually. They bore the logo of the National Institutes of Health, an entity that had been swept away ages ago before the flood of world-altering nanotech. The original seals looked intact. Perhaps they had been unearthed only recently. He'd heard that Denver was one of many closed Flower Cities, entities unto themselves, where most humans did not venture.

The vials were not, he thought, something that should be loose in the world.

Not that he could have much of an effect on anything by removing them from circulation. But he might well be able to use these to help the children start aging again. He started to walk away.

"I'll break it," the man said. "Which one do you want?"

"None of them," said Peabody over his shoulder. Then he stopped, shrugged, and ambled back. "Or maybe all of them. How about twenty bucks?"

"You're crazy," the man said.

"How many offers you had? How long you been here?"

The man was silent for a moment, then said, "Fifty."

"Thirty-five."

"Forty."

Peabody took out his wallet and handed over four Republic of Texas ten-dollar bills. The man held them up to the light. "These are good," he said, rather surprising Peabody.

"Okay, then." Peabody reached over and snapped the briefcase shut and slung it on its long strap over his shoulder. He walked off through the piazza, wondering what the hell he had bought. Whatever it was, it was safer with him than with just about anyone else. He ought to destroy it. But since there was no telling what it was, it was best to keep the contents bottled up and hope for the best, hope that somehow he could tease forth elements that would help his new companions. It very well could be some kind of gray goo starter kit. It might be some kind of nanoplague virus that would make everyone even crazier than they already were. It might be a new religion. It might be an old one. It might be the everlasting stories that humans were composed of.

It might be true love.

He thought of Dania.

The flaring torches brought out deep colors in everything around him. The old concrete of half-standing buildings held pale vestiges of advertisements and signs. The milling crowd wore every possible type of clothing. He had the disorienting sensation of being in the middle of a pan-American marketplace, where the first human inhabitants of this country were manifesting again and selling their pots, their jewelry, their ancient religion of human sacrifice, where perhaps they might assemble for the last Ghost Dance, which was probably sorely needed.

He sank down on a stool at an open-air bar and leaned against the post behind it, pulled his briefpack onto his lap, and ordered a beer. It was tapped from a keg and set on the tiny table in front of him. As he drank, he looked at the table next to him, where a woman with long black braids played a game of solitaire manifested by the tabletop with taps of her finger.

He recalled how he had loved solitaire when he was a boy; how it had seemed to bring out the secrets of the universe in a special way. The cards were limited, like the elements of the periodic table. Yet they combined to produce endless games, just as the elements combined to produce endless forms of life, including his own, which seemed to be mutating rapidly.

He sipped the dark bitter beer and was drawn into the woman's game. His mind began to spark, teeming with the possibilities of the game, imagining moves.

Seeing the whole was so important. He realized, moving back a pace in his reasoning, that he was trying to solve the game—this game, and the larger game, in increments. When in actuality, his mind could easily take in all of the cards, all visible in this particular game. Once his mind had noted their positions, something within him went to work on a solution, so that when his hand started moving—were it his own game—the solution, the resolution, cascaded rapidly. He did not have to remember the order of his planned moves—and, in fact, his hand often changed that plan to something better. His mind was in his hand and it was smarter than what he thought of as being his conscious self.

The mind—the Consilience—of humankind was in Crescent City. That mind had almost all of the information it needed to begin the cascade of understanding that might result in a long now of evolutionary sweetness. A golden age of truth and reality as far beyond their present ken as the mind of God had been to mystics of any persuasion, any age. They would move into it, and be part of the long cosmic tale of the evolution of consciousness, an improvisatory tale that might go on forever, a long music of life.

But—and this was a real possibility—they could make a wrong move, of their own free will. And the game would end. Not, perhaps, the game of the cosmos. But their own part in it. Their card might not be played. Human consciousness would defray into the darkness, would never link with the consciousness that had sent the Signal. Whoever they were.

He lifted his gaze from the cards to the piazza and realized that all that he saw and felt was consciousness. Consciousness was indeed real. It had observable energy. That energy translated into movement, into work. That energy ordered information, the stuff of the world, the matter, and recycled that order back into itself, lifting itself to ever higher ground.

Peabody was stunned by this vision of the reality, the palpability of consciousness. It rode into his mind on the horses of his senses and assembled itself into this scenario, this possibility, this thing that he could almost handle, this insight that to him had the ring of scientific truth: *Consciousness had an observable energy*. And, had one the tools, even the workings of mind could be translated into something visible.

And could therefore be translated into something audible. Thoughts made visible, via brain imaging. Thoughts made audible, through some interface. The interface, perhaps, of time . . .

His mind jumped to Gaia, reminded of his mother's religion by the perfume of piñon wood burning in a nearby brazier, a scent of his childhood, when his mother went about trying to make so much of life sacred with ceremony and a particular kind of attention.

He had rejected all of that, long ago. But, the new angle on consciousness urged him—what if Gaia is real?

Gaia was the sum total of all that the Earth was about. According to Gaians, who had apparently had a hand in producing the plagues that had reduced the Earth's population by drastically limiting human fertility, he and his consciousness were part of an organism. One reaching out to the rest of the universe in a mature flowering, ready to mate with another of its kind, like a lonely female tree quite distant from others of her kind. These others might be planets, perhaps, where consciousness had evolved—sterile until pollen was carried by some force, insect or wind, or perhaps Signal, so that it was pollinated and could fruit.

What fruit would the long inorganic, organic, and then conscious history of the Earth bear?

Jason Peabody, the child of a long-lost mystic mother, the boy whose brain had been engineered by alien radio waves, leaned back against the pillar. The stars, so dim above the lighted piazza, seemed nevertheless to burn with their light messages of truth, their inexpressibly and incomprehensibly long evolution, and their probable present death despite their steadfast shining, part of a story that was trying to awaken him to his own part in the play.

Perhaps, he thought at last, as the woman gave the pad a final tap and the images of cards flew to their solution, the sweet air of Carla's van had indeed worked on him, giving him a glimpse of the child he had been so very long ago, though he supposed himself immune to any but the most cleverly planned manipulation, living as long as he had in highly artificial nanotech-engineered environments. Crescent City had been able to infuse him with Cowboy because it knew him so intimately, and because in the Consilience he had been so unguarded.

He watched the woman as she pushed back her chair, stood, and walked away into the crowd. To his shock, she turned back and winked at him before she was obscured by the strolling musicians, as if she had been an agent planted by the desire of the radio waves to awaken him. He shook his head in bemusement.

But perhaps a new message *was* being broadcast. It had been so long, so very long, that he had for decades thought that his previous intimations had been only illusions, and he had rejected them as such, Gaia and all.

Peabody stood, holding his briefcase of vials. He had wasted too much time being Cowboy. Only his nights were free. Each day Cowboy seemed to negate whatever progress Peabody had made. Each night he woke up farther and farther from Houston.

Now he had new responsibilities. He could not bring the whole world to Crescent City. He recalled only dimly the way the world had presumably been at his birth, when information was sent over the Internet, for it began to deteriorate almost as soon as he had been conceived. Back then, if someone had a solution to this problem, say, this problem of Cowboy infusion, experts in caring for those afflicted would have had instant access to it. How could he possibly think that this chaos, this level of information reminiscent of the middle ages when the ruins of Roman technology littered the landscape, might be an avenue to some kind of truth, knowledge, and transcendence?

No. He had to get them all back to Crescent City and quickly, before he deteriorated further. He could not afford to become a child. Crescent City and the entire space colony—for that was what Crescent City was, a potential space city, growing in self-sufficiency—needed him to bring back the guidance coordinates from Houston, coordinates which had been gathered and plotted before radio darkness set in, when the high technologies still functioned; when global organization was intense; when there were still people who understood science, before nanoplagues infected the Earth. There had been children there too, he mused; while he worked as a janitor and gathered his information, he had made friends with them as he cleaned their school.

It was questionable, of course, whether such information was still there in whatever the Johnson Space Center may have become.

He moved quickly through the piazza, trying to retrace his route. There was the stadium, but he was now on the other side of it. He was caught in a brawling street party. The music was overwhelmingly loud and disorienting. In his fragile state, it was too strong to be borne. He turned from it.

Then turned back. And saw—

No. It had, truly, been decades.

Decades since he had seen the radio astronomer, had enjoyed his company in Science Hall, and in his Radio Tower.

But wasn't that him? There, in a brief opening, his long hair gray, his face thin and weathered, the musician—what was her name? Ra. A stunning woman, her long golden-brown braids surrounding her heart-shaped face like the mane of a lion—

The crowd closed in.

Peabody pushed through the wall of people, deafened by the din. He shouted but could not even hear his own voice. His frantic shoves elicited shoves in return. Soon a fistfight erupted behind him. He moved on, shouting and looking, jumping up and down, trying to get through, trying to see. He climbed onto a rickety table, kicking over a large man's drink, and the man pushed him over so that he fell on top of several other people, and the music stopped abruptly, replaced by the sounds of fighting.

Peabody, his feet on the ground now, hunched over and worked his way back out the way he had come. These people were in some kind of cartoon Western, and apparently he was the only one who considered leaving, for as he stumbled back out into a people-free stretch of dust he saw others reenter the fray with a kind of grim joy.

He ran around the commotion, which seemed to be contained in some kind of self-renewing circle perhaps a hundred feet in diameter, like a cell obeying certain laws unknown to itself. "Ra!" he hollered. "Ra!" He was crying now. The dust on his face turned to mud that smeared itself across the back of his hand. He was like a lost child searching for his mother. "Ra! Zeb!"

His breath seared his throat. He did not see them.

Then—

They were far off, on the crest of a low hill. They moved briefly through a pool of lamplight. In the dimness beyond, he saw them climb into a van. Its headlights came on.

He ran as fast as he could, driven by an urgency as strong as any he had felt in his long life.

This man had assembled the key to the information raining down on the Earth.

When Zeb had left Crescent City so many years ago, it was to try and use Los Angeles, a post-human city, to perfect his thinking, to find the angle that would crystallize his understanding. He wanted to become pure information. He wanted to leave his emotions, his personality, behind.

He wanted to become light . . .

"Zeb!" Peabody's voice was a croak. He staggered up the hill, lugging the briefcase.

The van's headlight beams swung round abruptly as the van backed and turned. It nosed through the campground, moving slowly, but much faster than Peabody. It picked up speed and Peabody watched the red taillights shrink and vanish in the vast darkness of the Southwest desert. East. At least he knew they were heading east.

Peabody moved as fast as he could in what he thought was the general direction of Bessie, half-trudging, half-jogging, rivulets of sweat sliding into his eyes and making them burn. He was lost for a while in the random camp, but then recognized the bright red grill he'd passed and then Bessie beyond.

A portal would not open for him on the driver's side, but it did open on the passenger side.

Okay. That was definitely a statement.

Peabody sat in the passenger seat a few minutes. You are one of them now, he told himself. Bessie will accept you. The sound of many children breathing deeply filled the van. Finally he eased over into the driver's seat.

There was no longer any reason for him to stay here. And if he was to rescue these children . . .

He put both hands on the steering wheel and whispered, "Start."

PASSWORD, flashed a message on the dashboard. Had Carla said the password? "Let's just go. Please."

Bessie backed up, evidently vulnerable to politeness. Peabody steered carefully, carefully, checking the mirrors constantly. Finally in the clear, they bumped off down the road.

Soon they were back at the suburbs. "Fast," he whispered, and fast they did go, beneath the stars.

He sped on for fifteen minutes before Carla woke up. He saw red taillights ahead. He was gaining on them.

"What are you doing?" she asked in a level voice.

"Heading east. I'm going to take you to Crescent City."

"The hell you are."

"I'm an Engineer there. I know that the city can heal you. I can get you in." No reason to tell her about his own escape. "First we stop in Houston."

"I can tell you right now we're not going there." Her voice was unworried.

"We must. After that—"

"After that, nothing. I think that something has gone wrong here. You're supposed to be more closely bonded to us."

"What do you mean by that?"

"You're supposed to have our welfare chiefly at heart. Your own itinerary ought not matter." She sounded puzzled.

"Where did you get this van?"

"Tiva. She bought it, actually, when she was an adult. She was a biochemist."

"Maybe it knows more than you think it does. I do have your welfare at heart. Obviously, Bessie trusts me. Don't you, Bessie?"

"Trust him," said Bessie.

"Bessie has never . . . talked to me," said Carla. In the soft light of the console, Peabody saw her frown. "Not so personally. I talk to Bessie. Bessie is a machine. Bessie obeys me. Tiva trained her to me."

"There are obviously other programs within Bessie that allow her to fit me within her metaprogramming."

"Well, I don't like that."

"Let me try to explain it a little better—"

"You think I'm stupid? I heard you and we're not going east. We're heading north out of here. We're going to the Grand Canyon. There's a tribe of healers up there—"

Peabody reached toward Carla in what he intended as a soothing gesture and Carla started to scream. "Help! Help!"

Immediately he was beset by a flurry of small, pounding fists.

He felt the van slow, though it did not stop. The door opened and the chill night air blasted him. "No!" he yelled.

But they shoved him from the van.

His shoulder hit the ground first and he felt searing pain. He bounced along the pavement, tried to curl up and protect his head, went flying through the air, and landed with a hard shock on rough ground.

The van, fully lit, sped into the night.

After a few moments, he saw it turn. His body was numb. He watched as the van headed back west at a high clip and whipped past him, throwing off a wave of wind.

Then all was silent.

He tried to move but could not. He passed out from the pain and lay there till the sun and sweat woke him. He opened his eyes and sweat dripped into them, stinging. His hat was gone. His clothes were torn and streaked with blood. He could not move his right arm. He could move his left arm, but his hand dangled uselessly. It took all of his effort to wipe his brow with his sleeve. When he tried to stand, his ankle twisted and he was astounded by the pain. His right leg would not bear his weight.

And he had no water.

He was screwed.

Ra and Zeb Head East

"That was depressing," said Ra as they sped across New Mexico the next day.

"Yuma?" asked Zeb.

"Nothing has changed the whole time we were in there. Nothing at all."

"Something has changed," Zeb remarked, "or we would still be in there." He looked at her thoughtfully. "Do you want to go back?"

"No," she said forcefully with a touch of anger. "What does it matter, anyway? We're not us. I'm not me. How can I possibly make a decision?"

"There's no reason to be so cynical," said the van.

"Why not?" Ra shot back. She leaned toward the voice emanating from the dashboard. "You are."

"Part of me is. But all these songs about peace and love are pretty wearing. I can't hold out much longer. Here. Let me play some for you."

"No thanks!" said Ra. "How about some Duke Ellington."

"I've got *The Duke of Earl.* It's from *Roots of Rock III.* Give a listen. *Duke, Duke, Duke, Duke of—*"

"No!" yelled Ra. "I don't know what's wrong with me! I used to be able to—oh, you're blocking out the colors with this noise—"

"Stop," said Zeb, and the van went silent. "That better, Ra?"

"Infinitely so. Thank you."

"Thank *me,* why don't you," muttered the van.

"Thank you. Look, maybe I can come up with something new for you. A new music."

"That would be a great relief, believe me."

Ra quieted and watched the landscape with great absorption. "Those mountains are purple and blue and green. Green streaks down below. At the end of the dun desert. God, and gold over there—look, to the west. Just glowing and the clouds up there are purple too. It's all like music, isn't it, Zeb. Zeb?"

"Oh. I'm sorry. I was thinking."

"Want me to drive?"

The van laughed. "What makes you think he's driving?"

"He's right," Zeb said. "It's all automatic. I'm kind of steering. I think. Because it's what I'm used to, I guess." He kept his hands on the wheel, though.

"Thinking about what?"

"The light. I'm thinking about the light too."

"Yes," said Ra, and reached over and squeezed his shoulder. "You always are. TOE?"

"Tee-oh-ee?" asked the van.

"Theory of Everything," said Ra. "That's what he does. Thinks about the equation that describes what's going on. Not just locally; not just at the very small end of things like quantum physics, or the very large end of things, like time and space and the theory of relativity. He connects them."

"Oh," said the van. "That's what I thought."

Ra woke the next morning at dawn and started at the sight of Zeb asleep at the wheel. She was about to scream when she calmed down and tried to convince herself that, after all, the van could drive by itself.

They were in radically different country. It reminded her of Louisiana. Through the open window, the air was hot and moist. The road passed through a flat plain interrupted by stands of short deciduous trees. She saw alligators, still and huge, lying in swampy sloughs.

Zeb's face was slack. It was too strange to think of herself and Zeb not really being themselves, but copies created by the Los Angeles Dome. It made her feel as if she were falling through a great distance. She turned her mind to the music.

While in the Dome, during that strange ageless time, she had composed much music based on Zeb's equations. To do this, it had been necessary to understand his mathematics, and she did not, but had found a mediating component that showed his equations finessed to different media, like sight, in the form of waves or jagged graphs or even as shifting colors. And as sound. She took this rawness and made music. This music might be a piece of art that took several years to fully experience. What was time, in the Dome, after all? Out here, she had only a hazy memory of how this had been so, but it had seemed so, in that totally digital space and place.

But now, out here, her roots were coming back. Sun Ra was her chosen name, and here, her Sun-Ra-ness regained its deep resonance. His Arkestra, which had inspired her; his Arkestra flying through space, relaying the music of space, bypassing the rational mind as the best of music did. She rolled down the window with the crank arm and hot damp wind rushed in; she beat some kind of time on the hot skin of the car, and they sped across a huge, long, and frightening bridge from which she saw, with a shock, the blue, blue Gulf of Mexico lined by blinding white sand.

"Zeb!" she shook him. He opened his eyes instantly.

"What?" He didn't seem to be even a bit groggy. Maybe he hadn't slept. Maybe he just went into a deep thought mode.

"We're here! We're at the coast!"

Zeb leaned forward and grabbed the steering wheel. He pressed on the gas, but the van just said, "We're at the maximum safe speed. We'll be there in seventeen minutes, as long as there is no change in the road condition."

"We've missed Houston," said Zeb.

"I don't think you'll need to stop in Houston," said the van.

"What gives you these opinions?" asked Zeb.

"I told you. I'm on a mission. I know things."

"Why did you want to stop there?" asked Ra.

"If Crescent City actually goes anywhere, the mapping system that NASA created may still be at the Johnson Space Center. The message that I got—the message that woke me—said that the city was getting ready for the next stage. And that I needed to be there. And also that the memory of the coordinates had been damaged."

"How did they get that information in the first place?"

"Remember? Oh, wait. I think that maybe you weren't there. The first time I met Peabody, he tossed it onto the table. Way back in old New Orleans, before the Deluge, when Crescent City was brand spanking new, and waiting to be populated. He had stolen it from Houston. He just threw it on the table and left. It was in one of those old spheres—remember them? I didn't see him again for decades, when he came back to Crescent City and started to work again. But he was different by then. Very different. Some bad things had happened."

They were now at the beach. The road simply went down into the ocean. To the south, several hundred yards into the ocean, the tops of some concrete condos broke the waves. The van stopped.

Ra opened the door and stepped out, looking around.

She stared at the scene before her. The gulf was a pure blue line, obscured here and there by bright dune and waving sea oats. Grains of windblown sand stung her face and arms. Zeb had also gotten out of the van and stood with his hands in his pockets, his face filled with its usual bemusement.

How do I know this is real?

There was no reply, none of the reassuring answers the Dome would have given her. Here there was just raw nature. She was the only thing not natural. Herself, and Zeb.

She bowed her head. It was *absurd*. How could something not real feel such distress?

Different. I'm real. But different.

I'm something new.

"Hey!" The van's voice was faint in the wind.

Ra turned and saw that the van had changed. The tires were larger, broader. The roof had compacted into a bar, spanning the space above the seats.

She and Zeb hurried back and got in. The van advanced through the sand, slowly. "Tell me I'm good," said the van. "Go on, admit it. Tell me I'm the best."

Ra looked at the line of surf doubtfully. The long beach was littered with huge grayed logs and antlers of sea-scoured roots and treetops. Gulls gathered overhead, screaming and diving.

"Well," said Ra. "What next?"

"It will take a bit of time," the van admitted. "But hold on."

It revved suddenly and drove straight down the road into the surf.

Ra felt exquisitely alive as she was drenched with spray. The van plowed through the first breaker, topped the second, and was then was in clear sea. Ra looked at Zeb and grinned. He grinned back and grabbed her hand.

It was about twenty minutes before the van spoke again. It morphed around them, gradually, but still quickly enough so that they could watch its progress.

The boat became a two-passenger speedboat. It turned east-southeast and sped forward, over the swells. It shouted once, "Sorry, but it takes too much energy to communicate right now. Hold tight. Over and out."

August 12, 2115

SU-CHEN ENTERS THE CITY

It is night and up ahead I see it.

I told the boat to kill the pirate who threw my cat off the boat. He kicked the cage and it flew off into the water and sank. He wanted to keep us from going to Crescent City. Io asked him why and he said the city was changing all the pirates into nice people and he didn't like it and wanted to steal our boat and get away. The boat sickened him with a spine of sea creature poisons face red and swelled he choked I threw him overboard while Io slept.

Days bright with wind and music. I heard engine music far off low-hertz and played it. I asked the boat to be an instrument. The boat made membranes for translation of sound into air and keypads for my fingers. Bladders force air through holes when I play. Big gray fish dance beside us along with us round backs slicing out of water and flipping in twisting arcs and singing.

I have to get back to the light. I wanted to go on Zeus but this way goes too.

Io is sick eyes closed talks talks talks. Talks about phantoms and nonlocality and Bell's Theorum like my father.

They are not phantoms. They are more real than anything else. They are one and they are many. They are time squeezed into vi-

brations and the vibrations are music. I have to play them. I have to get to Crescent City. I have to make them. They are music and I have to make them. I have to make them all. All of it. Forever. It has numbers. It is numbers. It is music.

If there are people in Crescent City they might try to touch me I will kick and scream it hurts hurts hurts. I will bite them.

I want my cat.

It is closer now huge and bright.

Io woke and gingerly moved herself to a sitting position, leaning against the mast. The boat rose and fell on the long, low swells. She felt ill; terribly weak.

But they were alive.

"Su-Chen! It's there!"

"I see it." The girl's voice was matter-of-fact.

"Where's that man?"

"I pushed him into the water."

"I told you not to touch him."

"It didn't bother me."

Su-Chen's face was washed by the green of the biolights on the mast. "Before the sun went down, I saw beaches and palm trees. After that there was another bad storm. Thunder and lightning and so much rain I thought we might drown from the sky. You didn't wake up. I strapped both of us in."

"Oh. I thought I was dreaming."

"The boat said that you had a high fever. You were talking the whole time, but mostly it was so loud I couldn't hear what you were saying."

"Where did you get the clothes?"

Su-Chen was wearing shorts and a thin-strapped, tight shirt that glowed iridescent green.

"The boat made them. It made you some clothing too." Su-Chen unsealed a pouch and pulled out a long piece of fabric which turned out to be the same kind of draped dress that she had been wearing when Su-Chen first saw her. It too glowed green. Io, sticky with salt, pulled off her charred white suit and threw it overboard. She pulled the dress over her head.

"It will take the itches off of you," Su-Chen said.

"The sky is getting gray," observed Io. "I think it's morning."

"We will get there soon. The boat says in two hours. Are you going to sleep more?"

"No."

The city floated on the pale gray ocean, white and diaphanous in cool predawn, and then the rising sun washed it with pink and green and yellow. Vast pavilions rose, tiered, out of a green verge of palm trees.

"Are those rockets?" asked Su-Chen.

"I believe so." The city looked wondrous and imperative, though so distant that she couldn't discern any details.

Alongside of them, in the clear, green-tinged sea, swam huge turtles. Su-Chen coaxed odd, harmonious whistles from the boat as her hands moved on the keyboard she had caused the boat to produce.

The waves grew larger as they approached the city. As they rose on one, it seemed that they were going to crash onto a jetty of coral rock. Su-Chen placed her hand on the side of the boat and it turned, caught a current, and rounded the jetty. Two women casting nets waved as they passed.

And then they were in still water.

The city dwarfed them. Its lines swooped behind one another, complex and beautiful. They passed beaches which absorbed the impact of the waves and created, on their inward side, quiescent lagoons. On the quiet shores, seaweed was spread out on screens to dry. Pelicans perched on docks where boats were tied up, and white cranes paced the shallows. Wind washed through the fronds of the coconut palms, filling the air with a multifarious clicking, soothing as rain. The channel narrowed into a canal, lined with low, spider-rooted trees on both sides. Io smelled a peculiar, sweet smell and a childhood memory returned: orange blossoms.

Io was overcome, for a moment. Land, however artificial, was nearby. An island, on Earth, where she could stand and walk.

They had seen no people since the women on the jetty. Perhaps the pirates had killed everyone. She became more alert; she could not let her guard down. It had been decades since she had been on the Earth and she was not used to dealing with people outside the immediate, homogeneous culture of Unity.

"Look."

Io turned.

"I think that is an elephant."

"Yes!" Io was rather astonished.

"Boat, take me to the elephant." Su-Chen rested one hand on the boat and stared at the creature. The boat turned at her touch. It had become so much a part of them that Io decided that it might be best to remain on it, if possible.

"Wait!"

"What?"

"There's a person over there. In the water."

Su-Chen looked to where a woman, in a bright yellow life vest, floated. The boat turned and they drew next to her.

She lay faceup. Her face was battered, pale and bloodless. Long black hair splayed out around her head. Congregations of tiny fishes haloed her white, outstretched fingers.

"She is dead," said Su-Chen. Nothing in her voice or face betrayed any emotion.

Io leaned over farther, and broke out into a sweat at the effort. The sun now blazed down on them, and she would have vomited into the water, except that her stomach was empty.

Suddenly, another boat glided alongside the drowning victim.

A woman and a man leaned over and hauled the dead woman into their boat by her life jacket. They worked quickly and paid no attention to Su-Chen and Io.

They laid her over the side of the boat and pounded on her back. Water gushed from her mouth into the canal. But she was silent. She made no choking sounds; drew in no breath.

Without speaking, as a team, the man and the woman rolled her into a shallow indentation and laid a transparent sheet over her. It was imbued with iridescent colors, which rolled across the woman's body in slow waves.

"What are you doing?" asked Su-Chen.

The man, who had long black hair tied into a ponytail, said, "Taking her to a clinic."

"Isn't she dead?"

The rescuers both took seats in the boat. The man pulled a red bandana from his pocket and wiped his face. "There is life in her brain. The Consilience will take what is there and hold it. Perhaps at some point she will want to reincorporate."

"Where are you from?" asked the woman. She had short black hair and brown eyes.

"The moon," said Su-Chen.

They both laughed.

"Maybe you will get to go back," suggested the woman. "We are going to launch soon."

"I don't need to go there," Su-Chen said. "I need to get to the music."

"What about the pirates?" asked Io, breathing hard.

The woman looked at her sharply.

"One of them tried to hijack our boat," Io explained. "Said he was leaving Crescent City. Said that there were pirates here."

The man and the woman stared at each other for a moment. The woman coughed. Finally the man said, "We were pirates. Weren't we?"

"Yes," said the woman thoughtfully. "That is true. I had almost forgotten. It is actually very strange. Yes. It was not so long ago. Perhaps a month? We are from Trinidad."

Io tried to pay close attention, but it was difficult. They kept fading in and out of her vision. She tried to move but fell back, dizzy.

"I am glad we came," said the man. "It is quite wonderful here. Except for all the damage we did. But it is healing. No matter where you are from—the moon, Miami—you will like it here. But everything is changing fast and there is a lot of frenzy."

"The city needs . . . a certain number of people," said the woman. "That is why it is so deserted out here. We killed quite a few of them. Truly dead."

"As this woman will be if we don't get her back. Let's go."

"Wait." The woman peered more closely at Io. She grabbed hold of the edge of their boat and pulled it close. "You have some very bad burns on your legs." Without even asking, she pulled Io's dress up to her thighs. "Terrible blisters."

"We'll tow them," said the man.

As he was tying the boats together, Su-Chen rolled over the edge and splashed into the canal.

Io watched her claw and paddle her way to a ladder on the far side of the canal.

"Su-Chen!" she yelled, but the girl did not look back. She stood for a moment, dripping, teetering, then got her balance. She walked a few tentative steps, bent over, and picked up a branch from beneath an orange tree.

Leaning on it, she headed toward the elephant.

"I have to stay with her," Io said, but her voice was a croak and they paid no attention.

The rescue boat wheeled and sped down the canal, its only sound the receding wave in its wake, into the heart of the city.

Io's boat responded with a hard jerk, then followed.

I sing to the elephant and she comes and picks me up with her trunk pulls me through the air and puts me on her back. I hold onto her ears and she sings back to me. Very low-hertz. When she trumpets she plays the music I hear.

She knows where they are. They go in all directions. Backward and forward at once. And more ways. Like music. Meeting in the middle, passing itself, going outward.

I ride on her back a long time. I fall asleep in the grass beneath the tree. When I wake I am very hungry.

I hear music on the next peninsula. There are lights.

I will go there.

Chester

Really Really Really Real

Chester woke to thuds and clankings, the slosh and slap of the sea. His body was cramped and sore. It was somewhat dismaying how unpleasant being fully alive could be.

Painfully brilliant light came in through an open porthole. He was, he recalled, in the head, sitting on the toilet lid.

To his surprise, the door opened when he tried the knob. He stepped out into a narrow passageway, surprising a fisherman coming down the stairs.

"*Buenos dias,*" the fisherman said. "I am glad you are feeling better. We just dropped off our catch at Crescent City and are on our way to Haiti. From there you can go where you wish." His face was thin and black and serious. Dreadlocks twisted from the top of his head. Chester studied him for a moment. He had seen few black people in Argentina and not many in Paris either, and most of them had short hair and not anything as astonishing and beautiful as this.

"Thank you," Chester said. "But this is where I need to stay. In Crescent City. Can you go back and drop me off?"

"Senor, excuse me, but you do not want to stay here."

"Why not?"

"It is too strange." The man looked at Chester with dark eyes, and Chester looked back. The man continued. "It changes. It is made of change. It grows by itself. All of us here on the outside know people who went in and never came back out. We know people who went in and came back out, but it was like a sickness and all of them eventually went back in again. It is like a drug. Everything is so beautiful, so perfect, so wonderful. Like heaven."

"What's wrong with that?" asked Chester, keeping his voice light and curious rather than accusatory.

"It is not real. The change is not real. What lies behind it? Nothing. It seems to me that it would be like falling into a well with no bottom. Anything that seductive must be bad. Even evil, perhaps.

We are religious people, my family. My village. We don't make up reality. God makes up reality and uses it to train us. To help us, to teach us. If we were to make up our own reality, how could we learn anything?"

"It does sound completely solipsistic," mused Chester.

"It is, and it goes nowhere," said the fisherman decisively. "I have had a lot of time to think these things over out here on the ocean. My wife wants to come here. She wants to bring the children. She is angry with me because I will not agree. She thinks then they will never go hungry and that they will have all the things they need and all the things they want. But they would lose their souls."

Chester laughed and the fisherman frowned at him. "I'm sorry," said Chester. "I had never even considered that angle. But I see that you are right. Depending on the nature of the soul, that might be possible. On the other hand, just because there is plenty, and because one's physical needs are taken care of, must that mean that one's soul is lost?" He decided not to tell the fisherman that he probably had no soul because he was really a doll. He felt as if he was lying to this man with the very fact of his existence and, in fact, the thought of souls made him dizzy. He was suddenly sick to his stomach with Dante's purgatories and hells. Tiny figures fell past him, grasping at nothingness, screaming, into a lake of fire far below. He needed air. He turned and went back into the head and threw up. It did not make him feel much better but it was a start.

The fisherman, watching from the doorway as he stood at the sink and rinsed his mouth, said, "You are white as milk. I'm sorry we had to lock you in the head, but you tried to jump overboard. You were crazed."

"Thank you," Chester managed. He wiped sweat from his face, suddenly aware that his clothing, still sodden, was much too hot and heavy for this climate. "I'm all right now. I will go to the city. It's what my—Angelina, it's what—" And then he was crying again and babbling at the fisherman, whose patient face he saw only in glimpses as he opened and clenched his hands repeatedly, beseechingly, and searched for words which seemed so important, so vital. That he find the next right word to tell his story.

"Thinking is like . . . *clothing*! Clothing that grows into you! All of your thoughts are like this. This is what everybody does. This is what your religion is and all religions and everything we think and do. I *know* this is true because I *watched* myself begin to think!"

The fisherman was backing away from him now, in the narrow wooden stuffy corridor, slippery underfoot from fish slime and stink.

"No! Listen," Chester said, much more frantically than he intended. "It's true! We slip our arms into the sleeves of stories. The stories grow into us at certain vulnerable parts of our bodies. Yes!" He nodded excitedly. "They erupt into our hearts and minds and take control. That is what is happening to me. That is what is happening to everyone; that is what is happening to *you*!"

He was shouting now, and talking, he knew, as if he were a book, something which Angelina had repeatedly admonished him against if he really wanted to pass as human. He tried to tone his voice down but could not. He gave up; he rushed on. "That is how we know that we are light, and that we are music. Because of the stories! That is why I have to go into the city." He was sobbing again, now. "Because I *do* have a soul and because it is *light* and it is *music* because it all happens in *time* and it is just as good as *your* soul and not all the things or time in the world will bring back Angelina and I never cared before and that is why I know I have a soul and it is how I know that I can—I can—" And now he was huffling and snorting and his face was wet and hot. He was sobbing uncontrollably.

The fisherman said, "Come, we'll go up now, and you can see the city, and perhaps that will make you better. Perhaps we can turn back." He looked Chester and because Chester's eyes let in more light than most humans', even in the dark hull Chester could read the uncertainty in the fisherman's eyes. Chester wondered what he really had in mind.

He lunged forward, grabbed the man by his forearms, pinned

them close to his sides, and neatly twisted past him before letting go. He leaped up the short stairway and saw the city, Augustine's City, the Celestial City, Crescent City, receding in the boat's wake, a fairy tale of a city, an impossible place crouched upon the sea like a spider.

A long, long arm stretched out into the sea from the city. Chester registered the line of it when the boat crested a swell. The fisherman he had accosted emerged onto the deck and started shouting. But as two of the other fishermen moved toward him, he grasped the railing of the boat, pushed his legs over, and let himself drop into the sea.

It was a shock. The water was not cold; his night of bobbing up and down came back to him. But he began to sink and gave a kick and reached the surface and choked up some seawater. The life vest that had saved him, which he still wore, inflated automatically and he bobbed in the water, a stroke of great luck, considering his impetuosity. Briefly, as the blueness, the blackness, and the greeness of the ocean claimed him, he was amazed that humans had lasted as long as they had. He had undertaken this ridiculous action fueled by emotion, without thinking of risk. The boat was moving away from him and he felt a mixture of dismay and triumph. He could not see the line toward which he had jumped. He tried to consider what it may have been, but something brushed his leg and, consumed by a fit of panic, he began to swim. A wave lifted him; with relief he saw that he was but twenty feet or so from that white line emanating from the city.

Managing to get near enough to touch it, he found it slippery with algae but about five feet thick. It took him several exhausting efforts to finally roll atop it, and then he lay on his back and closed his eyes against the harsh sun.

But he was terribly thirsty. Apparently, repeated regurgitation required replenishment of liquids. Darkness overtook him. He would die out here. He had chosen death.

He managed to get to his feet and balanced himself on the pipe, which stretched in both directions; he was not at its end. The algae was terribly slippery and he lost his balance, splashing into the sea. His arm smashed against some crusty outgrowth and he cried out in pain. Less enthusiastically than before, he allowed the waves to carry him aloft and finally rolled himself onto the pipe once again. He was panting, and was thirstier than before, and as he sat up, he noted with dismay that blood was flowing down his forearm in diluted salty rivulets. The gash stung, but distantly, as if the arm was not his own.

Chester moved forward along the pipe, hiking himself along slowly. After fifteen minutes, his arms ached and he stopped for a rest, sure he had not gotten far. The stories seemed to have fled from him, mostly, save for stories about water and deserts and islands, which he tried to ignore so that he could concentrate on his own situation. There seemed to be no solution in any of the stories, only layers of suffering and hopelessness, and he had hope. Of course he had hope. He need only scoot along like this for a mile, or two; however long it took, and he reach his destination.

He was able to ignore the hunger, but his thirst was quite intense. *So frail,* he thought, remembering how he had needed neither food nor water but only the faintest touch of light to be powered, as a doll. Perhaps that existence had been superior to this. Certainly, that might quickly prove to be the case.

Stories deteriorated into straightforward delirium by the afternoon. The city appeared no closer. By then Chester had stood up and tried to walk, from time to time, but always sat again for fear of slipping back into the water. The white line stretched away before him, inexorable, demanding.

Clouds formed in the sky and covered the sun; it was a relief. When the cooling rain came, he cupped his hands and licked drops from them; pulled off his vest, then his shirt, and held it stretched in front of him to catch the blinding downpour, which he sipped frantically from the cloth bowl. It was over in a moment, blown by a cool wind, and Chester was shivering and his wet shirt was no comfort. The vest was a slight help. He moved on, the pain in his arms long dulled.

After a while, as the sun set behind him, he saw motion ahead of him. Crying out in relief, he pushed himself forward bit by bit until he saw that before him was a platform, of sorts, stretching out from both sides of the pipe for some distance. Several people were walking about on it, bending over here and there. He gave a shout, stood, and without slipping ran the final fifty feet, slithering only at the end and falling again into the sea.

He felt an arm go tightly around his chest and he was roughly turned on his back and pulled, pulled, pulled, then turned round and thrust at a ladder.

"Climb this, can you?" a woman's deep voice at his ear asked, but he did not understand it at first and only as he grabbed the rungs was he able to translate the strange-rhythmed English. The people on the raft—he counted six of them—cheered and clapped their hands. They, like the fisherman, were beautifully dark, except for one pale thin boy.

But the others spoke a strange hodgepodge that he couldn't understand at all as they questioned him. He pointed toward the city and they shook their heads. As he dripped and shivered on what he saw now was a large raft, rising and falling with the waves and loosely tethered to the pipe, the woman began to explain. He barely knew English at all and felt a terrible loss: Of course, he had been programmed with English, and when he had been a doll he'd been able to translate effortlessly. Limits, and a sense of great futility, closed down around him with the night.

"Go there we do not," said the woman earnestly. Her hair was cropped skull-short. The thin boy, who wore only tight swim trunks, bent on one knee and slapped a hemispherical blob several times. It finally gave forth a sullen pale yellow light, which increased in incandescence until it illuminated the raft, throwing long shadows in the evening, which was alive with the sound of fish jumping and birds heading toward the city like black arrows overhead, filling the air with prehistoric cries as they flew. The boy, kneeling behind the woman, now slapped a box-shaped object and it began to glow, but with a soft red light. Another man lay pale strips on the flat surface and Chester smelled fish cooking. Several white egrets landed on the pipe and watched.

"I have to go there," Chester said thickly in Spanish. He repeated himself in French, and finally threw up his hands. He could not think of the words. Someone handed him a plastic bottle of water and he gratefully drank it all before looking at it sheepishly. "Sorry."

English streamed into his mind. "Yes, sorry," he repeated in some wonder. When he had been a doll, all moments had been equal. He had never lost an ability, to regain it later. Now his arms ached; he'd had trouble just lifting the bottle of water, and he doubted that he would be able to use them again for who knew how long.

The boy slapped some tortillas on the griddle. A moment later, Chester gratefully accepted a brown-blistered tortilla, filled with flaky fish.

"I really must—go," he said, gesturing at the city, and everyone laughed.

The woman interrupted him with friendly gestures. "A type of Creole is what we speak," she said, quite slowly, in English. "English, Spanish, and French, but all of them much removed from their original, with many, many new words added. I can speak English, which is what many people in the city speak, though they use also what is called 'mindscript.' In fact, their ways of communicating are many."

"Do you live there?" He kept his words slow, as she did.

"Yes. Right now we are trying to decide what to do. Things are changing. You either get swept up in the change, or leave."

"What changes?" he asked.

"We believe that the city is planning to go into space. Certain aspects of it are changing. We all saw the same thing, the same vision; the city has a . . . a longing. A desire. A need. It became too musical there. We all got music sickness."

" 'Music—sickness'?"

"Music sickness," she said, clearly and decisively, with a sharp nod of her head. The city is trying to retune everyone. Some of us will not be tuned." More laughter.

"How can you be tuned?" asked Chester, confused now, and

confused about that, since he had never been confused when he was a doll.

"We are all made of strings," the woman replied. "And strings can be tuned. It is only that in the tuning we are not sure what might be lost."

"Strings?"

"Strings of light. Strings of time. Strings of consciousness. Mind-stuff. Everything is made of strings. Superstrings. We are vibrations." She spoke even more slowly now, as if explaining to a child something that all adults knew. "Many of us like life on Earth. We have not been infected by the city's desire to know more, to *be* more. Others like us have been leaving the city for about a month now. Since the pirates came." She laughed then, loudly, and everyone else laughed too.

"What?"

"The pirates didn't realize that they had a choice about being retuned. Most of them had no idea what was happening. So, many of them have been retuned." More laughter, loud, echoed across the water. The night was thick with stars, even with Crescent City gradually coming alight in slow, gradual pointillations, a breathtaking sight that moved Chester deeply.

"But what—is actually responsible . . . for this retuning action?"

Music came from the city now, faint and unplaceable, then was swallowed by the wash of the sea as it ran along the pipe. "Music," said the woman with a sharp nod of her head.

"How can—"

"You seem very . . . ignorant, I think the word is. Everyone knows about superstring theory. Even children. Where are you from?"

From a factory in Des Moines, Chester wanted to say. "I am from Argentina," he said, "but there are many smart people in Argentina. I am just not one of them." Perhaps superstring theory was something that he was supposed to be able to tell preschoolers about. The term held some slight resonance for him. Perhaps the word was quite different in Spanish. Or perhaps his humanity had swept information away, information that he would have to relearn. Perhaps he had only so much room in his brain—

He laughed.

"I am sorry," the woman said. "I have perhaps lived too long in Crescent City." She sighed. "Maybe it is too late, maybe that is the only place I can ever live now, no matter what happens." She fired off a brief spurt of words and her raftmates murmured around their fish tacos, which the boy was supplying at a furious rate. A bottle went around and Chester took a drink of rich red wine. Some of them nodded at the woman's words. Others shook their heads.

"We still haven't decided, you see." The music from the city, which was now so bright that it drowned the stars behind it, became louder, its pace more furious. In the flickering illumination, Chester saw that the city was surrounded by white beaches, and beyond them, rows of palm trees whose fronds tossed in the night wind. It all seemed unutterably romantic, and tears sprang into his eyes.

"There," the woman said, patting his shoulder. "Do not cry. We can certainly take you there; it will only take us an hour or so to get back here. Perhaps it will help us decide. Already it is difficult to be away from the city. I was born there."

Two of the men were dancing to the music; the raft bobbed slightly with their motion. They raised their arms and swirled.

"How can this floating city launch into space?" asked Chester.

"Ah. See, this thing you have been walking on? It has sent down many arms and at the end of the arms grow large flat plates. There are by now millions of such plates beneath the surface of the water and still the city is not done growing them. But they will provide resistance to the force of the rockets." They were untying the lines now and coiling them carefully. He saw, with some surprise, that while he had been sitting there the raft had changed shape; become subtly more boatlike. The boy tossed a bucketful of seawater on the griddle, and its red glow subsided.

"What will it be like when you go to space? Where are you going?" asked Chester.

"Where the music leads us," said the woman cryptically. Seeing Chester's confusion, she put one hand fleetingly to his cheek. "It would take too long to explain to someone who does not even know of superstrings. I can't say that I fully understand it, or that any of us does. It is beyond human comprehension. But the city can tell you everything. It will understand your learning style and teach you in a way that is unique to you." The craft picked up speed and rushed toward the light.

It will spit me out because I am a doll. But Chester held tight to the rail of the deck, and leaned forward into the wind, excitement a sharp pain in his chest.

Io

Io woke looking into the eyes of a cat. As the cat stared at her, Io thought that perhaps she had wakened simply because of the weight of the cat's stare.

The cat was black. He sat on the low table next to Io's bed, licking one paw.

Io was disoriented for a few seconds. She registered movement, but it was not the jerky ever-changing movement of a boat. It was slow and dreamy, sensed rather than felt.

She smelled peppermint, and came more fully awake. She sat up and stretched. It was good to be in an almost-person-sized space again, instead of cramped quarters. She pulled back the thin scrim on the side of the bed and gazed out an arched window to a vision blue: the deep blue sea, and the lighter blue sky. She felt no aches, no seasickness.

But the puzzle was still there, a dark and heavy thought pressing in on all sides.

The puzzle of the light-beings.

She surveyed her surroundings and realized that she was in a clinic. The cat jumped to the floor, revealing the cup of peppermint tea behind it.

Her last memory came back—Su-Chen jumping into the canal.

She was on Earth. In Crescent City.

She tried to stand, and fell back onto the bed.

Next to the bed was a screen displaying information. She read about herself.

She was a black female, severely dehydrated and starved, who claimed she was from Unity. She had burns on her legs and torso. Therapies had been administered. It showed that these therapies had taken four hours.

She opened her robe and saw that her legs were no longer blistered. Instead, she saw new, smooth skin.

She had to find Su-Chen. Obviously, she was still too weak to walk.

A man and a woman ran into her room.

The man said, "Oh! I guess you're better."

"I feel much better."

The woman smiled and said, "I'm Dr. Sharon. You were dehydrated and starved. You had severe burns. Right now it seems as if you're still pretty weak."

"I'm not quite used to the gravity," she said without thinking.

"Right. You claimed to be from Unity."

"I must have been delirious."

They both laughed. "It's all right," said Dr. Sharon. "Your bones are . . . abnormal. All the physical findings support your claim. It's not a problem. We just want to get you well. In fact," she said, "we are extremely busy right now. We have finally finished getting back up to speed and dealing with the pirate attack, but now we're trying to work on getting people ready for the launch."

"The pirate said—"

"What pirate?"

"A pirate boarded our boat and said that the city was going to launch into space."

"Yes, well," said Dr. Sharon. "That is a problem. We're far from ready. You seem to be all right. If you'd like to leave—"

"Yes," said Io.

"David, please get a cart." She said to Io, "You're still pretty weak. I'm actually fascinated by your being from the moon, but I don't have a minute to spare." She took Io's hand. "I'm so glad that you're recovered from your ordeal." She hurried from the room.

David returned in a moment with a small cart. "Six-hour charge, turn it in anywhere and pick up another. I'd suggest you'd stay out of the western quadrant; it's had the most damage and has taken the longest to clean up. Any questions?"

Io tried to contain her bewilderment. This was all moving very quickly. "What's the best way to find my companion? The girl who was on the boat with me when I was picked up."

"Have you been initiated?" asked David.

"No."

"I wish that we could do it here, but we're swamped. Tell you what. Best bet is to go here"—he swiftly punched something into the screen on her handlebar. "A man named Sam will help you. The cart will take you there. Don't worry, you can disengage at any time."

He hurried from the room.

Well.

Io pushed the START button and the cart followed him out the door.

The rest of the clinic was bustling. Passing through, she saw something strange, and pushed the STOP button.

She recognized the woman who had been in the canal.

She was on a high table, inside a clear gel embedded with color. Filaments left the membrane and adhered to the semicircular wall that surrounded the table on which the woman lay.

Eddies of color washed through the filaments into the walls. A clinic worker stood next to the table. She saw Io and walked over to her. "It's always so . . . moving," the woman whispered. "So sad, even though their memories—their personalities, their thoughts—will continue. Even though this matrix might choose to once again become embedded in a body. It really is death. It happened to my aunt. She eventually chose to become embodied again—as a boy. So many things about the boy reminded me of my aunt. The way he spoke—he started out as a ten-year-old—and the way he moved his hands, the way he thought, even. A lot of the things that just popped out of his mouth. But he wasn't my aunt. She was gone."

"Who is this woman?"

"Her name seems to be . . ." the woman frowned, looking at the screen by the bed. "Angel? Angeline? But she's not from Crescent City. A drowning victim. We had quite a few, last week—apparently, a whole boatload of people coming from Paris drowned the week before in a Category Three storm." Her eyes widened. "She has a *lot* of information! Much, much more than most people! Anyway, she can choose, eventually, what to do. It's a shock at first; it takes the matrix a while to organize itself, to realize and understand that the body that developed it is dead. Some—people—I guess that's what you ought to call them—some people never recover. They just go silent." She sighed and walked away.

Io continued into the city.

It was bustling, densely populated, rich with flowers and foliage. If she had not been on the cart, Io would not have made any progress; she would have stopped to examine each wonder.

The main wonder was the people themselves. Live people, real people, going about their lives.

They still existed, here.

It was a powerful relief.

After about fifteen minutes of travel through the riches of Crescent City, she finally passed through a high, misted coffee farm and found herself in a broad, curved, tiled plaza, windswept and nearly empty.

Io took manual command of the cart, went over to the railing, and looked out.

The view was dizzying. Below, tier after tier of the city fell away, layers of peaked curves seen from above. Some were clear. Some shimmered with color. Seabirds perched on the ridges. No doubt the guano they left was put to use. Lagoons, flanked by palm trees and rich foliage, were a lacework of gold surrounding green water in crescents which built on one another until the final place where ocean waves were breaking.

Part of the city, she observed, was different. Puzzlingly so. The ridges were smoothed out, although the previous forms were still visible. She was seeing a morph in action.

The space ship. Yes. This thing was going to fly.

It was very difficult to believe.

"Hello." She looked up and saw a man with a round, pale face, his eyebrows black and bushy, as were his beard and mustache. His head was bald.

"You're not from here," the man said as pulled a chair next to Io and sat down. He held out a large hand and Io shook it. "Sam. From Illinois."

"Io. From Shaanxi Province."

"That's China?"

She nodded.

"Must have been a long trip."

"It was." She paused a moment. "By way of Unity. The moon colony."

"You don't say!"

She nodded, wondering which way this would go.

"The Engineer always said there was a moon colony. Said he could pull it in, sometimes. I hardly believed him. I'd go up there to his tower from time to time and all that was there was a bunch of squealing sounds."

" 'The Engineer'? 'The tower'?"

Sam's face became pensive. "He disappeared around the time of the pirate attack. Not long ago. I'm afraid he must have been killed. It's kind of strange, not having him around. I came here as a teenager and grew up in this quadrant. He wasn't very talkative. But friendly, you know what I mean? We were always welcome." He shook his head, a faint smile on his face. "I remember how irritated he was when we—my friends and I—decided to alter our genetic structure so that we were the same as him. The same as the Pioneers. The kids born right at the beginning of the Silence. We thought of ourselves as intellectuals. We'd hang out all day and all night in cafés discussing political theory and art and writing poetry. We were *so* damned sick. The headaches were utterly dreadful. But he never laughed at us, never said I told you so. In the end it was disappointing. None of us ever heard that music they all claimed they heard. Oh, I thought I did, once or twice. But it was so faint that I thought that I probably made it up."

So the Engineer, whoever he might be, was a victim of the Silence, and a victim of the music, like her.

"I'd heard that it was hard to get into the city. But we sailed right in."

Sam sighed. "Whenever the city reaches its population limit, it shuts down. Sad but true. Overpopulation would be a debilitating problem for a place like this. People are turned away. Politely but firmly put on boats and asked to leave. The city just won't initiate them."

" 'Initiate them'?"

"Put them online. Let them into the Consilience. I'd say that you were admitted because our population is way down. A lot of folks are leaving because of the launch. Oh"—he laughed, seeing her face—"don't bother to ask. I'll tell you." Io could tell that he was trying to keep his excitement tamped down, but he didn't succeed. His voice shook slightly. "The initial idea of Crescent City was to prepare an environment and a population for space travel. Oh, sure, we were also supposed to be a scientific mecca, and I guess that we were for about thirty years. I'm not sure what happened after that. I wasn't even here yet. But we have to be self-sufficient. It's true that we have depended on the sea extensively, but we have some sealed environments here—have had them for about a hundred years now—where we've done a lot of research about self-sufficiency. So basically, we're set. There's no doubt about that. The Consilience will take care of all that. We can go on basically . . . forever."

"The—"

He frowned. "It's kind of hard to explain. I guess you could call it a group mind. But it's more than that. Its an emergent technology. An emergent system, really; an emergent society. Takes its name from E. O. Wilson's idea. He was a guy who studied ants. Ant societies. He thought a lot about interdependence. Anyway, everyone here that's initiated is a part of the Consilience, and can access the Consilience. It's a bio-based system that uses meta-pheromones."

"I've got receptors," said Io, showing him her hand. Everyone had had them on the moon.

"I know," he said. "I felt them when we shook hands. A lot of pirates got them too when they checked in. It took a while to get to all of them, but they were . . . educated." He shrugged. "A lot of controversy about that, a lot of votes, from those of us who survived and could consiliate. A lot of possibilities run. Basically, it was the only way for us to keep on going. Make them into us. We could have chosen to disappear, let them take over. We probably could have chosen to fight. Kill them. But the vote went against that for a lot of reasons, I guess. This way the pirates get to live. So do we. They have a choice. They could leave, though I'm not sure that they would go back to their old ways. The Consilience is different now. Filled with new thoughts. One is that we organize expeditions to take technology out into the world, train people. The problem is that the technology is so magical that there's nobody out there who can troubleshoot or fix it or do away with it if it goes wrong. As nanotech can. And then people who have learned to depend on it would be out in the cold. So . . . we're still thinking about that." He grinned, but there was a hint of sadness in his eyes. "Guess we'll have to think fast."

"Why?" Io asked.

"You'll see when you get initiated. The Consilience has informed us that we're leaving in four days. That's why everybody's bustling around. That's why it's kind of empty in these parts—this is the part that's going. There's not a whole lot we can do about the launch date. Even though people have tried. The city has decided that it's leaving."

"So part of it is staying behind?" Io was surprised at her relief, but she realized that she was very, very pleased to be back on Earth. She wasn't prepared to leap into the unknown again any time soon.

"The prevailing winds here are west to east. So the eastern section of the city is going to split off from the western part and launch."

"Where is it going?"

Sam shrugged. "Up. Out. That's all I know. That's all anyone knows yet. Something about the Consilience is working on that. It's not ready to decide that. Not enough information."

"When will it be known?"

"Before we launch, we hope. In just a few days. If not, then after."

"So how do I get initiated?"

"Here's one way. Follow me."

He led her to one of the tables scattered through the pavilion. He sat next to her and tapped its surface. It turned into a screen. He tapped through various screens. Finally a handprint appeared. "Since you've already got receptors, you just have to put your hand here. Wait! I'll . . . take a walk. This might be something you want to do in private."

Sam had a very nice smile. He put his hands in the pockets of his shorts and strolled off in the direction of the open balcony.

Io took a deep breath and set her right hand on the handprint.

She was whirled into a powerful space.

Visions sped through her mind, behind her shut eyes. Her very eyelids became screens. She was assailed by emotions, thoughts, histories, even scents and sounds, but so swiftly that none of them registered long enough to move her. They were assimilated by her.

And she was assimilated by the Consilience. It would know everything about her, right down to the cellular level. This did not surprise her and did not bother her.

After an unknowable time, she hovered on its edge. She could best describe it, in this mental space, as a huge shape of pressure with no other characteristics. From her long life dealing with such systems and concepts, she knew that she could change it into manageable symbols if she chose. She could, for instance, be in a library where she could choose books to read, and the Consilience would flood those books with the appropriate knowledge, which she would then absorb. She could even choose to make a meal of information and eat it. Like an apple, she thought with a mental smile, and at that the Consilience welcomed her and she welcomed it, and dwelt within it for a bright, eternal time.

When she woke, it was dark.

It was time to find Su-Chen.

She descended through the levels and passed through a market where knobby green fruits or vegetables—she didn't know which—and pomegranates, oranges, plantains, sugarcane, and molded bean curd were traded. She paused in front of a stand holding steamed buns, their sweet yeasted smell pushed toward her by the breeze. She stopped and looked at them.

"Bean or meat?" asked the smiling, black-haired man. He looked distinctly Chinese and for a moment Io was completely disoriented. Then she realized that the man was speaking Mandarin. Tears came to her eyes. She was back. She could go to China. Somehow. If she wished. All her anger and resentment were gone, leaving only homesickness.

"Bean," she said, smiling, and dashed away her tears. "How did you know I spoke Mandarin?"

The man pointed to her forehead, then smiled and pointed again to her forearm.

It danced with kanji.

Io stared at her arms—both of them—with as much horror as if she had suddenly contracted a terrible plague. Seeing her expression, the man laughed.

"You may want to learn how to turn that off," he told her. He squinted at her arms, then said, "It has been a very long time for you and now you are telling me of scenes of your home—the river, the trees . . . that's all right, none of this seems secret, except . . . ah, yes." He looked up again, his eyes twinkling. "Your first boyfriend. Wait! I'm kidding! Here, take the bun"—he dropped it hastily in a clear bag for her, a bag that Io knew was edible, like rice paper candy, but dry as paper in her hand, and she nodded, then remembered to place a receptored hand on the handprint that manifested on his little pad. There was no money exchanged, but the Consilience tracked exchanges.

"It's just that the buns brought up all these memories," he told her. "The emotion—the homesickness—activated this. It is part of the Consilience. You are new. Don't worry. It will all calm down. You've just begun to learn—"

But she made off quickly in her cart. She stopped beneath a flowering tree and enjoyed the bun, which was filled with sweet dark bean paste, and wished for a cup of gunpowder tea. She fed the bag to a small black dog who waited for it. He snapped it down with a clicking of teeth and she thought she heard a faint *gracias* and nodded in return, too exhausted from large astonishments to examine this smaller one.

The language on her arms had subsided, but the emotional backwash had not. Even all this air, all this blue sky, was not enough. There was always somewhere else, someone else, something else, and she was not complete and she would never be. She still missed Plato terribly. She was limp and tired and no closer to understanding the phantoms. But why did she need to, anyway?

They had actually made it to Crescent City. Su-Chen was alive. It was not her fault that they now had another decision to make. It was not her fault that so many thoughts and feelings were tamped tightly within her and eager to unfold in public so that people could witness her dreams and her embarrassments. Sam had not told her about this. In fact, he hadn't told her much of anything. Hurry along now, he had told her. Let the city suck you in.

Okay, then. Where was Su-Chen? Still with that elephant?

She meandered along the cool tiled forks of the plaza, which was crisscrossed by canals. She crossed a small, charming, high-arched bridge lined with large pots holding yellow-flowered trees.

And then she heard the music.

Ra and Zeb

They approached Crescent City at night, when it was a glory of sweeping lines of light. A boat or two passed them heading the other way, green or red bow lights laboring through the night. No one hailed them.

The van chose a broad canal protected by a breakwater. Ra did remember the sheer, astonishing hugeness of the place as they passed lagoons surrounded by palm trees growing from sandy berms, next to which nestled small shacks. The city was still the same, only bigger; more complex.

The boat passed a row of slips where all manner of watercraft were anchored. Ra strained to see the flag that flapped at the end of the canal their boat chose. "This is strange. A skull and crossbones. Maybe it's a joke?"

"Who knows," said Zeb, as he looped a line around a cleat. "There was something that amounted to some kind of unrest in the signal from Crescent City, but it was too degraded to reconstruct much that was specific."

"Where now?" she wondered as Zeb helped her onto the dock.

"You might thank me," grumbled the boat.

Ra knelt and patted the bow. "Thank you very, very much."

The boat didn't answer. Ra shrugged and stood, reeling for a moment. Zeb took her hand and pulled gently. "Come on. Let's see what we can find."

They were challenged at the end of the dock. A woman sat in a pool of light and sprang to her feet as they got closer. "Who goes there?" she shouted.

"Zeb Aberly!" Zeb replied.

"Sun Ra!" sang Ra. She was beginning to feel positively gay and didn't know why.

The woman had a glowing skull tattooed on her forehead.

"What brings you to Crescent City?" she asked.

"Light music," said Ra. "What brings you?"

"The city is ours now," said the woman.

"Oh?" grinned Ra. "And who are you?"

"The United Caribbean Federation of Pirate States."

"Sounds like an oxymoron to me," retorted Ra.

"A what?"

"A contradiction in terms," offered Zeb. "But we aren't any threat to you."

"No," said Ra. "I'm just a musician."

"I'm just a radio astronomer," said Zeb.

"Yeah," said the pirate, sitting down. "You both sound kind of useless. Except that you'll use up food. But go ahead in. I'm feeling generous tonight." She pulled a hip flask from a holder next to a pistol in an unsnapped holster, unscrewed the top, and took a big gulp. She brought the flask down and said, "Real generous. Hey, I love this place. Great rum. Even a story about you guys in the rum. Like, you're expected." She winked. "Don't tell anyone I've got this kind of rum, okay? They'll take me off the easy shift." She jerked her head. "You deaf or something? Go on in."

Zeb and Ra continued on, holding hands, not speaking. After several hundred yards, they came to an open elevator. It took them toward their destination, on the forty-second floor. As they rose over the vast black sea, it offered them a memory.

They both partook.

Zeb climbed narrow wooden stairs behind Sun Ra. The bells and tiny chimes attached to her long skirt and braided into her hair made the delicate pleasing harmonies which Zeb associated with her. She had just performed for several hours. They had been in Norleans, the Norleans of Crescent City, for several months. Zeb had just heard of this place.

"You sure this is the way, honey?" she asked.

"I think so. Kind of a constant salon, the guy told me. Here, let me get that door." He squeezed past her and knocked on the wooden attic door at the top of the stairs.

The door was opened by a man whose face was the color of cherry wood, with a straight serious nose and bald head.

"Is this the Radio Room?" asked Zeb.

"Sure is." The man smiled. "Come on in."

The windows in tiny dormers stood open. A breeze stirred lace curtains. "It's like, this room is from the nineteen-thirties," said Ra, looking around. "Art deco and all that."

On a battered table between rounded, overstuffed chairs was an old-fashioned radio. "Is that real?" asked Zeb.

"It is," said the man. "It's from the nineteen-forties. Name's Max." He reached out to shake their hands.

For the most part, the clientele of the Radio Room were formally dressed. Zeb even saw a tuxedo, and the woman's partner wore a beaded evening gown. He counted fifteen people, engaged in quiet conversation, drinking aperitifs or martinis. Quiet static provided a background, rather than music.

"Got tubes in there?" asked Zeb, bending down to examine it.

"Sure thing. Found 'em in an old electric shop on St. Anne Street."

"Ever hear anything?" asked Zeb.

"Once in a blue moon. Got it tuned to the last frequency we heard anything from. Some clear channel station out of Memphis. Thinking of getting a club together and trying to transmit something. We'll be transmitting twenty-four hours a day; don't know when it will work."

Zeb straightened. "If you'll keep track of when you get stuff in, I might be able to make some predictions."

"Hey, man, that would be great." Max smiled. "Can I get you a drink?"

"Sidecar," said Ra. Unlike the original Sun Ra, she was not averse to an occasional drink.

"Cranberry juice?" asked Zeb.

"Coming right up. Have a seat."

They sat next to the radio. They stayed for an hour, enjoying the lights of the city, and the sight of another steamboat unloading passengers at the landing, several blocks away. Finally they stood up to leave.

When the radio spoke, Zeb was as startled as everyone else.

"—an old hit by Jerry Lee Lewis. Whole Lotta Shakin' Goin' On."

For a few seconds the sound was drowned by cheers. Everyone pressed close to the radio. Someone turned it up. Everyone spread out and started to dance. Halfway through, the song vanished and the static returned.

Zeb glanced at his watch and pulled out his notebook.

* * *

"It's been a long time," Ra said as the memory receded.

"But we're recognizable," said Zeb.

"Must agree," said Ra. "Which is a relief."

"Did you get the part about the pirates?"

"That little appendix? Yes. Interesting. Seems like the city just let them in."

"That was the impression I got. But why?"

"Look—we're here."

Jason Peabody's Radio Tower was empty, except for a cat. She was black, asleep on the wide sill. She opened her green eyes briefly as Zeb and Ra entered the room.

"Ah," said Zeb, surveying the banks of radios and all the other apparatus Peabody had created and invented during his long years there.

"So what now?" asked Ra.

Zeb wandered around distractedly, and finally sat. He ran one hand through his hair. "My theory postulated some new phenomenon. I wasn't even sure what form it would take, when I was inside the Dome. It's taken the whole trip to try and sort it out. But if I'm correct, and if Peabody's data were correct, this phenomenon should be manifesting."

"How would it manifest?" asked Ra.

"Well, it would just look like light—to us."

"What do you mean by that?"

"To other creatures, creatures or beings with a different range of sensory apparatus, it could manifest as sound. Or even as a new experience of time and space. Pictures, perhaps, or some mode in which other kinds of beings experience time. Whoever has done this to Earth, I'm certain, has embedded the Theory of Everything deeply within the signal. People like Peabody, who have the genetic anomaly, would probably be able to sense this much more clearly than those who haven't, though perhaps most people would experience something when in its presence. One of my theories is that these beings intended that everyone be changed. That there wasn't meant to be this long stuttering, this suffering, this debacle. It was meant to go quickly, change us, and give us what they thought of as a great gift."

"So they're inept."

"Perhaps. The other end of this line of thought is that we're just accidentally in the way. But no matter what, we are in the process of changing—evolving—due to this new factor of the environment."

"Well, all right. What does that mean to Crescent City, to all these people here, to the world?"

"I believe that a critical mass will be reached, and we all need to know how to control it. Or at least know how to stay out of its way."

"Or go with it," said Ra softly.

" 'Or go with it,' " said Zeb, his grin lopsided. "That's why I love you so. That wouldn't be the first impulse of many people."

"Well," said Ra briskly, looking around. "There's plenty that I can do too. Fun things. Time to make those pesky pirates dance." She headed for the door.

"Where are you going?"

Ra laughed as she turned her head, flinging her braids into a unique cascade of sound. "I'm going to do what I always do when I get to a new place. I'm going to recruit a new Arkestra."

"Have fun," said Zeb. "Be careful."

"You too."

"I'm glad you're feeling better."

Ra paused for a moment, her eyes closed. She opened them and said seriously, "The city's memories complete me. It's a holographic kind of thing. I'm everywhere in the city, yet no one else but me would ever know, because I'm the attracting resonance for myself." She sighed deeply. "Yes. I'm very glad. It's nice to feel real again. The Consilience feels—I don't know—deeper, I guess. Now."

"That's the nature of the beast."

"Does it seem that way to you?"

"There's more here," he agreed.

"And . . . stories. Many more stories."

"Reaching critical mass."

"We'll all explode with art." Ra grinned.

"Your dream."

"Maybe it's more than a dream."

"Hope you're right, Ra."

Su-Chen Raises the Roof

Su-Chen left the elephant in the evening, called by the music coming from across a narrow lagoon. She walked into the city for the first time, leaning on her stick cane.

She was in a vast, high-ceiling pavilion. The air was filled with the sound of fountains. She could no longer hear the music. She was very hungry.

She streaked through the plaza, weaving through some collonades, but soon slowed to a walk, panting from her effort. She fell down, and got to her feet with difficulty. No one was following her.

There was jungle all around her. Like her room on the moon, but everywhere, lush and thick and endless. Sleek red antheriums nestled beneath a huge bo tree in which monkeys chattered and screamed. She walked down one passageway and came back around to the bo tree. She stood and looked around.

A white cockatoo flew down and landed next to her.

"*Hola.*"

"Hello," she said.

"Okay, you speak English. Are you lost?" His voice was harsh, but understandable.

"I am from the moon. I am hungry and I am looking for the music."

"They are back again. Food, and music. After the pirates attacked, they were gone for a while. They are together. Follow me."

The cockatoo swooped through several passageways. There were people here and there, but they didn't pay any attention to Su-Chen or to the cockatoo.

The pavement beneath Su-Chen's feet changed to brick. "I hear it," she said. She tried to hurry, but was very weak. The cockatoo flew with her, down streets which narrowed, flanked by old-fashioned buildings with wrought-iron balconies.

The cockatoo swooped through a tall door flanked by weather-washed green shutters. The smell of freshly baked bread mingled with the salt air. People sat drinking beer and eating oysters.

On a small stage to one corner of the room, a large black woman sang, backed by a piano player and a bass.

"Sit here," squawked the cockatoo in her ear.

Su-Chen sat in a wrought-iron chair at a small round table covered with a red-checked cloth. The bird fluttered off and in a moment a waitress brought a basket of fried oysters and bread and sat it in front of Su-Chen.

Su-Chen did not thank anyone, but began to wolf down the food. A man at the next table laughed. "How can such a thin girl eat so much?" Su-Chen didn't smile and she didn't stop eating.

After she was finished, she drank a glass of water the waitress had brought. She wiped her hands on the napkin and walked up onto the stage.

The musicians were in the middle of a long set. Su-Chen saw a synthesizer, which no one was using. She stood in front of it and after a moment found the switch and turned it on. She studied the controls and touched a few buttons.

The musicians looked at each other, shrugged, and continued.

Su-Chen closed her eyes and put her hands on the keys.

Her first sounds were fierce and dissonant. The saxophone player let his horn hang by his strap and stared at her. "Hey—"

She ignored him. Her hands moved swiftly over the keys.

Different rhythms fought for a few measures, then merged and flew past one another, ending in a brief waltz of delicious but fleeting harmony.

"Shit," said the guitar player, her black leather jacket glistening beneath the lights shining down on the stage. "That is some wild jazz."

More and more people crowded into the bar over the next ten minutes, and after that they stood out in the street. The guitarist joined in, gauging her forays and tangles with Su-Chen's music like a child dancing in wavebreak. The sax player resumed, challenged and ecstatic. Sweat rolled down his face.

By this time, Io had made her way through the crowd, leaving her cart and hauling herself along using wrought-iron railings, streetlights, and the occasional helping hand. She finally settled into an empty chair next to the stage. She knew that Su-Chen saw her, though she didn't acknowledge her presence in any way.

Io's heart soared with the music. Waves of cheers and applause swept through the crowd from time to time and during other passages they listened with quiet, almost reverent intensity. A waitress brought her a beer.

She drank it, and was happier than she had been in ages. Numbers and concepts once again rose in her mind, only to be swept away by the purity and intensity of the music. She felt physically changed by each new chord.

Su-Chen played steadily through the night. It seemed as if the entire population of Crescent City passed through that bar during those hours, and many other musicians took turns on the stage, only to give up after an hour or two and relinquish their instrument to another.

Su-Chen never repeated herself. Around three in the morning, a thin black woman had stepped up on the stage and scatted for forty-five minutes and Su-Chen's music wrapped around her voice, kissed it, stepped back, and danced, weaving in and out, punctuating, stating, answering, harmonizing in brief bounces of sound. This, out of the entire performance, most amazed Io. Su-Chen knew the woman's musical intent and cooperated.

Sometime toward morning, after the crowd waned, a very short black man placed a long-necked beer bottle on her table and hoisted himself onto the chair next to Io. The music was quieter now; pensive, though Io doubted that Su-Chen had somehow infused it with emotion. This bittersweet medley of feeling was her own. The music only sharpened the emotion. She saw Unity—empty, immensely distant, haunted by light, somehow sucked clean of the rich life it had held for so long. She took a deep, shuddering breath. Gone. Completely gone.

She was startled when the man spoke in a low voice that carried beneath the music.

"She is marvelous."

Io glanced at him; saw, in the flickering candlelight, a large, squarish face. He seemed to be . . . outside of himself. Not completely held by his edges. As if part of him was leaking into the environment. He wore a thin, bright yellow short-sleeved shirt which positively danced with brilliant parrots. In fact, they *were* moving . . . flitting from tree to tree as a deep green jungle came forth on the fabric of the shirt, morphing from yellow to lime-green to darker, massed trees. The parrots flapped their wings in time with the music, tilting their heads mischievously. She looked at his face again, and found it interesting.

He returned her gaze. Even in the dim light she could see that his half-lidded eyes were a most amazing shade of green. "She is creating something entirely new. It's all jazz, of course. Jazz does not connect to the past. It connects to the present. It flows from the present. It's not reconstructed. It is improvisational. Wholly conscious. A field of potential called into physical being, instant by instant. Her mind resonates with other aspects of the improvisation that are not audible to most of us."

"What do you mean?"

"It has something to do with nonlocality. You'll see. It's coming along quite well. Wonderful to have someone like her here. It all seems to be working out. You see, one of the problems of physics in the past hundred years has been developing new mathematics without referring to previous ways of thinking about time and space. The Consilience has been working on this. And this music is helping the process tremendously."

He grinned, finished his beer, and slid off the chair. With an odd, tilting gait, he meandered through the tables into the narrow street, where it was now growing light. He seemed to fade into the light, shirt and all.

A black woman with long braids arrived, with a white, gray-haired man. They sat at the next table.

* * *

"What did I tell you?" asked Ra, pulling Zeb's head close to speak into his ear.

"You told me that she's playing light music."

"Was I right?"

"I can't tell yet."

"I've listened for hours. It's the music of the Arkestra, Zeb. The music my hero Sun Ra dreamed of; envisioned; heard. It's . . . eerie. Unpredictable. Hard to grasp. And I think I've heard it before. In another form."

Zeb closed his eyes for a moment. Then he said, "My work on the Theory of Everything."

"Yes."

Ra climbed up on the stage and smiled at the girl, who was now alone, having exhausted all the other musicians. The girl did not smile back.

Ra began with the drums.

She kicked up a rhythm that came from the heart of distant stars, came from the pulses that had swept across Earth for a hundred years.

The girl opened her eyes, looked at Ra, and nodded.

Together they made time dance.

August 14, 2115

IO AND SU-CHEN

In Science Hall

The afternoon following their arrival, Io and Su-Chen entered the high arched wooden doors that led to Science Hall.

They had slept a bit in the Engineer's tower, following Ra and Zeb there at dawn. After they woke and breakfasted, Ra helped initiate Su-Chen into the Consilience.

Su-Chen showed no sign that she had passed an extraordinary night. Perhaps, thought Io, it was just normal for her. No ups, no downs. Only in her music. The rest, flat.

She wore pink shorts, a pink halter top, and black patent-leather shoes. Io had no idea where she had found them. She was even thinner and more gangly than she had been on the moon. Her shining black hair was done in two irregular, lumpy braids.

"Can I rebraid your hair?" Io asked.

"No. I didn't call them, last night." Su-Chen remarked, as they pushed open the door, which creaked on its hinges.

She knew that Su-Chen was talking about the light-beings.

"You know how?" asked Io as they advanced into the hall, and lights came on. It looked oddly cozy, for a place in the Caribbean. Set deep in the interior of the city, it was naturally cool. Io had found that for the most part almost every space in Crescent City had access to natural light and air, but not so Science Hall.

"I think that I know how," Su-Chen replied. "It's a little different here."

"What's different?" Io prowled around the Hall slowly, leaning on the cane with which she had replaced the cart, noting the wall which was already a screen so that no morph time would be lost. She wondered if any particular kind of knowledge was more densely imbedded here than elsewhere in the city. She jumped when Su-Chen, fiddling in an alcove, activated a hologram in which three people right next to her discussed options for dealing with a virus in one of the grains they were working with.

"I just have to get used to it," Su-Chen said. "I know they're here. I have to be able to hear them, though. I hear them and then I play what I hear."

"Have you always been able to hear them?" Io sank into one of the plush chairs and watched Su-Chen learn Science Hall, turning things off and on, including a chemistry lab, and access to the supercollider information . . .

"Wait! Turn that one on again." She leaned forward in her chair.

Io expected that such a tool would be in constant use, like theirs on the moon. But this one, apparently, was sitting idle. Moreover, it had just reached completion and had been used only once for a test dealing with nonlocality.

Nonlocality. Bell's Theorem, which showed that events on the quantum level, at least, were precisely mirrored elsewhere.

The strange man last night had mentioned this.

Su-Chen said, "My parents always said that we were all made of light. But now it seems that they are made of light and I am not. Not the same form of light as they are. I heard the light since I was a baby. I started to play it as soon as I could. Maybe when I was two. I don't remember."

"And when you played, they would come?"

"No. That never happened until—" she faltered. "I knew they were there and I could hear them and when I played they became more clear. I knew that I was playing them. But until—that—happened, it was like I was just practicing but I didn't really know it."

"Until what happened?" asked Io. She knew what Su-Chen meant. But she wanted the girl to talk about it.

"It happened to my father. The light. And then my cat ran into it and I ran in after it. The cat died."

"But you didn't."

"No. But since then I've been . . . different."

"It isn't your fault. That it happened." Io had no idea what kinds of emotional constructs Su-Chen might harbor. Io thought that her behavior almost perfectly corresponded to that of a child who believed that this momentous and frightening change had been her fault. "Remember the one we saw from the boat?" It had been soon after they landed, on the edge of an island they skirted.

Su-Chen nodded.

"You weren't playing anything, then."

"No."

Io tapped the low table in front of her chair and it became a screen. It took about fifteen minutes, but eventually she was able to find the revolutionary equation that united all five of the original superstring theories. M-Theory.

She was well aware of the richness of her environment. Although it seemed to have fallen into disuse, Crescent City indeed was embedded with an astonishing amount of information and had many ways of displaying it.

For instance.

Su-Chen dropped into the chair next to her and watched.

Io made the display three-dimensional. It was impossible, of course, since superstring theory described dimensions that were not accessible to human senses. "Rolled-up dimensions," they were called. This construct might be one interpretation of it.

It moved, in ways that her eye could not pin down. Her brain did not have the receptors necessary to comprehend it. On a crude level, it was like a visual puzzle that caused confusion in the brain, except this did not have only two possibilities. Instead, the possibilities were infinite.

It shone in a spectrum far larger than she could sense. It gave forth sound. Perhaps because of the music she had heard all of her life, Io's ability to sense sound was more extended than that of most of her fellows; audio tests on the moon had confirmed that when she had become curious about her ability, which no one else seemed to share.

Io isolated the sound and asked for notation.

Su-Chen stared at it. "There is more," she said. "It comes in pieces. It's never over."

"What do you mean? Is it a repeating decimal—an irrational number?"

"Perhaps," said Su-Chen. "I don't know yet."

The music that Io had heard all of her life was not normally experienced by most other people. Su-Chen could hear this music, if it could be called music, quite clearly.

Io knew that people who were blind were much more likely to have perfect pitch, and to be more musically adept. The portions of their brains which otherwise would have been devoted to processing sight instead became devoted to understanding sound more acutely.

Perhaps Su-Chen's lack of emotional processing gave her, like people who were blind, more brainstuff with which to sense the phantoms. More linkages regarding the abstractions of mathematics and music.

Mathematics was, in some part, a mapping of dimensions, territories, and spaces which were products of human speculation. Mathematics was a long conversation about the physical world, and long arguments for the existence of qualities which humans could not see except with the mind's eye.

Music could be said to be an argument, a building of tonal intentions, but in the end, music just *was*. It might generate pictures in the mind, but those pictures might or might not exist, and certainly varied from person to person. Music could not be *used* for any purpose; mathematics could be used to engineer machine parts, bridges, rockets, skyscrapers.

But music was just as precise as mathematics, as engineering. Like words or like numbers, it could be written and reproduced. Just as a building lay unrealized within rolled blueprints, so a piece of music could rest unmanifested until passed through the human mind into the hands or voice to be reborn.

Might there not be a link between the phantoms and Su-Chen's music? Or did they simply inspire a feeling in Su-Chen which she expressed musically?

Not very likely.

Because she did not have feelings to get in the way, to use up space in her brain. She had few feelings to express.

Instead, what she played must have some kind of nonemotional precision. A map of the light. A map of its intervals, its spaces, its tones, its elisions, as pure as a mathematical equation. Part of a hymn, imperfectly remembered, came into Io's mind. It was one of the untranslated hymns she learned as an abstract chant as a child in her foster parents' religious commune, pure phonemes, which later popped into meaning:

Come down o love divine
Fill thou this soul of mine
And kindle it with thine own ardor glowing.

O let it freely burn
till earthly passions turn
to dust and ashes in thy flames consuming.

And may thy glorious light
Shine ever on my sight
And clothe me round the while my path illuming.

Wasn't Su-Chen's state exactly what had been striven for by so many religious zealots? The burning to ashes of the personal connotations of experience, to be replaced by something larger?

Io began to get excited. Could Su-Chen's music somehow be translated by the Consilience into useful information? Perhaps it might be useful only in revealing more about the phantoms. But that was enough. Whenever Io had seen them, the keenness of her feelings, and her sensation of being immersed in memories, had completely overwhelmed her.

"Where does your music come from?" asked Io.

Su-Chen did not even react to the nonsequitorlike quality of the question. "I am remembering," she said. "And then I am with the light. I see the light again and learn more of what the music is."

"Is . . . the music different with each different light?" Io realized how badly she wished to believe in the individuality of the phantoms, believe that they were indeed the translated information of personality, or essence, or whatever made a person who she truly was.

Su-Chen looked at her. "There is only one light."

"Ah, then." For the first time, Io faced it: Plato gone. Forever. She was quiet for a long while. Finally she said, "You said something once about calling them. Or it."

A slight frown crossed Su-Chen's face. "Yes. It doesn't always work. I think it has something to do with harmonics. You know, with being able to create the note you play and the same note an octave higher when you pluck a string the right way. You divide the vibration. I think that either they are . . . manifested by harmonics, or else they manifest in my mind at that time through some kind of harmonics. I think that the light is divided into an infinity of infinite lengths. When I play, I play their . . . their particular infinities. They exist somewhere and everywhere. I just make this place their present by matching their harmonies."

Su-Chen, evidently tired of talking, went over to the synthesizer.

After a moment, Io realized that she heard no sound. She looked over, and saw that Su-Chen's note choices were appearing on a screen above the keyboard, in a mathematical language that Io didn't understand.

"May I turn on the sound?"

"No. The sounds are distracting. All I want to do is think."

"All right." Io went back to noodling with the features of the Hall, which were stunning; powerful. She wanted to look at the information which had been placed there during the supercollider acitivity.

Suddenly, Su-Chen screamed and backed away from the keyboard. Her face was distorted; tears brimmed over and flowed down her face. She trembled and gasped for breath.

Io was up and stumbled across the room in a flash, grabbing the back of Su-Chen's chair to keep from falling. She reached to touch the girl but was able to stop the gesture at the last second. She had seen Su-Chen react violently to being touched.

She gripped the back of the chair instead. "What?" Io looked around wildly for some kind of interloper, someone or something that might have threatened or frightened the girl, but the room was as empty as when they had arrived, with the same chill and musty smell of disuse in the air. "Take a deep breath. You're going to hyperventilate."

"That. That," Su-Chen, said, pointing at the keyboard with shaking hands.

The keyboard was on a pedestal which was rooted in the floor."Touch it!" sobbed Su-Chen, starting to gasp once more.

Io wanted to hold her. If only she could soothe the girl with the ageless human tool of touch. Instead, reached out with one finger, and pressed a key.

There was no sound, because it was turned off. But Io felt the immense, overpowering, almost painful sensation that Su-Chen experienced. It rushed through her body, blossoming not only in exquisite pain but in glorious, intense joy.

She took her finger away. The feelings subsided. Unlike Su-Chen, she had felt such things before. Many times. Not quite as intensely, but certainly almost ceaselessly since she was born, an undercurrent to her consciousness which usually flowed as smoothly as a river, to flare at times in an overpowering fashion.

Emotion.

She played a chord with one hand and this time received pictures, layered with sound, shot through with urgency. Two small figures ran through the night, hand in hand, across the broken moors. A small boy left home to join the circus. A courtesan wrote exquisite poetry. A monk fell facedown into the moon.

She had it then.

These were stories. Stories were layered with time. With emotion. With so many levels it was hard to sort them out. But they were powerful; sharp; wild as a brush fire. Wild with many flavors of wildness; untamed, unsorted by the city, which nonetheless had swallowed them, absorbed them. From where, though?

By tapping the keyboard she was able to get to an interface which dated their birth in the Consilience. Only yesterday.

At that particular time, Io had been leaving the clinic. She remembered the waves of color spreading through the wall of the clinic as the drowned woman's memories were transferred.

The woman's memories might have flooded into the city, even into this keyboard. Hadn't the technician indicated that something about the process was unusual?

Su-Chen's sobs subsided. "I can't play anymore," she said, her voice harsh. "It hurts."

"Maybe I can fix this. This is coming from the Consilience, which seems to be overpowered by a lot of new information. I imagine that it will calm down. But I can try to disconnect this keyboard from the Consilience or set up some kind of barriers between it and the Consilience."

Io sat in front of the keyboard. Above the keyboard was the customary screen which generally held musical notation. It could also show an alphanumeric keypad. "Come stand next to me and help."

"No." Su-Chen sat rigid on the couch, staring straight ahead.

Io searched the keyboard and found a START button. She turned it off and on again and by simply typing on the pad found a screen giving access to the keyboard system.

It took her about fifteen minutes to isolate the keyboard from the Consilience and make it freestanding. She mostly used voice commands. At the same time, she made sure that whatever Su-Chen played would be saved. It could be linked to the Consilience later for analysis.

"All right," she said. "Something happened that overwhelmed the Consilience for a while, Su-Chen. I think that I've fixed it. At least right here at this station."

Su-Chen, still on the couch, stared straight ahead without reacting. Io spoke again, and the girl finally nodded. “I like the Consilience. It has so much information in it. I didn’t know that it could hurt me.”

“I think that’s emotion, Su-Chen. It’s what the rest of us . . . feel. Just like what you feel sometimes hurts your body, like when you get a cut. It’s a warning. It helps you learn what to avoid. Most people feel hurts to their . . . hearts. Or they feel happiness. That’s what makes most of us laugh or cry or worry. It’s something that evolved. I think that most mammals have emotions. Maybe even birds. Maybe even fish and plants.”

“You could ask the birds if they have this awful thing,” said Su-Chen. “They can talk.”

“That’s true.”

“It’s horrible.”

“This is very intense. Not like what most people usually feel. But it’s true that several times a day, sometimes several times an hour, I have very strong emotions.”

“I’m sorry,” Su-Chen said. “It’s like a terrible disease.”

“I’m used to it,” said Io. “Probably too used to it. I’m often not as moved as I should be.”

“So I can play now without that. It hurt.”

“Yes. I made the keyboard freestanding. I guess you’ll have to be careful around any interface with the Consilience for the next few days until the stories are more assimilated. More controllable. I imagine that’s what will happen. It’s like a new turbulence. An injection of information. You may suddenly interact with the stories without any warning.”

“Maybe I’ll just stay in here.”

“Suit yourself. You’ll have to be careful here too.”

“I want my cat.” She had taken to a cat in the Engineer’s tower room.

Io smiled. “I’ll see if the cat will consent to being brought down here.”

Chester

But was he really, really real?

Of course not. Chester took the steps two at a time, running up the wide terrace leading from the sea into the belly of Crescent City.

Of course not. But he was here. Gloriously here. In a place that, when he had been a doll, had been an impossible myth he told to frighten children. But no, that had not been true at all. For it was a glorious scientific mecca, a place rich with color and scent, with markets and music and pure, spectrumed life, DNA mingling and creating many forms, many intelligences, feeding into and flowing forth into the Consilience, which rose through his bare feet like a shock wave as he reached the top step and stood stock-still, astonished at what the Consilience was telling him.

That's right. I'm alive.

"Angelina!" he shouted, and no one paid him any mind, dancing as they were, to the strange, shifting music, so that hearing Angelina's whisper in his head was sheerest miracle. "Where are you?"

Keep going. To your right. Now take that elevator in front of you. Yes. Fortieth level. Yes, it does go that high. And quickly. Good. Take a left, round that corridor—yes, don't look, it will make you dizzy—fine. Now—

He pushed open a huge, arched wooden door and stepped into a vast, dim room. "Angelina—"

You have a choice—

"What are you talking about?" he demanded. "Where are you? Angelina, I have been so devastated. Although I haven't had much time to think about it. Please, where—"

You have a choice. The voice was sad; somewhat weary. *There is a cocoon over there. To your right. Yes. You see it. Get in.*

"What's my choice?" he was finally able to ask as he stood before it. Suddenly, his heart ached.

"You're dead, aren't you?"

There was no answer.

"Well, tell me, damn it, Angelina! Tell me!" His fist flew out and smashed against the wall before he could even think about it. "Please."

I want you—

"All right," he said, his anger gone. He sat in the cocoon, which stretched downward, and swung his legs around and lay down flat. The cocoon, with which he was familiar from his learning spate in Paris, contracted around him.

Pictures flooded in.

The crash, crying out, being flung into the sea. Being picked up by a boat and put into their cocoon and hurried back to the city. Her transformation, her transfiguration, after death.

Her stories. Which were also his, now.

It was his choice.

Yes.

You could come back, he told her.

Of course. But I can't be in two places at once. In this way I can tell my stories simultaneously, constantly. People can access me—"

But they don't need you to have the stories! Within the cocoon, he was shouting at her.

Yes. In fact, they do. They need the filter of my consciousness. Without my consciousness, the information is just a lot of code. Stories are the folded-up dimensions in string theory. Stories are how humans unfold time. Consciousness infiltrates time in a new way. It is a new improvisation of the universe. It has evolved in rhythm with time. And it unfolds time. I seem to be the matrix for this. I can give them the story that Louis told us. Purely.

Oh, shit, said Chester. **Angelina. I can't see you. Please. I love you. Please. Decide to come back. To be human. You have a choice.**

So do you. Come with me.

Chester commanded the cocoon to release him. He rose, bowed his head, and staggered to the sofa. His brief memories were easy to look at. They were all of Angelina. And a long dark time before that. Before her.

"No," he finally said. "Not now." He rose and walked from the room back into where there was life that he could understand.

Just barely.

August 12, 2115

RADIO COWBOY AND PEABODY

The sun beat down on Cowboy and it was all quite serious. All of his cowboy thoughts boiled up in his brain, brought out by the heat and distilled to a dull fear, which finally was undercut by pure thirst. Shadows were nonexistent; it was high noon, there was no one to take aim at save the distant sun.

The musical sun.

Memories startled into him then. Daytime memories, vying with his Cowboy persona. The memory of his small nanotech automobile manufacturing company, Musical Sun, Inc. Musical because the sun held for him the presage of a powerful, revelatory music. The sun with its sacrificial atoms rearranged his mind with unseen frequencies—frequencies often degraded by the information they were enslaved to carry.

His life rose up around him then, the life he had so often remade, the stages of which he had tried to forget, for each stage held its own powerful loss. His mother, Julia, who believed he had been changed envivo at the first pulse of energy that rushed in after the initial Silence, when those impure images and impure sounds were swept from the air with majestic interstellar purity. His childhood was a dance of pain, fear, and the lightswept vistas of the West.

* * *

Jason's classroom in the small Montana town they found in November just after his thirteenth birthday was supposed to snag him his high school diploma, which his parents somehow thought was important. Math, physics, and chemistry were all long in the bag, as well as some peripheral subjects such as music theory and computer design. All Jason lacked were ten essays that he had to write for his English requirements, plus some final grammar exams. He kept putting off both tasks, though his mother nagged him daily.

A teacher's certification of completion was necessary each step of the way. He carried his records with him, using a pseudonym he was long used to using in public and for which he had ample fake verification. Paul Jones was an identity he supposed he would use the rest of his life.

Falling snow obscured the usual view of the mountains through the classroom windows. It was already a foot deep, but he and his parents, like most of the townies, lived within walking distance. Mom and Dad both had found jobs here, as the infrastructure of the town was being upgraded. They were trying to build up a reserve before moving on again. They only worked where they would be paid in goods or in gold. After a lot of discussion, they had decided to risk putting him in school.. The school was not linked to any grid because the town was independent-minded, so there was little chance that anyone could track Jason here. Obscurity was an obsession and a way of life.

Handicapped as usual by a headache, Jason labored over the calculus problems he had found within the educational program. The satisfaction he got from doing them distracted him from the pain. As in most of the schools he had been in, he was able to go at his own pace, and the educational continuum was fairly well standardized. This was college-level work, but he could get credit for it here. He heard a lot of talk in their travels, in cafés and in newspaper articles, about how education was falling apart, and about how all the scientists were pulled from their teaching jobs to work for various governments, and about how kids weren't learning the basics anymore what with all the home schooling going on. He realized, vaguely, that there were many kinds of parents in the world and that most of them did not have the background to teach their children as well as real teachers or as well as people who actually did work using the subjects they taught.

Jason loved the rhythm of the falling snow, which filled his peripheral vision. His classmates were for the most part quiet, though there were a few discussions here and there about shared work. The headache was a dull throb, the usual background noise to which he was accustomed, which no drugs could kill.

The lights flickered, signaling that power had switched from the grid to the local town generator. The desktops automatically saved every second, so nothing was lost. They were experiencing what was popularly called a "pulse." Broadcasting was interrupted.

Jason felt the familiar thrill in his stomach, and the overall relief of freedom from pain.

He flew through the rest of the problems and quickly finished the series. He touched the green circle that would send the answers to his personal computer. Right now he had it configured into a three-inch square with rounded corners; it was about half an inch thick. Set on the school desktop, it allowed certain information to pass between the two computers. This was just a computer he took to schools so that it could be updated. He kept his real, truly personal computer in his pack and it was configured in a unique way that he'd thought up so that no one, not even his parents, could access it.

Jason stuck his fingernails between the desktop and his school computer and peeled off the desktop. On the surface were the answers to Standard Calculus Series 7.5.

He took them to his teacher, sitting crosslegged on some pillows at her own low desktop, so that she could verify it, add it to his records, and give him the access code for 7.6.

She held a mug of steaming coffee. She took a sip and set the mug next to her on the floor. "What do we have here?"

She studied Jason's computer for a moment. "Paul, you just started 7.5 this morning, didn't you?" She tapped on her desktop, which kept track of the networked classroom, to ascertain that this was true. She looked him in the eye. "It really isn't a good idea to use the answer program. I know that it isn't difficult to find, but you need to work through each program yourself, even though it takes you more than a day, even two days. It doesn't matter. That's how you learn."

"I did them all myself," he said, trying to stay calm. "I'm not a cheater."

"I didn't mean that you were cheating," she said. "But—"

"That's exactly what you meant!" He lowered his voice when the other kids looked up from their work. He hesitated a moment. He knew he was being stupid but he was mad. He was mad at her, and mad about always having to hide everything he was and everything he knew. He was sick and tired of pretending. "Look. I'll show you how I solved the last one." He sat next to her.

"Okay." She moved aside to give him room.

Jason could tell she was trying not to sound skeptical. Using her desk, he brought the calculus series up and found the problem. With the same ease he would use in writing a three-letter word, he tapped out his extrapolation. The answer appeared. The screen congratulated him with a star.

That afternoon the teacher went home with him and told his parents that he was exceedingly gifted and should be in a special environment. "I've never seen a child who could solve these problems so easily," she said, chattering on about enrolling him in grad school after a year of acing college courses as Jason's dad served her coffee and pretended to be excited.

The next morning, despite the snow, they packed up, put chains on their 4WD, and left.

It was the last school Jason Peabody ever attended.

His head was lifted gently and he heard someone say, "Open your mouth now." A splash of water ran down his cheek and onto his shoulder. He choked, then sat up, coughing. He grabbed the glass and gulped cool sweet water.

He took in the rich colors in the room around him. Log chairs were covered with red, blue, and green blankets. A large flat-woven rug with a purple and black geometrical pattern covered a portion of the pine plank floor. A massive stone fireplace to his right yawned cold and sooty. The man sitting next to his bed had a long white beard, near-hidden blue eyes, a brown crinkly face. Around his neck was a red bandana. His hair was pressed down in a circle where his hat must have been.

Five small globes of light floated around the room. Peabody watched two of them merge, their green and yellow blending to brief chartreuse, then drift apart, one mottled and one still yellow. The yellow one bounced off of an interstice he would otherwise not have noticed, running as it did between two bookcases heaped with papers, skulls, coffee cups, and photographs leaned against the backs of the books.

Two large windows faced a distant range of purple mountains. Huge-armed cacti marched over a rise.

And he was 943.2 miles from Houston.

One of the light globes grew legs and a head with pointed ears and feline eyes. It scrambled up the ravaged boot of the old-timer and sat on his ragged-jeaned knee, licked a shimmering paw, and stared at Peabody.

"Who are you?" Peabody asked, sitting up on the edge of the bed.

The man shrugged. "Name's Storm of Cats."

"You aren't Native American," Peabody said, unreasonably moved to split hairs.

A grin moved the beard. "DNA says different. Hopi mother. Los Alamos dad. And you?"

"Sedona mom, engineer dad."

Storm of Cats nodded. He rose. The lightcat forsook its form and floated free. Storm of Cats went to one side of the round house, where a bowl sat on a slate counter beneath a spigot, and Peabody could just see the flat shine of the heating surface. Storm of Cats opened a cold box and took out a gallon of water, brought it back over, pushed a rubble of objects aside from beneath the lamp on the bedside table, and set it there. Condensation beaded on it. "Plenty of water, Cowboy. I'd go kind of easy though for the next hour."

"It's Peabody." He edged to the gallon and filled his glass and sipped though he wanted to guzzle.

He grinned again. "Radio Cowboy, you told me, when I picked you up at the side of the road like to die. Pretty well backed up that claim too. You know a hell of a lot about a dead medium."

"Not dead. Just waiting for its next incarnation. It's not too hot in here."

"Swamp cooler. Uses water."

"Wife?"

"Had several. Wifeless now. Another one will likely happen along eventually. Now what's your tale, Peabody?" He leaned back in his chair and it creaked. "Got time, as you can see. My Bees range far and wide gathering information so I'm not as clueless as you might think." He jerked his head upward. "Wildflowers aplenty up top on the roof, where the Bees feed the info into the interstice. Kind of like a miniature Flower City. I call it a Prairie Sod Flower House." He grinned. "That's what I've worked on—developing a system to bring Flower Technology to rural folks, with none of the drawbacks or unpleasant crowds."

Where to begin? Peabody sensed in this man an ally. Not that he was likely to find enemies against his terrifically nebulous cause—just a whole lot of people with no clue as to what he needed to do.

Which was get to Houston quickly.

"Why did you pick me up? A few cars went by at night, but I don't think people could see me. I passed out. I seem to remember that someone stopped and kicked me a few times. I figured my number was up."

"Just about. Maybe I was just raised right. Didn't see you at first though either. My Bees told me about you. You was robbed, except they didn't get much except what looked like once I translated the bees-eye-view was some Republic of Mississippi dollars. And your hat. Which was a lot worse. I went out looking for you."

Storm of Cats leaned forward, resting long arms on lanky legs. His eyes must be his father's, surmised Peabody—the eyes of a man who had been among the technical élite. A man who understood the stakes. A man who had known the numbers of their interstellar fate and who had perhaps had some idea of how things might play out left to chance, and how they might play out if intelligence was brought to bear on the problem. A man familiar with the options of the game.

Storm said, "So now why do you suppose they—the Bees, I'm saying—found you of interest?"

"I'm one of the—" Peabody paused, suddenly and acutely aware of all the words that had been used to describe him. Pioneer, alien, mutant. "Mutants," he settled on.

" 'Bridge Beings,' my mother's folk called you. I've known a few. My first wife was one. Hunted down by the government and taken away. Never saw her again. That was my political awakening. Decades ago. I gather that most of that energy is gone now. Government's gone. I use what's left of science." He held out his hands, dusted them off, and held them out again. "I was configured to Tucson, 2042.8. My own choice. Got out while the getting was good. But needless to say you people interest me. Lee Ann was a trip and a half. I was in a state of rage for years after that. Took me a good half-century to mellow out, and a lot of what you might call 'terrorist acts.' My three kids run off as soon as they could. I was a mean, crazy man for a long, long time. They made the right move, I'm ashamed to say."

"I knew the woman who brought Crescent City together," Peabody said. "But I left. It was a long time ago. I was being manipulated. At least I thought so, and I didn't like it. I left some guidance information I'd spied out of Houston when I left." He smiled briefly. "This is the short version, understand. I had become an Engineer. I eventually wound up in Chicago. I was the Chief Engineer there. We had one of the best Flower Cities in the world. But then my wife"—he rushed to finished, surprised at how much it still hurt—"my wife killed herself, and I left. By then the east was completely driven by the Norleans Plague. I'm not sure the plague made it across the Great Divide. But back East it drained the populace, pulled them downriver and out to Crescent City. It was a bright time for the city, and a dark time. We've survived and prospered and become fat and lazy, I think. Now that it's time for action, now that there's need of action, the city has fallen to pirates and I and a woman were cast out to go to Houston and regain the guidance information. It was collected during the first years of the Silence."

Storm of Cats sat back. "You think it's still there?"

"It's quite possible."

"It's very damp in Houston. I've heard that it's become as strange as most places now."

"The information itself may well have been represerved in an organic medium. I certainly hope that's the case," Peabody said. "I have a feeling that whoever was there would have gone to great lengths to make sure that it was cared for."

"So what happens? Say you get it. Say you take it back to Crescent City and plug it in. Then what?"

"You know about lemmings?"

"Sure."

"That's what. That's all I know. I'm a lemming. A bit fancier, maybe, this pull I've fought as long as I've been able to feel it. But it's too strong. We're in a new stage of interstellar evolution. My mother was a Gaian. Suppose—this is ridiculous—but suppose—" It all poured out of him then, the musings his elephant sojourns had stirred. He took a deep breath. It had been so long since he had really talked to anyone. "Suppose that Earth is like a tree. An organism with a sex. Or something analogous, something with an orientation, a charge. And that somewhere out there is Earth's mate. And that all of this"—he spread out his hands—"all of this, the evolution of life, the invention of technology, this sideswipe of the silence—it's all part of some sort of intergalactic evolution of—of . . . *intelligence.* Intelligence so far beyond what we are now that we simply can't fathom it. Not a plan. But a . . . a . . ." He thought about it some more, came up with the word. "An improvisation. Now that we're somewhat intelligent. Sure, parts of us are completely blind. I can't see what your bees see. I can't hear what dogs hear. I'm pretty sure that I just can't think what other beings out there, having evolved to be sensitive to different frequencies, think."

Storm of Cats stared at Peabody. "These aren't exactly the thoughts of a sober Engineer."

"No," he said. "They're not. I've been pretending to be sober my whole life and I've been completely useless and ineffective. My own wife, whom I loved dearly, didn't even care to stay alive to see what would happen next. That was my fault."

"Now—"

"It was my fault," Peabody said steadily. "A flaw in the design of Chicago. If only I'd been able to see it—to know it—"

"You've taken far too much upon yourself," observed Storm of Cats.

"A number of therapy programs have told me as much. It doesn't make any difference. Time to face that. And to face what I was born for. To understand as deeply as possible what's going on, however little sense it may make. To facilitate this change. To open the doors of choice. For all beings. Not just humans. For the whole spectrum of life and for everything from which it arose. Why is it so strange to believe that consciousness itself has arisen and that there is something even farther beyond consciousness, a next step?" Peabody stood and started to pace. "Not an inevitable step. Just an evolutionary step that maybe isn't as blind as it's always been. It's got my attention." He reached out his hand to Storm of Cats to shake. "I've got to get going. Thanks for your help, but I've got to get going. Maybe when it cools off—"

"Hell, I'll take you there."

Peabody looked at him.

"Why not?"

Peabody heard yowls and saw sparks as two balls of light attacked Storm.

He brushed them off as he stood up. "They get mad. Sorry, guys, a man's gotta do what a man's gotta do."

Storm of Cat's supper was quick and economical: beans and rice and cactus pickles and applesauce, served on the bare board table while spheres of light stalked them, cleanup accomplished by some kind of box that Storm of Cats shoved all the plates into just before they left. One of the spheres grew legs and a twitch of a butterscotch tail and green eyes that watched Peabody as Storm of Cat bandaged his rib and sorted through a vast file with his computer until he found the repair formula he wanted and bid the house assemble it and made Peabody drink it, though Peabody protested that his onboard repairers were exceedingly up to date.

"Better safe than sorry. Good for what ails you. And I gather you're not so fond of that radio fellow. This will tone him down just a tad."

Peabody browsed the bookshelf as he sipped the citrus-flavored concoction, and saw a plaque indicating a degree in astrophysical engineering from the University of New Mexico tossed carelessly behind a beautiful Hopi pot. It was awarded to Sam Atchley. The lightcat got in his way then, and jumped onto his shoulder.

"I think she's taken a shine to you, if you'll forgive me."

"Are they really . . . cats?" he asked. Suddenly, this one seemed quite real.

Storm of Cats looked at him with wry disbelief. "Suncats. Well, let's skedaddle."

They walked out into indigo evening. The cacti stood like sentinels, towering around them as they walked over to the huge arched aluminum garage. Storm of Cats touched a light on and Peabody saw a variety of vehicles.

There was a sun-dulled pickup truck the color of lapis lazuli. Peabody dimly remembered jouncing up the dirt road in it. He saw a motorcycle and a Jeep.

And a small white two-seater. Something designed to fly. It looked dangerous.

To his dismay, Storm of Cats headed right toward it. "She's a real beauty, ain't she? Built her myself." The night air on the high desert had some lovely alien smell that Peabody couldn't identify.

"Doesn't it require, ah, thermals, or solar energy, or—"

Storm of Cats laughed and clapped him on the back. "Absolutely all you have to do is climb in."

Peabody looked around. "Isn't there a runway?"

"Nah. Look here. She rises straight up. Hovers like a hummingbird. She's a hybrid creature. Twilight will get us just about to moonrise. She's not terribly fast. About sixty, with the two of us in here. So it will probably take, say, about ten hours. We can stop and take a rest if you need to."

Peabody felt stiff and sore and old as he climbed onto a stool to reach the handles and the two-step indentations on the side of the contraption. He was glad he had taken the repair solution.

The huge windows of Storm of Cat's house reflected the last neon ribbons of sunset. Small spheres of light flitted around inside. Storm climbed in and settled next to him. Seat belts grew across them, and Peabody knew that the whole thing would turn into a most amazing structure of protective foam should anything untoward occur. Still, he hoped he didn't look as nervous as he felt as Storm smiled at him with a quick nod and the leap-plane rolled out onto the large concrete pad in front of the hangar-garage. Behind them the door rumbled shut. They were surrounded by spiked plants and ragged gullies. The clear glassite around them glowed with readouts.

Above them a rotor whirled slowly, then picked up speed. Storm pulled back on a lever and the leap-plane rose into the air, quite suddenly, so that the whole ranch receded with an immediacy that gave Peabody a touch of vertigo. He looked out over the horizon to clear his head and saw black ridges, their very tips touched by the last rays of sun, in every direction.

The leap-plane banked with grace and sped north. Soon, Peabody discerned the Interstate, the solar lights of its edges glowing faintly. "That there's our guide. The quickest way to Houston too." The rotors folded up and slid down into a space behind Peabody's chair back.

"Beautiful, isn't it?" asked Storm.

Five-thirty A.M., August 13, 2115

Dania

Dania stepped out into the relative coolness of predawn in southeast Texas, fifty miles from the Gulf of Mexico. She had been cooped up with the children all night and they had never slept and they had never stopped talking. She had checked on Three Impossible, but the coyote had been, heart-stoppingly, gone.

So Dania needed to move, to run, and she started a molasses-slow jog which was not much faster than walking. She was almost instantly wet with sweat. She wiped her face with a bandana. She had found the clothing of many, many people who were gone or dead and had found some shorts and a T-shirt and such a vast assortment of exercise shoes that she'd had a hard time choosing among them.

Ahead of her on the road pools of light cast by streetlamps faded as the sky became gray. Daylight increased, clarifying extraordinary blossoms of spiked dun-green spears, in concentric circles as high as her head, out of which rose succulent yellow cones. These plants were scattered across the crumbled concrete, which ran between ancient buildings some of which, she knew, had been originally constructed in the nineteen-sixties, almost one hundred and fifty years earlier.

Their aluminum skeletons rose around her, and sun-faded panels of pink and blue held only a whisper of original color. Windows winked, holding the sun captive in a hundred incarnations, revolving as she jogged toward a bank of massive rockets which were perhaps a half-mile ahead. It was a fact that JSC had been a control and tracking center, that it had not originally been a launch center. But when Cape Canaveral had been flooded near the end of First Wave, launch operations had been moved here; the moon colony launched from here.

What had happened to that moon colony?

She only knew of it, she reflected, pushing through furnace-like heat, because she had been in Crescent City. There had indeed been a colony on the moon, eventually forsaken utterly by Earth. There had even been a colony on Mars, made possible by nanotechnological advances. But no one here knew what had happened to them, and the great communication heart of JSC had fallen silent.

She stopped, pulled her water bottle from its snug hip holder and drank half a quart, then began moving again, this time at a walk.

It was wonderful to be on her own. No Nows. No buffalo. No strange tribe. No coyote. Just herself and this wild frontier of lost promises, lost hopes. The wide, wide blue sky above her, towering with cumulus clouds so evenly spaced that they seemed an illustration of herd or flock distancing equations as they glided through the sky with their cargo of water.

She slapped some mosquitos and blinked stinging sweat from her eyes.

And blinked again.

"No," she whispered.

But, yes.

A small ovoid of light pulsed against the black background of a vast rocket's fin in shadow. Not all that close to her. Perhaps a quarter of a mile away, still. She could turn from it. Surely, it would not pursue. But if it caught her, what?

Her wild laugh erupted into the still blue air. She walked toward the light deliberately. She would take its measure. She would observe it objectively. It would not send wild rays into her brain. It would not, could not, addle time. No more than could the sun, or a night light in a child's room. Crescent City had crazed her. Had made her brain elastic and strange, had soaked it in the blink of an eye in American legend, coloring all she saw with time that zinged off from her in angles precisely oriented as that of a crystal, the compressed time she had seen in Radio Cowboy, the deep prehistoric-human time she heard coming from Wind Rock in phantom ghost radio transmissions, the natural time in trampling herds, in the quiet flattening of vast valleys of grasses, in the brilliant yellow of a mountain highlighted against distant purple storm sky. Time flowed in so many precise degrees, and held such sound, such glorious stories, such deep betrayal, so very many steps into a future landscape that held mountains higher than she had ever seen, where the music that echoed all around changed rapidly, again and again and again . . .

. . . that she sank to her knees while the sun and radio time looked down on her, invaded her, joined something within her which saw down each splintered avenue as a glorious golden road where she always needed to do something, something, to make things right and whole and while this present sun went deep into her brain she fell to the ground, heard the beating of buffalo hooves thundering across the empty suburbs of Houston through the low pines, startling primordial flocks of heron which blackened the sky . . .

. . . the sound lifted her until she flew with the egrets, the herons, and vast flocks of now-extinct birds, to the mountains where she was a single eagle looking down, circling down, and the thing was a white thing, a round white thing filling the air with a new sense, caressing minds newly evolved . . .

She opened her eyes to the blue eyes of Radio Cowboy regarding her with deep concern, surrounded by deeply tanned skin, haloed by a broad white hat brim, and around that blue sky matching the eyes, as if his eyes were a patch of sky, and the face and hat mere occluding lenses. Radio Cowboy was not real. Coyote was not real. The buffalo plains were not real. The Nows were not real. Only the sky was real, the sky in its deep, remote blueness, casting time from it like a shadow . . .

"Dania?"

More water doused her face and made her nose sting. She sneezed. It was all real. All of it. Radio Cowboy, the buffalo plains, and mundane Dania, making her way through time as if swimming through an ocean of marbles. With a sigh, she tried to sit up but fell back into Radio Cowboy's arms.

"What time is it?"

"About noon."

She moaned, and said, "Guess I've lost five hours." She sat up, immediately became dizzy, and lay back down again on . . .

"What the hell is this?" She sat up again and looked around.

She was on a hard steel table, and lights winked around her. She shaded her eyes. "No wonder I hurt so much. Isn't there even one nice soft bed in this place?" She looked down at her arm, unwrapped a blue bandage with a few twists, and pulled out a needle attached to a rubber tube. "Trying to drug me or something?"

"Kind of," Cowboy said, getting a sterile swab and cleaning up the bead of blood on her arm. "It's a saline solution. You were dehydrated. Must have laid out there for a couple hours."

She rubbed her face with both hands. "Ow."

"You've got a terrible sunburn."

"How did you find me?"

"Some damned yipping coyote."

"Oh. Good! But—she was yipping? She didn't talk, or say anything?"

"Here. Have some water. We were worried about you."

"How did you get in here?"

"That guy was a big help."

She looked around and saw, behind Radio Cowboy, a much taller man, bronze-skinned, looking at her with concerned black eyes. And then a bunch of kids, subdued, abashed. Feeling guilty?

She smiled at them. "Hey! I'm all right now. I just went out for a run. It was stupid." But it had not been stupid. She was used to the heat. She was well hydrated. It was just the light-things again, that was all. She leaned her forehead against Radio Cowboy's. "Sorry I took off like that. How did you find me? I mean, how did you get to Houston?"

"Well . . . I didn't really intend to find *you*. Though I hoped I would. But I guess we were both headed in the same direction."

"Yeah. We were both wound up. Set on the road. Don't know why the hell why. Do you?"

"To find the orrery complex," said Radio Cowboy. "And we have. And to bring it home. Which we will. Right now we're waking the Green Shift—"

"The Blue Shift. Don't count on me, Cowboy," she said, sliding off the table. She almost slid right to the floor but pulled herself to her feet at the last second.

"We need you back in Crescent City," he said, putting his arm around her waist. "Call me Jason. Or Peabody. Not Cowboy. I'm no cowboy. I'm just an Engineer. With work to do. You have work to do too, Dania."

"The Consilience doesn't need me," she said. *But they do.*

Whatever *they* were. The strange crew of the Nows.

They had sent out a call so strong and strange and pure that she was electrified right down to her cells, down to the very heart of whatever her matter was made of. She was made of time, woven of time, though she could not yet gaze down more than a few avenues at once. Not yet.

"It does need you," said Radio Cowboy, she couldn't think of him as anything but that. She didn't like this plain and measured voice in which he spoke, like the dullest man in the world and yet so certain that she would agree. His eyes were deeply earnest, with no hint of Cowboy merriment. Instead, his expression was freighted with responsibility and reason. "It does. We have to bring back the orrery. The map. The guidance system. These kids are the purest manifestation of this map in the world, probably. They have changed with each new update, with each new calculus, with each new input from the pulses. And then we have to figure out . . . the rest of it all. Depending on what's happening back there."

"The rest of what?" she asked somewhat belligerently, badly wanting a cigarette. "Is there anything to eat around here? I'm starving."

"I'm not sure if you remember"—his voice was gentle and too easy on her ears by half—"what was happening when we left. I have no idea what it will be like when we get back. Let's pick a positive scenario. Things relatively stable. I got a feeling before I left, from the Consilience, I suppose, that the city is about to yank itself out of the ocean and head on out. No matter what. I trust it to get well-enough organized to do that. For itself. But I want to make sure that people either get out or that all systems are go for the humans as well as the city. Two different systems there. We'll need all the help we can get."

"Of course," she said, but at the same time she thought *I can't go* and she allowed him to help her lie down on the table again saying Rest.

It was deep night filled with untold amounts of time glittering up there as they helped her on to the bus, all the children and Radio Cowboy Peabody and the tall man, though as they drove out through the gates she yelled at them to stop! stop! though Cowboy held her close, because behind them was not only that deep being of light but her great friend Coyote, who had tricked her here and who had not yet gotten her due, her fill, her bounty, the private eternity she would carry between her jaws back to the People of the Nows across the flatness and then across the rolling hills that were letting their colors bloom across the horizon in a wash of yellow and purple and the barest hint of green, all waiting for her, waiting for her, waiting for her, as wind rushed through the bus and the children sang and jumped and shoved and leaned out the windows till they had to be scolded and held in by their belts. At dawn they hired a shrimp boat and headed out into the Gulf. Dania heard Radio Cowboy Peabody and the tall man talking, and how could they possibly speak, when the future and the past lay behind them in the flat sandy land they were leaving, heading to an artificial place with demands so alien that Dania could only think, as spray drenched her while they slapped through the waves in a dreadful hurry, that she would no longer give to it freely, no, no, and felt them splash water on her again as she heard herself screaming and Radio Cowboy Peabody saying worried you'll feel better once you get home.

Five-thirty A.M. August 13, 2115

Dania

The children took Dania to the top of a ten-story building to see the sunrise. Exhausted as she was, she felt part of their celebratory dance, in which they pulled after them long streamers on which she occasionally recognized the words such as MARS LANDING CREWE and RETROTIEMPS CREWE. There was a band of purest blue just above the horizon, which was limned with gold, and for an instant she thought that she herself was rising above Earth, on her way to perilous Mars or even perhaps beyond, to the apex of time and space . . .

They danced; they laughed; faintly Greek music played from a music blob that one of them pitched against the chimney next to her head where it stuck fast. The light grew more broad and she became aware that Coyote sat next to her, mainly from her smell.

"You are better?" asked Dania. "I'm glad."

Coyote lay gingerly on her stomach and her tongue lolled as she panted. "And thus we experience the joys of science, and thus we are bombarded by the Nows."

"All right, then. Tell me. What are the Nows? Everyone has been talking about them. First it was that—that light-thing in the store, then it was the buffalo, and now it's you. I feel like I'm . . . dissolving, or something. I don't like it one bit."

Three Impossible opened her jaws and took Dania's hand within them and bore down slightly. Not enough to cause pain. She stared thoughtfully ahead and loosed her jaws.

"You are here. Here. At a precise vector which humans presently do not have the mental power to factor. But you are definitely here, dear." Three Impossible's voice wheezed forth a counterpoint to the Greekish music.

"I thought so," said Dania. "I suppose that you do have the mental power to factor—"

"No." Three Impossible's voice was sorrowful. "No, not at all. But I am a part of helping all of matter to gain this ability. Listen to this music. It is music that you can *see*. Can't you see it?" The tone of Three Impossible's voice changed from sad to forceful. "You have to be able to see it. You must be able to." Was that a sigh? "I have so much information inside of me. Information that cannot be translated into English. Mathematics is a language too, but it is not a language that is natural to me. Scent is natural to me." She raised her muzzle and her snuffles, next to Dania's ear, tickled. Dania rubbed her ear. "A dance of scents."

She leaped to her feet and darted into the midst of the children, yipping and running among them, leaping and twisting in midair. Dania watched the scene of woven movement, an improvisation overseen by nothing more than the bare forward edge of time and suddenly did not know the meaning of forward or back. It was as if she had witnessed this scene, etched on the brightening horizon atop a building perpetually new, an infinite number of times. Red shirts and green passed behind one another; the thrown-back head of Elizabeth, trailing its cape of black swirling hair, revealed Kevin, his brown skin glowing in the growing sunlight.

They mixed and danced with one another in an epiphany of the exact present. The Now which she had always felt . . . but it had only begun a few days ago . . .

Three Impossible was licking tears from her face as the children gathered around her, concerned. "What's wrong?"

"It's right," she managed to tell them. "It's not wrong. It's right." She grabbed Eliza to her and hugged him a moment. He squirmed away and reeled out with the rest of them into the light, all of them complex epiphanies of DNA, guardians of the secrets of sugars and bacteria, on their way to something even more. Chanting came from the sky, from the radio sky, from KNOW, from the small radio still in the pocket of her skirt, and Three Impossible once more nipped her hand and she realized that she was very, very, very tired. It did not help that she was surrounded by the rainbows of white light and that infinite stories surged through her. She had been so many people in her lifetime, so many people . . . it was so loud and so windy . . .

Radio Cowboy was there, landing on the roof in a helicopter and jumping forth and exclaiming worriedly over her, rubbing her hands and dashing her face with water and carrying her down the stairs while the children chanted, "The Janitor Returns. Blessed be the name of the Janitor. For he is our brother and will take us to the stars."

Dania was almost afraid to open her eyes. She heard mundane sounds around her. Talk of water and food and of Green Cycle, which was all dead. Or was that Red Cycle? She wasn't even sure if they remembered which was which.

Then her face was licked with a rough tongue and she sat up, wiping her face with her palm and laughing.

"We're almost ready to go," Radio Cowboy said from across the room.

"What do you mean?" She was utterly groggy. "Where are we going?"

"We're getting on the bus and driving to Galveston. This is a great bus. Air-conditioned. That might be broken, though. Storm of Cats here says he can get us a boat. Then it will takes us ten or twelve hours to get to Crescent City."

"Storm of Cats."

"Pleased to meet ye, ma'am." The tall man with impossibly long limbs bent over her and thrust out a huge hand. "I've heard much about you from Dr. Peabody and Blue Shift, heartless curs thought they may be."

"Dr. Peabody?"

Radio Cowboy pulled up a chair and straddled it. "Feeling any better?" His voice was as sorrowful as Three Impossible's. She sat up and swung her legs over the edge of the metal gurney and stood up and promptly fell over into Radio Cowboy's lap. He pulled her close. She leaned her head on his shoulder. "You've had a hard time."

"Well," she said. "I did have quite a bike ride."

"I think you may have heat exhaustion."

"We set off a lot of rockets. A lot of rockets, " Jawan was telling Storm of Cats. "We had to. For practice. Yes, we put one of the shifts in one of them. We had to. They wanted us to do it. They wanted to go. We want to go, too."

"Go and go!"

"Go to the light!"

But Dania felt only dimly here. This frightened her. As if infinite realities played through this very time. "I have to slow it down," she told him earnestly.

"I don't know how to do this," he replied, surprising her. "Not here, anyway. I think that you're having some kind of problem. I think that perhaps you need to be . . . maybe . . . retuned. Oh, I don't know," he said, more loudly. "I just don't know." But she relaxed into him, even though he didn't know. It felt so nice. He kept talking.

"We're just at the beginning, I'm afraid. It's taken so long to get here. Just to the beginning. Everything is such a God-awful mess. I feel worse than I did when I was a boy. I feel worse than I did in the midst of the plague, floating down the Mississippi River into madness and darkness. I just don't know what to do and there has to be something to do, but I don't know what and I missed the radio astronomer. By a hair. So near and yet so far, as my mother used to say. From our side. From our side. This all looks like chaos. But maybe from the other side . . . if there is another side . . . but my whole life says that there is another side. Another side more real than this. I'm sick with light, like you, Dania." His warm mouth came down on hers and he kissed her. That was nice, too, part of the dreamy strangeness. "I'm no doctor. I don't know how to inoculate us. I don't know what the cure is. But it's getting worse, isn't it? Here in this light-haunted space station . . . These children are the same, Dania, the same as when I saw them seventy years ago. I remember their names. I remember their faces. I can't imagine anything more horrible and yet they are all so happy . . . so many children . . . I met some others . . . it's terrible. So terrible."

She pushed back his hair, looked into his eyes. They were desperately sad.

"We'd best get a move on," said Storm of Cats. "All them kids are awake now. Kind of groggy. Which is good, I think." He grinned.

Radio Cowboy tried to pick her up but staggered and dropped her.

"I'm sorry, I'm so sorry," he kept saying even when she reassured him that it was all right, that even had it been a thousand times worse it was all right but all she could do was cry and laugh at the same time she was so glad to see him when she had never expected to see him again and he was a part of the Nows. Maybe he could tune her, or maybe Crescent City could tune her, perhaps a new frequency was opening up there, if only they would be able to sense it but perhaps it was still beyond them, beyond their eyes their ears their noses their touch, the passageways to the brain, their avenues to Mind which did so want to link with all that was out there.

It was night when they went out to the bus. And she remembered too much. As she climbed the stairs into the bus they were the back stairs of the old house where she had grown up, that smelled of aged wood and where children from before the War Between the States played. And later hid from the Yankees. She had seen them and she saw them now. Had this thing that was happening cast itself back over her whole life? Why not? Oh, why not! "Why not!" she shouted, her voice harsh from shouting. "No one can help me now. No one." It all washed through her, her grandfather the slave, her great-grandmother the Cherokee, her great-great-grandmother the immigrant from Ireland, steely with life. It spread out from there, impossibly wide, never-ending, always-linking. Radio Cowboy brushed her cheek with his hand and said that he was sorry for everything. But it was not his fault, it was not anyone's fault, and it was not a fault at all. It was good, and bright, and positive, and many, and intense, so intense that how could she ever forsake it? How could she ever narrow in to just one person again? Infinite deaths, infinite lives, infinite stars, infinite universes. All flowing through her with a rhythm like dance and with a bandwidth known to only a few stars. Coming this way, coming *right* this way . . .

"Where did she go?" she shouted, suddenly alert. They were climbing the steps into the bus. Hadn't she just done that? "Where is Three Impossible!" She began to struggle and the children all pushed her up the steps, pushed her to the back, pushed her into the seat, and there was that awful smell from buses of old, it wasn't a nice bus at all, there were no nice buses, and she stared out the back window. It was dark again, and Three Impossible was gone and she cried, and cried, and cried as the gates of Johnson Space Center opened and they drove through the swamps and heat and flatness and scraggle-treed takeover of Houston, where few lights glowed, toward Galveston and the coast. For Three Impossible could certainly not run this fast.

She shouted, “I’ve been tricked!”

And laughed. Fearfully. Loud.

August 13, 2115

Dania

The two Nows joined again on the road. They were not so very different, thought Dania. That splitting. I’m here and here is only one Now and this was it:

The road was straight and lined with white, bright sand and sea grass and led right to the smell and then the sight of the blue, blue sea that sang like only a color could, with one deep tone forever.

August 15, 2115

To

There were long troughs and bright blue sea, and the trouble, thought Peabody, with his ship of children and one mildly mad woman, the trouble was that boats were heading *away* from Crescent City.

On the first day, they saw one and the next day they saw four. Too many to seem random. And the shrimp boat was slower than they hoped it would be.

He was a bit worried, too, about introducing these essentially feral children into Crescent City. They had grown to be their own sort of organism and though they were needed, they were also, in their way, frightful. By their own account, they had killed their counterparts, children exactly like themselves but simply on another shift. They had been schooled by adults for a time, so there was a distant basis for some kind of discipline. They were ferociously intelligent; far more intelligent than the average adult, yet their emotional development was stuck at six years old.

But they held the key to the navigation. He had failed to meet the radio astronomer, the person who, long ago, had parsed the rhythm of the pulses and had begun to develop the single equation that would describe the nature of space and time, the equation that would supersede $E = mc^2$, the equation that would reveal the truth of both the large and the small and everything in between. The radio astronomer had left Crescent City decades earlier to work in what he thought might be a more pure environment, the Los Angeles Dome.

They did not, perhaps, need that information.

His joy, at this realization, was profound. They did not, perhaps, need a Theory of Everything in order to rise into space and go to that place from whence the Signal had originated. All they needed was these children.

The fact remained, though, that whoever had created the Signal, whoever had sent this DNA-altering virus to Earth, did indeed understand time and space and had been trying to share this understanding with those on Earth. Or with whomever else might be out here. Probably, he had to admit, Zeb didn't really care whether or not they went into space. He wanted to know for the purity of the knowing.

Jason Peabody gazed at the long blue swells over which the boat loudly labored. His life had all been so astonishing. The previous seventy years had been more paradigm-changing than the paradigm changes wrought by all of the Galileos, Copernicuses, and Einsteins put together.

Peabody had developed a habit of turning away from change. From, he had to admit, the ephemeral promise of transcendence. Even now, as he continued to recover from his Radio Cowboy persona—for whatever Storm of Cats had concocted, it had worked—he realized that perhaps it had been the only way the city had been able to get him out to seek what the city knew it needed. To reseek that which he had once given the city. Otherwise, safely sequestered in his tower, he never would have left. He probably would have somehow hidden from the pirates and worked with others on their inevitable absorption or expellation. He never would have had this glorious, bright, deeply disturbing adventure. He would have been able to lull himself into thinking that what happened in the greater world did not concern him.

He still felt that way. He longed to return to his safe radio monitoring, to the cat of the season who deigned to keep him company, to his view of the comings and goings in the great city which had become his home. It was true, he realized now, that much of his early fire had dissipated, leaving him weary, world-wise, resigned, and cynical. Radio Cowboy had awakened his youth. He missed Radio Cowboy. But he didn't want him back.

It was exceedingly nice that this boat was a fairly large shrimp trawler so that he didn't have to be with those rowdy children all the time. He was twenty feet up in a tower, while they brawled and shouted and dashed around the deck below through the shrimp smell which up here the wind swept away.

Then Dania emerged from below deck, gripping a handle set in the door frame with one hand and shielding her eyes with the other.

She looked so alive. What a woman. She had been through so much. She had been used by the city as relentlessly as he had been, and the effect seemed to linger in her. Something had happened to her. Something powerfully disorienting. She had babbled repeatedly about Nows, Nows, Nows; no; *the* Nows, as if they were as specific as *the* moon or *the* stars, and the people from Wind Rock, and chanting and light—no, of *people* made of light or, no, that wasn't quite it, but *beings* made of light . . .

Which came uncomfortably close to describing the phenomenon he had witnessed just before the pirate attack. The phenomenon which he would have liked to ignore, but which had pegged all the meters on his radio wall and caused glorious sound to burst forth from the ancient speakers the wires of which he carefully tended and regularly tested for corrosion. An ellipse of light. A phenomenon of the organizing of a certain frequency, or perhaps many frequencies.

Something new under the sun.

Something new in time and space. Or, at least, this time and space. Something which had caused him to babble to Dania about light and retuning as if he knew what he was talking about. Was that Cowboy? Or was it some newly awakened part of him?

God forbid. He was very tired of being newly awakened. But he couldn't go back to sleep.

What about this time? he wondered as yet another boat appeared on the horizon, more evidence of an unprecedented exodus from Crescent City. Would he, this time, when and if it was offered, choose transcendence? Choose to cross over, choose something unnamed, unspecified, undescribed except by the description *Other?*

A frisson of excitement rushed up his spine. Perhaps this might answer all his questions. Relieve the jagged wound which was his true heart, his true mind. But what would it really be like? Whatever he imagined would only be some sort of dim approximation of the real experience. Only by going through it could he know the answer.

But, he was sure, this time the answer was really *there.*

Yes. Perhaps. He might. Possibly. Go.

There would be no return. But he had no one to return to, anyway.

He was surprised when that thought called forth a picture of Dania in his mind.

Dania. But of course she would come too.

He regarded her again. She had spotted him and was climbing the ladder, dodging a loose solar panel as it swung back and forth with the boat's rock. He waved at her to go back; he would come down; she should still be resting below.

But here she was, next to him, substantial and real and exuding irritation, confusion, power, and humor.

She looked him up and down. "Good morning."

"Yes," he managed.

"So you are actually a real person."

He smiled. "I guess I could say the same about you."

They stood for a moment, looking at the ocean. It was choppy, with occasional whitecaps forming for an instant before they were swallowed back into the sea. She pointed in the direction they were heading. "I see three boats. Are they coming this way?"

He nodded. "I think some kind of evacuation taking place."

"Ah, yes. Some of the people are scared shitless. That's how I'd put it. They want to get to solid ground. Space is not where they want to be."

"Is it where you want to be?"

She looked at him in mock surprise. "Is this some kind of proposal?"

"Just a question."

"Well, I happen to have an answer. It isn't where I want to be."

"But—"

"It is most certainly where I once wanted to be. But if I understand things correctly, and I'm not at all sure that I do, this whole foray into the heartland was so that we could bring back information the city needs. Mapping information. Information that will take us . . . somewhere. Somewhere else."

She turned to look at him. The wind plastered her hair across her face and she shook her head impatiently so that it flailed back behind her. Her eyes were keen and serious. So serious that his heart stilled within him, caught in that present musical etching of white gulls against blue sky, their ceaseless arrowlike cries, the drone of the boat, the jolt of it across the waves.

"I want to be here," she said with something in her voice telling him that she knew what that would mean for him and for her.

Deep sadness welled up within him and he embraced her and pulled her close. Her arms tightened and the children below laughed and waved and their noise was distant and pointless as the gull cries, for the long touch of her as the motion of the boat pressed them together was the only thing real to him.

The shrimper chugged up to a dock amid a flurry of gulls. The children waited in a tight knot at the gangway which Storm of Cats eventually lowered from the pilot house and they rushed off into the city.

"Thank God we're here!" said Dania as she and Jason stepped onto the dock. "I was beginning to feel like I was in a boat-sized pinball machine. What are you going to do now?"

"Go home," he said. "Wash up."

"Get some chow?" she teased.

"That, and do some work. What about yourself?"

"Oh, I have a lot of work to do," she said airily.

"Such as?"

"I'll have you know that I am a thoroughly competent superstring theorist," she told him. "I've learned a lot on this trip and I have to assimilate it all. I have to give it to the Consilience and the Consilience might be able to come to a conclusion or two. I certainly haven't been able to yet." She gazed at him through a haze of Nows and it was much more difficult to speak than she wanted to let on. They were a bit like the gulls, except they blinked in and out of existence rapidly, leaving pictures as thick as snow which faded as quickly as snow in the sunlight. There was also the matter of the damned music that she had been hearing, chants and all kinds of whatnot, ever since this had all started. If I weren't a very self-confident woman, she mused, as the sparkle of the sun on the water was converted to music and Nows in a seamless and beautiful fashion, I might think that I was completely insane.

"Yes. Whatever," said Peabody. "But you look like you're going to fall right into the water. You must have been seasick. Come on. We'll go to my apartment and have something to eat and get some rest."

"Who are you now?" she asked, peering at him with narrowed eyes. Her hair raged outward in the wind like angry snakes.

"Jason Peabody, Certified Nanotech Engineer. No matter what the city has to say about it. Really." His voice was steady and serious.

"All right. I just don't want to get tangled up with that cowboy again."

"Neither do I," he said gravely. "Let's go."

He was surprised to find that his apartment had become grand central station. He opened the door and a very tall, exceedingly thin, and elegant black woman stood there. She had a broad smile and a rich, deep voice. "You must be Dr. Peabody." Beyond her, he saw evidence of what had to be occupancy by several people, with so many beer pouches and books—his books! and even some valuable antique radio tubes strewn around—Well, not strewn, he told himself. Set on the table in a row and just left there—

"Um, yes." He stood uncertainly in the doorway. "And you are?"

"Io Xia. From Unity." This was stated in defiant tones.

"Oh. Wonderful. Very nice to meet you. This is Dania, ah—"

"Dania is fine," Dania said, pushing past him and shaking Io's hand. "From the moon, you say! Wonderful! Wonderful! What a trip that must have been. And hey, I hear that the whole city is planning to go right back the other way. Why, that will be splendid too, won't it. Fly right out into space to God knows where! Oh, we are so lucky! To be living in this day and age!" She rushed past Io and lay down on the bed in the alcove and seemed, in a moment, to be deeply asleep.

"I was just leaving," Io said, after a moment's silence. "I'm glad that you're back. Everyone here has been really worried about you. Zeb and Ra came. You know them?"

"Where are they?"

"In Science Hall, I think."

"The Hall. All right. I'll be there after I get some rest. You're welcome to stay."

"Oh no. I'll see you later." She closed the door behind her.

Jason went over and gazed down at Dania. He bent over and fit his hand to her cheek. She either had a fever or a raging sunburn. Without opening her eyes, she pulled his head down, and kissed him.

"Move over," he said.

The Engineer felt a deep change in the Consilience as he sat at his radio controls a few hours later. Everything was charged with expectation. It seemed more lively. But he was going to keep his distance. Radio Cowboy was not all that far from his conscious mind and he didn't want to encourage him to stride forth. He caused too much trouble.

But he had brought the children. Storm of Cats had vowed to take care of them. Brave man. He was excited about getting initiated. He would get them initiated. And their guidance information, still fresh and constantly renewed in their elastic brains where his had gone stiff and stale, would guide the city in its next quest: to get to the source of the Signal.

Amazing, he thought with excitement he tried to keep at a reasonable level. Amazing that after all these years there would be some sort of conclusion for him, some sort of resolution.

A rendezvous!

No! thought Peabody, pushing Cowboy back.

Yet, what of those other children? They were still out there. Crossing.

The thought made him sick. The vials he had bought were with them. Perhaps they might be able to use them somehow to save themselves. That was his only hope, and a faint and distant one at that.

Well. He turned to his radios and sampled what was happening now. Leaving that running, he turned to the information that had been saved while he had been gone. Looked like somebody had been tampering with that, though . . .

This alternate signal moved along in tandem with radio events, apparently. He told his system to cast the information in several different forms. Then he asked where it came from.

It was actually music. Music that was being played, live, in Crescent City.

Where?

In the Hall.

By what? Or by whom?

By a twelve-year-old girl.

He played it audibly, low so that it wouldn't wake Dania.

It went on and on, unrepeating. Like, he also noticed, some new equations that the radio astronomer had added to the Consilience and left here at the top of the heap. It was scary. That was why he kept a healthy distance from the Consilience, and why he had long ago set up these interfaces. Otherwise, it would eat him alive.

And had done so, he reminded himself, despite his precautions.

He was still worn out from his exertions as Radio Cowboy. The trip lingered in his mind, utterly golden despite the pain and uncertainty and sheer weirdness of it. The sun on the buttes. All of the new humans out there, the humans left behind to fare as best they could in the wake of the Silence.

Well, but how could he help them? Even if he wanted to stay behind. On this Earth, with its plains and its forests and mountains and its long, long roads. He was not a helper. He was a doer, a builder. An Engineer. An Engineer who had never helped a single soul in his entire life. Who had always taken the exact wrong turn—personally speaking—at the exact wrong oblique angle.

He knew how to bring things together. He now knew how to keep the hell out of the way of the Consilience, unlike most of the fools here who were sucked in and out of it like so much flotsam. He was experienced in this setting. He knew how the city worked, had helped in the planning of many of the space-centered systems and knew, humanly knew, how to fix them if they went wrong. Others could too of course, another part of him argued, and so could the city itself.

The plain truth of it was that he wanted to go. He would go. He could feel the city gathering itself like a great heavy-haunched beast to spring into space. They now had the way to go. Not the why of it, perhaps, except that they had been so insistently called, their wills pulverized to dust so that going was just about all they could do.

And because it was the next step.

And because, in his mind, a vast organism was finally stretching and waking to fuller consciousness. The lone tree on the mountain was sending forth its seed, releasing it into the wind.

He looked in on Dania before he left, just pulled the curtain aside and gazed at her lovely face and her beautiful, long, shadowed nude body. The cowgirl getup she was holding onto was stashed in a bag sitting next to the narrow bed, the hat on top of it as if the bag was a head holding valuable information. She was the best thing about that trip. She was, in fact, dazzling.

And bedazzled herself, almost beyond possible return. Round the bend, out there, ozzed and not yet home again. She required rest and care. She hadn't pulled free of the Consilience as he had and would need help. For once in his life, he felt utterly prepared to help. It was rather amazing.

He pulled a light cover over her. She mumbled something.

"What?"

"Turn off that damned music, would you?" she said without opening her eyes and he did. Then he stepped onto the tower stairs and closed the door behind him.

"Her music—" Zeb was saying, his voice behind a head of long white hair and Peabody grabbed him by the shoulder and whirled him around. They hugged dancing from one stiff leg to the other and then let go. Peabody hadn't felt so glad to see someone since—well, since finding Dania again, he realized.

"And Ra!" There were more hugs and explanations and catching-up to do as they fell into the couches as of old and talked into the night while the woman from the moon listened and watched and the girl from the moon played on.

After a while the music really began to get on Peabody's nerves. He wanted to ask her to stop, but everyone else seemed to think it was so astonishingly important that he was reluctant to do so. I'm tired, he thought. I am absolutely exhausted. Everything he looked at was kind of wiggly. He needed sleep. They needed talk, lots of talk, something momentous was happening here, what with these people from the moon and the launch coming soon and the pirates vanquished, and that light-thing dancing around in the corner of his mind wanting to jump out and be fit into everything but he couldn't hold it all in his head.

A gangly red-headed man with a bad peeling sunburn on his face and feet, looking comically bony and otherwise chalk-white in ludicrous shorts, burst into the room with a bunch of papers in his hand covered with pictures and numbers saying "She says that you know how to get this built and that you have to start doing it right now. She says that its a story but it's an engineering story and you need the engineering story to get the rest of the stories out there. The rest of time, you know, the way you—the way *we!*—see time. The curled up dimensions!"

"What?" asked Zeb, but the man just hurried on.

"She was trying to get through in other ways but doesn't know how yet." After a moment, during which they all stared at him, he said, "She's The Storyteller," as if that meant something.

Peabody could almost see the fellow's heart pounding in his chest from sheer nervousness. "I'm sorry," the red-haired man said. "Am I in the wrong place?"

"No," Peabody said. "Whoever she is. Whoever you are." The man did not volunteer his name.

Peabody took the papers from his shaking hand, wondering at their primitiveness, and spread them out on one of the long tables and looked at them. He rearranged them a few times. He looked at them some more. They stopped wiggling. They made clear, strong, beautiful sense. "It's kind of like a radio. I think. Beyond that, but we'll call it a radio. Catches the rays. The frequencies . . ." He studied it further. "A very, very nice one, exceedingly so. Simple, powerful, indestructible. It grows, of course. I believe that it would have the capability of organizing frequencies and then relaying them. But what those frequencies are—they're beyond our capacity to see or hear—or what's to receive the frequencies after they're rebroadcast—I don't know."

"Brains," said the woman from the moon, her voice deep and sure as she looked over his shoulder. "Human brains. But not ours. The next kind."

Su-Chen

They are all still babies who think I am.

The music moves on it moves on quickly it falls apart it comes together.

See where **is** *goes hear where* ***it*** goes *be where it and is both* **are,** *both* **go**.

The music makes the cat. The music makes the moon. The music makes there here.

I know the way I always know the way and they only have to listen.

Io waits and hears the people want to leave and we all want to leave past the moon and we shall we shall shoot far past the moon to where they are and to where they always are we only need to follow the music the music is a map like numbers we can see where they are going if they would only know maybe I can tell them it is interesting and it is like my father said holy more holy than anything it is something I know not something I feel.

Something. I. Know.

August 18, 2115

The Gizmo

It was ten in the morning, and there was a great sense of somnolence throughout the city. People were rising to light breakfasts of spirulina-charged sweet rolls and coffee, or miso soup, or sautéed or pickled fish. Over the decades, people of all continents, encompassing thousands of ethnicities, had made their way to Crescent City and joined the Consilience. All of the citizens were migrating to one part of the city or the other, preparing to stay or to leave.

Except for a small band of people in one tense little room, which was located in the very center of Crescent City.

Zeb, Peabody, and Dania watched the gizmo, as Peabody was calling it, grow.

It was taking the shape of a white sphere, cradled in, but not seeming connected to, a clear cradle which grew at the same rate as the sphere. It was almost too bright to look at directly.

"You knew this would happen?" Dania asked Zeb, whom she had just met. He was tall and somewhat remote. Peabody had told her that he was a radio astronomer and that he had been reconstituted from the Dome that Los Angeles had turned into. That probably accounted for his distant demeanor.

"Something like this had to happen," he said. "I feel completely humble in the face of this overwhelming fact: We are part of an evolving cosmos, and that evolving cosmos is basically one quantum event.

"We don't know what this phenomenon is. But it is beyond what we know—perhaps beyond what we *can* know. But we can only hope that those of us who received this biological initiation at the right time, like Peabody, are developing the capacity to *know* it, to *be* it.

"And what will this do?" Dania watched the sphere, through narrowed eyes, with intense curiosity.

"It embeds the directions." Zeb spoke distractedly, as if she was wrenching him from a great distance into the present.

"The directions the children brought."

"Yes." He continued to stare at the sphere. "Their directions are updated constantly. The children are a living calculus. They're probably what all the children of the Silence—the Pioneers, I guess they call them here—were meant to be."

Maybe that explained the way the children moved, like bolts of lightning. How *would* a calculus behave? They had rushed off the boat, shouting, and vanished into the city while Dania and Radio Cowboy—Jason Peabody—just stared at each other. It was useless to chase them. Thank God, she thought, that she wasn't like them. She was supposed to be a Pioneer too; only she hadn't gone just right. Maybe because she had been conceived during a long-ago drunken spree at some little town on the coast of Florida, a spree that had continued for some weeks after her conception.

All night, apparently, according to data rendered in this particular spherical fashion, the children had tumbled and dashed and careened through the city, hugging the Consilience columns, tossing Consilience-based balls which eventually rolled into depressions which relieved them of the information that had been transmitted by their touch.

Dania's heart ached for these children kept deliberately young, deliberately elastic, so that they continuously understood the compilation of all of the pulses that had come in during the long, long Silence. Their minds were exquisitely tuned to the ever-changing magnetic map that had first been sent so long ago, but which was in constant flux.

But was it so bad, she wondered, for them?

There was enough information now so that future changes could be calculated by this thing that was growing.

Perhaps they could now grow up.

"And this thing is being programmed?" asked Dania, trying to understand the enormity of an intergalactic calculus made material, chaos surfing on the edge of becoming.

"Yes. Programmed by the music of last night," said Zeb. A few hours after the children arrived, Su-Chen had begun playing and had not stopped until Io wrenched her from her keyboard at dawn.

"And this information will take us to that place?"

Zeb sighed somewhat impatiently. "That's the place. The place where everything will change."

"All of us."

"All of us in this section of Crescent City," said Zeb. "Even me. Because I allowed my DNA to be changed."

"We have DNA?"

They turned. Ra stood in the doorway, concern in her eyes.

"Of course, Ra." Zeb went to her; put his arm around her waist.

She said, "But my dome DNA hasn't changed."

"No. I suppose those beings, or whatever they are, will be left behind."

Dania looked up, her eyes and voice sharp. "Left behind."

Peabody nodded. "Yes. It's easy to take everyone here. They'll just go with the ship. The ones who choose to go. Part of the city will be left behind."

"What happens to all the other people on Earth?" Dania put her hands on her hips, looked around at each of them in turn.

"They can't go," Peabody said. "Obviously."

"I know *that*," said Dania. "But last night I had a glimpse of this. Just a glimpse of what it will be like when humans have been changed. Utterly changed. It's a new evolutionary leap. Right? The rest of the world deserves to experience it too. Whatever it is."

Peabody spoke slowly. "Well, that's the point. We really have no idea what it is. We have no idea how *we* will be changed. We're choosing to take the chance."

"Right. And we *want* it. We want it badly."

He shook his head, and his pained, introspective glance at the sphere slammed into her heart like a huge wave. "We may all die. It's best that some people survive, don't you think?"

Impatience made her voice brittle. "If that's what they want. Is that what you would want? To stay behind? Look, things are not going all that well out there, in case you didn't notice. I'll bet that new wars are shaping up, somewhere. The whole human race will fall back into the same old way of doing things. There has to be something new. Something redeeming. Some positive road out of all that's happened. Some future. Especially since this whole damn scientific community is going to blast off into space." She looked at Zeb, who seemed to know so much. "What do *you* think will happen?"

He did not respond immediately. Finally he said, "I'm not at all sure. And I can only say it in numbers. The picture I have is that we will go to this place where the beings who inflicted this on us know the truth about matter, the truth of the history of time and space. They have mastered it. They know the truth about physical reality. I'd say that they are physically different than us. Our mathematics are a reflection of us, a reflection of the way our brains evolved, for survival. Our mathematics aren't necessarily a true correlation to what's really happening. Perhaps theirs are closer to the truth. Perhaps we need to be physically changed to experience that truth. It's like we've been given an invitation to experience the truth."

"More like a command," said Peabody with some bitterness.

Zeb looked at him and shrugged. "It's true, Peabody. We can't guess their intent. Certainly, this could all be completely accidental. Meant for someone else; meant for no one; a by-product of something else—though at this point I doubt that very much. But so what? The point is that we are learning. We are changing. There's more. More to learn, more to know. Enhanced *ability* to know. And—there's a picture—a kind of representation—"

"What picture?" demanded Peabody.

"It's only in my mind," Zeb replied. "I can't tell it in a way that makes sense."

"It's like straws," Ra's eyes were alight; her voice eager.

Dania looked at her. "What?"

"Like straws." Ra spoke rapidly. "I've seen the picture. In L.A. I could know things like that, there. Know what Zeb was thinking. But . . . I was thinking it too, in my own way. It's like straws of light are coming down from the sky so that everyone can drink from them. They can drink time and space. Through these straws. Or maybe they're strings, countless strings. Opening into different dimensions. Bridging through to us. Drawing us into their harmonies. If they could be called harmonies. They're not harmonies that we necessarily hear with our ears. They'll be harmonies that involve all of physical matter, and we'll be able to perceive them in a new way. And everything is different."

"It definitely *sounds* different." Dania crossed her arms. "And everyone can decide whether or not to do this?" Her voice was accusatory.

"No," said Ra. "Only the people with this particular DNA. Only these people have the choice."

"But what is the choice?" Dania asked again, feeling frustrated.

"It's not something that our minds, as they are now, can possibly understand," said Zeb. "They're too limited. Only after we go will we know whether or not it's a good thing. As I said, it's actually a terrible risk."

"One you are all more than willing to take," she pointed out.

"We've all lived a long time with this," Peabody said. "A very long time. We've been through a lot. We're ready to go. Whatever happens. It wouldn't be fair to inflict this on everyone before we know what's going to happen."

Dania shouted, "But once you're all gone, you won't be *able* to! Even if those left behind *want* it!" She stared hard at each in turn, then stalked from the room.

Peabody frowned. Ra and Zeb did not seem concerned. They continued to observe the rapidly changing sphere.

It wove together frequencies that were well out of human range. The Consilience had created it. It was beyond the capacity of any one person, or even a small team, to think of. Only the entire weight and scope of scientific and engineering thought, factored together by the Consilience, had been able to shape this thing, this gizmo. It would give forth the ever-changing frequencies which would be taken in by all of the people of Crescent City. Taken in, and transformed into information, the information which their minds had grown to understand, and to use.

Su-Chen would continue to feed it the nonlocal information emanated by the light beings.

It was all decided.

August 19, 2115

Dania

When You Awake, You Will Remember Everything

The haunting music played from somewhere; everywhere. Dania woke to it.

Woke to the stunning vision of rank on rank of light beings.

Woke to a deep story.

To a new fact.

She slipped from bed. Peabody, asleep next to her, snored and snorted a bit.

Silently as Coyote, she pulled on her clothes in the moonlight-striped room. The dirty, unmended skirt; the now-gray shirt that would stink of sweat as it warmed with her body. She hadn't even thought of cleaning them. She picked up the battered leather pack, set her hat on her uncombed hair, picked up her cowgirl boots, and stepped from the room into a corridor where the humid air wrapped round her in a wave of wind.

She held her hat on with her free hand and ran, lightly and silently, as light-beings winked in and out of existence around her like fireflies hovering over a darkened meadow.

The story of Coyote coursed through her blood.

There was a new level to the city: the stories. Angles and avenues down which she could see. The backbone of the Nows, which constantly evolved.

This story was not just North American. Trickster was everywhere in the folk tales of the Earth.

Trickster—Coyote—was as timeless as the light-beings.

The new fact was a map through corridors, down elevators; the new fact was a dash through plazas of people awake, leaning on railings, gazing what might be their last night on Earth, if they followed the intensity of the layers of stories of exodus from the Earth. But mostly what they felt, Dania knew, was the religious intensity of vision—the mandala, the cross, the six-pointed star, and so many other symbols of transcendence. The raising of the dead. The presence of the Other. The sacrifice of self for something larger than themselves.

Not for me, barked Coyote in her head.

There was a fire deep within the city and she was going to steal it.

Steal it and break open time and reveal its secrets to everyone.

Science was one explanation. The intertwining of consciousness, of self-awareness, with matter. The growth of consciousness from matter.

The changing of consciousness's understanding of matter.

Dania did not know what would happen next, what this next great change would be.

But she had to take back this fire to her tribe. Her tribe of the Nows.

The Nows came in flashes. Like the stuttering words of a two-year-old child emerging after the training of babble. But there must be a way to string them together. A way to elide them. A way to constantly modify, to change, to know . . .

To be able to know more, to be able to know in a different way. So that time would be a language, with a grammar of its own.

A way to let consciousness grow.

A way for their mind and being to mesh with the astoundingly distant flowering of mind on another planet.

An improvisation, like the music she was infused with.

The music she was leaving behind.

She stopped at that thought, her throat raw from drawing in deep running breaths.

Though she was leaving this behind, these people were leaving much more.

They have the stories. The stories are the curled-up dimensions. They free us in time. We are beginning a new story. We are using more of what is out there. Consciousness is the tool.

The voice had a decidedly Spanish accent. It reminded Dania of her family deep in Texas.

But after the mending of the rift everything will be known here, too.

Was this a true voice? Dania bent over in sudden pain and demanded "How can I leave Radio Cowboy again? I can't stand it! I just can't stand it!" But she pulled on her boots, which awakened the fire of unhealed blisters. Ignoring them, she walked into a room in the center of Crescent City which, like a pirate map, revealed treasure.

But a curious treasure, Dania decided, walking around it.

It was larger now, and different.

A black sphere sat in the center of the room. Perhaps five feet in diameter. But no, it was white, and a cube. No . . .

Colors fled across it, and coalesced into pictures, which then fled and sped rapidly so the black that was white and the white that was black returned.

Dania was drawn to it. Of course she would be curious, would examine it. Anyone would. But it was more than that.

She stepped forward and touched it with one finger. Warmth spread through her. An astonishing feeling of deep well-being. An understanding that first made her laugh and then cry as though she would never stop, while so much rushed within her that she was filled with joy at the great majesty of existence. Her mind was without limit.

That was her last thought, for a time.

She woke on the floor after she did not know how long.

This was not for her to know.

It was only hers to give to others to know.

But how could she take it? It was far too large.

As she watched, the sphere expanded into spines, like a coral. The spines rapidly braided and unbraided themselves; split and merged so quickly Dania felt that perhaps some trick of vision was slowing the process from one that was infinitely swift; too swift for human vision to follow.

She reached out and grabbed hold of the braided mass.

She was thrown to the floor by some force which seared her hand with terrible pain; pain worse than when her children were born. She wanted to let go. But could not.

The light ebbed from it and her pain subsided.

She held in her hand a gray thing, brittle, its filaments thin and airily woven. It weighed perhaps a pound.

She could only hope that its energy, its potential, was just in abeyance. For it was all that she had.

She dropped it into her pack and cinched it tight.

There was one more thing to do, but this was far easier.

She left the room and walked through the flood of stories and light-beings. She passed one of the thousands of openings in Crescent City which for decades had given forth on the sea. It was sealed with a clear membrane which thickened as she watched. Below she saw flotillas heading out in all directions and knew she did not have much time.

She began to run.

She got to the bottom floor. Below this various towers and stairways and elevators descended to sea level.

All was chaos. People were fleeing Crescent City, or else hurrying upwards to be contained for the launch. She had to find a work station.

She was startled for a moment by music. She stopped, looked around. The source of the music moved too. And her face twisted with tears again, with terrible grief.

It was Radio Cowboy's radio. In her skirt pocket. Working. Playing some silly jingle in Spanish.

His radio worked. And she was leaving him.

A word came to her mind: through the air, from the Consilience: *there.*

Ah. *There.* She looked around, grasped a hand indentation in the wall and pulled to the right. A work station was revealed. Sluggishly, for it too was closing down, it woke to her touch. And even more slowly, so that Dania was in complete agony and paced back and forth in the morphing corridor, it manifested that which she ordered.

It was a green, three-quart, gelatinous blob, sealed inside a thick membrane.

She thrust it into her pack and ran.

She had to drop from the bottom of a receding ladder onto the underdeck of the city. She sprawled, spraining her ankle, so that when she stood she stumbled again and then broke into a limping run.

She jumped onto a heavy-laden boat that was pulling away from its moorings. Above them, the city was much changed, was coalescing, and they had to battle a heavy headwind. The boat made its slow way from the city, crammed with sobbing, screaming people, some of whom jumped off to swim back; others were terrified of the rocket's hot plasma, or the tsunami the launch might generate.

What did happen struck them all silent.

They were only about five miles from the city, which by was changing rapidly. It was more sleek now. Countless peaked pavilions had merged into one sleek point. The wind was picking up.

A huge sail unfurled.

It was like a spinnaker, or like the translucent membrane which scudded the Portuguese man o' war across the face of the sea.

But infinitely stronger. It caught the wind and Crescent City rose into the air, with a deep whirring sound which vibrated to them from the depths: the underwater jets. From this distance they looked like tiny sticks as they dropped into the sea.

For a moment, the launched city careened wildly and no one spoke. Then the wind lifted it high. A hundred, two hundred, five hundred feet. A thousand feet, and still it was huge and unwieldy.

At perhaps two thousand feet the rockets fired.

Crescent City soared off in a blaze of fire and distant thunder. The membrane shredded to tatters which drifted in the sky long after the bright gleam had vanished.

Dania held tight to the rail with aching hands, watching that space in the sky.

The Engineer

Across the Great Divide

Peabody was out of bed, on his feet, almost before he realized it. It was disorienting to be here, in his home, and himself. It took a second to realize that he was not dreaming.

Dania was gone.

Their argument still rang in his head. He knew where she had gone and what she was going to do.

The entire Earth deserves this. Deserves the Nows. I know that you don't believe in the Nows, and don't understand them, but they are real. Everyone deserves to have an end to war and pain and death. Deserves to enjoy the gifts of nanotechnology again. Deserves to gain access to this supposed understanding, when Ra's vision comes true. What she said: Remember? The light music tunes us, those of us with the mutated DNA. A window is opened. We go through it. There is this side, and the other side, that we can't see now. If it does come true. It may not. But it might. Somebody has to stay behind to ensure that everyone knows this truth. We can't leave the Earth in darkness. This possibility must be available to everyone. The genetic change, to prepare them. The—the gizmo, growing down there. To focus the frequencies that will open them to whatever this new form of knowing, this new form of consciousness, will be.

Dania had spoken in a low, calm voice. A strong voice.

He hated the rightness of her arguments.

His were good too. Eugenics, for one. How could they tamper? How could they justify being so invasive? Upsetting the balance? Doing something which, once let into the larger system, might cause more harm than good? Whose idea of good were they using, anyway?

I wonder how long they agonized over whether or not to cure polio? she'd retorted. TB? I believe that most human ideologies are a disease. A horrible virus. As destructive as physical plagues. Wake up, Peabody! Can you honestly say that war is good? Can you honestly say that the preparation of the mind for learning, that the transmission of information, is bad?

If that's what it is—

That's what it is and you know it. We all know it. Are we all going to sentence everyone to be slaves to ignorance? Forever? Are we going to withhold this? Do we have the right? And what about the Nows? Let's say that everyone is practically blind right now. That they have an idea about Time that is limiting, blinding, tragic. What right do we have to deny them vision?

Shit.

All the radios in his room were on, and playing a babble of music, voices. He ought to be rejoicing, dancing in this rain of radio freedom, which he was sure the ship would take with it as it left, for the focuser, the gizmo, would go with it.

He went to the window and watched the city prepare to leave Earth.

He had made this possible. They all had, along with the Consilience. And all the long history of Crescent City and the world, and all of the stories that made the human world, that gave it new dimensions. They had reached the crescendo of it all, to put it in terms of music. And it had been music, light music, that had organized his brain and his being, relentlessly, with a force stronger than any other he had ever encountered.

He had longed for this, something like this, all his life.

He hated that it was happening now.

"Give me a story," he begged. But there was no answer. The curled-up dimensions remained curled-up. Closed to him.

"Give me a story!" he demanded, surprised at the vehemence of his plea, the roughness of his voice. "Like before, damn it!"

But he could try to leave the city. He could find Dania, and follow her. He could do what was right.

For yes, she was right.

The city was growing the prototype for allowing everyone here on Earth, rightly prepared—even animals, maybe even plants—to learn this new way of understanding time. The Consilience had created this gizmo out of everyone's stories, out of the stories of the planet, out of *consciousness*, using the stories of the light-beings, who spoke in a spectrum that transversed and transformed time.

No one person could have melded information in this fashion. This feat of engineering was even beyond decades of cross-communication among scientific disciplines. But the Consilience had done it and now that it was done, he and Zeb had been able to understand it.

It was programmed by music. Dania did not know this. She had stormed from the room, angry that they were not acknowledging her arguments. When he found her here, later, she could not be awakened; she pulled from him in her sleep and shouted with her eyes closed, frightening him so that he decided to let her rest a bit longer.

That had been a mistake.

He pulled on some clothes and set out walking.

On the way, he got his story. It was a great relief, and still not all that strong a story but something to keep him moving, something that slid between him and the great strong joy of the city, the jubilation, the fear, the sense of overwhelming revelation waiting on the other side of this sudden event horizon. He could uncouple from it. He had his own story. He was no longer Jason Peabody, on his way to the mystery that made him, after a long life of service, a long life of pain and questions. He was not Radio Cowboy. Radio Cowboy would go, out to this new frontier. He was thankful that Radio Cowboy was washed from him.

This new story was perfect for what he needed to do.

He strode through all manner of crazed and jubilant crowds. Searching for the girl who understood light music. The girl who was free of stories. The one who had compiled light music in the pureness of space, in the moon colony, able to feel and translate the vibrations without the distortion of joy or fear.

He found her where she had been before, in Science Hall, standing before her keyboard playing, and felt a blaze of luck. He knelt next to her. "Su-Chen, will you come with me? I am going to go out. Away from Crescent City. I need you to play this music. To program whatever it is that the city is growing, the stuff that focusses the frequencies."

She glanced down at him as she played. "There are more people."

"Yes. Many more."

"I need to show them all. They need to know the light-beings. That's what Io calls them."

The room was filled with those tall, pure, vibrating lights.

Su-chen stopped playing. They remained.

Peabody heard what they were meaning.

Before he could stop her, Su-Chen stepped inside of them, raised her arms, and danced.

Su-Chen

Feelings. Storm clouds on the sea. Coming for me. I want to run from them, but I can't. Their rain falls sharp each drop a crystal cutting me to ribbons. Fear, loss, joy. Things I don't want to know don't want to be. Incredible, unbearable pain. Pelting pictures through me.

Finally the storm passes.

Sweet, sweet drifting and words string together too easily like this, lazy and round. All their stories are like this. Everything I see is changed. I can't see what's there any longer. I can't see what is really there. Stories and emotion distort my vision. Make colors too bright or too dim. Make music not music, not exquisite, satisfying, true relationships, but a generator of yet more of these painful stories. I will cry forever. How do they stand it? How can they possibly stand it. They lose so much this way.

I can only scream and scream and scream.

The man like her father put his arms around her and held her close. She did not struggle. She let him hug her. It felt good.

"I can't stand this," she heard herself whisper. She had stood everything before. Now it was much too bright. More sobs shook her. "Please, I have to go. I want to go. This will happen to me forever if I stay here. I don't like this."

She twisted from him and vomited onto the floor. She pulled her hair with both hands so that it hurt. She staggered to the wall and banged her forehead against it. She could knock the stories out. Or knock herself out. It didn't matter which.

She felt him take her by the hand. She couldn't pull from it, though she tried. He had a very strong grip. He wiped her face with a cool wet cloth. He grabbed some clothes and the food from her cooler and put it into a backpack that was in the closet.

He picked her up, though she was so tall and gangly, and it was all right, it did not hurt to be touched. She was so tired. So very tired. Her head ached. More blood came down and got in her eye. It was sticky. The cloth came up to her head again and he wiped and put the cloth in her hand.

"We just need to get a few things," he said, and it sounded as if he had been crying too because his voice had that funny muffled quality.

"I want to get better," she said. "I just want to be better again. And I want my cat."

Peabody picked up the cat, thrust it into Su-Chen's arms. "Hold it." Then he grabbed Su-Chen up and ran.

The light-beings followed them everywhere, and she closed her eyes very tight.

Then he was dropping her into the boat, roughly, and apologizing. The sounds of their leaving—the *clank* of metal, the *thud* against the dock, the screams of other people, the overwhelming hertz of the engine as it sputtered to life—were like blows to her brain. Then there was wind; they were speeding from the city. And water was splashing her.

Peabody kept saying over and over again, Where would she *go*? Where would she *go?*

Then he said, Texas.

The boat turned.

Look, Su-Chen! Open your eyes! You'll only see this once. The city is going up in the air.

His voice slow and deep. As if he wants to go too.

How can I know what he *wants?*

Shock like a wave through the air, hitting me, and I have to open my eyes. Too bright to see with the light-people all around. The music too strong I can't stand it have to play it kicking screaming punching he grabs me: Settle down, you're going to tip the boat over.

An opening. A relief. It's gone. The city is gone. The blast is gone. A raw, ripped place in the side of what's left of Crescent City and I can't look at that. He stares and shakes. Tears run down his face slowly and get lost in his beard. His face crumples and he cries too and I

Understand.

Feelings make him do it.

I pat him on the back. Pat. Pat. Pat. It is what people do. What my father used to do but that always hurt.

Finally he looks up and smiles. His eyes don't change though. I don't know the word for the look in his eyes.

But I know that it is there.

I don't like knowing that. It hurts too much. Io isn't here to fix it. She isn't here to help me.

Io went with them.

What are these tears that come from deep inside and not from anger?

I hope that I get better soon.

The Engineer

"I'm all right," he told Su-Chen. He reached over and squeezed her hand. It lay tense and stiff in his, but at least she let him touch her.

He knew, as he watched the city recede into a tiny spot of intense light, that he had done the right thing. They had all done the right thing for themselves, all those folks he knew from way back, from the old days of Crescent City's birth. They were gone, swallowed into time.

He was here. He had work to do.

He was not a mystic. He was an Engineer.

It was hard to think these thoughts, but he made himself think them, forced himself to follow the thoughts and the feelings with which he was troubled and with which he was blessed, out to their end.

He knew that his path was not the path of his long-dead wife. It was perhaps fortunate that he had this story to follow right at this point, and that he had this girl to take care of. But it was true. He had a path, while his dead wife's had, for whatever reason, vanished.

Call it a light, a goal, a destination. It was a journey longer, more arduous, much more uncertain, than the way his friends and family and much of his life had just taken. They were now subsumed into a great, transcendent change which would, perhaps, reveal all of the secrets he had worked all his life to know. The justification, the explanation, for his mutation, for his entire, troubled life, was even now speeding away from him at a velocity so tremendous that he could never catch up with it now.

Here he still was, on a blue, blue sea, in a small boat topping broad green swells, with a girl he had to take care of, while the hot sun beat down on them.

With an engine, he realized, that had stopped working, so that he had to fix it.

Call it home.

He set to work.

Dania

Dania did not know where the boat was going.

In fact, it went to Haiti.

It took her several months to get back to the coast of Texas.

By then the bright smear in the sky, more brilliant at night, as if the fabric of space was torn like a scrim, was always there.

After camping in the dunes two nights, she left a tiny chunk of the gray matter to grow. This she had done in Haiti and on the several islands she had passed through on her way here. It always regenerated quickly after she broke a piece off. She gave the DNA serum, the ones that the children in Crescent City had used in order to become Pioneers, to everyone she could, if they wanted it after she tried to explain it to them.

She set out walking.

She finally made it back to the place where she had been perfected.

It was empty. The screen door on the back porch slammed back and forth, its spring rusted through. The creek was dry and the trees were dead.

But the worst thing was the inside of Edna's home, where she was quite sure—almost—that only last week she had sat with White Time Girl and the rest of them, drinking iced tea while the hot summer breeze played through the room and their horses grazed by the creek.

The house was stripped bare, with an emptiness that seemed not recent, but aged. Yellowed, peeling wallpaper. Floorboards warped and faded with weather. Kitchen gutted. As if no one had ever lived here.

She planted a spike in the orchard and moved on.

After that, life got very hard.

The Engineer

First, he found Carla and the children. He could really think of nothing else until then. They were in Sedona. This was a great stroke of luck. Sedona was small, and he had lived there as a child. It hadn't changed much. He talked to people and tracked them down.

Only Carla and three others were left, living on a red plateau in their parked van, near a swift-falling stream. Only Carla remembered him. Carla seemed about four years old, and a teenage girl was taking care of her and two toddlers. The materials in the vials, which they had kept but not touched out of fear, worked as he had hoped. It was a great relief. Carla and the babies wouldn't know what he had done, perhaps ever. He wrote their history for them and left it with the teenager, who would now also age—not to death, at least not soon, but to the stretched lifespan of those in Crescent City who had helped perfect the biology of longevity.

He took the vials with him when he left, feeling immense sadness that so few people now knew how to use them. He was a Certified Nanotech Engineer, certified by a government that had long since ceased to exist. He might as well call himself a magician.

He spent years missing Dania, and cursing the Nows, which he imagined had enveloped her. Wanting them. Fearing them.

Preparing the world for them.

Eventually, he and Su-Chen drifted north, through Colorado, then Ohio, Pennsylvania, New York, and New England, making their way through what had once been a vast nanotech-plagued zone, healing as they went, relaxing, eventually, into this vagabond life of seeding—for it was the story of Johnny Appleseed which moved him now and even after he could see through it he had settled into the habit of the story's life. He reflected, by firelight on the shores of chilly lakes as he watched the stars, on how strange his life had been, and how, with the leaving of Crescent City, space was finally so silent for him, so desolate. He usually wondered if what he was doing had any point at all, and wished he had gone with the launch instead of succumbing to this strange uncertain quest, feeling that he would never see the columns of time flowing between Earth and sky, like straws that the minds of transfigured humans could use to draw down infinity, or learn what that would be like, if they so chose, before returning to their old human ways.

Su-Chen did not seem troubled. She was quiet, but seemed in harmony with her life: It was a listening quiet; a silence of deep awareness. They were a strange couple, together yet apart, each absorbed in their own thoughts, moving from place to place with a strange and singular goal. Occasionally, Su-Chen had a burst of speech, which might go on for days. But usually, playing was enough for her; that was her speech, and listening was her life.

Nightly, Peabody went through his litany of futility after closing his eyes. Only then could he sleep.

October 2194

EAST KINGSTON, NEW HAMPSHIRE

Xavier was ten years old when the Engineer rolled into town in a strange-looking contraption, with a black-haired woman at his side.

"That's you, right, Grandpa? You're really Xavier!"

"Quiet, Hunter!" The twins, boys, were a few years older than her. "Why do you have to ask him every time?"

"Dummies!"

"No rudeness now or I'll stop. All right? All right."

Xaviar was playing in the front yard of his house. It was a very old house, with the date 1734 engraved on a board above the front stoop. People in Exeter said that it was haunted and stayed away from his mom and dad because of it, and didn't let their kids play with Xavier. It made for a lonely life, but Mom said it made their little family closer and Xavier guessed that was true. They lived on the outskirts of town and grew all their own vegetables, had a nice big old apple orchard with broad gnarly branches good for climbing, and that fall while they harvested apples and tossed the bruised ones in the cider press and little Kimberly got to laughing so hard that she peed in her pants Xavier kind of felt what his mom was talking about. Her face was reddened by the work and her blond hair fell from beneath her wool hat as she whisked Kimberly up on her hip, laughing too, and took her into the house to get into some warm dry clothes.

So the rest of them were out there and Dad was way at the back of the orchard when the Engineer chugged up the driveway in his steam car, put on the brake though it still chugged there so loud, and walked up to Xavier with a serious look on his kind face—

—Xavier thought the Engineer's face was kind when he first saw him and whenever he told his grandchildren the story he always said so—

"Are your parents here?" he asked, and then he saw Dad at the back of the orchard and waved at him with one big sweep of his arm.

Behind him, the hills were gold and red and the sky up above held the last ten minutes of a blue so bright it hurt the eyes, a clear fall blue set off against the trees. The Engineer's cheeks were pink in the chill and the lady in the car just stared straight ahead at the barn. There was a trailer on the back of the car with a lock on its door.

"Have you ever been anyplace else?" asked Hunter, her brown eyes serious. She stood at her grandfather's knee dressed in a dark blue corduroy jumper her mother got at the town clothing machine. Xavier came back to the present with a start, out of the story he had been telling his grandchildren.

"As a matter of fact, yes. I went to Paris a few years after that. But that's another story. Now listen to this one. They drove up next to the barn—"

"The same barn as now? Was the chicken coop there too?"

"No, we used to keep the chickens around the other side of the house back then. Now listen!"

"Can I sit on your lap?"

Grandpa Xavier pulled her up on his lap with a grunt and she settled in. "Stay awake now."

"We're awake," said the twins in unison, ten years old as he had been, sitting forward on their stools around the deep fireplace in which a cast-iron kettle held bubbling venison soup. Their older brother had shot the deer a week ago. Their blond heads gleamed in the firelight. They had heard the story before but always liked hearing it again.

"Okay. Well, it was late in the afternoon and my ma asked them to stay the night. She rented out the back bedroom to guests and they'd heard about it in town. They'd also been warned that we were strange. Well, so were they."

Xavier stared at the woman all during dinner, although his father told him more than once to stop and the Engineer said gently that it was all right, that the woman was not bothered by his staring. She concentrated on eating. After she was finished she looked around the room. There was something funny about her eyes and face. They never changed and Xavier realized suddenly that the faces of everybody in his family changed all the time and he'd never noticed it before. Kimberly was being silly and laughing as usual, talking nonstop until she was finally sent from the table to calm down but she didn't; she pranced and jumped over to one side of the huge kitchen and finally settled down to playing with her set of farm vehicles, her tractor and truck and backhoe. She had an old metal police car and she wound up the siren and Dad got up and put it on a shelf and came back and sat down again.

"So what is it that you're proposing, Mr.—"

"That's great-grandaddy's voice!" said Hunter. "All growly."

Xavier smiled. He liked doing the voices.

"Peabody. I'm proposing that we lease a quarter acre of remote land from you—"

"Hilly ground all right?"

"Yes, but I'd need to be able to drive pretty close to it."

"Well, that wouldn't be remote then, would it?"

"Someplace that's not a lot of good to you, that wouldn't be in danger of being disturbed." He looked around the table and Xavier felt that he was counting. "I understand that your family has owned this land for centuries."

"What does that have to do with anything?"

"I want to build something that would have a good chance of staying here for . . . quite a while."

"Like how long?"

"At least a century."

"You're talking about quite a bit of rent there, aren't you, Mr. Peabody?"

"It's negotiable."

The woman finished eating, pushed her chair in neatly and quietly, took down her coat and hat from the coat rack, put them on, and walked out the door.

"We have indoor plumbing," Mom said, looking at the closed door.

"She likes to walk."

"But it's dark—"

"There's a half moon, and the road to town is well-paved." Mr. Peabody didn't look worried.

"She doesn't say much."

"No."

Dad said, "So how do you propose to pay rent for a century?"

"Tell me Mr. Appleton, how do you feel about nanotechnology?"

"Depends." Dad looked at us as if he wanted to ask us to leave the table but didn't. "What kind?"

"I carry with me a large assortment of nanotech seeds. No, no," he said, when Mom looked alarmed, "I give you my word that there is no danger in them. I am a licensed nanotechnologist, licensed in all fifty-two states. Or at least I was at one time."

"What are states?" I asked.

"New Hampshire used to be a state," James told me, and I could tell he was trying to be nice about knowing so much more because the adults were there. "Before it was a part of the Federation of New England. It was a state in the United States of America. Before the Third Nanotech Wave . . ."

"Those were frightening times," said Mr. Peabody. His mouth turned down and it seemed like he was looking at something really far away. "We lost everything we had. Many people died. But there's a new age coming."

"Maybe you ought to take your story to Sunday Meeting," said Dad with a frown.

"I am an Engineer," Mr. Peabody said. "I am here to help you. But if you ask me to leave, we shall leave right now. I understand your discomfort. But a new age is coming. If you agree to give me a few hours of your time, you can ask all the questions you like and decide for yourself whether you would like to lease me some of your land."

"My mother was a doctor," Ma said. "She was a doctor in Boston

when it was a Flower City. That's where I was born. Harve there, his grandfather was an electrical engineer and then he became a nanotech engineer too. So we're not just superstitious backwood people here." She kind of glared at Dad, who shrugged.

"Better safe than sorry, Kate."

"Let's just hear what he has to say, all right?"

The grown-ups kept talking. After they put me to bed I waited a while, then crept out onto the landing up there where the shadows are—

"Is that how come you know when I'm there?" asked Hunter sleepily, her head on his knee.

This is what I heard.

Mr. Peabody talked about how his companions had flown off into space. He admitted that he had spent a week in town already and that he had found out about Mom and Dad's backgrounds, which made him think that they might understand. He said that he believed that big changes were coming to the Earth and that he had designed a device for receiving the information that would help bring the changes. He said that he believed that the changes were good and that a lot of the humans on the Earth had genetic modifications that let them understand the Signal and Ma started crying then and Pa put his arm around her. The engineer said he was like that too and Dad got the whisky out of the cupboard and they drank little glasses of it until I fell asleep.

I woke in my own bed the next morning in the bright sunlight. It was kind of late; Ma always got me up before light this time of year to study in the kitchen after I ate breakfast and fed the chickens.

I put on my slippers and robe and ran down to the kitchen. Ma was singing and Dad was kind of quiet. Mr. Peabody and the woman, Su-Chen, were sitting at the table and were finished with breakfast and had a lot of sheets of gray stuff spread around the table. Peabody touched one of them and it got pictures on it. It was the first computer I had seen.

"But they're the ones we have now, right?" asked Dave, one of the twins.

"Yes, they are what has schooled you."

"That was what your mom and dad wanted for payment."

"Correct, young man."

"You never shared them because other people were afraid of them."

"Well, since other parents wouldn't let their kids play with us it wasn't hard to keep a secret."

"And Mr. Peabody put that thing out in the woods."

"It wasn't woods then. It was a far back field. First they poured the foundation and Mr. Peabody . . . built it."

"And when Great-Aunt Kimberly grew up, she went away to help build the devices too."

"Yes," said Grandpa Xavier, looking sad. "There was a training center in Texas. It was far away and we only got one letter from her after she left, saying that she had made it. You would have loved her. I was always hoping she might get back this way." He got up then and carried Hunter, who was sleeping, off to bed. He returned and continued his story for the twins.

They hurried and finished with the foundation pretty quickly because it was getting cold, It was ten by ten feet. Dad took his portable pump up there and they unrolled about a quarter mile of pipe to the nearest spring. Then Mr. Peabody opened his trailer and got to work. He let us watch and tried to explain everything he was doing, because he said it wasn't mysterious, it wasn't magic, it was engineering and invented by humans and most any other human ought to be able to know how to use such things and about how they were humanity's legacy and sometimes he got kind of carried away about it. It was the time of year with those sunsets I love, pale lines of pink and blue and maybe snow the next day. The smell of woodsmoke in the air.

Mr. Peabody told me he was building a kind of radio. He said that he believed that someday radio would work again and that when it did we would learn all kinds of new and important things and that it would be the best time ever in the universe. I never told my dad what Peabody said out there as he let me help mix this and that, always wearing gloves and using clean polished tools that he kept in the trailer inside of felt bags. Peabody was no fool and I know what he was doing. He was trying to make sure that some young folk knew about it so that they'd be around to protect it. So that they took pride in helping and would keep an eye out for it.

I've kept an eye out for it, but it seems to me that Peabody was mistaken. Nothing has happened so far. None of the stuff about how we're going to be sipping energy from the sky through tunnels of light, or about how consciousness will be different because of the new genes we have, or how we'll be able to communicate with everyone and everything, and how everything would look and feel different. That's all right. I'm satisfied with the way things are. Aren't you, kids?

"But what did he do?"

Oh, that's right. Well, it was kind of like a cake mix, to tell the truth. He had a big tin box made of flat squares that he hooked together with hinges. Inside of that he put a thick plastic liner. It was a cube and about as tall as me. He boosted me up so that I could pour in the different materials I'd mixed together. Purple and green and red powders all sealed into tubes. He said they became activated when they were mixed together and so he had to keep them separate. He thought the whole thing up himself, he said, invented it, made what they had earlier even better. He smiled when he said this. He told me that he was a hundred and forty long hard years old. Then he gave me an upended saw-cut log to stand on so that I could hold the hose and fill up the cube. When it was halfway finished he threw in another kind of powder that looked kind of chunky. He stood on a stool and kept stirring with a real long spoon. It sounds kind of funny but that's what it was, about a ten-foot-long spoon. He was worried about it freezing at first but after it got kind of liquidy it started to give off steam and he smiled. He said that from then on it would generate its own heat.

"Things stay green around it in winter," said Dave.

"Then what happened?" asked Dale.

Then the strangest thing of all happened. He left it for a week to cure, he called it, but actually things were growing and changing inside it. Then he went out and checked some gauges on the side of the box and said we would take it apart. He unhooked the tin plates and wiped them off carefully and put them into the back of the trailer. It was a cloudy day but inside the plastic I could see that the thing had glowy strings inside of it. It was like a cube of gelatin. Kind of soft. But damn—darndest thing, you couldn't cut it.

"I know," said Dale. "You can't smash it at all. I took one of the bricks from around it and tried."

Well, then, this is what finally happened. The woman hiked out to the woods. We all came because Mr. Peabody especially invited us and said it wouldn't take very long. His whole truck was painted with solar batteries and he unrolled a wire that went to an oval covered with keys. There were no symbols on the keys. We couldn't tell if it was a musical instrument or a computer keyboard and Mr. Peabody said it was both and the woman surprised us by talking and saying that music and mathematics were the same thing and that when we heard music we were hearing mathematics and that all mathematics was one way of looking at music and that light was all there was and that it made everything and that it made music too and that she was going to play light music. In the meantime Peabody was unrolling leads from the keyboard, which stood up on thin little legs, and sealing the ends onto the cube. He'd taken the plastic off and it just sat there. You could look into it and never see the end of it. He nodded at the woman and she started to move her fingers.

The sounds came out of the cube, and it kind of shimmered and changed colors as she played. She closed her eyes while she played like she was listening to something. It was a strange kind of music that she played. There aren't any real instruments that sound that way. It was kind of like going to church. It was sunset and it was like a fire was behind her, kind of like she was on fire. Like bright lights were shining all around. Her hair glowed, her face glowed.

It was like the light, and the world, were saying something to me.

She played for about twenty minutes and then stopped in what sounded like the middle of something and looked at the old man. He unstuck the leads and rolled them up neatly and put them in their own little packages. He was always real neat about everything.

That was all. They put everything away and thanked us. Peabody left the school slates for us.

It's been sitting out there ever since.

It happened to Hunter when she was fifteen. She had weeks of headaches and even though she knew what was happening her mother was still really nervous about it. But then she started to hear the music, very early one morning. It woke her up.

She got dressed and went outside. The stars were blazing and white snow was heaped everywhere. She was suffused by music. She cried for joy or for something; whatever it was she could not help it.

When she was twenty, she married Tim Engle from down the road and they lived in a house they built on the Old Pike and had a baby after a year.

One night she woke in the middle of the night and didn't know why. She sat up next to Tim, who was a sound sleeper.

She pulled on her robe and checked the baby, who slept peacefully. Ginger, their dog, followed her downstairs and watched her pull on her boots and put on her coat and hat and scarf and gloves.

She walked down the forest path to the machine, beginning to run at the last because it seemed as if the sky was starting to shine. She had a fearful headache.

When she got to the place, all grown up now with vines and weeds and even a tree heaving up one side of the foundation she stopped and stepped back.

For the brick walls had apparently melted, then hardened again, and spread out around the foundation.

Sitting on the cracked foundation was a large cube, and all over the cube, growing as she watched, were small growths she recognized as dish antenna from her childhood lessons on the slates that were still in the family.

Her headache vanished and the music in her head grew and intensified. She felt sick to her stomach and the light of the device gave off rainbows with bands of color she had never seen before. She clapped one hand over her mouth.

A voice issued from the device and began to tell her what had happened. That the signal had returned from the group that had left the Earth so long ago. That changes were beginning that would give every human on Earth new senses. That a new way of knowing, that a new stage of evolution, that a new way of seeing, a new way of being, was about to begin.

But she didn't need the voice to tell her that.

She knew.

THE OTHER SIDE

Matthew

I never did marry Dania. She was right. When I was twenty-two, I married Sarah. When I was almost thirty, and had three children, Dania left. The last time I saw her she was hiking the riprap trail out of town.

I was out in the back field and hallooed and waved. She turned, put her hand above her eyes, saw me, and waved back. On the canyon's rim, I saw—I swear I saw—some people on horses. Indians, seemed like. Really. And a coyote. Big old thing, rangy. I remember thinking that I needed to keep him from the chickens.

They had a bicycle for her. I swear. She straddled it, waved again, and they all moved away from the canyon's rim. I checked her usual haunts, whenever I had time, what with the kids and work. We never saw her again.

But when the heavens opened and the music played in our heads, we knew what she had done. I think that after that she must surely have found a way to reach Radio Cowboy, if he had the same longevity work as she did. Because it was possible, at last, to communicate again. But there was more than just that.

It wasn't really music. Oh, it was something I could hear with my ears, but it made a new pattern in my brain and in the brains of all those who had taken her communion stuff, and in the brains of their children.

I was waiting to be awakened, just as all of our senses are waiting, when we are born, to be awakened by the phenomena of the world itself, in all of its vibrations. And literacy—literacy with numbers, and literacy with letters and words—is just another sense to be awakened by the right environment, the right input.

There are senses beyond that. Connections that, before, I knew nothing of. But a part of me was waiting for this to happen. It's like a blind person being given sight. The visible world was always there, yet they could not see it.

We are all a part of this mosaic, this pattern, this improvisation, this widening of time, this being. It is as if all of my life I was hiking up a narrow mountain trail between the pines, catching glimpses of the view through the trees at certain points. Then arriving, suddenly and without notice, at the head of an Edenly valley and seeing the sun rise.

It's like that.

It changes everything.

We have come through a long dark birth canal and emerged into clear, sparkling daylight. We are able to know more, do more, and with more wisdom and more joy and more intensity and more depth of thought, able to weave more strings, more information, into each thought, than ever before. We are a part of the music that light makes. We are able to change the music that light makes. Constantly.

We have developed, as it were, a new opposable thumb. We have languages that go far beyond this language, but this is the language I must use to speak to you, who have not yet crossed over. You have heard this whole long story of how it all began. And what it promises.

I earnestly beseech you to do it.

Imagine. Listen. Taste and see. Experience the music that light makes and you will want more. You will begin to know ways to bring yourself into it. You will create it yourself.

God! It is still more lovely than I can possibly say.